IT WAS A NEWLY DISCOVERED LAND . . .
A VISION OF BEAUTY AND A DESCENT INTO HELL . . .

Escalante saw a firearm blaze and heard its flat boom. Olivares' head seemed suddenly to have been pulled backwards. He clamped a hand to his forehead and blood trickled, shining, between his fingers.

Miera ran his horse into the formation. Its hooves chopped at chests and thighs as Miera's stabbing sword moved in swift figures of eight, down one side, up, down the other. The man who had shot Olivares fell back, his head cloven.

Olivares was rocking back and forth, still erect, shouting, "It's all right. All right!"

Escalante pivoted in his saddle, tight with fear, feeling sweat soak his body beneath the heavy woolen garment. He was looking for Coronel. He would drag him away too, end his perfidy and betrayal. Coronel was in sight for a moment, his face lined with rage . . . then he was swept back toward the lake and Escalante lost him in smoke and shadows. . . .

Miera was hanging down the side of his horse now, hacking the ropes that bound Andres Muniz to his cross of wood.

"Cut, man, cut!" Muniz yelled hoarsely.

Miera swung his blade and bits of rope flew.

Muniz kicked the last ropes free, then kicked his cross, too. He stood for a moment alone, with no one near him.

Then Escalante extended his arm and Muniz caught it with both hands, catapulting himself over the horse's back, riding Escalante's arms as a pendulum . . . to safety.

ESCALANTE

WILDERNESS PATH

Peter T. Blairson

A Dell/Banbury Book

Published by

Banbury Books
37 West Avenue
Wayne, Pennsylvania 19087

Dell ® TM 681510, Dell Publishing Co., Inc.

ISBN: 0-440-02402-1
Printed in the United States of America
First printing—January 1983

H. J. GILMET
DEP. SHERIFF
STAR ROUTE
ALPENA, MICH.

H. J. GILMET
DEP. SHERIFF
STAR ROUTE
ALPENA, MICH.

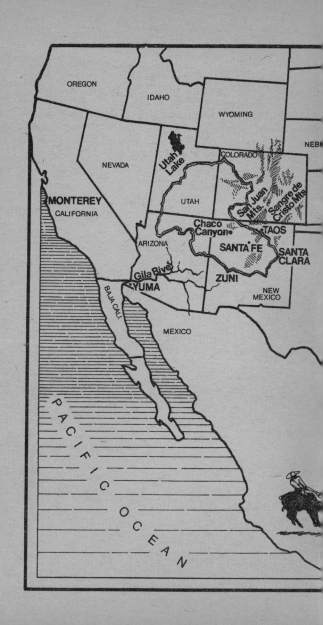

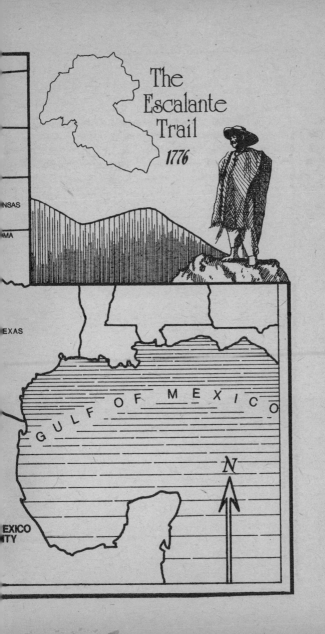

The
Escalante
Trail
1776

NSAS

MA

EXAS

GULF OF MEXICO

N

EXICO
TY

Chapter 1

From the crest of a cedar ridge, Father Silvestre Velez de Escalante finally saw the adobe walls of the presidio of Santa Fe. It was early on a June evening in the year 1776. The troop of soldiers he had been following for hours had just galloped into the city between a pair of ornate gateposts.

Escalante had been traveling for more than a week. Dust covered his hair, his beard and his long Franciscan robes so thoroughly that only his eyes and the insides of his lips showed any color at all. His horse, a bay mare, was dun-colored with dust.

Indians passed him on foot, bending their heads for his blessing, mumbling and touching fingers to their lips. He hardly noticed them. He was too busy staring at Santa Fe and the lingering dust that the soldiers stirred up.

Escalante reflected upon Santa Fe, its brooding presidio and its obsession with military force and commerce. He sighed. He didn't like Santa Fe, nothing but a dirty, dusty town.

He touched his saddlebag. Inside the weather-beaten sack were a map and a pile of papers. This map, he reflected, was perhaps the most significant one in all of New Spain. No doubt it would bring many more soldiers and settlers to Santa Fe. And when they came, Santa Fe would be a crowded, dirty, dusty town. No, Escalante would never like Santa Fe.

Just inside the ball-and-pediment gateposts, Escalante nudged his horse. The litters of three wounded men had been unslung against a wall covered with crude religious slogans and tiny red crosses. None of the three soldiers seemed seriously wounded, but two had their eyes closed and the third stared anxiously at Escalante.

The soldier had only a gash on his forehead, but his clothes were rimed with sweat-salt and stained with blood. As Escalante moved his horse closer, the very smells of blood and dust and animal viscera swelled toward him in a wave. The man was staring at Escalante's foot in the stirrup as though it were an icon.

"Has the Hopi uprising been put down?" Escalante's voice was a croak.

The man heard him, however, and nodded. "At more cost in good men than it is worth," he wept.

"Can I say I share your bitterness over their deaths? But can you not perhaps believe that worthwhile things often take their toll in good men?"

The soldier was pushing himself to his feet. "Tell me next, Father, that the Hopi must accept the word of God or die by the sword and suffer eternal damnation." He grunted, stabbing the bayonet of his rifle into the dust to use the weapon as a crutch. "Then also tell me that the suffering and death are the will of God."

"I believe they are," Escalante replied. He was aware how foolish and pious and comfortable he must appear. "But I realize the words sound empty to you. I have not taken a bullet or seen friends die for the belief. You have."

The soldier plucked the bayonet from the earth. "You, Father, are too young and green to know the difference between God's will and the mule dung in the streets."

Escalante suspected what the soldier was going to do. He rolled from his horse's back, off the side away from the man. When the man pulled the trigger, Escalante was no longer sitting in his saddle.

The lead ball hit the steeple of a church and flung out a geyser of masonry. Escalante's bay horse kicked the air in fright. The boom of the weapon killed the rest of the noise of the street. Everyone stopped and stared.

Escalante hurled himself beneath his leaping horse, dived between its hooves trailing his grey robes and rolled against the soldier's legs just below his knees. Falling backward, the soldier slashed and speared his bayonet through the wool of Escalante's tunic.

The Franciscan felt the burn of a deep cut. He dug his feet into the street dust and pushed hard to sustain the momentum of his attack. Priest and soldier rolled together for several turns. Escalante turned the rifle. The soldier countered, turning in the opposite direction. Instead of resisting, Escalante turned the rifle with him, exerting far more force. At the same time, he planted a foot against the soldier's midsection and pushed.

When the two split Escalante was first on his feet, holding the rifle. He teased the soldier's brass buckle, bright as the sun, with the bayonet.

The soldier could not conceal his surprise. He turned his empty hands over, looking at them as though expecting the rifle to reappear. Then he sighed. His arms dropped as a marionette's do when the operator releases the strings.

The commotion attracted a lieutenant of horse dragoons. He cantered toward Escalante and the soldier, lifting a short stabbing sword from its saddle boot and leaning low to chop open the enlisted man's head.

"No!" Escalante leaped into the path of the horse, forcing it to turn. He swung the rifle, caught the lieutenant's blade between the muzzle and the bayonet stud, then twisted.

The lieutenant had little choice: break his grip or break his wrist.

The sword arced end over end, flashing bright stars of light. As the soldier had done, the lieutenant stared at his empty hand, then at Escalante, who laughed. "How must this seem, a Franciscan priest with a sword and a rifle?"

The lieutenant's face was a silent reproach: Franciscan Fathers are not supposed to be skilled at close combat. But the lieutenant said only, "I saw the man assault you and try to shoot you. That cannot be tolerated."

"Lieutenant, Lieutenant, you misinterpret what you saw."

"He must be charged with assault and punished, Father."

"Assault?" Escalante looked puzzled. "You only imagined I was being assaulted. It must have seemed that way. But how do you know I was not assaulting him?" Escalante chuckled again and ground his sandal into the dust as though embarrassed. "The fact is, Lieutenant, we were assaulting each other. Horseplay. Had I not become a priest, I would be an officer such as yourself. I have always been fascinated by soldiers and soldiering." Escalante gestured at the trooper. "It was mock combat, Lieutenant. I was vain enough to believe I could show this man something he might not know about disarming an enemy. The fact is, I could not have taken his weapon at all if he were not so weary after a hard fight with the Hopi." Escalante paused. "It was a childish game on both our parts. The gun went off by accident." Escalante tossed the rifle to the trooper.

The lieutenant was persistent. "You are bleeding, Father. He tried to bayonet you. I witnessed this."

"When one engages in horseplay, one must expect to be hurt a little. The cut does not amount to much."

"Am I to believe this?" the lieutenant cried out, searching the faces in the crowd.

Escalante looked at the officer for several moments. When the man at last glanced away, Escalante snickered, "You had better believe it, Lieutenant, if you expect ever to receive my blessing.'' He indicated that what he had just said might really be only a jest. Someone in the crowd laughed. Soon it caught on and witnesses and passersby alike were joining in the mirth.

No longer knowing what to believe and feeling a bit foolish, the lieutenant leaned low from his saddle, snatched his sword from the dust and cantered off as he had come.

Escalante mounted too, but not before taking measure of the soldier's face; it was awash with relief. He was not going to die after all for foolishly shooting at a priest in anger before witnesses. His temper is volcanic, Escalante realized. He's humiliated. He will not thank me for my play-acting.

The soldier held the rifle as though he no longer had any use for it. He was doing his best to stop his tears, but failing.

"One thing I said was true, soldier. You are tired. Bone tired. You wouldn't have shot at me if you weren't so tired."

Traffic brawled again, raising dust in sheets and billows. Escalante's horse picked its course and nudged people and other animals aside with massive shoulders.

Thinking still of the incident with the soldier, Escalante grew frightened. His breathing was labored. Could his injury be more serious than he wanted to believe? He held the reins so tightly his knuckles whitened. He could not will them to relax.

He recalled that Roman soldiers had been known to assault their own commanders after terrible hand-to-hand battles with Gauls and Germans, berserk with fear and grief for fallen comrades. The Roman commanders frequently forgave such assaults; they understood stress.

Could I do less than a barbarian Roman commander?

Escalante turned and blessed the soldier. The man still stood watching in the dust.

Escalante supposed the battle with the Hopi must have been more brutal than was immediately apparent. There were wounded everywhere. The commanders had dispersed them into small groups, it seemed, so their numbers wouldn't seem so great.

Escalante found still more wounded men stacked outside a *carniceria*. How appropriate, he thought. How ugly. This must be someone's idea of a joke, setting the wounded down outside a butcher shop.

A stout man who walked with a cane was approaching the group, nodding first to Escalante with preoccupied respect.

One of the injured men opened his eyes and suddenly reached out to Escalante. Lifting his arm, he revealed an arrow broken off in his side. The stench of infection was evident in the air.

"Save me, Father."

Escalante reined his horse. The man with the cane was calling to a boy, ordering boning knives from inside his carniceria. Wealthy women in mantillas stepped around the wounded men and fled. Bareheaded women in dirty peasant skirts crowded about the hurt men, offering comfort. A scream pierced the death-filled street. A mother recognized a young soldier as her own.

The boy ran back from the shop with the butcher's boning knives fanned out aloft. The butcher slid one hand down along the shaft of his cane to kneel beside the soldier who clutched the broken arrow. The butcher selected a knife from the boy's offering.

Again the soldier yelped, "Please, Father, save me."

Escalante trembled as he considered the wounded men before him. Do I stop to tend and speak with all I see? I shall never reach Father Dominguez. I shall never deliver my messages concerning Monterey. My instructions are to hurry, to stop for nothing.

Flies circled the stump of the arrow and danced on the soldier's hand as Escalante spoke aloud. "Father Francisco Atanasio Dominguez will have to wait."

Escalante swung his right leg across his horse's rump and dropped from the stirrup. His back wound lashed at him.

Escalante clapped a hand on the butcher's shoulder to delay the incision. He knelt beside the man and smiled. "Do you know what you are doing?"

The butcher looked at Escalante, at the ring of street people about them, then at Escalante once more. He shrugged, touching the splintered shaft of the arrow. "I believe so, young padre. If I can bone animals, I suppose I can cut an arrow out of a man."

"Begging your pardon, it's not at all the same," Escalante countered, holding out his hand.

The butcher shrugged again and placed the knife gently on Escalante's palm, wooden handle first.

Escalante ordered the boy, "Quickly, fetch me a marrow bone from the carniceria."

Escalante squatted, spreading the skirt of his robe as a woman might, and carefully examined the wound. He tugged the broken shaft gently, praying the arrow had not twisted. He knew that if the head lay at an angle to the cut, deep in the muscle, the extraction would be even more difficult.

The man's back arched at Escalante's touch and he let out a groan. Inflicting more pain upon the young man was unavoidable; the priest probed on. At last Escalante got the answer he needed—the arrowhead and cut were still in alignment.

Finally the boy emerged from the butcher shop. "I have it, Father. I have it!" He ran through the street, crowded with bodies, turning and staring occasionally at a wounded soldier before continuing on his mission.

"Hurry, boy!" shouted Escalante. He grabbed the marrow bone and reeled off a list of instructions to the boy and the butcher. "Pry open the man's mouth. Put the bone between his jaws. Make certain the tongue is not between the bone and his teeth or he'll bite it off."

The wounded man objected, but the butcher grasped upper and lower jaws and pulled them apart as he might have stripped cowhide from a carcass. The boy pressed down the tongue and dropped the bone into a cradle formed by the soldier's taut cheeks.

Escalante motioned for assistance from the crowd of onlookers. A concerned older gentleman sat on the soldier's hands and another fellow held down his feet. Escalante took the boning knife and steadily lengthened the wound, working away from each edge of the arrowhead. He swiftly pushed the knife-point in deeper, deeper, until he no longer felt the grinding of steel against arrowhead. He had come to the tip. He cut deep in the same manner along the opposite edge of the arrowhead.

"He'll kick like a mule now," Escalante warned the others. "Hold him. Hold him. Hold . . . him. . . ."

Escalante wrapped his fist tightly about the stump of the arrow shaft, then pulled quickly and firmly. The soldier's eyes bulged, his face purpled and the muscles of his jaw stiffened as he sawed his teeth against the bone.

Before long Escalante stood triumphantly with the arrow in his hand. Enormous cheers rang out from the crowd. There followed a snapping sound, like a dry twig in winter, then a terrible cry. The soldier had crushed the marrow bone between his teeth. Splinters and saliva glistened in a paste of marrow on his cheeks. He fainted.

Escalante knelt again before the young soldier to probe the wound. "Someone, anyone, get me some brandy to clean this wound. And a clean cloth, too, for a bandage."

Finally the wound was bound and the young man was coming to. Escalante rose and dusted himself off. "Well, Father Dominguez has been patient enough. I'll be going now," he muttered.

"Excuse me, Father," inquired the crippled butcher, "but how does a priest know so much about removing arrows?"

As he parted his skirts to lift his left foot to the stirrup, Escalante smiled. "A long time ago I spent much time among the Hopi myself, nearly a year. When one lives with the

Hopi, one learns how to remove arrows—a daily hazard, you know.''

The crowd once again parted to permit his passing. A woman who knelt beside the wounded soldier cried out her blessing. Several on the street applauded and crossed themselves.

One man who arrogantly kept his hat on remarked as Escalante's horse brushed him, ''If there were more priests such as this youngster, the church would not need soldiers to spread God's word.''

Escalante pretended not to hear him. The remark disturbed him for the church's sake, but pleased him for his own. He had meant to ask some of the soldiers what news there had been of the vanished Father Francisco Garces. There had been no word of Garces since months before, when he had gone into the northern wilderness among the Hopi. Escalante grieved for Garces. He was a good friend.

His back bedeviled him. He touched the place where the bayonet had gouged him. The cloth of his robe was wet, but the muscle seemed intact. The wound could wait, then. He had a message to deliver, of a dream of glory for God and for Spain.

Chapter 2

Oxen hauled a tumbrel before the Cathedral of Santa Fe as Escalante crossed the plaza. Doves swooped through paloverde trees at the mansion of Governor Pedro Fermin de Mendinueta. Escalante dismounted at the rectory and paddled dust from his grey robes with the brim of his hat. He removed his bedroll and pack from his saddle.

Looming suddenly in the rectory doorway, Escalante scared the young sacristan, who dropped a bouquet of flowers. They were mountain roses, somewhat wilted. It was too early as yet for candles; the sacristan had just carried the flowers to the window to examine them more closely in the last light of day when Escalante startled him.

The sacristan was not the only startled person. A tiny man who had given the flowers to the sacristan for Father Dominguez let out a stifled cry, then bowed his head in embarrassment. As Escalante passed him at the center of the rectory, he noticed the small person nervously twisting his cap in his simian hands.

The sacristan timidly approached from the shadows. "Are you Father Escalante?"

"Yes, my son. I've come from Zuni to meet Father Dominguez."

"I know. We have been expecting you for several days. We have your quarters ready, over there in Father Dominguez' residence."

"I would like to say vespers and Mass first."

"I expected you might, Father. Your reputation for prayer among the common people has reached us here in Santa Fe."

"Then I look forward to seeing you tonight in the old mission church."

"Oh yes, Father. You can count on it. I'll be there," chimed the young Indian boy in elegant Spanish.

Father Francisco Atanasio Dominguez, the commissary visitor of the Custody of the Conversion of Saint Paul in New Mexico, was watching the birds through a window in the governor's mansion just across the plaza from the rectory. His moon face seemed to generate a pale light. Bernardo Miera was ushered into his presence. Dominguez turned toward the door. "Welcome to the territorial offices of the Holy Evangel of Mexico."

Even in the gloom of early evening, Dominguez could see that Miera's dwarf had accompanied him. The little person was waiting for his master on a bench in the hallway, feet not quite touching the floor. Miera came humbly forward to Dominguez, but there was something happy and expectant about his face that immediately worried the priest.

"Father, I have good news."

Dominguez motioned toward a chair across from his desk. Miera, his leather breeches creaking under his brilliant sash, sat down heavily and right away leaned forward. "That explorer-priest who comes from Zuni, your Father Escalante, has word of a route to Monterey, an actual way, a veritable northwest passage, so to speak, overland. Can you imagine? From here in New Mexico to the Pacific in only twenty days! Just think, Father. Only twenty days!"

Dominguez had been arranging his Franciscan skirts with great care over the pillowy bulk of his legs. He pretended not to hear Miera.

Don Bernardo ran one hand impatiently through the brush of his greying hair. "Your famous Father Escalante has some Indian map of the northern lands, Colorado and beyond. He also has word that Father Francisco Garces has himself seen a way through the sierras, clear from here to Monterey. Think of it." Miera's hands danced in the air. "A safe overland route all the way from the Gulf of Mexico to Spanish holdings on the Pacific Ocean in California. Forgive my repetition, Father, but you appeared not to hear me."

"A route to the Pacific. In only twenty days."

"Yes. Escalante arrived just this afternoon with the soldiers from the punitive expedition against the Hopi. My dwarf just saw him at the rectory." Miera paused. "He seems young to have accomplished so much. Only twenty-six. His youth disturbs me."

Dominguez looked out at the paloverde trees. They were enveloped in dust shrouds raised by a slight breeze. Beyond were the bell towers of the Cathedral of Santa Fe; he had to close his eyes to them, they reminded him so much of Mexico City. He longed to be there. "Jesus was also quite young, as I recall. No more than thirty Himself at the time of His crucifixion, I believe."

"No criticism intended, Father, only concern."

Moments passed in silence. Then, with eyes still shut, Dominguez declared, "And on the strength of a map and a few reports that no one here has even seen, you agree with the bishop in Mexico City and with Governor Mendinueta himself, and with every official and his dog in New Spain. In fact you wish me to plan, mount and lead an expedition to find this so-called Northwest Passage. Is that not so?"

"I do not suggest this myself, Father. I am told you have already been so informed by your own superiors."

Miera had been leaning back in his chair. Now he leaned

forward again. "Father, you must understand how important this northern route to Monterey is to the crown. The Russians have built their barbaric churches just north of Monterey itself. Their seal and whaling vessels operate only a few miles off the harbor roads. And English frigates boldly anchor in the harbor. Understand, Father, Monterey is at this moment vulnerable to both the Russians and the British. It is but one small, isolated garrison in California. It has no presidio worth the name as yet."

Miera slapped his knees and continued boldly. "Father, if we cannot connect the New Mexican frontier with our holdings in Monterey, then neither New Mexico nor California can be protected. Our galleons from Manila need a Spanish port in California. With a road to Monterey and with troops making the trip in only twenty days, we can hold California. Without the road we cannot. It is that simple."

Miera shrugged. "And if we cannot hold California, Father, Spain and her church in America will never expand."

"I realize this," admitted Dominguez.

"Then you are as hopeful as I that a route will soon be opened."

"I said I am aware of all the political and economic implications, Don Bernardo, nothing more. The Hopi and Apache will not let us pass to the south, as you well know, and there are Indians to the north too."

"Yes, but they are waiting for the word of God."

Dominguez acknowledged this. "One would hope."

"The northern route is our only chance, even though most of the territory is uncharted."

Smells of cooking from the governor's kitchen drifted up through the open windows. Ahh, my favorite soup, Dominguez thought, made of the native black bean. The flavor was like something never tasted before, but somehow familiar and enticing.

"Please, Father, we cannot delay too long. Think of Fathers Kino and Serra and their heroic exploits."

"I do—with great dismay."

"The church and the crown must unite for this great undertaking," Miera proclaimed, pulling himself up for one last try at winning Dominguez' enthusiasm. "Father, think of all the lost Indian souls. You must mount the expedition and you yourself must take command. You and Escalante can lead us toward the greater glory of New Spain. I know the bishop in Mexico City would wish you to do so."

Dominguez nodded. He too knew the bishop in Mexico City would wish him to do so.

"After all, Father, on all of the frontier, you are the highest-ranking priest." Miera stood ready to take his leave. "Both Governor Mendinueta and I await your decision, Father. We pray it will be the one we all expect of you."

Dominguez wearily waved Miera away. "I must think, Miera. Forgive me for seeming rude, but I would like to be alone now for a while before I meet Father Escalante. Good evening and God be with you."

Miera left. An Indian boy came with word from the sacristan that Father Escalante had arrived and would be saying vespers in the original mission church. Dominguez pictured the dusty, dark-featured young man standing in the small adobe church just a little distance away. He welcomed the additional delay. Dominguez did indeed wish to think some more.

He sat at his desk and bade the Indian boy to bring him some chocolate. The boy returned with a cup quite hot from the kitchen fire. Dominguez pushed back his chair and beckoned for his footstool. He suffered from gout and had grown fond of propping up his feet whether he was really afflicted with pain or not.

Now, Dominguez wondered, what to do about this Father Escalante? He was annoyed because the explorer was directly changing his life with his map and his reports of a highway through the sierras to California; Dominguez liked his position as highest-ranking priest in the territory and looked forward to comfortable retirement. He was also amused at the man's so-admirable precocity.

Dominguez knew very little of Escalante except for two things. There was the basic physical description, which was indeed impressive: tall and hard as a log; dark blunt features; thick, short hair as black as a wire chimney brush.

And there was his reputation, which for a man of only twenty-six was considerable. Dominguez was hardly better known and he was almost forty. Clearly, Escalante was an unusual man.

Although Dominguez wished Escalante had never appeared with his maps and dreams, he was nonetheless curious to meet the famous traveler.

Settling back with his chocolate, Dominguez heard Miera's last words once more. Yes, Bishop Diego Nadie de Escobar in Mexico City did indeed wish Dominguez to mount an exploration of an overland passage to California with this adventurer of a priest. The bishop had made that clear to him only a few short days before.

The two had met alone in the bishop's study. The tapestries hung like hides covering the walls and furniture. Escobar drew two chairs close together and leaned across the dimness to Dominguez. "One of your missions is to pursue the quest for overland passage from Santa Fe to the Pacific. Develop it, Father. And one of your crosses to bear along the way may be Father Escalante." The bishop spoke in dark, secretive tones. "Repeat a word of what I am about to tell you and I shall deny we ever had this conversation."

Dominguez nodded. He would not.

Escobar went on, "Escalante's achievements are well known, and well they should be; they are most impressive. His reports on the history of the Hopi to our beloved governor and captain-general of New Mexico, His Honor, Pedro Fermin de Mendinueta . . ." The bishop paused. Dominguez imagined the very air to be charged with the man's distaste for the governor. ". . . Escalante's reports on the Hopi are impressive for their thoroughness and insight. As chaplain, Escalante has accompanied diplomatic as well as disciplinary expeditions to these Hopi. His battle reports: again, brilliant. With it all, he does not forget he is a priest first. He is one of our most accomplished harvesters of souls. He has even been known to sit with the Hopi and share his *cigarros* with them and speak to them on their own terms to win them for our Lord."

Escobar sighed in wonder. "He is not afraid to become one of them. He learns to farm as they do, brew beer from maize as they do and treat wounds and sickness as they do." The bishop chuckled without mirth. "It is also said he beds women on occasion as they do." He waved as though dismissing the idea. "Nevertheless, he tries to understand their gods in order to bring them to our God. The thing is, Dominguez, Escalante succeeds with his unorthodox approach. You should see how the Indians flock to his mission at Zuni to hear him whenever he says Mass." The bishop fell silent.

Dominguez waited. Conspiracy was not to his liking. He had learned the best way was least involvement, to say little or nothing when others were plotting.

"The man apparently believes he can singlehandedly convert every savage in the territory from here to California, if we will only unleash him with the mandate to do so. Perhaps he is close to correct. I know of no one who believes in the word of God for itself alone and in its truth and beauty as this Escalante does. Further, he is indeed the man divinely fitted for the work. He truly prefers wilderness hardship and plain rusticity to the things that more mature and worldly men such as you and I seek out in our cities." Escobar sighed once more. "In short, Dominguez, Escalante is explorer, chronicler and priest of the first order. As some others do, he believes in the overland passage to California as fiercely as he believes in our Lord. Such zeal is alarming, especially in one so young."

Dominguez finally spoke. He was growing irritated with Escobar's roundabout approach to his obvious dark thoughts. "You speak so well of him. Now you are going to tell me he is a leper? Is that why you squeeze me for a promise of secrecy?"

Bishop Escobar did not like the mild sarcasm. "It is because the very intensity of his good qualities is an embarrassment to us, Dominguez," he snapped, moving his head closer still. "An embarrassment. The unorthodoxy of his ways, to be specific. He sometimes moves ahead of us, sometimes around us, to achieve his ends. Men in high places sometimes wonder and ask, what is the truth? Is Escalante so marvelous or are we so mediocre?" There was another pause. "He is too young to be permitted so much recognition so early. Older men have built our plans of action and worked out our methods for decades, Dominguez, decades. Eventually we will succeed in bringing God to the territory and power to Spain. We have hundreds of years of history to support us, Dominguez. We cannot permit ourselves to be undone or outshone by one untested young genius. He and his work will not stand the test of time. We cannot permit them to. We who are more experienced shall prevail, no matter what. He must learn to accept this."

"In other words, he must learn to heel." Dominguez smiled in the shadows, unseen by Bishop Escobar. He understood the stress upon secrecy. Like Christ, Escalante was proving a threat to the power structure. He nodded and said nothing more.

"One problem in curbing such headstrong ambition," the bishop went on, "is that we here have nothing he wants or needs. He would not care for advancement in the church. No post in Spain or Mexico City seduces him. He wants only his simple life with his Indians. God spare us ambitious men who want nothing for themselves. They are the most troublesome of all."

Dominguez silently agreed and the bishop went on. "Furthermore, Escalante is an embarrassment because he does not tolerate fools, and we have so many of them in church and government. No prudent diplomat, this young man. He will criticize anyone, the Pope himself, I do believe, if he sees it is justified.'' He waved a fat hand. ''You should read what Escalante wrote during a misunderstanding last year with some Hopi Indian traders over tariffs. One should not tell the governor that his closest aide does not have the intelligence God gives a clam. I was delighted. Delighted.'' Escobar chuckled fruitily. ''Perhaps when he is older, Escalante will have learned the art of conflict and compromise and will accept our Franciscan system and its ways with the grace necessary for its continued success and his own.''

Dominguez exhaled heavily as sadness touched him. Yes, he reflected, play the game of church politics, wait your turn, do not create controversy by being too good too soon. Best of all, marry mediocrity the day you marry the church.

The bishop was now whispering to himself as if no one else were with him. ''So then. One way to handle such a young rebel is not to handle him at all. Send him off somewhere. Let him sway in the wind as a pennant does. One who is not seen and heard cannot create any disturbance.'' He swiveled around in his chair and spoke as he stared out the ceiling-high windows behind his desk. ''As I told you a moment ago, repeat a word of what I now say to you and I shall deny I have ever said it. My rank alone would protect me against you.''

Escobar turned back to face Dominguez with a most serious expression. ''We must sweep Escalante under the rug for a while, so to speak. We will give him what he wants so badly, a long trip into the wilderness. We have named him to follow Father Garces, to go as an emissary to the northern Indians with special instructions from our superiors to assist in the discovery of the route to Monterey.''

Dominguez waited.

''Unfortunately for you, Father, you must be the one to

lead him. We want you to take him out to open the overland route and keep him there as long as possible. As long as possible.'' The bishop repeated the phrase slowly and heavily, with a certain savor. "Give us some relief from him and give him some time to season in our ways and learn humility. That is, if in your estimation his maps and reports really do show a way.''

"Judging by what you say of him, they probably will," Dominguez sighed.

"As always, your optimism is admirable. You will lead the expedition in name, but let Escalante do all the work if he must. Put his admittedly great talent to work where it is most valuable and least visible. Let him convert souls and find overland passages in the name of the cross and the crown. But you, Father Dominguez, will be there to receive the lion's share of the credit and glory for your leadership.''

Yes, Dominguez thought once more, and to keep Escalante in check and in obscurity. Marvelous, simply marvelous. I have perhaps been in the church too long, he thought, for I suddenly feel I have too often seen good men ground to paste in her name.

"It will be an arduous and risk-ridden test for all of you.'' Escobar's manner grew even more clandestine. "It is even possible that one could lose one's life. Who knows? A fall from a steep trail, an Indian arrow out of the night— Escalante is one who seeks tests and risks.''

Dominguez filled with a terrible chill of anticipation. The bishop's need for secrecy was now plain. His mind was even darker than Dominguez had imagined.

Escobar took a deep, deep breath. "If Father Escalante should come to some harm, or even death . . .'' Escobar's words became almost inaudible, as if he himself found them unspeakable. '' . . . if he should come to some mortal harm, then we could not help viewing such misfortune as God's call for another martyr to His own will here on earth. I sometimes have the intuition that that may well be God's plan for this particular young man. Escalante has been critically ill for years, you may know, severely so at times. Some intermittent fever, I understand. And twice he has taken Indian arrows. Do you know what he did? He cut them out himself while still in his saddle and went on with the troops. It does seem he has a death wish.''

He was done. The plan was intact. For a moment the bishop's face gleamed in the candlelight. He was pleased with himself; he was actually smiling.

Dominguez reeled before an onslaught of conscience. "You are talking about murder, Bishop.''

"Oh, Dominguez, Dominguez. Not murder, but God's will.''

"You are playing with words. No matter how you express yourself, you are still talking about murder. I'll not be part of that, not even in God's name.''

"You usually hold your peace more diplomatically.''

"I find it difficult at this moment. I resent what you are doing to him. And I resent what you are doing to me, dumping him and his maps into my life just three months before I am to retire.''

"And I resent this talk of murder,'' the prelate cried out. "How dare you? I am not suggesting that anyone actively bring about his death. I too remember the Fifth Commandment, Father Dominguez. I am merely saying what is in the mind of everyone: namely, if God sees fit to take him while he is out in the wilderness, so be it. He would be of more value to the church as a martyr on a quest than as a live priest. Quite frankly, any one of us wearing these grey robes would be. Oh, Dominguez, Dominguez. . . .'' He pressed the priest's arm.

Dominguez' anger gradually dissolved, leaving him empty. He found himself believing in the bishop. And with some distaste he realized that he agreed with Escobar's assessment and management of Escalante. The same treatment Escalante was to receive had been given countless others over time. Dominguez had never liked the game, but this was how it was played. And there was no way he himself could escape the play, for there was no way he could not be a priest. No doubt he would do the same in Escobar's place. Practicality and discipline demanded it. He therefore silenced all his doubts but one.

"Are you sending Escalante on the expedition because he is best suited? Or are you sending the expedition because you wish to be rid of Escalante?"

Escobar did not reply.

"Either way, you are asking me to keep this young Father searching for an overland route as long as possible, no matter how flimsy the evidence that such a route exists."

"Not quite correct," Escobar retorted. "Do not go off unless you are convinced his maps and reports do have merit." The bishop formed a steeple with his fingertips. "This seems to be your day for misunderstandings, Father. I mean what I say. Do not go unless you are convinced. That is an order. If we must, we can abide Escalante alive and at his parish in Zuni forever. For the fact is, both you and Father Escalante are far too valuable to waste on a fruitless exercise. No, first and foremost your mission must promise a profit. That is the primary consideration. If God chooses to bestow additional benefits, so be it."

Dominguez prayed God would not be so hypocritical.

The bishop examined the steeple of his fingers. "I am saying you are to plan an expedition. I am saying you are to lead it yourself. I am saying I leave it entirely to your own judgment as to whether you actually go or not. That is all I am saying. You have proven yourself wise and prudent. And I tell you this." He looked at Dominguez. "If after you meet with Escalante you decide the quest is folly, call it off. We shall accept. We shall not view you with prejudice, I promise you."

Diego Nadie de Escobar stood. The meeting was all but ended.

"There is one other embarrassment to emphasize concerning Father Escalante's character. Women." The bishop carefully tiptoed over his words. "There was a recent unfortunate liaison between a distant cousin of Governor Mendinueta and Escalante. The girl became obsessed after she offered her body to Escalante—and he took it, I am told, a number of times—and insisted Escalante deny his priesthood and run off with her to Belize. Of course he could not; once a priest, always a priest, as we both well know. Escalante had no choice. But this girl would not understand. She tried to hurt him by informing her father. We cannot tolerate such scandal. So you see, it would be politic for this reason too to let him run about in the wilderness he so loves. The matter is still a source of tension at Zuni and here in Santa Fe." The bishop laughed. "But I marvel at the man. No remorse over the matter has eroded his capability for work in the least. It seems to bother him about as much as—well, as much as an arrow in the side."

Dominguez' anger flared anew. "Your Excellency, Escalante has only done what so many of us have done—yes, yourself included, I believe. You are not punishing him for sinning, but for allowing himself to be caught at it and exposed."

"Your frankness is not becoming."

Dominguez imagined their glances to be clashing blades.

Escobar studied the guttering beeswax candles. "I only point out to you, Dominguez, that—"

Dominguez completed the thought. "—that sin forgiven in ourselves is not forgiven in this man. Bishop, his only sin in your eyes is that he took up with the cousin of the governor instead of some Indian woman out behind the cactus."

Dominguez stood to take his leave. "I will do as my superior bids me, although it pains me. No one but you and I shall ever know the purpose of this expedition. I bid you farewell."

Chapter 3

Dominguez was so caught up in his reflections that he lost track of time. It was nearly an hour since Don Bernardo had left. The birds had flown from the paloverde trees for the night. Bats were ducking between the rain spouts of the governor's mansion. Farther off, up on the hill, Dominguez could see candles flickering in the windows of the mission church and fireflies sparking in the middle distance. Streams of faded purple and yellow still lined the evening sky, but it would be only moments before total darkness set in. In Mexico City he had loved these glimmering twilight moments; in Santa Fe they made him sad.

He turned back to his desk to look at his papers. He read reports from the various outlying missions, trying to imagine the conditions they described, making notes for his own report to the bishop and Governor Mendinueta in Mexico City. He worked until it was nearly dark and then he went outside, careful on the wide short stairs down to the first floor. The events of the day had tired him beyond his measure.

He had only three months more as the commissary visitor. This assignment to Santa Fe was to have been his last away from the graceful living and easy duty of Mexico City. To Dominguez, Mexico City was a place of aesthetic riches, enough for any man. Now he feared the stint at Santa Fe would be his last as a priest.

Dominguez worried about his ability to make it through the sierras. Escalante probably welcomed the test of will against body, but he himself did not. The doctors had assured him his condition was due to poor blood circulation. With proper diet and rest and absence of stress he should live another thirty years.

Comfortable retirement, well earned and much desired, awaited Dominguez in only three months. For the sake of his health and in recognition of his service, it had been promised.

He was looking forward to the role of priest in retirement, with everyone pampering him and paying overblown respect and hollow court. The most pressing question facing him on any given day in the easy future might be, ''Father, do you think the sacramental wine is perhaps a little tart?'' There would be enough simple religious duties to give him priestly purpose and to hold him safely in the warm embrace of the church.

For such riches and rewards he had had only to wait three months—but then Escalante arrived to pull it all from his grasp. The very contemplation of the name filled him with dismay and anger.

But there it was. If this Father Silvestre Velez de Escalante did indeed possess a valid map and supportable reports of a northern overland passage from New Mexico to Monterey in California, then he would have to forgo retirement for another few months and take this Escalante out to look for it.

The bishop had allowed him discretion to decide. Indeed, it seemed as though the bishop had even shown Dominguez a way to stay at home if he wished to break the faith just a little. Whether the map was good or not, he could simply say he found no merit in it and that would be that. He could stay at home and retire in three months as planned.

He would never be criticized. He could simply argue quite reasonably that the judgment had been left to him and in this case his judgment had been faulty. No one would chastise a priest in retirement in such circumstances.

So why was he unable to seize the bishop's option? Because when the greater glory of God and Spain was involved, there was no reprieve from such a mission short of disability, insanity, death or some miracle in the form of a countermanding order.

Dominguez wagged his hand impatiently. He understood clearly the need for such an overland passage. No more would Spain have to sail her men and supplies across the Atlantic to Panama, transport everything overland through the jungle to the Pacific, then reload onto other ships heading thousands of miles north to California.

There was still the alternative eastward route around the Cape of Good Hope, across the Indian Ocean to landfall in the Philippine Islands and across ten thousand miles of Pacific Ocean.

No more of that either, if there was a direct overland route from Mexico to Monterey.

And while British and Russian ships floundered about in two oceans, Spain would keep California by simply riding there on horseback in twenty days from Santa Fe.

Dominguez smiled. With the overland route Spain could keep California; the church could keep her western missions and the uncounted souls of the Indians.

Success, achievement, world power—all would depend in substantial measure upon himself and upon this Escalante.

If this Escalante had a good map. . . . Of course he had a good map. Dominguez knew it.

Somewhere a fly was caught buzzing in the folds of a curtain. Light cast upward from a tinwork lantern speckled the ceiling.

He fell to his knees and prayed fervently that God would

find the grace and generosity to delay the expedition another three months for some reason, any reason, for he himself could not do so.

In three months his replacement would come. He would be back in Mexico City, where he would pray long, fervent prayers for he who led Escalante into the wilderness in his stead.

On his way to say vespers at the old chapel in the early Santa Fe evening, Father Silvestre Velez de Escalante walked wide streets among the settlers' low adobes and the Indians' thatched huts.

A woman threw a pale sheet of water from a pan into the street.

A crow flapped up from a pile of barrow staves.

A naked child came to stand at the head of an alleyway.

Escalante passed a tavern. The soldiers inside were braying their laughter.

A very pretty woman in a shawl watched him pass her window. She smiled at him but did not bless herself. This pleased the handsome young cleric very much, that priest or not, women still smiled at him, thinking but one wicked thing. Some, Escalante liked to imagine, even had power to see through his woolen robes.

Man of God or not, he himself thought of this wicked thing so often he sometimes thought he should never have entered the church. The thought and sometimes the act itself interfered with prayer and with God's work.

Escalante had long ago come to peace with lust and its fellow traveler, guilt.

He had often wondered whether it was a trial decreed by God Himself. And what an exquisite trial indeed, to be sworn to celibacy in both mind and body and yet forced to go about God's business plagued by hard-working lust. He recalled the nonsense riddle of the monastery, put to all novices: What is the most difficult trial facing a Franciscan? To be a Franciscan with a love for women.

Mortally sinning possibly too often for the safety of his soul, Escalante had long ago decided not to torture himself looking for a solution to the unsolvable. That was indeed a waste of God's time, interfering with God's business.

He knew well how much and how often women dreamed of seducing their priests. Sobbing with guilt, they had many times told him so in their confessions.

Priests in their supposed unattainability were among the most desirable of men. Even the most innocent women, pure and steadfast in virtue, conjured visions of the priests' bodies inside their robes.

The cousin of the governor had been one such woman. Escalante sighed and winced. Eliza had taken, with pain, the fact that he could not run off with her to Belize. He believed that if he had sinned with Eliza, the sin had been his poor judgment of the young woman's worldliness. She was simply not ready for illicit love with any man, let alone a priest.

She had seemed ready. The way in which she had slowly removed his robes, as though peeling a fruit, had seemed bold and eager, but he suspected by now that it had been mainly superstitious curiosity. Some people thought the oddest things about priests' and nuns' bodies.

But for himself, before his God, once he had confessed the sin, done was done. And did not God Himself truly test those He loved with tests they could not pass so that in forgiving, He could love them more? Escalante had been taught that and he believed it.

He sighed. If God had not meant women to be tempting, he contemplated, He would not have made so many of them so beautiful and so willing. He crossed himself and prayed to heaven that he was correct in his thinking.

Boys ran beside him for a distance. They comforted him, but he could not determine whether or not they wanted some-

thing from him. They seemed not to be simple and true as
were the sons of settlers he had known and befriended in
Zuni.

He reached the adobe and brick church on the hill. It was
the original Santa Fe mission in New Mexico, dating from the
time of Juan de Onate. That was long ago, Escalante thought,
in the 1590s. He wondered that the Indians had allowed the
church, or Santa Fe itself, to stand. Onate had come to them
as the classic conquistador, vulgar, cruel and avaricious.

A coolness was descending the slopes of the San Juan
Mountains, moving in broken, lacy mists from the sandy
arroyos. Escalante went inside the church, beating the ever-
present dust from his robes.

In the low light of the vaulted church a figure in the
smock of an altar boy approached from behind a pillar. He
helped Escalante unpack his stole and vestments. The familiar
smells of incense, altar wine and beeswax candles made
Escalante feel as though the love of God was actually a
palpable lump swelling in his throat. I am a man who simply
likes to pray, Escalante thought.

He asked the Indian altar boy to light candles throughout
the church. Then he celebrated vespers for a few shawled
women, several Indian men and the young sacristan from the
rectory.

So few, he thought, so very few. He sighed. He envi-
sioned vespers at that moment in his own parish at Zuni,
miles away.

I built Zuni, he thought. Aware of his near-blasphemy,
he amended. As God's instrument I built the church in Zuni. I
love Zuni. And although the Zuni themselves still love their
own gods more than mine, they nonetheless come to my
church to learn of Him.

Escalante did not much mind the nearly empty church in
Santa Fe. He prayed for God's help in mounting the expedition to Monterey, the expedition he so fiercely believed in,

the search for the route both God and Spain needed so badly.
He prayed for His guidance, to be shown the way to California. Escalante was convinced it existed.

I am driven, he thought.

When he finished vespers and Mass and dismissed the
Indian boy, Escalante slipped into the carved confessional.
The restfulness of the small dark booth was in keeping with
his mood. Several women confessed their sins in low voices
that shook when they asked Escalante for the mercy of God.
One of them, an Indian, did not seem to have committed any
sins at all.

In time he found himself thinking of the wounded soldiers and whether or not they would recover, and of Father
Francisco Dominguez and what he might be like.

An old man came into the confessional and spoke brief-
ly. After he left there was a long silence. Escalante closed his
eyes and rested in the darkness. He was about to leave when
the kneeling pad in the chamber on his right creaked. He
heard breathing.

"Bless me, Father, for I have sinned," a male voice
began. Escalante immediately realized that it did not match
any of the faces in the pews at vespers. "It has been a few
months since my last confession."

There was a pause; Escalante had to urge the man to
continue. He spoke of a few minor sins and then stopped.
These clearly were not the matters he had come to confess.

"Speak up, my son," Escalante intoned.

"I can't, Father. I am full of tears."

Escalante waited a moment. Hearing the man weeping
aloud wearied him. Of all human failings, self-pity was the
one Escalante tolerated least; he had long wished he could
muster more charity for it. He saw his inability to do so as a
priestly failing.

Escalante recalled the encounter with the soldier that
afternoon upon entering Santa Fe. The wound still scorched

his back. Escalante appreciated and respected the man's anger;
as a response to adversity and stress, it was more to Escalante's
understanding and personal liking than this blubbering in the
dark.

Escalante took a breath. He knew his duty regardless of
his feelings. "What is it, my son? Put your heart in the hands
of God and tell me what it is that you have done."

"It's my wife, Father. She was unfaithful to me."

"That is her sin, my son, not yours."

"She has lusted after other men, Father, many men. She
has told me this and I have seen many times how it is true."

"But what sin have *you* committed?" Escalante asked,
suddenly tired of mankind altogether.

"She taunted me, Father, made fun of me."

"How did she do that?"

"She spread word my children are not my own."

"Are they?"

There was a pause. The voice now was really wretched.
"I don't see how they could be."

Escalante passed his hand over his brow, his chest tightening in anger. "What do you mean?"

"That particular part of the sacrament of marriage I could
not fulfill, Father."

"That is no sin," Escalante said impatiently. "Why
have you told me so much of all this when you have not
sinned yourself? Perhaps it was not God's will that you
should marry, but I cannot absolve you of that."

"But Father, I murdered her."

"My son," Escalante began, "you do not actually take
the life of a woman by being unable to give her children—"

"Father, I killed her. Truly I did. She is dead by my
own hand."

Escalante sat back in the confessional booth, strangely
relieved for a moment. This was no waste of his time after
all.

Then he drank in the man's meaning and stiffened. Murder! He snatched open the curtains of the chamber, but the confessor was gone.

Escalante jumped from the booth and ran along the church aisle. The man was a shadow in the doorway to the night. Lifting the skirt of his robes, Escalante leaped from the top step and soared, arms outstretched. Air billowed his soutane round and wide as he came down. He splashed into the dust just behind the running man.

Another lunge slammed Escalante into the man from behind. The murderer's back arched and then his body recoiled, swinging forward, slapping the earth with the sound of a strap slapping a table. He grunted with pain.

The man knew how to fall safely, however, for he allowed himself to roll with Escalante's weight and used the priest's forward momentum to catapult him over his own body.

Escalante came down on one side of his head and his shoulder. He groaned. Tears of pain filled his eyes. He was certain he had broken bones. He yelled at the man, "If you have murdered you must deal with God and the authorities both."

"I should not have confessed." Each trying to be first on his feet, they pushed against each other on hands and knees, looking like pit dogs.

"At least stay to deal with God. I cannot turn in a man who confesses, you know. The secrecy is absolute."

"It was weak to confess. I must bear this alone."

"If you have murdered your wife you must—"

Escalante never finished the sentence. The man spun swiftly, balancing himself on outstretched arms. He reared and kicked hard against Escalante's chest.

Escalante imagined he could feel the imprint of his own crucifix on his chest. A shout of pain escaped him. He fell onto his back in the dust, arms flailing. The bayonet cut he had taken earlier opened and he had lost his breath.

The other was on his feet, a shadow flowing through the darkness. Escalante leaped and caught one of his boots with hooked fingertips. He held for a moment, but only for a moment. He was too far off balance. He fell against the bricks of the church steps. He barely got his arms up to protect his face; his head hit hard. His cowl muffled the sound.

He was stunned. Everything seemed brown. When Escalante's head was clear again, he saw he was alone. No one had seen his scuffle with the man from the church; or if anyone had, they chose not to remain to bear witness.

Escalante sat on the steps, knees apart, supporting his head to clear his senses, wishing he knew more about alley fighting. The other man apparently knew quite a bit.

Lanterns shone from the windows of the many houses of Santa Fe. Against the vast darkness of the mountain night the city seemed welcoming, almost poignantly so, but not to Escalante. All that he feared and disliked about cities—the presence of violence and complicated sin—had reared up like some poisonous snake to strike him.

On the threshold of an expedition greater and more important than he had ever imagined he would make, a phantom in the confessional was casting a shade of doubt upon his heart. He had fought weakness and doubt all his life.

But this strange, invisible man troubled him greatly. Was the man a symbol of weakness in himself? Was Escalante too willful? Was he a good priest? He had not even been able to hold the man there when he had him to minister to his spirit and persuade him to justice.

Shaking his head like a dog aggrieved by flies, Escalante tried to dislodge his doubt. He wanted to deceive himself, to believe he had dreamed the man's confession out of his own expectations of evil in the city, home of all that was false.

He had not dreamed it, though. The confession had been

loud and clear: "Father, I killed her. Truly I did. By my own hand."

Escalante stared into the candlelight that shimmered in the empty church. He was angry and disturbed. It all might just as well have been a dream.

Chapter 4

The two priests met for the first time that evening following vespers.

"Father Escalante." Dominguez nodded, extending his hand.

"Father Dominguez." Escalante grasped it.

They sat in the paneled vault that was Dominguez' study, sipping sherry as dry as sand to Escalante's taste. The smell of dinner made Escalante's saliva surge. He realized that he had once more neglected to eat all day.

He offered Dominguez a cigar from a badly stitched leather case. Dominguez refused, saying that anything so black and bitter only dulled his taste for sherry, but he begged Escalante to smoke if he wished.

Escalante took a light from a beeswax candle. He allowed the smoke to fill his mouth and nostrils. The bitterness was pleasant. It also made his appetite for food behave.

In silence, each took measure of the other.

Dominguez opened their dialogue. "I understand you said vespers and Mass at the old chapel. A fine and thoughtful gesture. The people appreciate such things. I should do so myself more often. I assume you found everything in order.''

Escalante was both vexed and amused by the man's glib way. In all things, even exploration for wealth and kingdom and glory and power, small talk came first.

''Not quite, Father. There was a man who confessed—'' He did not get to finish.

''They are sending you out into the wilderness to sweep you under the rug, Escalante, and I am to be your sweeper.''

Escalante flinched, jerking his head backward. This was not small talk.

''You are undisciplined, you are worldly, you are a womanizer, you are arrogant and you have no respect for rank, or so I am told. You are an embarrassment to people in high places in Mexico City and elsewhere in New Spain. And so they are sending you out as much to sweep you under the rug as to find the blasted overland route to Monterey. Do you already know this? Yes, you probably do.''

Escalante sounded a low whistle. ''Are you always so blunt, Father?''

''I try not to be. It is sometimes the only way. . . . No, do not speak, Escalante.'' He drew in a breath. ''Furthermore, should you happen to ride your horse off a mountain along the way, or take an arrow through the eye into your brain, they—those of whom I speak—would not actually mind. Exit a brilliant but troublesome priest. Enter a new martyr for the greater glory of God. New martyrs are always welcome.''

Escalante marveled. Dominguez said so much with so few words. The hint of intrigue excited him even as its meaning depressed him. He did not like being its focus. ''Can you tell me who 'they' are?''

''No. I am telling you a lot as it is. Never mind who. And can you imagine why all this is?''

''I know I have displeased many people. And from their point of view they have good reason. But I did not imagine they were annoyed enough to put so important a thing as this expedition second to back-stabbing.''

"Well, they are. I swore I would tell you none of this. Rubbish. If we are to travel together, you must know all of the facts and terms. Your response to them does not matter, nor does mine. If things are right for going, we are going, no matter what.''

Dominguez took Escalante's arm and sighed. "There. It is said. Now I can sit you down to dinner with good conscience.''

Escalante started to speak.

"Later," Dominguez chided. "We talk later about business. Dinner first.''

As they moved arm in arm toward the dining room, Escalante suddenly laughed from deep inside himself.

Dominguez observed, "It does not seem to disturb you, knowing this.''

"No, not really. Although the pettiness does, and the malice and intrigue. Why cannot grown men simply come out and say what they're thinking and what they are going to do? I don't think I really care what their reasons are for wanting to send us. The important thing is, we are going.'' He gripped Dominguez' hand. "Thank you for telling me these things. I like the honesty. An earlier impression I had of you was incorrect. I like you, Dominguez.''

"Humph. I am not yet certain whether I like you.''

The Indian servant laid before them beef so tender and fragrant that Escalante gasped at his first bite of it. He had heard of such meat but never eaten any like it.

The wine was so deep a red that it appeared black in the candlelight. It came from Mexico City, Dominguez mentioned. The flavor surprised Escalante. Its texture was velvety, but it possessed a lurking ferocity that brought broadswords to Escalante's mind.

For dessert they had a pastry in sheets so broad and light

that Escalante imagined they could fly. Streaks of powdered sugar looked like feathers to his mind's eye.

Escalante thought to mention the man who had confessed murdering his wife and then run away, but he decided to remain still. The secrets of the confessional were sacred, after all, no matter how sensational—even within the clergy. Besides, he might not be believed.

Escalante wished for a bowl of homemade Indian beer, cool and gently bitter, to drink with another cigar.

An Indian boy appeared in the dim candlelight to say brandy and coffee would be served in the study if the Fathers so desired.

Dominguez poured brandy into two glasses. He made a whirlpool of his own, turning the glass, studying the liquid for a moment. Then he probed, "Rumor has it that there is a highly credible map showing what appears to be a way across the desert and the mountains from here to Monterey."

"There is."

"And you have it."

"I do. You sound doubtful."

"Not doubtful, Escalante. Hopeful the rumor may be false."

"I do not understand."

Dominguez waved. "Never mind. I have my own private reason. I'll explain it to you someday, but not now. Escalante, knowing what I already know of you, I knew you would have such a map. I knew it would be credible."

"How can you be so sure?" Escalante was amused. "Reports have proven to be dreams in the past. Maps have turned out to be rubbings of the imagination."

"Escalante, Escalante," Dominguez sighed, "listen to me. You have the reputation of a man who accomplishes things, a reliable man despite your faults and appetites."

Escalante did not acknowledge the remark.

Dominguez continued, "You are in charge today of all

the Pueblo Indian missions in New Mexico. It's an enormous administrative and pastoral responsibility, hmmm? You were not given this responsibility because you produce unreadable maps and chase fantasies. You are no Coronado, chasing the dream called the Seven Golden Cities of Cibola, God forgive his dizziness. You follow no such myths. When you produce maps and reports of a way to Monterey in only twenty days, we consider them seriously."

"Nonetheless, certain individuals wish to sweep me under the rug, as you say."

"Nonetheless. However, their reasons have nothing to do with this talent of yours. But enough of that now."

"Yes. Done is done. And I might do the same with me if I were they."

"There's further support for your reports," Dominguez added, "and firmer than you might expect."

"That's a pleasant surprise. What is it?"

"Not what, but whose. We've heard that Father Garces has confirmed much of what you show on your map. There's a report that Garces has actually seen what may be the very passes between the mountains. Escalante, you cannot find stronger confirmation than Garces."

"First they ask Garces to look about and seek it, and now me. It is very likely that Francisco Garces is dead, you know."

The reference made Dominguez uncomfortable. "Yes," he fretted, "so it is rumored."

"He has not been heard from in some time, not since his last trip. I ask about him frequently. No one, neither Spaniard nor Indian, seems to know of him. You know, Dominguez, it is as though the mountains between here and California have taken him prisoner as he tried to learn their secrets and that they have thrown the key away."

"A pagan fancy on your part, Escalante," Dominguez admonished smiling. "Careful, then. The mountains may imprison you for the same reason. I understand both you and

Garces, thinking independently, have explored New Mexico and west with the notion of establishing a string of Spanish missions between here and California as a means of keeping communications open.''

"Yes, Father, that was Garces' intent, too. I cross myself for his sake and safety.''

Dominguez waited, studying Escalante. The man is such a mix of piety and independence, he reflected, rubbing one's nose in his rebelliousness one moment, praying as fervently as a novice for a lost brother the next.

"It's a good plan,'' Escalante continued. "Along the Gila River lies the Valley of the Sun. That river flows clear from New Mexico to Yuma in Arizona. The valley itself is fertile as well as fine protection.'' Escalante thought for a moment. "There is another factor to consider. There is no better time for Spaniards than now, this summer of 1776, to be establishing new missions and footholds. The British in California may be fencing and threatening now, but they may not be able to afford to for long, as you must know. They're about to lose their colonies in New England and farther south, are they not? There is talk that independence is inevitable. After a year of fighting, the British still have been unable to crush the rebellion. This man Washington seems to lead it well.''

"Yes,'' Dominguez acknowledged. "Ever since the first skirmishes in the Massachusetts colony last April of '75—Lexington and Concord are the place names, I believe—the British have not been able to contain the revolt. There were terrible British losses at some place called Bunker Hill.'' Dominguez' tongue was awkward on the foreign names.

He sipped brandy and leaned back in his chair. "Our reports on affairs in the East are quite thorough. In light of them, it's expected that you're correct in your assessment. Once we open an overland route to California, the British will give up. We'll be too strong for them. They will realize that they cannot hope to deal with strong enemies in two places a continent apart.''

"It is true, then, that the colonists' Continental Congress is about to publish a unilateral Declaration of Independence that severs relations with Britain forever?''

"I'm surprised you know so much about it out here, Escalante.''

"Even in Zuni we hear things, Father, even in Zuni.''

"It seems you do. Well, yes. The latest reports we have, now almost two months old, say the declaration is due right around now, in early July.''

"All the more reason to break open the way to California right now. As we agree, the British will be too busy in the East to invest much in stopping us in the West.''

"Precisely.''

"What about the Russians?'' Escalante asked.

"What do you think?''

"I don't know. I've never met a Russian.''

"No one knows. No one. When it comes to Russians, one never knows which way they will jump. Russians are mad. You talk of revolution; there, in Russia, is where they will one day have a revolution. And when it comes, stand back. What a revolution it will be.'' He shook his head. "But we digress.''

Escalante nodded. Both sipped brandy. Dominguez spoke once more. "Escalante, no matter how you may embarrass people in high places, you and Garces are not called explorer-priests without good reason. You are a valuable, very valuable breed. You do what others cannot, and speaking for myself, do not want to do. As you do, I pray Garces is not dead. We need him.''

"The reports are not confirmed.''

"And I hope they never are. The church would be losing a fine shepherd and a bold champion extending its reach. Smoke?'' Dominguez offered Escalante one of his special imported cigars.

"Thank you." Escalante sniffed the long, thin panatela. "In my opinion, Dominguez, our Father Garces is more than just one of a breed, much more. If the route to Monterey really does exist, and we won't know until we actually find it, it is Garces who deserves the credit. He was out there first. He pointed the way."

"No quarrel with that," Dominguez agreed. He lit his cigar. "But the fact is, you are the one who possesses the map." He stood and blew a cloud of smoke into the dark chambers. "Well, let's have a look at it, shall we?"

Dominguez summoned the Indian servant and asked him to be so good as to bring Father Escalante's case. When the boy returned Escalante was moving candles onto a large table to see the map more clearly. The document was hand-printed on cured skin and smelled of animal, oil and charcoal. Spread out, it covered half the table. It delineated a vast region north and west of both Mexico and the territory of New Mexico and showed rivers, lakes and mountains in great detail.

"One mountain pass is said to be here." Escalante pointed with his unlit cigar.

Dominguez bunched two fists and leaned on them, lowering his face to the map, the better to see the red lines marking routes. "Tortuous," he murmured, "so tortuous."

"No one ever said it would be like sailing a ship into Vera Cruz. And in reality, these passes may not even be there. One cannot drive mules on the red lines of a map."

"These mountains, these lakes, no one has ever seen them? Ever?"

"Not white men, certainly."

"Do these places have names?" Dominguez was filled with wonder, recalling how wild and excited he had felt the first time he had seen a map as a child. "Do these places have names, Escalante?" His hand tapped across the map.

"The Indians call this area Utah. As you already know,

this region is named Colorado for the redness of the mountains.''

"I understand from Governor Mendinueta's man Miera that the Indians gave you this map. Miera was here earlier.''

"Yes. They were Hopi who befriended us.'' Escalante tilted his head back and laughed. "Or at least they did not send arrows at us as often as the other Hopi did.''

"That was a terrible trip.''

"No.''

"But one of your worst, I understand.''

"No worse than any others, begging to differ with your sources of information, Dominguez. And the Indians cannot be defined as terrible just for resisting. Not all of them want our ways or our messages of God, as misguided and dangerous for their souls as such thinking is. Some of our people, the soldiers in particular, are brutal. They steal and rape and kill afterward, bayonet the women's bellies while they are still in the bed wiping themselves clean.''

"Force is the tradition of the conquistador.''

"It doesn't pave an easy road to God, Father. The Hopi often rebelled. They saw us as invaders; many still do. They fought before and they will do so when we go among them again. We have our wounded paving the streets of Santa Fe this very day as sign of it.''

"I am told, Escalante, that some of what you learned last year about removing Hopi arrows was useful today.''

Escalante hooted with laughter. "Your spies were out, Father. Yes, I removed an arrow.''

"You also engaged in some horseplay with one of the soldiers, I hear, although some seem to think it was more serious than horseplay.''

"Erroneously.''

"And the bullet hole in the steeple is erroneous too, I suppose.''

Escalante felt a tiny jump of fear at the reminder. He thought once more of the man who had confessed killing his

own wife, the faceless whisperer of perfidy. He thought to
confess to Dominguez concerning the incident; he did not.
For one thing, he was not certain Dominguez would think the
matter serious. Indeed, he himself could not swear that it
was. For another, he was certain he would meet this man
again. He was so certain that the thought chilled him. Could
he divine the future? Dominguez would think this blasphemy.

The priest was tapping the map. "And you trust this,
considering the hostility of those who gave it to you?"

"Those who gave it were friends."

"And they would not lie?"

"Let me put it this way, Father. Rather than a false map
they would have given me nothing at all. I can trust them that
far."

"Let me ponder all of this for a moment." Dominguez
paced, gently punching a palm with a fist. His cassock whispered. Escalante noted how well he moved despite his bulk.

A ponderous clock, thick as a pillar in Rome, struck ten.
Still Dominguez paced and thought. A few more minutes
passed. Escalante lit his panatela. Then suddenly Dominguez
stopped, flung his arms wide and faced Escalante.

"If you believe in this map, I believe in it." He sighed.

"But? There seems to be an unspoken but."

"No but," Dominguez assured him. "My orders are
clear. If you believe there is hope of finding the route, I must
believe it too. And if I believe, I mount an expedition. That is
all there is to be said. Miera will be pleased. Governor
Mendinueta will be pleased. Bishop Escobar will be pleased.
So. On to Monterey."

Escalante smelled sarcasm. "But are you pleased, Father
Dominguez?"

Dominguez bunched his lips. "Frankly, no."

Escalante tilted his head, questioning.

"I hoped you would not have this map, that it would be
a joke." He looked at Escalante sadly. "I speak to you
candidly, Escalante. It is no secret that I do not wish to make

this journey. I am tired. I am ill. I could retire in three months but for this—'' He pounded a fist down hard on the map. "But you need not know all this for now. Before we leave, yes. You're entitled to know the best and the worst about any man you travel with. I'll say this: even if I were young and not worn out, this sort of runaround would not be to my taste as it is to yours. I am no explorer, Escalante. I never have been. I serve the Lord in other ways. You are the sort of man who captures forts from the heathen. I am the sort who holds them forever afterward."

Dominguez filled their glasses with brandy once more. He touched Escalante's with his own, generating a lingering soft bell tone. "I shall authorize and promote this exploration with every resource I can muster. But be clear on one point." Dominguez sipped. "You will be its leader."

Escalante said nothing as he lifted his glass to salute Dominguez. He had not expected the man to abdicate so fully.

"Now it's you who do not seem pleased," Dominguez chuckled.

"I am pleased. But I'm surprised, Father. It's my preference to be in charge; then I can blame only myself for mistakes. But I am not used to men giving up power voluntarily, especially men of our order. Franciscans are deprived of the pleasures other men enjoy, so I think God makes it up to us by giving us power to play with. And infighting for power is a Franciscan way of life."

Dominguez was nodding. He knew Escalante was right. "Don't misunderstand. You are the leader because I could not be even if I wished to, which I do not. My instructions from Mexico City are clear. Bishop Escobar and Governor Mendinueta are aware of my shortcoming also. I firmly believe they are. They say I am to be leader but they know you will really lead. You have the experience and the ambition. To my dismay, I am to accompany you to play Mark Antony to your Caesar, to provide authority and presence, and to take command should something happen to you. I am merely a figurehead.'' He grinned. ''Don't worry, Escalante, I'll be busy in my own way. Although this is at bottom a military and political expedition to secure a power base in California, it is also an evangelical mission. We are to harvest all the souls we can along the way. I shall be working for Christ.''

"Then I am truly pleased," Escalante answered, gripping Dominguez' hands, "and deeply honored by the trust, despite the other reasons they have for sending me."

Dominguez studied Escalante across the rim of his glass. "Then I inform the bishop it is done. We'll leave Santa Fe as soon as you can put men and animals and supplies together. Return to Zuni tomorrow and get busy. Get everything we need. Get the best. I can guarantee unlimited funds for whatever we need." He paused. "One last thing. See that our men carry as few weapons as possible. I know, I know, we shall be passing among some viciously hostile Indians, but this order holds. As few firearms as possible, Escalante, and preferably pistols only. Enough of them for hunting and self-defense, but that is all. We go as a party of peace and love with the word of God, not as conquistadores."

Dominguez laid an arm on Escalante's shoulders. "Now off to bed. Get a good night's rest, God willing. You leave first thing after matins. Don't feel you must find everything you need in Zuni or even Santa Fe. Go where you must to find the finest men and horses, but get them all back here to Santa Fe as soon as possible. We must try to leave early next month, in July."

"I'll go to Zuni first, yes. But I'll probably go to Taos for the horses. The ones they breed there can climb straight up the mountains. But that's not what concerns me now." He was frowning. "It's something you said a moment ago."

Dominguez nodded, indicating he should speak his mind.

"This restriction on firearms is crazy," Escalante admonished. "And it's dangerous. Suicidal. I mean this,

Dominguez. Don't mistake my moderate tones to signify indifference on this subject."

"I understand."

"Hunting for the cookpot requires rifles."

"I understand."

"The Hopi put no restrictions on their own firearms nor on the arrows with which they can skewer a man from beyond pistol range."

"I understand."

"You understand, you understand. Is that all you can say?" Escalante suddenly stopped and sighed. "Father, never mind firearms for now." He had decided that he would solve that problem himself. Later, if necessary, he would simply hide the rifles in burlap and take them along, saying nothing. He smiled, savoring the disobedience. Of course that was one of the very reasons he was being sent out to California to begin with.

He was too pleased to argue about firearms. He had been given the one thing he wanted most for his church and for himself. The expedition would go, and for that moment, that was enough.

He raised his glass. "Father Dominguez," Escalante toasted.

"Father Escalante." They smiled at each other and their crystal glasses met, ringing out the coming of a new era for Spain and the church.

Chapter 5

At dawn Don Pedro Cisneros rolled over in bed and looked at his sleeping wife. Her personal musk wafted up as he moved his arm out from under the sheet. Greenish early light streamed through the window, illuminating only the upper part of the room, the top of the crested armoire and the heavy lace curtains his wife's family had brought from Spain.

Slowly, as his eyes adjusted and the light changed, the form of his sleeping wife grew clearer. Dona Estella's bulk lay against her downy sleeping gown like muscle under skin, but there was a fullness to her curves, a certain delicious swooping. One arm with its surprisingly small hand lay behind her on the pillow. A rooster crowed in a faraway jacal. In his mind's eye Cisneros could see the sun pinking the rims of the Sangre de Cristo Mountains. His wife moved and grunted. The sound of her nightdress sliding over one thigh aroused Don Pedro, who rolled onto his stomach. He slid his fingers beneath her palm and moved closer across the mattress. She was truly asleep, however, or feigning well, for her hand showed no reaction to his fingers and the rhythm of her breathing did not change. A horseman passed outside. For a moment Cisneros wondered who it was. Then his wife's hand closed around his fingers and she woke, or pretended to, and turned her head on the pillow.

Even in the dimness of the dawn light he could clearly see her large onyx eyes staring at him, the slackness of her face drawn ever so slightly into a frown. He rolled over to reveal his expectations. It was suddenly so quiet he could hear her eyelashes move against the pillow as she looked down. She sighed and raised up on one shoulder, then took away her one hand while reaching for him with the other. She touched his chest and let her hand press there a moment, more a halting action than any manner of caress. He turned against the hand and raised the hem of her muslin gown. With another sigh she lay back, whispering that it was all right. If he wished to, she wished to.

For an angry moment Cisneros wished his wife would admit wishing to herself, just once, before he wished to. Cisneros sighed. Women were not raised to appreciate and concede lust as men were. He knew that. Calming himself, he accepted the unchangeable once more.

Cisneros eased himself inside her. She sighed once again, this time trembling, and as he began to move she whispered, "Hail, Mary. Hail, Mary. . . ."

Sweat dribbled down Cisneros' nose onto her chin and soaked without trace into the whiteness of her nightdress. Her breasts moved like great rubbery mounds as the rhythm of her rosary grew forced.

Outdoors the dogs were barking. The sun's rays must have reached a long way over the mountains; a portion of the wall above the crested armoire was turning golden. "Don Pedro, my husband, the mayor of Zuni," she was grinding out between her teeth, "Don Pedro, my husband, the mayor of Zuni." Her eyes glittered with intensity. Her hair had grown damp on her forehead.

For a long while they rested at peace, watching sunlight

make the room glow. Eventually Estella spoke, touching an old topic that was sore to them both.

"You would not have been chosen by Escalante were you not the mayor of Zuni."

He nodded into her neck, listening with greater interest to the noises of early morning. Voices were floating between the adobes of Zuni like bits of ash floating from a fire. He tried to identify them but could not, and then no longer cared to.

His wife slid out from under him and pulled her nightdress down in a motion that forced her breasts to bulge between her arms. The sight of them aroused him again as much as her rounded white legs did. Don Pedro rolled into her depression in the bed and looked at her as she straightened her nightdress.

"Escalante is my friend," he reminded her. "Were I only a drayman, I would still have been chosen for the journey to find Monterey and the sea. After our trip to the Hopi he knows he cannot do without me. I am his eyes."

"But you are not a drayman," insisted his wife, untwisting her plaited hair.

Cisneros rolled to a sitting position. "That's true. I am now the mayor of Zuni."

"In no small thanks, though," boasted his wife, "to my cousin Joaquin Lain."

Cisneros shrugged. His wife's cousin had been generous with his influence, but Cisneros did not like to be reminded of his obligation.

Estella turned to him and took his hands in her own with a fervor that surprised him. "I have plans for us, my husband, so you must come safely back to me. I can see great things for your future. This is only a start. Much glory will come to you from this journey, you and Don Joaquin both." She seized his head and pressed it between her warm breasts. "I know you shall make me proud."

"I shall try," Cisneros huffed, removing his head from

her clasp, fearing suffocation. His heart was sinking. How often had Lain been in her mind? Her thoughts should include only him.

One of his daughters had come to stand at the open door. Cisneros' heart went out to the child, who did not see him. Then she was snatched up by her Indian nursemaid and carried off squealing.

It was still not fully light outside, but now the patch of gold had spread from above the armoire to color much of the wall.

"Conchita," Dona Estella called to her servant. "Please come assist your mistress." She was holding a dress against herself and staring into the greenish waves of a poorly silvered mirror.

Cisneros, now at the window, spat outside.

Conchita came into the room. A dollop from the bowl of warm water she was carrying slopped onto the wooden floor, giving off an incense of wet cedar. Cisneros did not turn around but heard the two women pass into his wife's dressing room.

Cisneros again spat out the window and scratched himself. A few Indians and several men in buckskins were standing against a distant wall. Among them was Lucrecio Muniz, his rather stupid servant. He stood by his brother Andres, who spoke Hopi, Ute and a little Havasupai and had trapped for years in the mountains. Andres would serve as the party's guide. Along with Joaquin Lain and his servant Juan de Aguilar, the priest Dominguez was coming from Santa Fe with Captain Miera and his dwarf servant, Simon Lucero. Cisneros felt a swell of pride. He would miss his wife and his children, but he dearly wished to get started.

Mist was rising from the bare beaten track that ran from one horizon to the other right through the center of Zuni. Under a giant piñon were the pack animals, tied to a railing before the smithy. Their long tails hung down behind them wet with dew. Smoke rose from the blacksmith's adobe chimney and Cisneros could hear the ringing of a horseshoe beaten on an anvil.

"Say, Cisneros," one of the men called from down below. "We're still leaving right after the noon meal to meet with Father Dominguez?"

Cisneros hooted affirmation.

"You know Escalante has already left Zuni," the man said, "early this morning. He was only here for a few days."

"Yes, I know," Cisneros yelled.

"What the hell for? Can't he wait? Is he going to try to find the passage all by himself?"

Cisneros laughed. "No, he's going to Taos for a few days. He's heard there are some good horses for sale there. He'll join us in Santa Fe." The man at the fire slapped his forehead with his palm.

Cisneros laughed. He turned to a big wall calendar on rough paper and lifted the pages to the future. The scheduled departure of the expedition to Monterey from Santa Fe was only a few days off. They would leave on July 4, 1776.

Simply thinking of the importance of the expedition made him gasp. That will be a day to conjure with, Cisneros thought, the beginning of a trip to glory. If they succeeded in finding the overland passage to California, July 4, 1776, might indeed go down in history.

In Taos the frustration and disappointment lay deep as night.

Just before noon Escalante was preparing to leave for Santa Fe with his new horses. As he adjusted his saddle and tack he thought to himself, Suddenly I do not feel well. Is this the old pain again in my right side? Within minutes Escalante was prone in the dirt, so sudden was the onset of his old illness.

Escalante clutched his bridle. He tried to haul himself from the dirt hand over hand along the leather, but he fell back sucking wind. The pain was curling him up like a leaf in the noon heat. The horse slathered Escalante's face with his tongue, evidently seeking the salty sweat that ran down his face.

Escalante bellowed, "Get up, get up! You are my body and you go where I tell you to go. This expedition will leave on schedule. I will *not* be ill."

The others at the corral did not understand that he was reprimanding himself. They imagined he was talking to some being they could not see and were certain that madness was upon him.

Then he passed out. Escalante did not saddle up for Santa Fe that day or for many days thereafter.

During the illness Escalante's body sometimes grew so hot and dry that the Indian brothers of the Taos mission said one might boil water upon his chest. At other times they found him cold, soggy and shivering. Any food he ate he almost immediately spewed back out onto his lap and bed-clothes. At times he slept so deeply and breathed so slightly they thought he might be dead, and when he did not sleep, he raged in delirium. His blasphemies and curses made his nurses weep. They feared that listening to Escalante's rantings put their own immortal souls in jeopardy.

Some of them said Escalante's voice was no longer his own; he was possessed of Satan. And they said Satan could be heard playing with his cloven hooves on Escalante's ribs like a xylophone.

There was talk of exorcism and flagellation. The superstitious maintained the entire expedition should be called off and all of the saddles and supplies burned and the ashes thrown into deep canyons, for Escalante's affliction was surely God's own curse upon him for his worldly ways and sins. They said that God was rejecting both the man and his expedition.

Some even insisted that dark clouds had been seen above the very route the expedition was to take on its departure from Santa Fe to the mountains. At the very moment Escalante had fallen, they said, lightning had sundered the rocks beside the trail. However, this was not taken seriously since neither witnesses nor sundered rocks were to be found.

At dawn eight days later Escalante's fever and chills left as suddenly as they had come. He talked coherently once again and the first thing he asked for was food. Light broth, bread and chicken were taken to him. He ate voraciously for almost an hour while all who watched gave thanks to God.

His only complaints were of weakness and exhaustion and residual pain in his right side.

His second request was for Father Dominguez.

Early in Escalante's seizure the middle-aged priest had recognized the condition as an acute episode of the chronic illness that had troubled the young man for several years. No doubt it was exacerbated by infection in the bayonet wound he had taken in Santa Fe. Dominguez had told everyone to cease being foolish and talk no more of possession. He told everyone to have faith instead and soon the illness would pass and Father Escalante would be well once more—until the next seizure.

Dominguez decided that since the expedition could go nowhere without Escalante, he himself would go to Isleta to attend mission business while Escalante recuperated.

He was still in Isleta when a messenger on a sweating horse caught up with Dominguez with word that Escalante was well again and asking for him.

At once Dominguez saddled up and hauled his bulk onto a mount.

Chapter 6

Father Francisco Atanasio Dominguez guided his horse along dusty alleys among houses not much larger than commercial ovens. The animal lurched from one side to another. Footing was difficult. The paths were so worn that they were no longer streets, but troughs worn into the earth by feet and hooves.

This was Taos.

Outside the community he crossed wooded ridges and grassy knolls. For once in his life he was happy to be outdoors, away from a city. To Dominguez Taos was an unhappy place.

A woman in Taos had described the house Escalante had chosen for his recuperation, and as he rode through the deserted streets he watched for it, wishing it would appear. It was many miles from town.

He prayed Escalante was well enough to begin the expedition. The men of the troop, which Escalante himself had mustered, were chafing under the delay. It was now three weeks after the scheduled departure. Dominguez wanted to begin, if only to end the trip sooner.

With his good will Dominguez brought sad news for Escalante. He had received word in Santa Fe that Father Garces had never returned to Yuma. Traders and scouts coming in from the wilderness knew nothing of the adventurous priest. He was presumed dead. The men of the Monterey expedition now had the added responsibility of searching and inquiring along their route for Garces or his remains; Bishop Diego Nadie de Escobar in Mexico City had ordered it so.

As he bounced along on his horse, Dominguez saw evidence of the warfare plaguing the region. Beside him were fields of maize, put to the torch so recently they seemed planted with tendrils of smoke. Arrow shafts littered the roadway, where puddled blood had chipped and flaked away like mud. The carcasses of butchered animals seemed ready to float in the air, so ballooned were they with fetid gases. Carrion birds wheeled above.

Dominguez' heart felt as though it were lifted from him by wonders of pain and suffering he could not have imagined had he not seen this debris of the war. He reflected that God's great plans had often moved him strangely.

Hopi and Santa Fe garrison troops were chasing each other up and down the cliffs of northern New Mexico. The Spanish soldiers laid siege rings around the Hopi strong points, frequently finding their rifles and cannon unable to reach the distant targets. Cannon balls and rifle shot fell back on their own positions.

Confident field reports described the Hopi uprising as all but crushed. Dominguez snorted. Looking about the countryside, he doubted it. His eyes smarted with pity for the men of both sides.

Dust was taking the place of smoke, swirling continually out from the hooves of Dominguez' horse. Traces of the Spanish troops were more evident here than signs of the Hopi they pursued. Bucklers and sword weights lay where they had fallen. Injured horses, recently revived, stood curious and attentive among the sagebrush.

Motivations for it all were so beautifully, tragically simple, Dominguez realized. The Hopi wanted to rid themselves of Spanish law, levies and religion. The Spanish troops were sent to force them to accept. There was no compromise; the war was destined.

It was just after midday and Dominguez was hoping to reach the mountains before dusk. All of Taos seemed deserted. The heat was intense and dry enough to parch the breath. Children played a game in the shade of an adobe, throwing the knucklebone of a buffalo against a wall. A woman came out to make them stop, but instead watched Dominguez ride by on his slow-moving horse.

"Bless me, Father," she begged, "and bless these little children."

It was the stillness, Dominguez thought, that made these people appear to strain without movement against the awful space of sky. It seemed only the wind could move them, as though they were only bits of larger things, of rock, grass and tree.

As Dominguez rode toward the foothills, he saw grasshoppers jumping at each step of his horse and tiny pocket rabbits darting across the animal trails. An occasional jack, twitching ears the color of flesh, ambled through the sage, stopped, then bounded away.

An hour before dusk he reached the tiny stone house the woman had described. There was a spruce tree cleft by lightning and then the house on a wind-bared hillock. He led his mount up the hillock to the stone house, where sheep had cropped the grass to the fineness of baize. Dominguez sheltered his horse in a small corral.

The doorway was low and he had to duck to enter the house. Escalante was propped up on his pallet, a blanket at his feet. Dominguez, who had some experience with fevers, knew immediately that Escalante's was gone, although he still looked glassy-eyed.

Escalante pushed himself slowly away from the wall and onto his knees. He bowed his head to Dominguez.

"Please, Father," Dominguez urged, "don't exert yourself so. I'm glad to see you're not looking as bad as one might expect. Except for being unwashed and unshaven, you don't seem like a man possessed by Satan."

Escalante chuckled. "Yes. I heard that had happened to me."

"I can see where people might have gotten the idea. Your feet are so dirty they might be taken for cloven hooves."

"Father," Escalante said wearily, "when you're as ill as I've been, clean feet are your last concern."

Dominguez noticed Escalante's legs trembling beneath the thin nightshirt he wore. "Please lie down, Escalante. Your exertion is making me tired."

"It's good for me to stretch the muscles as much as I can. It prepares me for exercise."

"I feel sure we can find a hair shirt for you too, since you like stress and discomfort so much," Dominguez replied.

Escalante smiled, then looked stern. "I think I am angry with you, Dominguez."

"For not coming to you sooner? Lord, what would have been the point, man? In your delirium you would not have known me from a baboon."

"No, that's not the reason."

"What other?"

"For not getting the expedition on its way on time. You should have left without me. This is far too important to delay for the sake of one man."

"Should have in theory, perhaps, but in fact could not have. Escalante, can you see me with my sparse knowledge of the wilderness leading those men? Can you see me, this doughy, overfed, aging priest, catapulting into a saddle each morning and crying, 'Forward, comrades. On to Monterey'? Can you see me, who don't even want to go, managing the men, a herd of cattle and all those supply animals?"

Dominguez leaned forward and wiped perspiration from Escalante's face. "No, Escalante, we could not have left without you."

"God's truth is, I'm glad you didn't."

"Even the bishop would approve the delay, I believe."

"Perhaps he has even more reason than you for wanting me out there in the wilderness."

Escalante creaked, forcing himself to stand. He did waist bends and arm twirls while Dominguez watched, shaking his head, silently chiding. Escalante gasped, "I'm ready to leave now, today. I'm fit. Send word to the others in Santa Fe, Father. We'll join them day after tomorrow and leave two days after that." Unable to remain on his feet, he fell onto Dominguez, who sat in a gristle-thong chair.

Dominguez whispered, "Even if I had not just seen you all but faint like a girl in my lap, I would still say no. You'll rest and eat and do your mild exercise for another week— more, if I think it necessary. You don't move until you're restored."

Escalante wheezed, trying to answer.

"Don't even bother to argue. You have no say in this matter. You may be the leader, but this expedition does not move out the gates of the Santa Fe presidio without my orders." He helped Escalante stand. "If we left now, considering the shape you're in, we'd be back in an hour with you draped across your own saddle."

Escalante sucked in air, feeling as though he would never again get enough of it.

"I'm staying here until you're strong enough to return to Santa Fe," Dominguez concluded. "Then we'll go together. I'll send word of the delay by one of the Taos mission brothers."

There was silence between them for some time, until Escalante finally managed weakly, "I'm happy to see you, Father. And now I'd like you to hear my confession."

*   *   *

Afterward the two sat for a while, comfortable in the silence and the weakening light of day. As the shadows began to take over, Dominguez spoke.

"The things you have just confessed to me point clearly to one thing, Escalante. I think I know what you're going to tell me. You believe your sudden sickness might have been a sign of God's displeasure with your ways and your behavior in the past. The women, the—"

"Was it so obvious? Am I so transparent?"

"Others seem to have thought it was a sign also. I'm not surprised at them; I am surprised at you."

"You don't consider it a sign?"

"No. That's rubbish."

Escalante shook his head. "I guessed what others might have thought. I suppose I'm not surprised, either. To the superstitious my illness was a perfect sign from God."

Dominguez nodded. "I've known of your recurring illness, and even though one cannot name it, one knows what it means. It is not a sign. It is just an illness that has struck you before and will probably strike you again."

"You are probably right," Escalante admitted. He repeated the words, bellowing them at the ceiling. "You are so very right. I long ago learned to control such self-doubt. Perhaps it was fever that weakened my defenses this time." He paused. "Father, I've been here all alone with my fever and my thoughts and I've been thinking."

Dominguez waited.

"Oh, don't look so wary," Escalante chuckled. "I'm going with you. Don't ever doubt that. Nothing can keep me from trying for Monterey, not even a sign that God Himself does not wish me to go. I'm that determined."

"I know God's will is not involved in this. Nevertheless, I don't like hearing you speak so defiantly of His wishes."

Escalante disregarded the rebuke. "I've found that self-doubt and guilt over such things are boring and interfere with God's work. All my life I've believed that a Franciscan priest cannot effectively go about God's work feeling guilty about his every sin. So I've successfully ignored a lot of what bothers other men who wear our grey-blue cloth." He crossed himself. "Now, that perhaps is the greatest sin of all. Nonetheless, it's been my decision. I've never told anyone of it and I pray you do not. There's no point in discussing it. It's a personal issue that no one else can resolve for me. I've never confessed it because I don't believe an attitude of conscience comes under the heading of a confessable sin. Right or wrong, I have decided to dismiss my guilt. I could not work if I didn't."

Escalante shook his head. "But Father, since I've been alone here, recuperating in this hut, I have questioned my own resolve to be so independent. I've been certain at times during the past days that my sickness may really be the working of His holy will."

"That's rubbish, too, Escalante. Get a grip on yourself, man."

"Father, there are times when I need guidance as much as any man. This is one of those times, and I turn to you, Dominguez. You seem wise and generous, in spite of our first meeting."

"Yet you did like me despite your impression that God gave me about as much brains as he gives the village idiot?"

Escalante laughed weakly. "Do you have any advice for me on this matter?"

"Yes. I've been thinking on my ride here. If God's will is evident anywhere in your sickness, if God's hand is directing you in any way, I believe it is this. Your sickness and this trip coming up are God's way of testing you. Succeed in overcoming your illness one more time, succeed in our mission, and you will be better able to succeed at serving Him."

"You believe it's that simple. God is testing me."

"That simple, Escalante, although more accurately, you are testing yourself for the greater glory of God." Dominguez laughed sympathetically. "So what if the others, the flock, see your illness as a sign that you should not go? They're superstitious. If they were wise enough to know better, they would not need priests to show them God's way. They would see it and simply know. They would be priests themselves.''

Escalante nodded. This was close to his own sentiment.

Dominguez stood. He began pacing, pounding and grinding his palm with his fist, as Escalante had seen him do before when he was excited.

''We're going into the wilderness to convert savages for God as well as for commercial and political and military reasons. All of this, as I see it, is the means by which God is giving you an opportunity to achieve self-control, to prove your own worth to yourself, perhaps to become content.'' Dominguez paused. ''An opportunity, not a sign.''

Suddenly Escalante was curious. ''Why do you say prove it to myself and perhaps become content?''

''Because you do not really believe in your own worth, despite what you said a moment ago about controlling your guilt. You do feel lacking in many ways, you know.''

''And how do you come by that judgment?''

''You wouldn't otherwise take such pains to be a maverick. You make an art of independence and disobedience. If you really believed in yourself you wouldn't have to.''

''Touché,'' Escalante laughed. ''You have no right to know me so well.''

''Then you have no right to be so young and vulnerable. Escalante, practice what you preach and accept what you are.''

Escalante laughed again. In his weakened state, the laugh was more cackle than boom. He whirled his index finger as if it were a rapier and tapped Dominguez' chest. ''Touché once again.''

''On to Monterey, then?''

''I suppose you mean, do I accept your concept of God's tests? Yes, I do.''

Dominguez gave his palm one final punch and announced,

"I'm famished. I've been riding all day and you've kept me blathering another twenty minutes besides, trying to beat some sense into your head. Now it's time to eat." He strode to the doorway and pulled the canvas cover aside.

Escalante protested. "Now, how much food do you think a city man like you is going to forage out there?" He pushed himself from the bed. "The brothers from Taos have set rabbit snares for me. I'll go and look at them. We're pretty certain to find dinner hanging by one foot from some tree out there."

Dominguez gentled him back to the bed. "In your condition you'll not make it so far as the traps. Besides, I wasn't expecting you to provide anyway."

Escalante continued to protest but Dominguez interrupted him. "Enough, Father. What sort of man do you think visits a sick friend without bringing a couple of roast chickens, a loaf or two of fresh bread and some of that red wine that travels so well?"

Everything was outside on his horse. He would be right back with the ingredients for a feast.

Escalante collapsed on his bed once more. He was shaking; he hoped Dominguez would stay outside till his body relaxed. He was on the threshold of sleep when he heard Dominguez' voice, weak and thin. "Escalante." Then again, "Escalante."

There was something desperate in the tone; it brought Escalante immediately to his feet, reeling toward the fireplace for the rifle above it.

"Escalante!" This time the fear was naked in his voice.

Escalante almost fell, stretching to reach the weapon. The effort dizzied him and blurred his vision. He fell toward the door, the rifle a crutch.

In the harsh late-afternoon sunlight, a breeze fluttering his grey-blue robe, Dominguez stood stiffly beside his horse, his hands frozen inside the saddlebags. He dared not move a muscle. "Escalante," he quavered, "Es . . . ca . . . lante. . . ."

The young priest felt a thrill of horror when he understood what was happening. "Lord, give me strength," he muttered. He needed both hands, bracing the butt of the rifle against his groin, to pull back the hammer. It clicked into firing position, seeming as loud as a blacksmith's sledge on the anvil.

"Lord, give me eyes," Escalante beseeched. He lifted the weapon to his shoulder.

"Father," Dominguez groaned, "I'm frightened."

Escalante's arms trembled beneath the weight of the rifle. "Keep quiet, don't move. In my condition, I'm apt to shoot you instead." As he talked Escalante was allowing his legs to give way slowly and his back to slide down the door frame until he was sitting. He steadied the rifle barrel across his knees. "Lord, give me a true aim."

He sighted, held his breath, prayed for steady hands for just one moment, then squeezed the trigger.

The recoil lifted the rifle from his hands and only the door frame at his back prevented him from spinning into the room.

The rattlesnake became bloody spray. Badly shaken, Dominguez opened his eyes. "I didn't even see it. Suddenly it was just there, between my horse's hooves, rattling at me."

"You can move now, Dominguez."

"Was it going to bite me?"

"Almost certainly. But who really knows? It was probably snoozing. They find any shade they can. Even a handrail post will do. You frightened it."

Dominguez slapped his hands across his face and bent his head forward. "I'm such a coward."

"You did the correct thing. Your instincts are good. You didn't move and you called for help softly." Escalante tried to stand but could not. "I said you can move now. For God's sake, do it and help me back to bed."

Dominguez gripped his wrists and rocked backward, lifting as Escalante pushed with trembling legs. As the two moved toward the bed, Escalante sighed. "You were wrong about one thing, Dominguez."

The older man grunted.

"I wouldn't last even an hour in the saddle right now."

Reaction had set in and Dominguez felt beside himself. "How can you joke at a time like this?" He dumped Escalante onto the straw. "I almost lost my life. What if you had missed your shot? The exertion nearly killed you. And you make jokes." He raised both hands above his head and howled, "Escalante, you are maddening."

"Yes," Escalante smiled, "I know."

Rain struck. It flattened the sparse grass outside the door. Darkness arrived early, with the rain. Escalante struck a fire and lit lamps.

Dominguez revealed the sad news he had brought while they ate chicken, bread and wine. "Still no word of Garces." Dominguez sucked at a chicken bone in the comfortable gloom of the hut.

Escalante crossed himself against a wash of sadness. "I expected this news. You probably did too. Had you brought it earlier, when I was looking for signs of His displeasure, I might have rejected this expedition completely. Garces is a great loss. Beyond that, there's little else to say. Without Garces, if indeed he does not live, one could easily say the rest is not worth a peseta. I have prayed for Garces. I shall continue to pray."

"So shall I. And . . ." A crucifix hung on the wall, and Dominguez thought he saw two dark round spots like blood beneath it on the floor. "Forgive me, Escalante. I repeat, there would be no journey were it not for you and Garces. Furthermore, you dare not desert me. You are willful even to consider not going. The office of the Holy Evangel has made me lead this expedition, and I require you to lead me."

Dominguez sat back heavily in the chair. A thong snapped beneath his weight. "I'll have no more of your penances,

Escalante. Already this expedition has constituted the worst of mine." He continued to eat as he spoke. "At a certain juncture after you did not appear for our departure, Miera offered to scour the territory for another priest, but then the Hopi from Oraibe attacked and the expedition was put off. Miera went and I believe your men from Zuni joined the soldiers also. They are all back now." Dominguez shifted his weight and threw a chicken bone into the fire. After a moment the bone popped and the marrow hissed into the flames. "A man from El Paso who volunteered for the expedition has been discovered to be a murderer."

"Whom did he murder?"

"His wife. The woman's father followed him to Santa Fe. He wishes to bring him back to El Paso for justice."

Escalante sat up suddenly against the warm adobe wall. "Our Lord in heaven, I heard his confession."

"In Santa Fe?"

"Yes, the night I arrived there. I thought sometimes I might have dreamed it, as I had fallen asleep in the confessional booth."

Dominguez nodded and picked at another bone. "It was no dream."

Escalante's hair stood up untended from his long, thin head. His knobby face looked burnished in the firelight. "What has happened to the murderer?"

"Gone into the wilderness, I believe. Lorenzo Olivares is his name."

The fire burned down and Escalante finally prevailed on Dominguez to accept his pallet. Escalante wished to sleep outside to toughen himself for the journey. The effects of his fever, Dominguez noted, even the lingering ones, seemed to have faded. Still, he made Escalante accept part of his bedroll before he would allow him outdoors.

Before he slept Dominguez prayed before the crucifix on the wall. He discovered through the pressure of his knees that the spots he thought were blood were only indentations in the stone; were they from Escalante's knees, he wondered.

Escalante prayed outside in the starlight. Dark, massy clouds rolled over the plain. Lightning flashed in the distance and an occasional far-off rumble of thunder could be heard.

Escalante thanked God for showing him His mercy, and as he did a sense of mission came to him, expanding his heart and raising the hair on the back of his neck. Once more he had bent himself to the will of God and once more the will of God had bent him further. God had tested him, had not found him wanting and now had granted him his wish. As he prayed Escalante could see in his mind's eye his life forming into an arrow, moving upward to a purpose that merged far in the glowing future with the golden purpose of God.

He lay for a long time in his blanket on the ground, staring into the darkness. He tried to imagine what was out there: scenery, the faces of strange Indians, animals he had never heard of. The one image that kept rising from his thoughts was the sea pounding on a rocky coast, an ocean he had never seen. God rolled him in the waves, cast him over the rocks and onto the beach. Again and again God rolled him and cast him. . . .

He had a fitful night's sleep. In his dream the chalice and paten of beaten gold changed to sticky lead and pewter. They were slippery and they soiled his hands. A woman came with him into the confessional wearing a mantilla made of human hair. She breathed in his face. Her breath was sweet, her laugh inviting. A strong pleasure pierced his sleep and awakened him.

Ah, there it is again, Escalante thought smiling. A skulking dream-memory of the first woman he had ever known. To fall once is to keep falling forever, he thought, when the stumbling block is woman.

Such complacent thoughts, he mused. Having achieved the reputation for rascality, which one can never shed, how often have you played the game?

He knew the count exactly; there had been so few. He liked to recall them though, especially his first.

They had met at a most vulnerable time in his life, just before his ordination. He was not alone in his inability to resist the temptation. He recalled how the difference between his age, seventeen, and hers, thirty, had made no difference to her.

"It is the soul that determines the man," she had murmured. "Yours is strong enough and sensitive enough for ten."

Escalante recalled that this woman had also given him much pain. It was for her that he had almost rejected his calling and fled the seminary life at Convento Grande in Mexico City only weeks before he was to be ordained.

She had been outraged. "You will do no such thing, for you belong to God much more than you belong to me. I only pray that God will forgive me for borrowing a small piece of you for a while." It was then that she told him she was returning him to God. She would never see him again.

And it was then that Escalante had decided he would do his best never to blame himself over this woman or any of the others who were sure to follow. He would have preferred not to need women, but he did.

As he rolled in his blanket, he smiled to himself. I still do need them. And God has not yet questioned my willingness to serve him because of that need.

Escalante smiled, remembering the riddle once considered so naughty among certain novices in the seminary.

Question: What is a Franciscan's heaviest burden?

Answer: A working lust. He can't use it and he's never allowed to get rid of it.

Dominguez again promised Escalante he would remain until he was strong enough to travel to Santa Fe. Wiping a sudden rush of perspiration from his face, Escalante was deeply grateful. Although he disliked admitting it, he knew he should not be alone. The fever still held him and the pain still attacked from time to time low on his right side. But yes, he was going to go. His body belonged to him. He would take it where he wished.

Having Dominguez with him during convalescence was a blessing. Besides, there was still plenty of the man's wine to drink. Escalante grinned and winked at the sky.

Chapter 7

Juan Ignacio galloped into Santa Fe, lather pluming his horse's mouth. His own mouth and nose were caked with trail dust. The young Franciscan brother had ridden hard from Taos to find Pedro Cisneros. He had no trouble locating the mayor of Zuni, for he stood in the middle of the plaza surrounded by a crowd.

Juan Ignacio leaned from his saddle and handed Cisneros a letter from Dominguez. The coarse paper was flattened and damp from the rider's body heat.

Cisneros bid farewell to his friends and began to read. When he was finished he looked out over the streets. Animals, wagons and people struggled around each other, sending towers of dust shimmering about the steeples of the church across the plaza. He read the letter a second time, then cursed.

"Escalante is ill and the journey is delayed until the end of the month." He spoke to no one in particular. He remembered with the filling sensation in his groin his last night in Zuni, his wife's body, the folds of her nightgown. "I could be home with Estella during this delay instead of marking time here."

"You said something?" the young monk asked. "I couldn't hear over the street noises."

"It's unimportant, Brother . . . Brother . . ."

"Ignacio."

" . . . Brother Ignacio. I'm simply grumbling about things I cannot control. I'm not angry with you. I'm not going to shoot the messenger who brings bad tidings."

The man smiled, shifting in his saddle. "I know what the letter tells you. If I were you I would be irritated too. No offense."

Cisneros pointed to the church rectory. "You've ridden hard. You're covered with dust. You look like a sugar pastry. Take your horse and go eat and rest. You both deserve it."

Brother Juan Ignacio saluted and wheeled his mount.

Cisneros walked toward the presidio barracks and the corral, spitting street dust, to tell the others that July 4, 1776, would not go down in the history of the Monterey expedition after all.

Bernardo Miera wiped his paintbrushes clean and squinted at the altar screen he was rendering for the San Miguel chapel. The pigment glistened wet on the section showing Christ's feet. He sighed. The feet were always the hardest part to paint.

The mixed scents of burning beeswax candles, turpentine and paint were as pleasing as the bouquet of good wine.

He imagined Escalante off in the low hills near Taos, ill and weak. Miera knew Escalante's low opinion of his art-work, even though their relationship was still one of distant politeness. However, in Miera's view Escalante was a valu-able priest and a good man in the wilderness. These impres-sions had been gained during the few weeks since they first had met at Dominguez' rectory in Santa Fe.

Miera crossed himself. Facing the altar, he asked God for Escalante's speedy recovery.

Cisneros came in, blinking and unsteadily feeling his

way forward while his eyes adapted to the dimness of the chapel. Only at the altar, where Miera worked, was there good light inside the place.

Miera joked with Cisneros. "You're back with more news of our Escalante. By the look on your face I'd say at the very least he must have been consumed by scorpions."

Cisneros grunted. "No. Now that I've told all of the others, I have to discuss the expedition with you in particular."

"Don't tell me that now you're seeing signs of disapproval from God in Escalante's illness?"

"No, no, no," Cisneros snapped. "You know I never believed in omens. And neither do any of the other men."

"So then discuss." Miera was wringing turpentine from his brushes, squeezing them in folds of soft cloth.

"It's nothing to treat lightly, Miera. As Governor Mendinueta's representative on this Monterey venture, Escalante's illness concerns you greatly. You were chosen to lead the trip in the first place. If Escalante doesn't soon recover, you may have to take it after all."

"Let's get one thing clear," Miera demanded, poking a soggy brush toward Cisneros. "I was never considered to lead this expedition. That is rumor. I have no idea how it began. Escalante himself has buried the rumor. He wants me along only to map the land we cross on the way to California. The young priest has said so himself. 'Only for this do I consider Miera useful.' Remember?"

Cisneros nodded. "I remember. Even so, if Escalante doesn't recover we must consider another leader."

"Of course."

"And you, Miera, you're the only one with the right credentials. You've been an army captain and an engineer. You've traded with the same Indians we'll meet out there. You've beaten them in combat. You know how they fight and make peace. You've done well ranching cattle in this unforgiving country. You've traveled much of it on government business as territorial agent. You're the only one in

Santa Fe who really understands how to use that astrolabe you keep so shiny and well oiled." He gestured toward the altar screen in progress. "And, for God's sake, you're the only one who's draftsman enough to turn out a map that makes any sense of our routes and the country we'll see out there."

Miera chuckled. "Thank you for the glowing litany of my accomplishments, Cisneros, but I'm only in my mid-fifties, you know. I'm not yet addled with age. I think I can remember them myself without flattery from you." He chuckled again. "Even a few you've left out."

"You still take this too lightly. I hope you'll be more serious about the responsibility. It may yet fall to you whether you want it or not."

"Let's worry about responsibility when it falls, hmmm?"

"But what of the weather, man?"

"What of it?"

"The longer we delay, the deeper into fall and winter we'll find ourselves in the end."

Miera dismissed this. "Oh, it may mean we'll be in the field deeper into fall than I might like, but not dangerously so. Three weeks more or less probably won't make much difference. Cisneros, if there is indeed a way to Monterey through the mountains, we'll probably find it before fall or not at all this year."

"Your lack of concern distresses me."

Miera draped an arm across Cisneros' reluctant shoulders and spoke so close to his face that Cisneros recoiled. "Cisneros, I want to get started all right. But the truth is, I am not so much disappointed by the delay as you are. Lack of disappointment, not indifference, is what you see." He drew away. "With the delay I can probably finish my altar screen before we leave. Three weeks also gives me an unexpected gift of time with my family. We've lived in Santa Fe more than twenty years now, you know, my wife and I. We've come to like the place, rowdy as it is. Each departure becomes a little more difficult for me than the last."

"Then why are you going at all, Miera?"

"Curiosity, Cisneros. Adventure itself. We're going to places I have never seen. There are things there I have not drawn. Those things are for myself. For my government and my church, there is the possibility of finding minerals and other resources. I hear stories of mountains of copper and silver. The poorest of the Hopi certainly seem to have enough of both to squander on pots and jewelry finer than those of some of the nobles back home in Spain."

"You're still too frivolous about it for my taste."

"And you too sober for mine." He put his arm across Cisneros' shoulders once more. "Put your mind to rest, amigo. If Escalante cannot lead us I shall, if it is so ordered. Willingly, even zealously. There. Does that satisfy you?"

"As a beginning."

"I don't think the matter will ever come to pass, though. From what I know of Escalante, he won't allow a small thing like near-fatal illness to keep him down. If he says he'll be here by the end of the month, he'll be here even if they have to carry him in on a stretcher. I've known him only a short while, since he came to see Dominguez that one night last month. But since then, Dominguez and I have both had one singular impression of him."

Cisneros waited.

"Unstoppable determination and pride override whatever doubts he may have about himself. And I say he has plenty."

"I know, but—"

"No buts. I guarantee it. We won't have to worry about replacing Escalante as leader. I didn't think much of him at first, I admit, but I'd follow him anywhere now. Thank you anyway for honoring me with your suggestion that I stand ready to lead. I do if necessary." He extended a fan of brushes. "Now if you'll excuse me, I still have some cleaning up to do here."

Bernardo Miera once more studied the details he had painted on the feet of Christ that morning. "It's a good painting, Cisneros. Even Escalante himself would be obliged to agree.''

Joaquin Lain propped himself on his elbows across the body of the Hopi woman he knew by the name of Hunger. Sweat glued the skins of their bellies. Lain lowered his face within inches of her chest. "When I see breasts like these, I know the Hopi wars are worth fighting.''

"You have always had a disgustingly childish manner of speech in bed. You've known me for two years, since I came from the pueblos to live your Spanish way of life in Santa Fe.'' She seized his head to bury his face between her breasts. "And after two years, you still do not call me by my right name, only the soldiers' name Hunger.''

Lain laughed. "It's a pity we ever taught you Indians Spanish.'' He struggled to free his face from the suffocating flesh. "We wouldn't have to listen to you complain if we hadn't. Besides, for what you and I do together, names are not necessary.''

"I sometimes hate you, you know, and wish I really could suffocate you between my breasts.''

"They're big enough,'' he gasped. She bit on his ear until he cried out. "Why do you stay among us, then? Go home to the marvelous misery and disease of your Hopi pueblos.''

"That is no longer for me. I have lived as a Spaniard. I am dead as far as my people are concerned. If I returned now they would probably kill me. The cliffs are high in Hopi territory. One could never survive the fall I would take.''

Lain could see that his taunt had troubled her.

Teeth still clamped on his ear, she hissed, "I hope you die out there looking for Monterey. The Apache sometimes throw a male prisoner or two to their women for sport. Do you know what the Apache women do to men?''

"No. Do I care?''

"You will care if they ever have you. They strip a man's

skin. Those who are skilled at doing this can roll a hide up like parchment in one piece from a man's chest. The pain is greater than even a watcher can imagine. Death is certain. Weak men beg for it quickly. It takes a long while. Without skin, I am told, every part of the body is so much more sensitive. Even a cool breeze is torture.'' She ground his ear hard with her teeth. "I pray the Apache women get you. I pray they ignore your whining and begging. I hope they skin you and keep you alive for a week.''

"You are a bitch, you know.'' Lain was sobered by her anger. He kissed a nipple. "If you hate me so, why have you bedded me for two years? Why don't you kill me yourself? A knife in my back while I am in your arms . . .'' he shrugged.

"I would be put in a Spanish jail and hanged for it. You are not worth it.''

"Also I am better than anyone else for you in bed.''

"Better than most,'' she conceded. "And why shouldn't I use you for that? You do the same to me. If your pious and pure Spanish virgins would do the things I do for you, you wouldn't go near the Indian slut.'' She jerked his head up to look into his eyes from about six inches. "Have you ever cared to speak my true name? Do you even know it?''

He lied, trying to annoy her. "I knew it once; I've forgotten it. No matter, I tell you. We don't want names from each other. We want only this.''

He opened his mouth wide and engulfed her breast. She lifted it to him with two hands. "I hate you,'' she snarled.

After they had made love once more, she teased Lain. "Have you thought that I might be the last woman you will ever have before the Apache take you and your entire group?''

This time Lain was deeply troubled by the image of capture. Twice he slapped her hard, forehand, backhand, so that her head jerked right and then left.

"You could stay at home,'' she taunted him. Her tongue sponged up a drop of blood welling from her lower lip.

He shook his head: no.

"And go often to Zuni to console your cousin Dona Estella." Sitting cross-legged, she made a mocking bow as she spoke.

Lain backhanded her once more. His knucklebones ground against her cheek.

Hunger shook her head from side to side. She refused to acknowledge hurt but her laugh was vicious. "You talk sometimes in your troubled sleep of this cousin. You wish she had married you instead of this Cisneros."

Lain raised his hand one more time. She waited defiant for the strike. Lain exhaled, then collapsed against the wall. "Go on," he fumed, "torture me."

"It is true," the woman chanted like a teasing child, "it is true, true, true."

Then her mood changed and she stroked his face with genuine tenderness. "We have become so skilled at hurting each other, Joaquin. How awful. I can't stay angry with you for long, though. I don't understand you. Why must you go on this expedition? There is nothing out there for you."

Lain did not answer. Why indeed? There were times he nearly wept thinking of the importance of such a quest for the church and Spain. To Hunger, though, such ideas would sound hollow and foolish.

"You have nothing to prove to anyone. You're a merchant of great respectability. You're a generous church contributor. And why do you arrange for your cousin's husband, this Cisneros, to go? Such generosity to the man who has the woman you want." Her laugh became vicious and hurtful again.

Again Lain did not reply. Why Cisneros? Because he loved his distant cousin Estella enough to advance the career of her husband as best he could, even though there were times he wished the husband did not exist. It had been Lain's endorsement of Cisneros that had won for him the mayoral seat in Zuni. He had only to suggest to Cisneros that any man who joined the Escalante expedition would forever be garlanded in glory such as a Caesar could command. It was the sort of glory that could make a mayor into a governor.

Cisneros was a political animal. He snapped at the bait. He had rushed to sign the articles of the expedition.

Hunger was whispering at Lain's ear, jeering. "Bringing Cisneros along is a fine way to take him from his wife. Do you not see how naked you are in your thoughts? Perhaps the Apache will even flay him instead of you. How nice to come home and console a widow. Who knows? If you console her well enough she might even marry you."

Lain winced and continued to brood in silence. He conjured up images of Estella Cisneros, a woman with riches enough to satisfy any man. Cousins or not, Lain thought, we are the ones who should have married.

Lain had dreamed often of her for himself. He knew that she too had sometimes dreamed of him, but she married Cisneros. He had asked her first.

All that had happened so long ago. We were both sixteen, Lain thought. Now I am twenty-eight and life is passing me by.

But one could not be a poor loser. For Joaquin Lain this was important on principle. In a perverse way that he sometimes did not comprehend, this principle directed him to do as much as possible with his money and political influence in both Santa Fe and Mexico City to advance the political career of Pedro Cisneros.

Cisneros made it all worthwhile, however. He was a dedicated and competent man. He had the potential to do good for the church, Spain and New Mexico.

Hunger's mood grew more vicious in response to Lain's brooding silence. Finally Lain could stand her no longer. He bundled his clothing and fled naked and barefoot from her room. "You win, you have driven me off. You win." He hopped from one foot to the other, trying to jump into his breeches. Her heinous laughter echoed down the hall.

"You would like Cisneros flayed, you toad," she railed.

"To marry your cousin, the grieving widow, you would like him flayed."

Lain clamped his boottops to his ears so he would not hear. Deep in his heart he knew her charge held the truth. He would be pleased if God saw fit to allow the Apache women to take Cisneros as long as he, Lain, survived to come home.

Chapter 8

It was night at the garrison settlement of Pajoaque, north of Santa Fe.

The man had the look of eagles about him. He sat with his back tight to a wall, away from the door of the tavern, left foot forward from his bench, right foot back, the posture of a man prepared to move quickly. He spoke only to order wine and dried beef, not sharing the good-nature of the soldiers lurching drunkenly against one another. He sat brooding in gothic silence, concentrating on the soot of lamps that blackened the adobe walls.

Two pistols hung in leather holsters beneath his left armpit, one above the other, convenient to his right hand.

A short cavalry stabbing sword shared his right boot with his leg, its handle protruding from the boottop. A short-barreled saddle carbine stood propped against the wall supporting his back. The barrel was bruised and the wooden stock bore scars; it had been used as a club and chopping weapon as well as a firearm, but barrel and stock were oiled and polished. As were all of the man's weapons, the rifle was as well cared for as a child.

85

The few soldiers who noticed him shrugged. One muttered that it was best to leave his kind alone. For they plainly wished it and meant violence to anyone who disturbed them.

One of the women decided that this advice was nonsense. She said every lonely man wanted a woman. She approached him, smiling and swinging her hips in a motion as old as time.

The man turned from the soot patterns to watch her as she neared him through the foggy, smoky light. Her smile fractured as she approached and was better able to see his face. She stopped and backed away, turning to the soldiers as if for safety. She muttered that the man's eyes told her he was not the man for her on this night.

The solitary stranger looked off again into some private distance. Three men entered the tavern, two young fellows and one about fifty. Looking at the shared face and stooped physique, it was plain they were a father and two sons. They formed a triangle as they entered, the older man at the point.

All three carried pistols and knives. The bearded older man carried a rifle as well, slung muzzle-down from his right shoulder.

The man against the wall set his wineglass down on a table beside him. The movement was his only sign of recognition or alertness.

The three newcomers shifted to form a line abreast. They moved slowly toward the man sitting at the wall. The men before them moved from their path. One young soldier came from the wooden bar as if to intercede. Twisting his collar, his sergeant pulled him away. The matter did not concern him.

The three stopped before the seated man, looking hard at him. He ignored them.

The father stood between the other two and finally spoke. "Lorenzo Olivares. My son-in-law." He added with deep weariness, "I loved you once."

The seated man kept silent.

The two sons looked to the speaker, who continued, "With your wife's brothers, I have sought you all over New Mexico. I have two reasons."

More silence.

"One is to lift the burden from your heart and tell you your wife is not dead, as you may have believed. Your bullet wounded her badly, but in the end it did not kill."

The seated man nodded, just one tilt of the head. His face showed no change in its darkness.

"Two is to kill you for shooting her."

Olivares finally responded. "She slept with others."

"I know that."

Olivares shrugged. "So, then?"

"You do not injure my daughter," the father growled, "no matter what the crime."

Olivares sat waiting.

The older man sighed. He gripped his rifle barrel, lifting the weapon to firing position. The brothers' hands only tightened on their pistols. The right of execution belonged to the father, who moved slowly.

Olivares sat like a rock, as if accepting passively the judgment upon him.

Then it happened. He kicked. His foot sent the rifle spinning in an arc on its sling. The butt end levered around and over the shoulder to hit the father in back of his head.

As the older man toppled forward, bellowing in pain, Olivares leaped up. His own rifle seemed to spring from the wall into his hands. With it he hammered the pistol from the hand of one brother, breaking the wrist bones. He followed the swing through, breaking open the face of the other brother. The second brother's pistol fired, blowing out the end of his holster. The ball opened a hole the size of a saucer in the floor.

Olivares hurdled their falling bodies, smashing two lamps that hung on chains from the ceiling. The tavern darkened.

Some of the crowd rushed to the action and some fell to

the floor away from it. Olivares had now become one of the shadows. No one saw him go.

Later, when the tale was retold, no two people in the tavern could agree in detail what had happened, it had happened so quickly.

Andres Muniz was dissatisfied. He stood in the tack room at the Santa Fe presidio, loving its smells of wood and hay and dung and leather. In the noon heat the place was a sanctuary, cool and dark. He walked the line of pegs suspending harnesses and bridles on the wall. He patted saddles on their dummy horses. He stroked the wool of the saddle blankets lying in neat piles.

Everything is ready to go, he thought. But I'll still polish and oil and fuss over everything one more time. As good as it all is, it is never perfect.

Outside some horses sought the shade of the paloverde trees around the corral. The midday sun was cruel. They snorted water over each other's flanks. Other horses were pacing the exercise circle, led by the men who would ride them.

Lucrecio Muniz shuffled into the tack room, raising small clouds of gritty dust with his boots. He gulped deeply of the cool water in a bucket. "Tell me, big brother," Lucrecio chided Andres. "How often do you intend to put all of this gear into perfect shape?"

"Once a day until we finally leave. You should know by now I am a pefectionist, little brother. You've known me for twenty-five years. And you should be out there paying the same attention to your horse as the others do."

Men walked the corral with heads low and faces covered with cloth masks against the dust they and their mounts raised in the exercise circle. The cloud of grit was rising steadily, fed by their feet and the hooves of their horses. At times the dust masked the leaves of the paloverdes. Andres Muniz stared dully at it. "Santa Fe means eternal dust."

"And my horse and I have both eaten enough of it for one afternoon, Andres. Any more and our lungs will be plugged." He gulped more water. "Speaking of the trip, you've heard Escalante is well again and on the way back here with Dominguez?"

"I'll believe it when I see Escalante leading us out the presidio gate. It's almost the end of July. We're three weeks late as it is."

"I'll never understand why you're so anxious to get back out there, big brother. Haven't you spent enough of your thirty years trading with dirty Utes and sleeping with mountain lions? I would think you'd had enough for a while. The Utes don't have the women and wine and fun we have in Santa Fe."

"I've explained so often," Andres sighed. "If you must still ask, little brother, you'll never understand, so there's no point explaining again."

Lucrecio frowned. "You emphasize my lack of understanding in just about everything far too often."

"Don't display it so often, then. One reason I'm anxious to start, I suppose, is that I'm like Escalante in many ways. I like life out there better than life in here." He pointed from the tack room toward the city. "I like trading with Indians. The excitement and uncertainty make my blood rush. And when I talk to them in their own language, I feel as though we are really speaking to each other, not around each other, as our fine Spanish manners require us to do in the name of civilization."

"I've always been jealous of the easy way you learned so many dialects."

"To me it doesn't seem as though I ever had to learn. It seems the words were always there in my head. I knew them all the time." He began yet another oiling of one of the saddles. He looked at his brother. "Feeling as you do, Lucrecio, why do you want to go at all?"

Lucrecio Muniz grinned. "Where you go this time, big

brother, I go. Listening to all of your talk of last year's trip, it's occurred to me that I might enjoy the life. I might even get more out of it than you do. Certainly I'll have more fun spending the trading profits than you do. In fact," he added, "I think I might even be better than you at Indian languages and trading, once I apply myself."

Andres Muniz frowned. "The rivalry is never far from the surface, is it, little brother?"

"Not so long as you call me little brother."

"You've wanted to fill my boots since we were boys in Embudo. Forget it, Lucrecio. You haven't got big enough feet. You never will. You like the wine and women too much, and for a man of twenty-five you're too dark and beautiful to resist the temptation."

"The afternoon's suddenly turning sour, Andres."

"Afternoons always do whenever the subject takes this turn."

"Which can be just about any afternoon."

"We're brothers. Our mother said all brothers are Cain and Abel, remember? Born to challenge each other, and often to the unhappiness of both."

"God forbid we ever decide we want the same woman," Lucrecio snickered.

"Cain slew Abel."

"We'll never do that, big brother."

"No, little brother, we never will."

They looked into each other's eyes, knowing how easily each could hurt the other and knowing they were unable to stop.

Juan de Aguilar imagined he heard a cry of someone in terror and pain. It was dark. There was no one ahead in the dancing light from the street lamp and no one behind.

Again the cry. There was an alley to his left, funneling the sound to him. He lifted one leg across his horse's flanks and jumped from the saddle, landing lightly and quietly on his toes.

Trotting along the alley, he wished to heaven he were armed with more than his ten knuckles. He turned his ankle in a rut that ran with sour water. He grunted and hop-skipped forward, favoring the ankle.

The yelp sounded once more and was cut off by the sound of a hand slapping flesh. Aguilar turned a corner and saw a light. An oil lamp flickered in an alcove beside a swaybacked wooden door.

Aguilar saw two men pressing a bulky old woman to the wall. What they were doing to her was plain. She fought wildly as shreds of torn blouse fell from one breast.

The woman grunted and kicked but her foot missed. The momentum of her leg lift levered her over backward against one of the men. He stepped aside, allowing her to fall, hastening her with another slap to the head.

Aguilar saw that the two wore the buckskins of mountain men. He spat. Only mountain men would rape old mothers.

Then he bellowed. Always yell when attacking a man, his father had once advised. The yell has no force and does no harm, but it distracts your enemy, if only a little. A little may be enough to give you the edge you need.

Aguilar charged, bending low. He flew from the alley floor and rolled into one of the two men, hitting him between ankles and knees. He wanted to press the man's feet flat to the ground while forcing his legs to hinge backward at the same time. One could pull the tendons of a man's foot out by the roots that way, Aguilar knew. His father had taught him that attack also.

The man twisted away from Aguilar's weight and clawed the wall for support. He screamed that his feet had been torn from his legs. His fingers plowed eight furrows in the adobe wall as he slid to the ground.

One man was all Aguilar could handle. The other stood

before him and drove his boot heel into Aguilar's mouth as he might have kicked in a door.

Aguilar imagined his neck had been broken. He became aware of deep pain spreading from his face. He knew he was spitting blood and splinters of teeth. He watched the lamp in the alcove pass across his field of vision as he went down. He rolled and pushed himself to his knees.

The man was waiting. He hammered the boot heel into the side of Aguilar's head. Aguilar roared in pain. He was sure he had lost most of his ear. He rose to attack again.

The other stood on Aguilar's neck and ground his face into the alley dirt. He looked at Aguilar and at the woman, who was showing signs of fight again. He spat and started to haul his howling comrade away.

Aguilar watched them flee, unable to lift his head. The two seemed to gain propulsion bouncing from building to building. The man Aguilar had hurt was holding onto the belt of the other and yelping to God to spare him further pain.

The last thing Aguilar saw before unconsciousness took him under was the woman. She was reaching out as though to stroke his head. She was younger than he'd thought and almost pretty. It was her size that had made her seem old. The breast was still bare and quite lovely. . . .

Juan de Aguilar woke up on a mound of straw filling a clean but rough cotton sack. He was in a room somewhere, the woman kneeling beside him. She sloshed a clean cloth in a clay basin of water. Aguilar realized it was the sting of cold water that had roused him.

She had put on a maroon blouse. The light in the room was poor. Her head appeared to be a free-floating moon over the blouse as the color and the darkness became one.

Aguilar saw too that she was Indian. No wonder, he thought. They'd never have tried to rape a Spanish woman. Another violated Indian woman caused little concern in Santa Fe. According to some, rape was just forgetting to ask them to do what they would do in any event.

Aguilar tried to lift himself. She gently pressed him back into the straw. He welcomed her firmness. He did not really wish to get up just yet.

She squeezed some juices from an aloe plant onto his bruises and scrapes. The touch was fire at first, but then it gradually became cool and pleasant.

She spoke little Spanish but they managed to communicate. She had brought him to her house from the alley some distance away slung across the back of his horse. She had carried him to her living quarters on her own back. She was a house servant to a Santa Fe merchant, had no family and lived alone.

Aguilar managed to convey by sign and word his thanks to her for taking him in and nursing him. He asked whether she might be able to keep him for the night. Every time he raised himself he fell back. He knew he was too dizzy to find his way back to his own quarters near the presidio corral.

She nodded as though she had intended him to stay all along. She made him understand that it was she who had to give thanks. He had saved her at enormous expense to himself. Since she had neither money nor gifts for him, she knew of only one way to show her gratitude, providing he was not too weak to accept.

She was undoing the fastenings of her blouse and smiling at her own jest. She stretched her arms so that Aguilar could pull the blouse over her head and shoulders.

She lowered herself onto the sackful of straw. She pressed his hand to the breast he had seen in the alley. She pressed his fingers deep into her flesh.

Aguilar was filled with wonder. Who on the expedition to Monterey would believe such a thing?

Simon Lucero climbed onto the bench, looking for all the world like a struggling infant. He stood before the table, pounding with both fists and calling to the innkeeper, "I may be a dwarf, but tonight I have the appetite of Goliath. Keep bringing me food and wine until I tell someone to stop.''

"Even Goliath needs money in order to eat in this place,'' chortled the woman tending the stove. She sounded good-natured but firm.

Simon Lucero bounced a five-peso coin onto the table. He rolled the gold piece back and forth, scoring goals with it in chubby palms worn hard from working horses.

The innkeeper elbowed his wife and wagged his head, indicating she should say no more. "He's Miera's dwarf. Even if he had no money, Miera would be good for the bill.''

"Oh,'' the woman nodded, "Miera.''

She took Lucero a plate of rabbit stew made fiery with jalapeña peppers, half a loaf of bread and a mug of cool, thick beer. Lucero stood on the bench and ate. The table came up to his waist. The dagger at his side took on the proportions of a saber next to his legs. It hung almost to his boottop.

Though he stood to eat while others sat, somehow Lucero's manners with knife and fork spoke of dignity and determination not to appear grotesque. Some were silently amused by the sight of a dwarf standing on a bench to make himself tall enough to eat from an ordinary table, but the innkeeper's wife was impressed and remained respectful. "I've never seen a dwarf,'' she told her husband. "Certainly I've never watched one eat. His head is so large and his body so small. Do you imagine he stores food in his head?''

Her husband's neck was reddening. "Shhh. Not so loud!''

"Why sh? I like him and I think highly of him. He has the table ways of a gentleman.''

"I shall tread on your foot,'' the innkeeper whispered.

"I show no disrespect, so don't you shush me. Some of those who are so amused could take table lessons from this one.'' She peered from the kitchen at Lucero again. "Tell me, husband, how do you think he manages on a horse? Or in bed with a full-sized woman?''

Her husband choked.

Simon Lucero knew he was under scrutiny. He knew he amused some of the customers. He did not trouble himself about it; he felt no resentment or anger. Always he had been different; always he would be different; and always he would be an object of attention. He knew it well.

He did appreciate the inn wife. In her innocent fascination she remained without malice. Lucero liked her.

And knowing that at least one person in the room viewed him as human, Lucero felt happy. He found he was standing taller than he otherwise might. The fact that the one kind person was also a handsome woman especially inspired him.

His ears were very good. As he ate he fancied her in bed, demonstrating how well he managed with full-sized women. He had been amused by her speculations.

Lucero called for more stew. The woman brought it covered with a napkin to imprison its warmth. Lucero loved her forever for this thoughtfulness. He did not look for long at her face. He feared he would blush and she would read his thoughts.

He concentrated upon enjoyment of food and was content. He had thought about such a dinner all day long. Lucero wanted to eat until he vomited from excess, then eat again.

The expedition was to start any day. Whereas most of the others on it would have last nights with women to sustain them on the trail, he, Simon Lucero, the smallest man in New Mexico, would have to think of food.

He would not even be in the expedition's number, he knew, were it not for the fact that where Miera went, he went.

He looked at the inn wife once more and dreamed. If there were more women like that one, and if they were not all married to normal men, and if there were more time before we set out, I too would have memories like the others. She knows I am small. She also knows I am a man. She likes me.

He viciously speared some meat. Pain and frustration suddenly were palpable in his throat.

Forget it, Lucero, and forget her. Concentrate on food. It is so good. Mmm. It is so very good. Make the most of it, for food will be the only memory you'll have to sustain you on the trail.

No innkeeper's wife for you, or any other woman for that matter. Forget how badly you need them and want them; it doesn't matter how hard you try to seduce them or how worthy you may be even among the best of men.

You are three feet tall, Lucero. You have a keg for a head. You have little half-moons for legs. You are a dwarf. Dwarfs are not for loving. Ever.

Chapter 9

On an oppressive day toward the end of that month, Escalante and Dominguez rode hard into Santa Fe. Escalante was well—a little unsteady still, but well.

They found the expedition horses fit and the slaughter cattle plump and restless. Six of the seven others were ready and departure was scheduled once more: July 29, 1776.

The tenth man on the roster was not among them, for after it was learned that Lorenzo Olivares had tried to kill his wife, he left Santa Fe and had not been seen since. There were reports that the fugitive had also tried to kill his wife's father and two brothers in a tavern north of Santa Fe. It was said the three would require long recovery.

Dominguez was relieved to find Olivares absent, but Escalante was not.

"Bless the man for disappearing," Dominguez said. "We have enough problems without a hunted man along. Even if he showed up now, we'd only have to press him to turn himself over to the authorities. We couldn't take him. We'd have to remove him from the roster and leave without him."

"But he hasn't actually killed anyone, as I first believed when he confessed," Escalante argued.

"You'd take him, then?"

"I'm not saying that. I'm simply saying I'd like to talk to him before deciding."

Dominguez snorted. "A man of such violence. He's wounded just about everyone in the entire family but the dog—the wife, her brothers, the father. Would you really have such a man with you?"

"Men who feel trapped and guilty do behave violently sometimes, even when it's not in their nature. The trapped animal always fights. And besides, I've seen far worse. Soldiers butcher entire villages, including the dogs, and we call them heroes."

"I say it again, Father. You are mad sometimes."

"All I'm saying is, his sin is now a lesser one. He hasn't killed his wife. Perhaps the sin could be rationalized, even forgiven, if he were here to make a case for himself. Perhaps he could take his place on probation, with the condition that he surrender himself on our return."

Dominguez was shaking his head. "No. The other men would refuse to travel with a man who's shot his wife, no matter what the circumstances."

"They might shoot their own wives under similar circumstances."

"They might shoot Olivares also. He was not a man in the marriage bed, you're aware. They would give him scant sympathy, might even feel he drove her to other men."

Escalante countered, "Still, he's a man in pain. Criminal or not, we haven't been able to help him. He turned to me and I let him slip away."

Dominguez was right after all. Throughout that day in Santa Fe, it was made plain that the other seven would not tolerate Olivares as a member of the expedition, though no one spoke a word about it.

Escalante finally approached all seven as they worked over their horses at the corral that afternoon. He asked bluntly how they would feel about taking Olivares along if he should appear before departure and explain himself to their satisfaction.

No one answered. They turned from Escalante to their horses and became busy combing and tending to leatherwork.

Escalante asked again and finally Miera answered for all. "Olivares? Olivares who, Father?"

The name was never mentioned again. Escalante found the denial fascinating and frightening. It was as though he had never existed. The men divided Olivares' chores among themselves. They set aside no kit or provisions for him. They asked for no one to go in his place. And on the morning of departure, they left the horse assigned to Olivares standing in its stall as though it did not exist either.

That morning, July 29, 1776, the company chose for its patron saints the Virgin Mary and her husband Joseph. Escalante and Dominguez said solemn Mass in the original Santa Fe mission church, where Escalante had first met Olivares weeks earlier.

Just before noon the party mustered in the old plaza. The horses became restless and struck sparks from the cobbles with their shoes. Cisneros shouted that he was finally going to have a look at the Pacific Ocean. Andres Muniz responded that he should have a bath too while he was there.

Hundreds turned out to watch them leave, bearing the heat and dust for the importance of the day. Boys burdened the branches of the paloverde trees. Birds fluttered in and out of the church belfries, unable to find rest with so much noise below. Soldiers sat in rows on the church steps. One of them shouted to no one in particular, "Better you than us."

Women threw flowers and sweetened bits of cactus wrapped in cornhusks. Old men wiped away tears, wishing to God they were going too.

Escalante was forced to shout every order, the noise in the plaza was so great. Finally he simply stood tall in his

stirrups, his hat hanging down his back on its leather thongs,
and pointed the way to the presidio gate.

The cattle moved out first. Simon Lucero the dwarf
drove his horse among the beasts, hanging down from one
stirrup to flog them along. The animals formed a huge wedge
and split the crowd.

Birds fled from the church tower as the bells rang out the
departure of the adventure. People cheered.

Bernardo Miera reined back his mount so it would not
paw the children at the edge of the crowd. The animal reared,
slashing air, then galloped after the livestock.

The other men followed Miera in single file. Pack mules
bounced along behind on tethers, raising still more dust to
blanket the day and darken the sun.

A strong voice called out, "God bless you." Others
picked it up. Soon the entire crowd was chanting, "God bless
you, God bless you, God bless you. . . ."

Escalante shouted close to Dominguez' ear, "Let's get
out of here. The women are beginning to cry, and I can't
stand that."

They too wheeled their horses and galloped on with the
train.

At the presidio gate, the two sat in a sea of dust and
people watched the train pass. Dominguez pointed. "Father.
That mule, second from last. What's in those leather sheaths?"

Escalante replied, "Just some odds and ends and implements we might need along the way."

Dominguez covered his eyes. "I may not be experienced
at all of this, but I have come to be able to know what most
of the bundles contain. These sheaths, I don't recognize
them."

"Does it matter, Father?"

"My Escalante, they're oiled leather. Waterproof." He
slapped his thigh. "As if they're rustproofing something inside. They're rifles, by God."

Escalante grinned. "Father, you indicated to me that I

could settle the firearms problem in my own way. Well, I did. I thought about it at length and concluded only that the bishop preferred no firearms along. You did not quite say that he absolutely prohibited them. I am sure he would rather get us—most of us—back than send us out unarmed.''

"You are quibbling over interpretations. And exaggerating."-

"You yourself led me to these thoughts."

"You are deliberately twisting more than one of my words."

"I know, Dominguez."

After a moment Dominguez asked, "How many are there?"

"Twenty. Two for every man plus. Unlike our companions, I count Olivares in rather than out." He grinned. "They're not long rifles, but shorter—saddle carbines. They don't fire a ball quite so far and so they're a little less deadly. That might placate the bishop some. Besides, they're better for infighting. Handier."

"Never mind that. Just answer one other question."

Escalante nodded.

"Did you also have the foresight to supply plenty of powder and shot?"

"Did Moses lead the children of Israel into the wilderness without unleavened bread?"

Dominguez was amused. "So. You claim your rifles do not have long range, so the bishop should be pleased because they're slightly less deadly, though better for merely hurting at close quarters."

"I don't understand what's so funny about that."

"Only a Jesuit reasons that way, Escalante. Only a Jesuit."

Escalante tilted his head back in his characteristic way and laughed raucously, mimicking the many dogs that ran barking and chasing after the last of the pack mules.

Chapter 10

The party rode toward the snowcapped peaks of the Sangre de Cristo Mountains. They passed white cottonwoods, royal pines, dwarf oaks, lime trees, bushes of chokecherries, fields of wild blue columbine and crisp blankets of piñon nuts on the ground. Geese and eagles climbed into the silvery liquid sky, so blue at times it hurt the eye. The snow on the mountains blazed in the sun.

Escalante stood in his saddle, dropped his reins and raised his arms in affection for the beauty of it. "Notice one change taking place already," he called out to Dominguez.

"Tell me."

"No dust. Once outside the city, no more dust. You wipe your mouth and your hand comes away clean."

It was less hot riding north in sight of the mountains than it had been on the dusty plains around Santa Fe. Breezes worked like playful fingers among the manes of the horses and their thick bobbed tails, curled back the skins over the provisions and dried even the sweat beneath the pack saddles on the caravan of mules. Sunlight glinted off the silver saddle horns and ran along the bridles. The horses' shoes struck sharp music against bits of shale. Otherwise the hoofbeats thudded in a way that lifted one's spirits at the ease of passage, releasing from the ground the richness and variety of mountain aromas.

The Chain of Cranes was the Spanish name for the western mountains. Across the intervening blue they often did seem as grey and angled as flying cranes. In the foothill meadows the men saw cranes standing one-footed in the grasses, tall as children, thin as saplings. Lifted up in flight, they seemed to Escalante solemn as the human heart, brittle, dusky and straining. Their cries echoed over the landscape like voices from another world.

Once the expedition had passed the foothills, Escalante felt the constriction of life in Santa Fe loosen and fall away. His body had been purified by fever and privation. His will had been reduced from flabby fullness to a slender, active rod. He felt scoured and flooded with clear light. The memories of Santa Fe women in satin dresses, their musks and heavy odors, had vanished for a while in the quickening mountain air.

Monterey and the missing Father Francisco Garces seemed somehow directly before them, pushing ahead just over the next hill. The women in the plaza and the streets of Santa Fe had shrunk to tiny patterns.

Cisneros rode beside Escalante, idly slapping at his legs in *chaparejos* with the end of his reins. From time to time he would whistle at the dogs that ran on ahead. A breeze scented with pine and piñon pushed back the hair from his forehead and made his features move apart, as though in joy or laughter. However, he was concerned only with his whistling and the rhythmic slapping of his reins. His horse above all others rocked with the steadiest motion and had the finest and easiest gait. It was a fact for which Cisneros took no credit. Like his own good looks, it seemed just part of nature's way.

"I wonder how far we shall have reached by the end of each day," he said to Escalante. "I imagine it will vary."

"May God provide us always with weather just like this."

Cisneros laughed. "You know he won't, Father. His intentions are much broader."

"We should all grow bored, I suppose, if they were not."

The voices of Escalante and Cisneros joined chorus with the saddle noises. The horses nickered and the men discussed the climate.

Bernardo Miera rode slightly behind, accompanied by Joaquin Lain. The breezes were such that neither pair could hear what the other two men were saying. They hardly listened anyway; their heads were full of their own thoughts. Miera had an image in his mind of being ushered, dusty and sun-blackened, into the court of King Carlos the Third of Spain. Carlos would wave away all the others who had gathered there so he could talk to Miera alone. Impressed by his humility and daring, Carlos would say nothing, but his eyes would. We shall hear of this man again, the silent message would run. Miera then thought of his wife and how long she had cried when he left. She had said she was convinced she would never see him again. Now, however, imagining King Carlos, Miera felt much more at ease. A hard, sinewy man, Miera had a face full of folly, but not unkind.

Joaquin Lain's face was another matter. Not half so handsome as Miera's, it was strong but irregular. Lain was tall and too lean. Women did not find him handsome. His eyes showed his true temper. They were black and anxious, pitiless as a raven's. One of the reasons he thought so highly of his cousin Estella was that her eyes were like this also. Her allure, he was thinking now, studying the shadow he made with his horse, was more than love or kinship or the shapeliness of her body. Something about her seemed profoundly familiar, and was wasted, Lain swore, on Pedro Cisneros.

Andres Muniz' shadow crossed Lain's on his way back

from the head of the column. He wore a beaver hat low on his
brow and his sleek glossy beard looked like beaver also.

Andres had found a ford a few leagues away where the
cattle could be crossed. He was on his way back now to see
how well his brother Lucrecio, Miera's dwarf and Juan de
Aguilar were herding the cattle.

The pack train was about two miles behind the men on
horseback and the cattle a mile or more behind that. Andres
found Aguilar leading the mules through two strands of
timber, Dominguez following behind. The priest was saying
his rosary, which he immediately tucked away.

"Where are you going, Andres?"

"To check the cattle, Father. Why were you praying?"

"I was praying for my stomach."

Andres looked at him and his stomach. "It is ample,
Father. I can see that it may not like to travel."

Dominguez sighed and returned one hand to the rosary
looped over his belt. "Very funny," he sneered. "But I fear
a stomach fever has begun to rack me."

Andres snorted. The two men rode on awhile in silence.

"Have you heard the cattle behind you?" Andres asked
finally.

"Not for a time now."

"Does Aguilar lead the pack train well?"

"He seems to."

"Good."

With an air of finality, Dominguez took his hand away
from his rosary. Unbeknownst to him, the loop had slipped
and the crucifix was slapping his horse's flank. He burped
and passed his fat pasty hand over his forehead, his face quite
pale.

Andres grinned. "We are hardly a day out."

Dominguez' face was impassive and heavy-looking. Andres wondered how a horse could ever carry the mammoth
priest. "The majesty of God is in the strangeness of his ways,
but our way is not to question," Dominguez intoned.

"Ha!" Andres shouted, whipping his horse into a fierce gallop after the wandering cattle. Coming over a rise he saw them spread in all directions, pursued by Lucero and his brother Lucrecio. They were bulls, with a huge old longhorn to lead them, but he was standing alone in mild consternation while the herd scattered behind him.

Andres joined in the chase, shouting at his brother, who he knew could not hear him. Simon Lucero was jouncing in his saddle like a merry piglet. Andres topped another rise and saw six head of cattle crashing down a bald gully. They were being chased by a mountain bear. Andres stopped his horse. The bear was a good-sized one, brown and shaggy. A leather lariat trailed from its shoulders. As the bear went lumbering down the draw the lariat kept catching in the sage, jerking him upright. The bear swiped the rope free, reminding Andres of a noble lady he once had seen flipping her ermine cape behind her as she walked. This made him laugh, but then he was angry, having realized that the rope was his own.

"Come here, you idle chubwit," he screamed at Lucrecio, approaching behind him. "That's my lariat. You shall remove it from that bear and then at once return it. And you'll never have use of it again."

The eagerness died in Lucrecio's eyes, but he kept smiling. Andres started after the cattle.

The animals finally slowed down and began to graze and Andres gathered them up and turned them around. He watched for signs of the bear in the behavior of the group leader, an older bull with a slightly bleeding pawmark on one flank. As they neared the bald gully, Andres could see riders gathering the rest of the cattle on the high sage crest. As he approached, his six went bawling up the hill faster than a summer cloud. He yelled for the help of Lain, who rode off in another direction. Andres motioned to Escalante and Dominguez, standing on the ridge. The two priests responded, moving toward the cattle as though their very presence would attract them. Andres smiled; priests were so very arrogant.

Lain, Cisneros and Miera were together in a copse of tall cedar on the side of a nearby hill. Andres saw them only because the buckskin color of Miera's horse was so conspicuous.

The bear was no longer roaring. They were all watching the animal, swords at the ready. Andres grunted aloud, "Attack him, attack him!" Then he saw the reason why they did not, and a chill as deep as winter came over him.

Lucrecio Muniz, his breeches torn and his legs bleeding, lay nestled between the bear's front paws. At first Andres believed the bear was mauling Lucrecio's dead body, swatting it back and forth. He cried out for one of the carbines.

Then Andres saw that the movement was Lucrecio's own. It was the bear in Lucrecio's control. The servant was working the lariat off the animal's head. The bear was growling and watching Lucrecio closely, but he was peaceful and gentle.

Andres stopped his horse dead and felt his heart grow quiet. His chill deepened. Was this God at work or the devil?

Andres heard other growling sounds. Clutching his chest in fear, he realized they came from Lucrecio. They were sounds Andres had never heard.

Sunlight fell through the trees. Birds twittered in the branches. From far away, almost in another world, it seemed, came the lowing sounds of the cattle.

The bear was now still. Lucrecio had nearly freed the noose of the lariat from its head. He was petting the bear along the side of its jaw. Andres could not see Lucrecio's face, but he could hear his little brother still speaking to the bear in its own growls.

Once the lariat had been removed, Lucrecio placed its noose around his own neck and then rolled away from the bear. The bear stayed on its back and did not move. Lucrecio came toward his brother. The bear got up when Lucrecio left him. The horses snorted and stamped. The bear growled and shook itself back to wildness, growled again and lunged back into the woods.

The horses were all moving now, the dogs barking, the men crying out in amazement.

"In truth I have never seen such a thing," Miera marveled.

"God's mercy be upon you," said Cisneros.

Lucrecio, striped and bleeding, had now reached Andres. With a smile he handed back the lariat, sunnily indifferent to what had happened.

Miera was still caught in amazement. "We chanced upon him with the bear and thought he was dead."

"I have not seen the like." Lain looked up to heaven.

"Nor I," Cisneros concurred.

Andres was examining his lariat, wrestling with residual awe and fear. Glancing at his brother, not caring to look at him directly, he saw Lucrecio was in turn watching him. "Fool," Andres muttered under his breath, then tossed the lariat back to him. "Can you somehow explain any of this?"

Lucrecio shrugged shyly. "No. First he pawed me and I thought I was dead. Then suddenly I just knew I could make him be still and remove the lariat. And I did it."

"I'm stunned, younger brother."

"I didn't know I could talk to bears either," Lucrecio smiled.

As the group rode away from the copse toward the priests on the ridge, the extraordinary impression of what they had seen began to fade. Each man was already deciding how he would tell the story, but Miera spoke for them all. "I don't think we should tell the priests what just happened. Priests often make trouble when they meet magic."

The cattle crossed at the ford Andres had found earlier. It was late afternoon and sunlight falling through the pines turned the river molten in its shallows and black along its

deeps. The cattle kicked up rainbows of spray as they forded.
Droplets of water settled on the men and made them shimmer
until they dried. The sound of animals in the river sounded
like thunder far away.

That night they camped in a sweet-smelling mountain
meadow. Dominguez was stricken with a stomach fever. The
cattle sifted through the forest like falling leaves. The birds
were growing quiet. Fireflies began to spark, lovely and
hopeful, against the darkness of the trees.

Miera brought the elderly priest water in a dripping
goatskin bag. Dominguez lay propped against his saddle, his
back fat enough to hold him upright, a blanket warming his
legs.

"Here, Father," said Miera, "your thirst will need a
slaking."

Dominguez seemed to be thinking about something very
far away; his eyes turned inward to memories of another
place. He took the goatskin, pulled off its pitchy cap and
drank. "Thank you."

"Sickness at the onset of a journey often bodes well for
the middle portions and the close."

Dominguez sighed. "That's superstition, but still a comforting thought."

Miera had been squatting but now eased onto the grass beside
him, staring out toward the dimming mountain peaks. "For
myself, death among this splendor would not be such a bad
thing."

"I suppose not."

"You would wish for another place?"

"Very much." Dominguez sighed again, a droplet of
water falling from his chin. "All my months in Santa Fe I
have been longing for Mexico City. My heart is there. It is
my birthplace. The memories of change live so much in its
walls that I can see myself at different ages as I pass through
certain streets. Old as you and I are now, Don Bernardo, we
tempt the hand of fate."

Miera smiled. "I have had this feeling often, though we are not so very old."

"I wish only to return to what my heart yearns for, and yet my course has lately taken me away."

"So it seems." Miera got up suddenly. "I know you shall recover, Father."

Dominguez looked up at Miera, plaintiveness crossing his face. "I am almost reluctant to do that as I get older. I know myself as I am now. I like myself. I do not wish to change. But after a trip such as this one . . . I know I cannot, will not, be the same afterward."

"That's almost too deep for me, Father." Miera nodded and returned to where Simon Lucero was making a fire. The dwarf was chuckling and shaking his head. "Bearbaiting and the supernatural—what a fine beginning for an exploration in the name of God and the crown." He snapped a few sticks of kindling across his pudgy knees. "If this is any sign of things to come, we'll handle ourselves just beautifully the rest of the way, won't we?"

Miera ignored the sarcasm and studied the snow on the mountains, the orange of the fire. For some reason they turned his thoughts to Santa Fe.

"I hope we do, Simon," he murmured in a wistful, faraway voice. "I hope we do."

Later, when the evening meal was done, Escalante set his writing desk on a rock near the fire. The stone radiated the heat of the day's hot sun, comforting him.

With his knife he shaved a point on a goose quill, then split it so it would retain ink. He spread a blank piece of parchment on the desk top. He sat thinking for several minutes before he began the first entry in his journal of the Monterey expedition:

This is the diary and itinerary of Father Francisco Atanasio Dominguez and Father Silvestre

Velez de Escalante on their quest for an overland route from the presidio of Santa Fe in New Mexico to Monterey, California.

On this 29th day of July in the Year of Our Lord 1776, traveling under the shield of Our Lady the Virgin Mary, who was conceived without original sin, and under protection of her husband the most blessed, the three times holy Joseph the Patriarch, we, Father Francisco Atanasio Dominguez, incumbent commissary visitor of the Custody of the Conversion of Saint Paul in New Mexico, and Father Silvestre Velez de Escalante, minister of doctrine of the mission of Our Lady of Guadalupe of Zuni, in the willing company of Don Juan Pedro Cisneros, high mayor of the aforementioned community of Zuni and his servant Lucrecio Muniz; Don Bernardo Miera, army captain (retired) and honored member of the community of Santa Fe and his servant, the dwarf Simon Lucero; Don Joaquin Lain, respected citizen of the same community and his servant Juan de Aguilar; and in addition, Andres Muniz, accomplished linguist and woodsman and brother of the aforesaid Lucrecio. All, having dutifully beseeched the protection of our high, most holy patron saints, and having received the Holy Eucharist, have now set forth from Santa Fe, capital of New Mexico.

After traveling approximately twenty-four miles northwest, we encamped close by the village of Santa Clara, where we spent the night.

Escalante brought his draft copy of the journal to Dominguez. As he wrestled with the torture seizing his insides, the titular head of the expedition read carefully and with great concentration, squinting in the dancing firelight.

Putting the document down later, Dominguez remarked that it could not have been clearer or more complete if he had written it himself.

Chapter 11

Escalante and Dominguez and their men rode north along the Chain of Cranes through territory that Andres and several others had seen before. Beaver was plentiful in the mountain streams and elk and mule deer abounded on the hillsides. The terrain varied as the party moved higher and more to the north; the passes were easy and the rivers shallow. Under Simon Lucero's direction they lost the cattle several times, so Lain and Dominguez were put in charge, and Lucero was sent to ride with his master, Miera. Dominguez had recovered from his fever, although the expedition had had to remain at its first campsite for several days while he recovered.

Now, with Dominguez healthy once more, the caravan moved on, sometimes covering thirty miles in a day. But they weren't the first Europeans to travel these mountains, for nearly a century earlier, Spanish explorers had mapped this rugged terrain. Andres Muniz told the others that he himself had passed through on the expeditions of Juan Maria de Rivera several times, most recently in 1775.

What the newcomers found most interesting was the richness of the Indian land. Minerals crowded the rock walls.

Smoky lignite wisped in buttes of yellow stone. Some rocks cast a light greener than sunbeams under water. Often what looked like lichen was actually pure copper. At dusk, in greying canyons, sunlight struck traces even of gold.

These minerals interested Miera very much, so much that he began collecting samples of the glittering rocks. It wasn't long before these samples filled his saddlebags, forcing him to discard those he considered least valuable. He inspected every promising rock with a lustful eye.

Andres Muniz observed, "No one I have ever traveled with has collected samples so gluttonously as you, Miera. Why are you doing it?"

"For my church and king, of course," Miera answered simply.

Something in his seriousness squelched Muniz' ridicule. "I suppose that's acceptable," he mumbled instead.

"You once came for beaver, didn't you?" Miera questioned accusingly.

"And found them in great numbers."

"Well, if my rocks prove valuable, they'll bring not only trappers, but also men looking for gold and other metals, and they in turn will bring priests, women and cattle, the main implements of civilization and conversion to God's way."

"Miera," Muniz asked, "are you really as dedicated as all that?"

"Yes," Miera answered, "really. And if we can establish a road to the sea at Monterey, then all we find in this wildnerness shall be forever Spanish, not English or Russian. Our language and our church will reign and our names will be spoken with awe."

"And from all the wealth of these minerals, you want nothing for yourself."

"I already have plenty for myself."

"It's hard to believe, this selflessness of yours."

Miera laughed in genuine good humor and confidence.

"If you have to question it in the first place, you'll never understand it. Just believe me. Those are my reasons."

In the heat of midday they passed through a chalky canyon full of Spanish dagger. A trail through the yucca had been cut by animals along one crumbly edge. Aguilar and Cisneros now led the caravan. Extra horses, linked tail to bridle, swayed along unburdened. The pack mules followed grunting, their harnesses and panniers creaking, rocks rolling and chipping away beneath their hooves.

The lowing cattle followed, lining up in order of herd status for narrow spots in the trail. Mostly, though, the cattle overran everything in their path, punching through chamisos and willows wherever it pleased them. At the banks of small arroyos they purled like water at a drain. They seemed more like voyageurs than any of the explorers, more curious and understanding, ready for every new turn of the trail.

"Escalante, what's this?" Cisneros pointed at something resembling a spear drawn in ocher on a canyon wall.

"It almost looks real," Escalante observed. "Look, here's another."

Suddenly they realized they had passed other spears and arrows drawn on the rock faces as well as Indian men painted in red. Leaving the pack train to care for itself, Escalante and Cisneros rode back through the canyon.

There in the shimmering heat of day were drawings of spears, knives and lances. There were running men and thick-legged bison. Escalante began to laugh. "How simple and endearing."

"The canyon is alive with these symbols," said Cisneros. Lain, at the head of the cattle, had ridden up beside him.

Dust rolling forward from the cattle began to rise toward the painted walls.

"A battle, I would venture to say," pronounced Lain, "some sort of commemoration."

The cattle proceeded past the three men, bringing

Dominguez, Lucrecio Muniz and Juan de Aguilar. They joined the others, moving slowly along the canyon.

Finally Andres and Miera arrived from the head of the column. The sun and the heat made this discovery too dreamlike, too unadorned to be real. Escalante chewed at his finger. There was more here, he realized, more time and history than he had ever imagined. God in His heaven did not look down over all the world. He bit his cheek and prayed for forgiveness for the thought. The wonder moving in his heart had brushed against the grain of his religious belief once again.

The men trotted calmly over the mountainous terrain and the cattle, horses and mules drifted from the canyon and fanned out onto a higher plateau. Then it happened.

Cisneros' horse shrieked wildly and clawed the air in terror, nearly lifting Cisneros from the saddle. Escalante yelled to his friend, "Don Pedro, it's a rattler! Under your horse!" Escalante reached for his knife, but he was too late, for Cisneros had slipped his saddle carbine from its sheath and fired. But he missed. Escalante watched in horror as the scene unfolded before his eyes.

The old longhorn boss leaped straight up from the ground, all four hooves airborne. When he came down he bounded straight for a pair of mules and gored their exposed behinds with his four-foot horns. The injured mules screamed and ran, panicking the other animals as well.

The stampede headed for Miera. Before he could respond, the herd hit his mount broadside, knocking it flat on the ground.

Miera pulled his feet free of his stirrups and leaped clear as the horse rolled over and over, screaming and screaming. Seeing Miera go down, Andres Muniz spurred his horse to outrun the herd, but he was too late. The bellowing animals all but ran up the horse's back and Muniz too went down.

Cisneros, the cause of it all, tried to cut a hard-ridden line across the leading edge of the herd, to turn it and slow it down. He was clubbing the noses of the bulls with his carbine. Juan de Aguilar and Lucrecio Muniz drove their own horses among the animals to help Cisneros.

Dominguez yelled to Escalante, "What do we do?"

"We get out of their way!" Escalante seized the bridle of Dominguez' horse and pulled it aside a moment before the humping cattle charged past.

It was over as quickly as it had started. Once in the clear, the animals forgot they were frightened and slowed down to chew on a meadow of fresh grass.

Tasting the fear in his mouth, Escalante rushed his horse to the place where Muniz and Miera had gone down. As the dust cleared the fear changed to the sweet taste of relief.

Lucrecio Muniz was lifting Andres and brushing the dust off his clothes. For once Andres permitted it, seeming dazed but comforted by his brother's attention.

Miera was trying to punch Cisneros and two others held him back. Miera struggled and cursed. "You empty-headed son of a priest and a whore, what in Satan's name were you doing shooting off a carbine in the middle of the herd over one little snake?"

Escalante galloped past, his cassock fluttering. "You two can fight later, but get the herd rounded up right now."

Most of the animals had not gone far and were easily gathered in. At the final tally, two mules were missing—vital ones, it turned out. They carried flour, sugar and salt.

"How are we going to travel without bread?" Miera bellowed. Everyone turned to Cisneros, as though he could answer and make the loss right.

Cisneros looked from one face to another and said nothing. As angry as Escalante himself was at Cisneros, his heart softened as he looked at Cisneros' face. The man was in an agony of guilt and humiliation.

After an hour of searching for the mules, Escalante announced that it was time to move on. The party only ran further risk of scattering itself in prolonging the hunt, he reasoned. There were flour, sugar and salt on other mules. They would make do with short rations on bread until they could replace the flour somewhere. He suggested that the Indians along the way might be willing to barter for some. "Thank God it wasn't the guns," he concluded.

The party crossed the plain and passed into stands of mountain timber. The men's anger at Cisneros for starting the stampede diminished as they bragged about their own quick thinking. After a while they were even laughing a little, as often happens among men who have shared danger.

Toward evening they hobbled the horses and gathered the mules and turned the cattle loose to graze.

When the party made camp, Escalante rode farther still into the mountains. Behind him the men were busy gathering firewood, drawing water from a nearby stream, unpacking mules and checking the provisions to see what was lost. Escalante broke through timber, not particularly thick, following an animal trail toward a distant rustle of wind through the trees. The wind eventually dropped to a breeze, cooling the sweat on his face and drying his horse. Pine needles swirled from the ground.

Escalante had no idea where he was going. He knew vaguely the direction to the plain. He hoped the two mules had wandered into this wooded fastness, but he had no real expectation of ever seeing them again.

In his saddlebag was the journal he was keeping, which he now read as he rode. They had been gone two weeks from Santa Fe and had covered nearly two hundred sixty miles. The trail the party had taken was well marked and obvious, but Escalante had a nagging feeling they could have gone in any direction—down any barranca, across any ridge—and still have been going in the right direction.

The expedition had not yet reached the wilderness, but it seemed to Escalante they had already passed into something new. A new presence, another order, seemed to govern their actions. The door of the wilderness, the land no white men had ever seen, was now only a few leagues away.

In the forest before Escalante the animal trails were fainter, the timber not so uniform. The forest seemed to be breaking up, although there was still no sign of the plain.

Escalante rode deeper into the timber. Soon he was traveling through a grove of large pine and fir trees. The dusk had deepened and the wind had come up again. It was a fresh, cold wind now, the type that brought rain.

Sure enough, the rain hit as he was crossing a clearing, turned to hail and collected in the folds of his robes. Thin young trees bent like whips under his stirrups, further soaking his legs.

By the time he got back to camp, the rain clouds had dissolved into a pervasive mist. The men had stretched the cured-skin tarps between trees at the edge of the clearing, leaving a crease at the center to allow rainwater to run to the ground. The fires under the tarps were barely alive.

Escalante turned his horse out to graze at the edge of the forest and came dragging his saddle across the meadow to one of the skins. He ducked into a shelter shared by Miera and Father Dominguez. Miera was smoking a pipe and Dominguez was contentedly chewing on a bar of chocolate. Escalante could see other members of the party dragging pack saddles about and covering them with leather to keep the seams dry.

"Where have you been, Father Escalante?" asked Miera quietly. "I'd sooner lose those missing mules than half our churchly guidance."

"The mules haven't returned yet?" Escalante felt unusually tired and discouraged.

As he often did, Dominguez was sitting upright against his saddle, a blanket over his legs. Gnawing on his chocolate, he watched with tired fascination a spout of rainwater stream from the creased skin to the ground. "That must mean you haven't seen them either," he surmised.

Escalante shook his head. "I'm afraid not, Dominguez."

Miera laughed, peering in the dimness at Escalante, who was shivering with cold. "I believe this rain will last, the way the clouds have lowered on us. We've lost our mules and now our weather."

"Please don't try God's patience any further, Don Bernardo," Dominguez said testily.

It was nearly dark. The rain abated, increased, then steadied. Water now dripped from various points on the stretched animal skins and hissed into the fire.

Aguilar came into the tent. "My master Lain cares to know whether any dry stores remain. Our meal is such a cold one, he can hardly bear to eat it."

"Tell him please to come join us," said Dominguez, "but also to bring another skin, preferably a dry one."

"What about Cisneros?" Miera asked.

"He seems to be quite fairly situated. I saw him eating with his dwarf," Aguilar sniffed.

Simon Lucero came into the tent next, his head misshapen beneath his wet hair. He threw down a load of firewood and began to shave back the wet bark from the wood.

Escalante changed into a dry robe, a heavier one made specially for winter, and stood at the fire trying to warm himself. He stared into the darkness. A flash of lightning revealed five mules and a horse, still saddled, among the trees. Someone would have to put them to bed. He glanced around the tent, but everyone seemed busy. Even Dominguez was helping Lucero shave wood for burning.

Escalante inhaled deeply and felt for the iron of his will to pry him out of the tent into the rain. He would have to unsaddle the rest of the stock himself. There was no sense in more than one man being drenched.

He opened the flap of the tent and suddenly felt a terrible chill blow through him. He inhaled in fright and muttered, "God help us!"

The other men stopped what they were doing and turned to him. Escalante was peering across the leaping flames. Only a moment before all he had been able to see was rain and darkness. Now there was a man standing there.

The man's face seemed ghostly white in the firelight. Water ran from his hair, nose and chin and from every article of clothing.

Startled, Escalante lurched back among the others about the fire. The saddled animals were moving closer. He realized they had come with the stranger.

The young priest did not recognize the face. There was, however, a familiarity of bulk and posture that heightened his tension and fear. He knew he had met this man before and had the impression it had been an unpleasant encounter.

The newcomer stood dripping onto the fire. Escalante thought his eyes had the look of an eagle's, cold and defiant. For a long time there was silence; six pack animals seemed less of a presence than this one man.

Lain finally spoke. "Who is this stranger? Hey, you! Identify yourself."

At that Miera bellowed, "Oh, heaven's blood upon my fingers, it's Olivares from El Paso."

And then, of course, Escalante understood why the man looked so familiar; it was indeed he whom he had wrestled and lost outside the church in Santa Fe. Escalante flinched; the recognition was a shock, though he thought later he should have been prepared for it.

"The man who would murder his wife." Dominguez spoke with outward calm that belied his distress at Olivares' appearance.

It was Miera who made the first move.

He pushed past the group and dropped to his knees beside his baggage, then leaped to his feet again and whirled toward Olivares, cocking an army-issue pistol. Gripping it with his right hand he hauled back on the flintlock striker with his left.

"Miera," Escalante warned, "put it down."

"Murderer," Miera spat at Olivares. The outlaw did not

reach for his own weapons, seeming resigned to execution. Escalante knew better, though. He saw Olivares' right hand move slightly toward a pistol kept dry under a leather cover beneath his left armpit.

"He did not kill her." Escalante moved quietly to block Miera's aim and path.

"I'd have shot him for what he did before; I'll shoot him now."

"Miera."

"Out of the way, Father."

"You'll have the mortal sin of murder on your soul."

"I am only executing a criminal, Father."

"No, you're not, Miera." He spun on one foot so hard his sandal squeaked on the damp earth. He lifted his fist up from the hip and straight out, connected and felt Miera's nose and upper lip give way under the power. Miera loosed a grunt of pain as blood covered his mouth and chin. He did not resist the punch. Instead, he allowed himself to fall backward with it to lessen its sting.

Miera rolled and came up in a crouch. "I'll not strike a priest, Father." He lifted the pistol before him. His message was clear to Escalante. "But I'm still going to shoot Lorenzo Olivares."

For a moment there was silence except for the rain, drumming on the skin tent.

Everyone reacted at once. Olivares' hand shot to his armpit holster. Andres Muniz pushed Lucrecio to the earth and covered him with himself. Dominguez moved his pillowy bulk with surprising speed to seize Olivares' arm. And Miera's knuckles tightened on the trigger.

Escalante lunged at Miera, arms outstretched. But Miera didn't move. Then, just as Escalante seemed about to tackle him, Miera pivoted away.

It was exactly the move Escalante was waiting for. While Miera spun, he was off balance. Escalante was on him in a second. He took Miera's elbow in one hand and his wrist in the other, put his shoulder in the man's armpit and flung himself forward to one knee.

Escalante cartwheeled Miera over his shoulder and slammed him to the ground. Miera's pistol blew out flame and smoke. The ball plowed a furrow in the dirt.

Escalante let go of Miera and he lay sprawled on his back, looking up at the soggy skin tent above, holding his twisted wrist. "I did not expect that, Father," he admitted.

Escalante was furious. "Don't you ever question my authority, Miera. And don't let these robes fool you. I am a man of God, but that doesn't mean I can't outsmart and outfight the likes of you. And believe me, I'd do it again—with pleasure."

Olivares had let his own weapon slide back into its armpit holster. He stood and watched everyone, waiting for the tension to ease before he talked. "I've come here to take my place in the expedition—with your permission, Father Escalante." He spoke confidently and calmly, certain that permission would be granted.

Miera spoke up immediately, before Escalante had considered his answer. "He was anathema in Santa Fe. He is anathema here. No."

Looking at the faces of the others, Escalante knew they still felt the same. He knew what he had to do.

"Listen to me, all of you, and do not mistake my gentleness for weakness. No one will harm him." To Olivares he said, "And you will do nothing to provoke them." He turned to the rest again. "When everyone has cooled off, then we'll decide whether Olivares joins us or not. And if any of you disobey this order, I promise you, I'll move heaven and earth to have you excommunicated. The man is a felon, yes; he shot his wife. But he has not killed her and that's reason enough to reconsider his case. Lord knows, if any of us were Olivares, we would pray for equal consideration and justice."

Escalante looked at the others and perceived an unspoken threat. He added, "And no one is even going to think of deserting this expedition. That is that, my final word on the subject. There will be no further discussion. That's an order. In the name of God, amen.''

Escalante studied the faces. The men looked straight at his eyes. They resented him and what he was telling them. No one spoke. Escalante wondered, what do I do if they rebel?

Then Miera spoke up. "I'd be obliged if you had a dry cigar, Father." He offered his pistol as well, acknowledging his obedience. Escalante took the cigar but not the pistol, and Miera packed the weapon away.

Then tension began to dissolve as one by one the men turned their backs on the scene and buried themselves in the remaining tasks for the night. He knew Miera's graceful and diplomatic acquiescence had returned to him the control of the expedition. He silently blessed Miera; such integrity, loyalty and maturity. Escalante sighed. That was a close one.

Chapter 12

In the renaissance of good will, even Lorenzo Olivares attempted to contribute to the peacemaking process. "I've found your mules and brought them back," he offered, "along with some provisions of my own.

"I found them here in the forest," continued Olivares, turning to Miera. "I've been following your party now for several days and wish to take my appointed place. I could think of no better way to approach than with your missing mules and supplies." Olivares smiled and cleared his throat. He wore a leather jerkin several sizes too large and his hands shook as if with ague. He showed no fear, however, and seemed insistent, almost rude. All eyes were on him. "I realize I have broken the laws of God and man. As soon as we reach Monterey I'll place myself before the bar of justice and accept whatever punishment comes for what I've done. That I promise you, whether or not you accept me for the rest of the trip." He thought for a moment. "I truly wish to join this expedition. I'm not here to escape justice. I think you'll find me a valuable partner." He pointed to the pack animals in the rain outside. "That is only my first contribution."

Olivares looked about the fire at the assembled faces. There was a common feeling that this Olivares was a troublemaker. Still, they were stunned at his sudden materialization and were not yet ready to speak objectively.

Olivares continued to plead his case to Escalante. "Father, I'd like to complete the confession I began in Santa Fe. I'd also like to apologize for roughing you up that night. Now, please hear me and tell me my penance so my soul may be saved before God."

"Your penance may keep you on your knees for years."

Olivares shrugged and nodded. No matter. He was ready.

Miera spoke up then. Escalante realized his submission to Escalante's orders would not last forever; anger still invaded Miera's voice. "How did you come to track us so well, Olivares, without our knowing you were about?"

"I have more powers than you would suspect, Don Bernardo, and greater competence." This was no boast but a simple fact.

Miera reddened and began to splutter. To avoid another confrontation, Escalante spoke hastily. "Let's go off, Olivares. I'll hear your confession in one of the other tents, out of this weather."

Olivares nodded. "Thank you, Father."

Cisneros persisted. "But first, I'd like to know how you did find our missing mules."

"I came upon them grazing in a clearing," Olivares answered. "I might have waited another day or two before coming in with them. I wasn't certain how you'd accept me. I thought the longer they were gone the gladder you'd be to get them back. That would have been another betrayal, though." He looked at Miera. "I would have done as you did. Please believe that I hold no grudge."

Escalante marveled. The man was like a child with his arrogance and humility.

"It was the rain that finally drove me to take shelter with you," Olivares added. "A man can stay wet only so long."

"Well, the return of the mules does tell in your favor," Cisneros grumbled. "It was due to my own carelessness that the mules ran off in the first place."

"They seem to have broken their halters."

"My thoughts have been on them ever since," Cisneros reflected. "I was greatly distressed by my own carelessness. And now my stupidity seems to have been redeemed by a criminal."

"A crime of passion, however," Olivares insisted.

Cisneros stared at him. "I could kill my wife sometimes, out of sadness and jealousy."

Startled at hearing this, Escalante was about to scold Cisneros but then thought, I am no one to rebuke another for sinful thoughts, considering the nature of some of my own. He let it drop.

Escalante and Olivares left for Escalante's own soggy tent, bending their heads into the winds that chased the storm. Escalante rekindled his fire there. He draped his stole across his shoulders and nodded. Olivares could kneel and begin his confession.

The fire crackled and it seemed as though Olivares was not truly confessing, but telling a story. It was terrible, to be sure, but told as if it were about someone else, not Olivares himself. Escalante, turned sideways and bending his ear, stared across the flames into the dripping darkness. The man was clearly a tough one.

The priest saw the lights of the larger tent and imagined the men there talking of what they wished to do *with* and *to* Olivares while he, Escalante, would exert himself *for* him.

Escalante pressed Olivares to recall other sins since the shooting. He noted to his satisfaction that there had been relatively few since Olivares had left Santa Fe. Injuring his wife's relatives had been about the worst of it, and since that had been done in self-defense, it was forgivable.

He asked Olivares whether he was truly contrite and repentant. Yes. He asked whether he was truly determined not to repeat the sin against his wife. Yes. He demanded of Olivares his promise to make amends to the wife if possible. It was given.

Olivares gave Escalante his assurance that he would never commit such sins again. Still, to the young priest, there was something about him that seeded doubt. In the end he gave Olivares absolution only because he believed the man incapable of deliberate dishonesty, even though he might not recognize truth.

Sincerity was the most Escalante hoped for.

The penance Escalante levied was simple but harsh. Olivares was to dedicate one half of his total income for the rest of his life to his wife and her father and her brothers for the injuries he had done them. Olivares was to pray on his knees for two hours nightly for as long as the expedition lasted. Finally, Escalante made Olivares swear before God that he would indeed surrender to civil authorities when the expedition was finished.

"Ego te absolvo," Escalante pronounced.

Later Lorenzo Olivares told Escalante he had expected penance more traditional and conventional. "No walking barefoot through the wilderness or scourging myself with cactus or hanging upside down from a tree, Father?"

Escalante did not know whether Olivares was teasing or serious. As usual, his face was without readable expression. "No, but if that would please you, go right ahead. I shall not stop you." He did not explain that he believed such penances were medieval and nonproductive.

Escalante told Olivares to spend his first night in the priests' tent. He could not be certain Olivares would be alive in the morning if he slept with the others.

"Doesn't it strike you as being hypocritical, Father, that what your men propose as punishment for my violence is only more violence?"

Escalante nodded. Of course Olivares was right, but no doubt he deserved a little violence. "Perhaps so, Olivares.

Now stop your chattering and get some sleep." After a few minutes Escalante added, "You're lucky to be alive." He rolled up in his blankets and tried to sleep before the dampness and chill soaked through them to his skin. He prayed for sunshine for the duration of the journey.

In the morning it seemed Escalante might have his wish. The day dawned cool, bright and dry. He unrolled his blankets with the sensation that mildew was caking and drying on his body. A fire was blazing in the large tent, generating smells of sharp smoke and sweet breakfast chocolate and yeasty bread.

Escalante stood and stretched. Lorenzo Olivares was already awake, sitting on the ground with a tree for a backrest. He hunched beneath his hat and cape and stared at his judges across the way. Escalante noticed he was wearing his pistols in their armpit holster once more.

The mood of the men seemed different this morning. The passing time and the night's rest had leavened their tempers. For this Escalante was grateful to God. His authority was strengthened and so was the chance for success.

The others were all sitting on their heels or standing about the fire, yawning and scratching and drying themselves and their wet clothes. They were discussing the possibility that Olivares had stolen the mules so he could bring them back and gain acceptance by the expedition members.

"That is not true." Olivares had overheard the hushed discussion. "I do not need to win approval with deceit or a coward's ways."

Andres Muniz and Joaquin Lain laughed, teeth shining in their dark faces. They seemed to be the most eager for punishment.

"What do you men think should be done with him?" Escalante asked the party.

"We have decided only not to kill him," Lain replied. "The rest is still in question."

Escalante had not hoped for even that much so early, but he did not say so.

"We've voted," Andres Muniz went on. "It comes out a tie. Four of us say he should be ostracized and abandoned. The other four, including Father Dominguez, are in favor of letting him come."

"As far as I'm concerned the priests shouldn't have a vote," Lain shouted.

"Your priests happen to be in charge of this expedition," Escalante reminded him, his face close to Lain's. "It is not for you to say whether or not we vote—or even if there will be a vote."

Lain did not reply, nor did he look away from Escalante's eyes.

Miera asked, "Do you vote, Father Escalante? Will you break the tie?"

Escalante nodded. "Of course, I stand with Dominguez. It is God's mercy; need you ask?"

"It is four to go and three to stay, Miera. How can these priests hold sway?" Joaquin Lain heatedly insisted. "The man has been to confession; his soul is saved. That should satisfy them. I say we keep our mules and one of his and send him back to Santa Fe."

Olivares' face was set and his voice grim. "I would not go."

"You won't have to, my son." Dominguez broke in, using a strange, quiet voice from deep inside himself. "You shall pay your price in Monterey."

Lain stepped forward. "How can you subject our souls, Father, to the contamination of one who has fallen? What you propose does not take into account the wishes of good Christian men. I say we remove this wickedness from our midst. At least give us the opportunity to dispose of him through a game of chance."

"The woman's father seeks h, does he not?" asked the dwarf of Bernardo Miera.

"After God's justice comes the King's, not a father's," Dominguez told Lucero, ignoring Lain. He turned stiffly against the saddle so that he could better face Olivares. "As you have not escaped God's mercy, you shall not escape His vengeance. Father Escalante or I myself shall escort you before the bar."

"Thank you, Father, but I won't need your help for that. As I promised, I'll go there myself when the trip ends."

Listening, Escalante thought, the man seems so sure of himself most of the time. It dismays me.

"What about the dice?" Andres Muniz asked once more.

"Why, we'll throw them, of course," Escalante answered. "We must settle this." He did not look at Dominguez for fear of the expression he would see. Escalante had been thinking of this moment and was prepared for it. He knew exactly what he was going to do to have his way concerning Olivares.

"You'll throw them?" Muniz asked in amazement.

"Yes. You seem surprised."

"I am. I did not believe you would approve. It does not seem holy, in a way."

"I'm a man of many surprises and God is sometimes very flexible. I don't think He'll mind. He can use even dice to show us His will." He paused, then said casually, "If no one objects, I'll use my own. I think it's my right. Besides, I think God might prefer it. They've been blessed."

Dominguez was too stunned to say a word. Olivares squinted at Escalante, studying him with suspicion. A priest with dice?

Escalante dug into his saddlebag for them. Miera took them, held them up to the sunlight for inspection, then thrust them back at Escalante. A blanket was spread on flat ground. Olivares' fate was to be tossed three times to chance. If the first cast totaled an even number, two of the three rolls had to produce an even number. If the first combination was odd, two of the three had to be odd. Then he could stay.

Escalante knelt with the others, passing the dice back

and forth from hand to hand. He seemed so certain of himself, so much at one with the will of God, that Dominguez did not say a word. He watched with the rest the first tumbling roll of the dice from Escalante's hand onto the blanket.

Double six. Even.

Simon Lucero rolled the dice back to Escalante, who scooped them up as they bounced, before they could come to rest.

He rubbed them between his palms. They made dull rattling noises, grinding together. He tossed them onto the blanket once more. They rolled side by side to the center and stopped.

Three and four. Seven. Odd.

This time Escalante plucked them from the blanket himself, not waiting for Lucero or anyone else to return them. He rubbed the dice once more, holding his hands as if praying, and rolled.

Double six once more. Even.

Everyone concentrated on the dice. The wind sounded in the trees. The birds above gave faint screeches. Finally Escalante spoke. "Olivares comes with us. As long as he obeys our rules and does the penances required of him, he stays. He promises he'll accept justice upon return. I believe him." He looked about at the faces. "Two even numbers out of three rolls. And two of them the same, too. Double sixes. They come up seldom. A good omen. Is everyone satisfied?"

Everyone nodded by ones and twos. Even those who especially resented Olivares did not complain. As agreed, all accepted the decision of the dice and perhaps of God.

No one congratulated Lorenzo Olivares, but then no one cursed him or abused him either. Escalante saw the acceptance as a positive sign for the expedition's future. They were satisfied that justice had been done. They began drifting from the big shelter to their own smaller ones. It was time to pack up and move out.

*　　　*　　　*

Olivares went to Escalante's tent, where he kept his own packs and saddlebags and weapons. He then returned to the large tent. Miera was there, examining maps and wiping his astrolabe clean. Olivares sought Miera out. He was carrying a potsherd as he would a gift. Not looking directly at Olivares, Miera took it and examined it, turning it over several times. "You found this?"

"Yes," Olivares waved toward the hills. "There's an entire city nearby, quite strange and very old. The people who made the pot lived there. No one lives there now. No one has lived there for centuries."

Miera rubbed the potsherd against his whiskers as if shaving, absently dredging his memory for recollections and facts to explain the deserted village Olivares described. The major places of antiquary Pueblo Indian culture were Mesa Verde in southwestern Colorado, Chaco Canyon in northwestern New Mexico and the Kayenta district in northwestern Arizona. They were all far away. Still, there were some smaller Pueblo communities nearby. He himself had seen some of them. He pulled out his maps and studied them carefully. One village named Chimney Rock was quite close by, possibly only twenty-five miles. The community near Chimney Rock could be the one Olivares was describing.

"Tell me," Miera asked excitedly, "does a rock as tall as a chimney stand nearby?"

Olivares shrugged. "Maybe. I couldn't say for certain."

"One taller than the others, standing alone?"

"So many of the rocks are tall and standing alone."

Miera questioned suspiciously, "Why does this interest you?"

"It occurred to me that perhaps treasure is buried there."

"There's something ugly about your attempt at ingratiation. How dare you imagine you can purchase my favor and good will for a bit of pottery, interesting as it may be?"

Olivares at once looked stone-faced. "It's a contribution

to the expedition. I don't need to curry favor and don't intend to."

Miera stared into Lorenzo Olivares' face. "Would you have murdered my wife had you stayed in my house?" He sighed bitterly. "We were friends once, Olivares. Oh, don't be surprised. I've mentioned it to the others. They don't hold it against me."

Miera held out the potsherd. *"Were* friends," Miera emphasized. "But no more, Olivares. I can never trust you again. Take back this piece of clay. I have no interest in anything of yours, even a single idea. You abused my respect, Lorenzo. And my friendship. Do you know, each time Escalante rolled the dice, I prayed they would order your expulsion."

Olivares took back the pottery bit and put it away in the pocket of his shaggy leather jerkin. Miera turned his back, peering intently at his maps. Olivares stood and stared at him for a long time, wondering if he shouldn't ride off right then and return to El Paso and the criminal charges awaiting him.

In another tent, Escalante and Dominguez were in a confrontation of another kind. Dominguez was angry. Escalante was amused and trying not to show it lest he anger his friend more than necessary. Escalante knew the issue was particularly important to Dominguez, who was addressing him formally. Dominguez called Escalante Father only when he had serious business on his mind.

"Father," Dominguez chastised. "What got into you to leave the decision to the dice? The vote was bad enough. For God's sake, what sort of insult to God Himself is that? What sort of lesson in self-determination for the men themselves?"

"None," Escalante acknowledged. "It was simply a case of the best means to a good end. They would have been debating over the morals of Olivares like lawyers from now to Michaelmas and there would have been no peace. You saw that. They could not even agree on a simple ballot."

"You could have simply exercised your authority and decided."

"It means more if God decides. Or appears to."

"They'd have obeyed you."

"They obey God more readily. It saved me a test of authority, too. It's better if it seems the decision was His."

"You've just turned God into a gambler."

"It was no gamble, Father. The outcome was preordained. God had nothing to do with it."

Dominguez looked shocked. "Stop blaspheming, Father. I am extremely disappointed in the way you've handled this." He sighed, then cocked an eye. "What do you mean, it was no gamble? And what are you doing with dice, anyway?"

"They amuse me in idle moments. I don't think the rest matters now, do you?"

"What you're saying is, you'd rather I didn't know."

Escalante smiled and spoke patiently. "Oh, Dominguez, Dominguez, if I must tell you . . . Dominguez, you cannot live among soldiers as I have and not learn how to make the dice do as you wish. First you fish them from your pack during a rainstorm in the night and shave them down, just a hair along one edge, with your knife."

"Escalante!" Dominguez seemed more shocked at shaving dice than at blasphemy. "You anticipated it would come to dice and you encouraged it. And you used deliberate fraud and stealth in the night."

"To all of these things I confess, Father," Escalante admitted. "Furthermore, in the throwing you hold the dice in a certain way, like so, your finger this way and both sixes pressing against it. And when you toss, you make certain they do not bounce on the blanket, but roll gently side by side. This takes much practice. If you do it correctly the dice will come up your way nine times in ten."

"Tell me no more. I don't want to know these things," Dominguez cried out, pulling his hood above his head and pressing the cloth to his ears.

Escalante bent his head to study Dominguez' face beneath his cowl. "You don't seem as angry as you were a moment ago."

"I wish I could still be, but I confess I'm not."

"In fact, I think you may even like what I've done after you reflect upon it. You might even wish you could do such a thing yourself, Father. Accept it. My ways of serving God are mine, and different from yours sometimes, but they *are* serving God."

Dominguez was silent. Finally he smiled just a little. "Escalante, you are not only maddening, you are a bandit."

Escalante laughed. "I know."

Chapter 13

The party left the forest and returned to the prairie. The country changed gradually as they progressed to a wonderland of tall and lonely buttes.

At midday they halted in the shade of a particularly fat butte, low and wide. There was a curious stillness in the air. A buzzard, suspended in a column of air, floated above them in total blueness. The men debated whether the bird was actually a hawk.

"Its wingspan is too wide for a hawk. Perhaps it's a bird none of us has ever seen," Miera speculated.

"I doubt that," Andres objected. "We're still too close to home."

Olivares had ridden up to the group of men, who stayed mounted while the servants prepared the noon meal. Even the cattle had moved into the shade of the butte, along with their flies and fierce stinging insects.

"It is a very large species of hawk," Olivares put in, "but the head is covered with white feathers as though the creature were bald. I saw one like this on an earlier trip."

"Some sort of eagle," Andres Muniz offered.

"Perhaps it is the spirit of your vengeful wife," Joaquin Lain remarked to Olivares. The other men laughed.

"Do not blaspheme, Lain," Escalante enjoined him.

Olivares ignored Lain. "Where do you suppose the trail has gone to? I've seen no markings for several hours."

No one answered him. Lain and Andres Muniz drifted away. Cisneros got off his horse and stretched his legs. A burl of white smoke rolled from the cook fire, followed by the smell of food.

"We aren't far from where I saw the city," Olivares said to Miera, "maybe fifteen miles, as I remember." Then to Escalante, "I passed the party in several places in these mountains. I didn't ride too near for fear of getting caught."

Escalante noticed a large rattlesnake asleep under a bush. He cautioned Olivares, whose horse seemed to be moving in that direction.

"Thank you, Father, thank you very much."

A rock flew into the bush, thrown by Cisneros. The snake coiled and rattled, and after another rock, slithered up the hill.

Escalante saw Dominguez watching, a bowl of soup in his hands. He seemed to be fending off the snake with his powers of concentration, making it slide away. The snake continued up the rocks, while those below watched with murky fascination. Tiny bits of shale tumbling down from its path nearly reached the horses' feet.

Olivares spoke again. "We're soon to pass where no white man has ever passed before."

"Silence, fool!" Miera snarled savagely.

Olivares did not react. It was as though he had not even heard Miera.

As the men ate clouds loomed on the horizon, not storm clouds, but the sort caused by rising heat. Oppressive heat had built up in the butte country, which was completely without the promise of rain.

Cisneros and Andres and Escalante went over the maps.

"We have not quite lost our way," said Andres. "According to Miera's astrolabe we're moving due north, but this is as far as I've ever come before and past the limits of whatever else I've heard of."

"To move north and west is our objective," declared Escalante.

"The time has come, I think, to send scouts ahead." Cisneros rolled up their best map and pushed it into its leather tube, which he capped by means of a buckle.

"The way of God shall lead us onward," intoned Escalante. Then he smiled. "But you're right, it wouldn't hurt to have a scout."

The butte country had changed to a single dry riverbed cutting through a high plateau. Escalante and Andres had scouted ahead to find where the riverbed opened into another plain. While the party waited for their report, a few cattle wandered away.

"We had better make camp here," sighed Escalante when he heard there was stock missing.

Lain and Cisneros had already ridden far up one of the dry tributaries of the riverbed. Andres returned announcing there was water ahead and the pack train and remaining cattle headed for it. Escalante, Miera and Olivares spurred their horses up a canyon.

Escalante soon grew impatient with their cautious pace. He waved good-bye and cantered up between the walls of another canyon, leaving Olivares and Miera. Indeed, Escalante thought, some time alone together might be good for them. They had been friends once. Perhaps, with some talk, they could be again.

Escalante's horse picked its way along the steep and scaly rock, making the only sounds in the canyon. The heat of the day had diminished and a peculiar sort of shade had fallen. Even insects were absent here.

The canyon rose and gradually receded. There was no trail, but Escalante could see a passage onto the high plateau.

Thinking he could see much better from this vantage, he guided his horse up and out of the canyon.

Once he reached the high plateau, even though it was covered with low scrub juniper he could see for miles. Given the freedom of level ground, he raced his horse through the powdery dirt between the trees, pounding along the edges of the canyons. He stood on their very rims and peered down into them for miles. The heat clouds they had seen earlier had rolled up from the far horizon and now were turning blue. No storm was coming, but the sky had changed shape and color. Shading his eyes with his hand, he saw no sign of cattle.

Escalante imagined the canyon to be big enough and grand enough to hold the moon. He was certain the river meandering its floor was the Colorado. From this height the river resembled a rawhide string, it was so far below him. They were probably in Arizona.

He rode farther along the plateau, leaning out from his saddle to peer downward, aware of the danger of falling and liking it. He wondered about Lain and Cisneros. He did not see them following. He speculated that the cattle might have climbed up as he did to wander over the plain. He kept riding. To his great surprise, he came upon still another canyon on his left. At first he could not see how this could be. Then he realized another dry riverbed had cut through the plateau. The lowering sun was in his face and his horse was growing cautious. He stopped. His eyes took a moment to focus as he stared down into the canyon. A huge geometric design, it seemed, had been painted on one wall. Then the sun dropped another degree and the light changed. The giant painting became an ancient city built into the canyon wall. It was depth—an enormous shallow cavern—not darkness painted into stone.

"Our Lord and saints in heaven," he exclaimed, "what is this wonder I behold?"

Light caught in the trees all around him and Escalante imagined himself pierced through with it as if by golden wires. Gloom kept rising from the canyon as the cliff top turned a reddish gold. He found a passage and plunged down among cedars and mountain pine, the cliff city growing clearer. Escalante nearly expected to see smoke rising from what looked like chimneys. He called for Lain and Cisneros, but there was no response. He was alone, riding deeper into the canyon, dropping so far below the level of the city he did not see how he could climb high enough again to reach the cave.

At the bottom he tied his horse to a tree and used a dead tree and handholds in the rock to climb up to the enormous cavern. He could see the buildings quite clearly now. They were made of mortised rock. Some were several stories high. He scrabbled through the crumbly rock, the smell of cooling dust in his nostrils. He reached the level of the lowest line of houses and walked through the spaces between them. He was amazed at the tiny doorways and moved by the sense of time standing still.

Then a rock fell somewhere, starting a small slide that as suddenly stopped.

Escalante suddenly was chilled by apprehension. He slipped into deep shadow and carefully looked around, ready for fight or flight.

He was definitely not alone.

Chapter 14

Escalante paid most attention to the direction of the falling rocks. The noise they made did not echo, but seemed more forlorn than all the little houses. He reached to his waist for the crucifix of his rosary, took a step forward and was startled at the sound of his own tread.

A breeze came up in a row of aspen standing below the cavern and now was working its way through the giant cavern, pushing ahead of it a certain smell, pervasive and somehow familiar. It was sinew, Escalante realized, moving toward it. Entering first one and then another of the small houses, frustrated by the changing breezes, he tracked the odor.

The houses were completely bare. Centuries of dust had packed into the corners like mounds of driven snow. Whatever wind had brought the dust had also carried away all the contents of the city. Escalante kept looking for some Indian fetish or dead bird that might explain the meaty smell. Each ruined house was bare, however, and with the sun dropping lower in the sky, a preternatural gloom was reaching up the walls of the cavern. The rock houses were turning grey.

Escalante was staring into the shadows, sure he had seen

something move. He stood still. Then, stronger than before came the odor. A flicker caught his eye. He turned and saw a tiny candle flame inside one of the dark houses. He blinked, disbelieving, but the candle was surely there. He went to the window of the house and saw some yellow object just inside the rim of light.

"Who's in there?" he called.

There was no answer; now there was no wind either, not the slightest breeze or rustling. Searching out the doorway and ducking low, Escalante entered the little house and moved slowly toward the candle.

"Show yourself before God," he intoned. He reached the candle and the yellow mass on the earth-packed floor. He had to examine the mass very closely before he could believe his eyes. This thing lying on the floor was indeed a decaying body.

"Oh Lord God!" he shouted. What kind of inhuman heathen savage could leave a body to rot like this? The candle went out. He was in total darkness. He stumbled, reached out, touched the still, withered flesh of a decomposing hand.

His heart froze. He stumbled backward, flinging the candle away. In sudden runaway fear and revulsion he wedged himself through the tiny window, wildly kicking to squirm out of horror. He thrust his hands out to break his fall, conscious of a man in dirty grey tatters running wildly away. Escalante lurched to his feet and ran after the fleeing man.

His quarry loped in a sideways scrambling gait, like an animal with a head wound. His beard and hair were matted and grey, his dark eyes ringed with white. Ducking around the low roofless buildings, he scrambled up terraces and over walls. He was calling back gibberish over his shoulder as he ran. Gradually the babble changed to halting Spanish, as though the man had not spoken it for a long time.

"Go away, monster, get behind me, do not follow. You'll be sorry if you do."

He had reached the end of the cavern. By way of handholds and footholds and a leaning tree he descended with the grace and speed born of constant practice. Escalante was much slower. Halfway down the cliff, without thinking, he leaped just as the man was running away. His last image before the impact was of branches and berries caught in the man's hair.

Escalante knocked his target forward. They rolled over each other like quarreling squirrels. The man did not move. Escalante rested a moment. Birds were twittering again in the canyon. Dusk had settled in the trees. The man untangled himself and sat upright. He seemed very old at first, his face riven with seams and wrinkles, but Escalante soon saw he was not ancient. Two little children in rags similiar to his own, but of mixed parentage, stood close together not far away under a piñon tree. They stepped forward now.

"Who are you, sir?" Escalante asked the hermit.

"I was once a Spanish trapper."

"A trapper. Unbelievable. How did you get here? When— I—Oh, I want to ask you so much now that I've caught you, I don't know where to begin." Escalante loosed a healthy laugh. "You scared me to death, you know, old rascal. Tell me first, how do you live?"

The man shook his head. "I live by my wits, Father. I live in peace with my son and daughter."

The two children, the girl slightly larger, had come to stand behind their father. The little boy held an old matchlock pistol, long useless.

"If you are a Spaniard you know it is not Christian to venerate the dead."

"I know, Father."

"And these children, do their souls belong to God?"

"They do not."

"At peril to your own, you understand," Escalante chided.

"It is their mother by the candle."

Escalante knew he should remind the hermit he was blaspheming in not burying his wife. He did not. It seemed neither the time nor the place for scolding. He started to ask, "How long ago did she die?" He did not demand an answer.

The vacant expression on the man's face told Escalante the man was not listening.

Loco, Escalante thought. Functioning, but crazy.

The man was looking around as though he were in an unfamiliar place. The brief light of menace had gone out of his eyes. His voice seemed frail and empty. "With whom do you come, Father, and from where?"

"From Santa Fe. We seek a northern route to California."

"Where is that?"

"On the coast of the other ocean. You must have come here once yourself."

"Only trapping, Father," the man said almost pleasantly, "trapping and lost."

"When?"

"I really do not remember."

Escalante heard the sound of horses echoing in the canyon. He could hear voices too, as clear and poignant as the calling of doves. It was Miera with Olivares and the rest of the party. They were marveling at the city in the cliff, at the size of the giant cavern.

"This is not the one at all," Olivares was shouting. "This one is much bigger and far grander. God knows, an ancient tribe, and by looks, a rich one."

"I would imagine those are your comrades." The hermit's voice was losing a little of its rust.

"Yes."

"You've come farther now than any party has before?"

"Yes, and we have much farther still to go. The souls of these little children, though, must be saved."

"You have nearly killed me, Father," said the hermit, holding his chest.

"Consider it your penance for worshiping the dead." Escalante was grinning at his jest.

"It's only an Indian custom."

"But you are not Indian."

Escalante turned to watch the riders dropping lower on the trail. He could hear their voices even more clearly as they argued between exploring the city and searching further for the cattle. They stood at the base of the cliff mulling over how they would possibly ascend. Strangely, Escalante wished for them not to visit the city.

He called out. "Come down farther to where I am. Follow the cliff base and you shall find me."

"Are you injured, Escalante?" asked Miera.

"No," Escalante's voice lilted, "and I've found a man."

The men came around a brake of cedars, intensely black in the growing dusk. Escalante stepped toward the hermit and put his hand on the man's head.

"Lo, what is this?" Miera demanded.

"Where did you find him?" asked Cisneros.

"Above in the ruins."

"Does he live there?" Lain inquired.

"No," answered the hermit for himself.

"Take us where you live, man," cried Miera, "that we may see this wonder of subsistence."

The hermit shook his head.

"The light is failing," Cisneros pointed out.

Andres Muniz got off his horse. He approached the hermit and looked into his face, pushing the hair off his forehead, the beard away from his neck. Muniz held the man's head between his hands, stroking and probing as if uncertain it was really a head. Escalante realized Muniz was more than just curious about the man; he was sighing and clearly moved emotionally. "Prospero," Muniz said finally, "Prospero Garcia Marquez. You're alive."

"You know this man?" Escalante asked in amazement.

Muniz released the face, gently patting the cheeks. "Yes, I know him. We were together with Juan Maria de Rivera on one of the explorations into Colorado several years back. I cannot believe he is still alive—after what we did to him. Is this not one of God's wonders, to find him here now?''

"What happened back then?" Escalante urged.

Muniz shrugged. "How do those things ever happen? One day Marquez dropped from a tall rock. When we found him his head looked as a melon does when dropped from a roof." Muniz wiped his eyes with his hands. "It was my opinion that we should bring his body back with us. Young as I was then, my opinion did not count for much." Then he turned to Marquez. "We buried you." This was as much a question as a statement.

"Not deep enough." Marquez gave a disturbing three-beat laugh. "I pushed the rocks away and climbed out."

"And we were gone."

"Probably for several days, judging by the way the wind had scattered the ashes of your last fire."

"Surely he cannot be a ghost!" But the speaker, Lain, backed his horse off and crossed himself.

"You're right," Escalante scolded him, "he cannot be. He was more likely deeply unconscious and nearly dead at the time. Stop being frightened. You know better."

"And you've recovered, I see." Muniz touched the dirty beard once more, disregarding Lain.

"Prospered," Marquez answered.

"And sired children too, it seems," Muniz added. "We left you for dead in good faith, Marquez. We really thought you were dead. Believe me. I am truly sorry."

"Don't be sorry. I believe you. I *was* dead. But now I've come back to life."

Lain spoke up again. "There. Make him stop talking that way. It's that talk that frightens me. This isn't to my liking, I tell you. A man who everyone, including himself, agrees was dead should not be sitting here talking to us."

"Lain, Lain," Muniz said patiently. "What he says is true. There's still a gash on his neck where he fell from the rock. He didn't move when we found him. He wasn't breathing either. So we buried him. Father Escalante is correct, Lain. We simply made a terrible error. Thank God we were a terrible burial detail, too. If we'd covered him properly he wouldn't be here.''

"I was not dead.'' Marquez contradicted himself. ''But now my wife has died and I am left alone with my children.''

"There could have been no wife,'' Miera said softly. ''The woman in that house cannot be his wife. There were no sacraments. He confuses a wife with a woman who simply bears children.''

"Wife or not, he couldn't have come by these children without her,'' Cisneros snickered.

Ignoring the conversations about him, Andres Muniz asked Marquez, ''And how have you come to be here, Prospero? Tell me. Never mind them.''

"I wandered, sick and weary. The Indians found and tended me. I've been to many other places in this wilderness and finally settled here.'' He gestured in despair toward the house in the community arched over by the cave. ''Where I must now leave my wife. She was Indian, you know,'' he said brightly, as if they could never have guessed. ''It doesn't matter what she was now.''

Cisneros had ridden to the children. He gently brought them back to their father.

"Could you tell us, Marquez,'' Escalante asked, ''what do you imagine we'll find ahead in this country?'' He was gentle. He had already decided that the man should stay behind in his wilderness when the party moved on. Marquez would no longer fit into life anywhere else. ''You must have learned a great deal during your years out here.''

"I'll tell you what you'll find where you're going, all right.'' The man perked up. ''Also some of what I've heard about the wilderness even beyond that, if you'd care to know.''

"Yes, please. We want to know everything.''

"Perhaps you'd come along with us and show us yourself," Andres Muniz proposed.

"No, but I will tell you what I know if you will forfeit the souls of these children. Don't insist on baptizing them."

"That cannot be," Dominguez exclaimed.

Marquez nodded. "I suppose not. Forgive me my sins, Father, and I shall tell you all I know."

Dominguez and the hermit drew away for privacy in confession, which took a surprisingly short time.

A fire had been started. The men dismounted while Marquez drew a map in the sand. "These are the ways to the ocean and this is what I have heard," he began.

Escalante decided to delay instructing the children and moved closer to the fire.

"You are entering the country of the Sabuagana Utes. Moving northward, you will find the lake people, who are fish eaters, and perhaps in time the bearded Utes. The rivers flow thus; the mountains lie here." Marquez brushed smooth what he had drawn to show the course of the rivers. "I have heard these things more than I have seen them, and in truth the Indians do not know so much themselves."

"Will we find Hopi and Comanche?" asked Miera.

"If you are unlucky you shall find something stranger still."

"Stranger?"

"Yes, and perhaps as dangerous, too. There are Indians past the country of the bearded Utes who are not Indians at all. They wear blue clothing and speak a language no one knows."

"Perhaps they are Spaniards, settlers moved east from California," Escalante suggested.

"They live where no white man has ever gone."

"The more conversions the merrier on our way to Monterey," Escalante hooted, laughing. And for a moment, he marveled at finding in the wilderness this man who was so closely linked to Andres Muniz' past. He found he could almost believe that God had put Marquez there years before to point them in a certain direction today.

"Is conversion the purpose of your journey?" Marquez asked.

"It is and always shall be," declared Dominguez.

"As well as to find a route to Monterey," added Escalante.

Marquez nodded, then peered into the darkness as if afraid. "I do not know if the sea exists, nor if it does how far away it lies. I have only general knowledge of certain routes, as I have said." He paused. "Those others I mention. Those are not Spaniards, those wearers of blue. That much I know. They are not Indians either. Your way, I gather, does not pass through their country. But if you get lost and find them, you shall never escape. I have heard this and I believe it." Marquez looked about. "Where are my children?"

"Gone to heaven, I presume," came a mocking voice from the darkness. It was Olivares, who had slipped away without anyone knowing and just gotten back. "I'm sure by now they've fallen and their souls are soaring aloft. Where they climbed the canyon there is no way to go and the incline nearly perfect."

"I must follow. I know the way."

"There is no way," Olivares declared.

Marquez stood and moved quickly into the darkness. Cisneros followed a short way into the brake of cedars but came back after he lost his trail.

"What shall we do?" asked Lain. "It's too dark to go far."

They mounted and rode farther into the canyon by the light of torches. They looked for ground and water that might allow a camp. Their horses stumbled. The way seemed not so clear. Then, rounding a buttress of rock, Cisneros saw a light far ahead.

"Look there," he called softly.

"We have our way marked," Escalante beamed. "Perhaps that's our Marquez the hermit."

It was Marquez' hut, a jacal made of brush and piñon sticks. The light was from a smoky glass lantern.

"Where has he gone?" Cisneros asked. "And how has he come by this lantern?"

They looked inside the hut, finding rags, tools, matting and pieces of crockery. There were knives so worn they seemed shrunken and fragile. Escalante found the matchlock mate to the rusted weapon the little boy had held. The handle of a cutlass lay nearby.

"These armaments are very old," Miera whispered. He was stroking a flint knife, still perfect despite its age.

"Who could have brought these here? And why are they so ancient?" Escalante asked aloud.

Andres shrugged. "Trade goods, maybe. I've seen none so old as these, though."

Cisneros held the lantern aloft, casting its beam wherever light was needed. By that light and in the canyon stillness, the faces of the men were haggard with wonder and fatigue. Most had beards now and their mouths were lost in hair.

Escalante asked Olivares, "Where were you earlier while we talked with Marquez?"

Olivares turned his stubby face into the light. "Looking through the ruins, but in the falling darkness there was very little I could see."

"Looking?"

"For signs of wrought metal and artifacts of gold. I plan to look a good deal more tomorrow."

Escalante stared at him, slowly shaking his head. "We've lost cattle, you know. I'll mark this place on my maps for you, but that's all. You can't eat gold, Olivares. We leave here at first light tomorrow. I plan to find those cattle. We will need every hand for the search and neither desertion nor side trips will be tolerated."

The men had unsaddled their horses and were making beds on the ground. They quickly fell asleep. Escalante huddled beneath his own blankets, thinking about Marquez' old weapons. Where had they come from? Some Spaniards had clearly passed this way once before, more than a century before, judging by the age of the matchlock firearms.

Escalante pondered rumors of lost caravans, disappearing without trace of man or animal or even a lost scarf caught on a piñon limb. But then, Escalante thought, there have always been rumors of lost caravans and of the cursed lives of their descendants, living as nomads in the deserts and wilderness.

Escalante refused to believe such rumors. He was his own authority. He had spent too much time in the wilds without seeing even a sign of such lost tribes. They were merely frightening tales to be told around the fire late at night—or so he hoped.

Chapter 15

They found the cattle late the next morning in a stand of cottonwoods, placidly grazing. The lantern at the hermit's hut had burned through the night and was still glowing at dawn. Sunlight had not yet reached into the canyon and the day had a quality of denseness. The horses carried the men up through the canyon, hooves clinking against the stone. They emerged one by one onto the rosy plateau so early that the giant cavern and the ancient city below remained in total darkness.

The men herded the cattle into the dry riverbed through the canyon Lain and Cisneros had traveled. They reached camp in the glare of early afternoon, the air thick with the sound of insects.

Escalante, idly wondering how Dominguez and the others had fared, was not prepared for what he saw. Three Indians dressed in beaver quilts and looking more like bears than men were standing in the camp. Escalante was only surprised to see them; they were stunned at the sight of the white men.

"What do you think they want?" he called out to Dominguez.

"Who knows?" Dominguez never shifted his glance from the Indians, who were now turning to watch the approach of the cattle.

Escalante could hear Andres and Joaquin Lain riding up hard beside him. They wisely reined in their mounts and did not go plunging onward. The Indians had for a moment given signs of flight. But now the cattle were gamboling toward the camp, lowing and throwing their heads back. The Indians began talking, gesticulating and laughing.

"They seem to find Simon Lucero rather strange," chuckled Cisneros. One of the three Indians was slightly taller than the others and had a narrow face. His right eye was badly scarred. He carried a hooked stick covered with copper sheet, studded and sharpened at the curve. His straight coarse hair was plaited and intertwined with leather thongs.

"Sabuagana Utes," Andres announced, "and one who is something else."

"Greet them for us, Andres," Dominguez suggested.

Miera, Olivares and Escalante had ridden up. Andres dismounted to approach the Indians. Escalante looked around at the butte rims, the banks of the dry river. They were empty but for Aguilar on a hilltop, watching the cattle. Sunlight caught the flame of his red hair. There were no Indians other than the three, no rear guard.

"Who are you and where do you come from?" The Sabuagana dialect slid smoothly off Andres' tongue, its alienness on the familiar voice disturbing Escalante.

He spurred his horse forward and leaned down to Muniz. "Don't tell them we're explorers," he whispered. "Say only that we're seeking Father Garces."

Miera glanced at Escalante, approving his strategy. He nodded to Muniz. "I wish I could speak their language," he said wistfully.

The tall Indian was a Uintah, as it turned out. This fact excited Escalante and Andres Muniz.

The dialogue lasted nearly an hour. During this time the

Sabuagana said they had encountered Comanche signs on their way down from the higher country. The Sabuagana warned that if the party proceeded farther, it would undoubtedly meet these Comanche and they would certainly attack.

"What are we supposed to make of this?" Lain asked Andres after the translation.

Andres shrugged. "Make of it what you will. It scares me witless, although that may well be their intention."

Escalante asked, "Will he lead us, this one with the stick, to his people? You said he is a Uintah. The hermit told me they live by the lake."

Andres spat a perfect bullet into the dust. He thought about this for a moment, then spoke to the Indian in Sabuagana, going slowly and using gestures; Andres spoke it better than the Uintah. The man nodded eagerly, but Dominguez, moving away from the conclave, shook his head. "I wouldn't believe him if I were you. Somehow I don't trust him."

The light in the dry riverbed had diminished and some of the men drifted away with Dominguez toward the animals. The immensity of the land and the sky had reduced the wonder of their first wilderness meeting with Indians to the trivial.

The Sabuagana insisted that the white men come to their rancheria. They implored them to stay until the country was no longer full of Comanche. Escalante pondered this proposal. Their rancherias were not so far away, and perhaps they could find a better guide than this bizarre-looking Uintah.

The pack animals, dozing in a margin of sunlight narrowing in the riverbed, caught the Indians' attention. They watched with great interest as Lain and Lucrecio Muniz and some of the others began to load them.

"Ah, I see now what it is they want." Escalante followed their gaze as he spoke. "They think we're carrying trade goods."

"How is this possible?" Cisneros was looking uneasy.

"They have a devil's eye for valuable objects."

Cisneros turned to Andres. "Must we follow them?"

"When do we depart," Olivares put in, "where are we going?"

The Sabuagana were ignoring the Uintah. They stared at Olivares as they had at the other white men; they seemed to think there was no distinction among the whites, as though all were the same man. The explorers unconsciously responded by moving closer together, including Olivares in the party for the first time.

"Let us follow them to their camp," Escalante suggested. "We can spread the word of God, part with a few shiny objects and be on our way. I trust this Uintah to guide us."

"We could use a guide," added Andres.

Miera spoke up. "I am sure we're being tricked. It is always this way with Indians, even those with garnered souls. They're never honest, but speak only to confuse."

"By God's will we are moved forward on this journey," Escalante said sharply, "not by feats of men. The least suspicion or doubt casts shadows on His providence. You must not think this way, Miera, for the sake of your soul." He looked searchingly at Andres, then at Cisneros. "And you two must not either. Are we such cowards we cannot take risks? Are we so weak we cannot defend ourselves in a trap?"

Escalante caught the eye of one of the Sabuagana and nodded. He couldn't tell whether the man understood, but when Andres asked to be taken to the Sabuagana camp, they didn't seem surprised.

The cattle were gathered and the pack train was loaded. Andres, Escalante and Cisneros went with the Indians, who led the party through the dry riverbed to another plain. This crumbled before the distant blue of the mountains into the remains of another dry river even more ancient than the first.

The camp was in a grove of dwarf cottonwood and aspen and manzanilla bushes. Cottonwood logs had been tented over a spring, their cut ends bright with the hacking of simple tools.

The dwellings were very much like the hut of the hermit Marquez—mud structures with grass roofs.

It was nearly dark and in the sky behind him Escalante could see faint stars. He turned back to see a young girl running toward them. She stopped by a tree and peered around it, eyes flashing like those of a cat ready to pounce. A little boy's head popped up some distance ahead of her; she was obviously chasing him. At the sound of her approach the boy turned and nearly stumbled, his breechcloth of skins falling almost to his knees. He picked himself up and held onto his only garment with one negligent hand.

The Indians walked past the children, who turned and saw the white men. The girl's face became a mask.

Indian women and men came out of the brush huts. It was a small rancheria, only a few children and dogs, but Escalante had never seen anything like it, not even on earlier explorations. The grassy huts, the blackened stones in circles on the ground, the silent, staring natives seemed mysterious and moving. Andres bumped Escalante's horse with his own to get his attention.

"Go steady, my friend," Andres muttered. "Your eye should be prepared for treachery."

Escalante nodded. "I am always prepared, Andres."

The elfin grey blindness of dusk, which the Indians seemed so much part of, made Escalante want to edge much closer. The three who had led them ducked into one of the mud-grass houses and emerged with an old man. Cisneros and Andres dismounted. Andres indicated by gestures and a few words who they were, where they had come from and where they were going. The old man listened carefully until

Andres was finished; then he shook his head. Escalante felt a twinge of fear at the finality of the gesture, but Andres, he noticed, seemed almost relieved.

Miera was the first of the herdsmen to arrive in the camp, swaying his big black mount into the clearing as though crossing the plaza in Santa Fe. "Let's break out our trinkets," he suggested, "and then get rid of our Uintah."

"Not so quickly, Don Bernardo," Andres objected. "I fear we may well have to stay."

The others arrived and Escalante and Dominguez paired up and rode forth to show themselves. The Indians gathered closely in curiosity, touching their cassocks, cinctures and rosaries.

Escalante and Dominguez made the sign of the cross over the Indians and explained through Andres the birth and death of Christ and the power of God over all.

The Indians listened quietly, but all the time their eyes strayed to the horses, the cattle and the mules packed high. In the gathering dusk their faces were blurring. The men of the expedition dismounted and with several Indians made their way back to the stock, which had been tended and put out to graze. There were fewer cattle now, after two weeks of travel, and as the journey tired them the edge wore off their orneriness.

The men walked through the cottonwoods looking for a spot to camp and finally selected one near a timbered spring. The Indians stood back and watched solemnly as the men pitched their rolls and coverings, gathered tinder for the fires and unpacked their cooking implements. Strangely, they did not seem to care much when the bits of trade cloth and beads were displayed. They were far more attentive to how the Spanish made camp. They seemed comforted, as though watching something familiar.

As it grew dark, more Indians came from the rancheria. The women stayed away but the men and children gathered at the brightening fires to hear the priests tell stories about Jesus. Andres Muniz, Miera and Lain sat by, Andres working the translations. Escalante calculated that no harm would come to them, but this security did not extend to the rest of the party. The Sabuagana continued to insist that the Spanish stay with them. The priests ignored this and continued to preach the gospel. Lain stood up from the fire and looked out into the darkness.

"Why do the women not come forward?" he asked Andres.

One of the Sabuagana shrugged when Andres relayed the question. The moon seemed to detach itself from the lowest fringe of cottonwoods, defining a distant mountain. Everyone sat in silence above the crackle of the fire.

It had been decided the party would move on to a great lake said to lie in the northern mountains. The Indians said raiding parties of Comanche would send the Spanish back in ruin, but Escalante said no trinkets would be distributed if the party were hindered by the Sabuagana. The Spaniards began discussing the question among themselves.

"If we go on," Andres informed the others, "these people wish us to send a letter to Santa Fe saying our demise, if it should come to pass, did not occur at Sabuagana hands. They are afraid that if we do not return, Mendinueta will send out soldiers. They care not to accept the word of God at the sharp end of Spanish vengeance."

"We must go farther," bellowed Lain. "Not to do so would be our disgrace. To hell with the Comanche. We have enough rifles to make that point."

"I concur indeed," said Olivares. "Commerce alone deserves that route to Monterey."

"Perhaps we could send the letter," Andres mused. "It seems not to be impossible."

"How so?" Escalante demanded.

"Three men could return while the others press on. Once

the letter is delivered, those three could follow the rest, perhaps with Indian guides. Surely you do not expect, especially in the service of your calling, to travel straight through and never stop to bring these heathen souls to God.''

"Of course not," Escalante exclaimed. Dominguez looked stricken. "But how do we divide the party so that your plan succeeds? I do not see how we can spare you, Andres, since only you speak Sabuagana.''

Andres shrugged. "Aguilar speaks some Indian also." He looked at Dominguez and Lain, even at Cisneros. "Perhaps some of the others wish to go. Father Dominguez?" he asked slyly, raising one eyebrow.

Dominguez sighed and shook his head. His lips parted to speak, then closed.

"You haven't been well," Andres went on. "Perhaps on a trip back you'd get better."

"This is preposterous, Muniz," Miera sputtered. "We dare not divide these priests."

"I knew the way out for more than two hundred and fifty miles, but I've been lost now several days." Muniz shrugged. "You have no need of me."

"We must press onward," insisted Miera. "I would not believe these Indians even if they were already Christians."

"They are God's children," said Dominguez in a tired voice. "But He doesn't seem to have put the truth in them."

"I could return with a small party," put in Lain. "Were it so decided, I could come back with soldiers—not for these miserables, but for the Comanche."

Cisneros laughed and spat into the fire. "We don't need to send a letter; we could always leave one here."

Escalante glanced at him thankfully.

"If by chance we lose our way," Cisneros continued, "or do not come back at all to Santa Fe, any party or group of soldiers would have testament we passed through here unscathed." He fell silent and stared at Andres and Lain.

"We'd ride hard," Lain was saying eagerly. "You won't be much farther than you are now by the time we return."

Escalante was wagging his head angrily. "No." He stood and towered over Andres Muniz. "We're all equals under God. I speak to you as an equal. I tell you, you're not returning to Santa Fe. What are you, Lain, some sort of postman, delivering letters personally?" It was then that Escalante realized he had to dominate the others also in order to dispel their fears of these Comanche whom they hadn't even met. He smelled doubt and mutiny, even rising panic.

He circled the fire, hands clasped behind him, head thrown back as though he were about to talk to the stars. Everyone grew still. The Indians sensed a showdown and watched grinning.

Finally Escalante took the initiative. "Listen carefully. I say this to you: no one is turning back. You all have courage; you've just lost it for a moment. But whether you find it again or not, as God is my witness, every last one of you is coming to Monterey if I personally have to drag you there. Lord, does it take only one rumor of danger to turn such a fine company into milkmaids? I won't speak of this again. If we're to die in the wilderness we shall die before God, doing our duty and working His will. Yes, there are Indians who reject God's mercy. Perhaps the Comanche are among them. If God wills it, we shall perish at Comanche hands. But I personally believe he does not will it. And personally, until I see a Comanche arrow flying at my chest, I do not intend to run. I will not permit myself to be frightened of a rumor." He paused, then finished, "And neither will you." With that he turned his back and strode forth into the darkness.

He allowed the men some time to think about what he had said and reclaim their grip on their courage. When he returned Miera and Andres were talking in low voices near the fire. Indians were passing singly into the darkness. There hadn't been so many Indians in this village as Escalante had first expected—maybe twelve or thirteen, a few children and several dogs—but the women would not show themselves. They remained in Escalante's imagination, shapes in the darkness, giving off certain esoteric scents.

The other men in the party were getting up, stretching and disappearing from the fire. Escalante was delighted. It was as if they had never been fearful of the Comanche at all. It takes so little encouragement to restore them, he thought, but it must be timed and worded just right.

By the light of the moon Escalante made his way to the edge of the spring, where he had decided to place his bedroll. In time came the sound of two people passing through a thicket.

One was Lain. He stood beside Cisneros' bedroll. "Are you awake?"

"Yes."

"These Indian women entice me. No matter how much I wish it to be otherwise, they entice me."

"How do you know, cousin? We have seen nothing but their shadows."

"I know. But I can smell their sensuous perfume from out there. Can't you?"

The silence told Escalante that Cisneros could indeed smell the women. Then he heard Cisneros say tenderly, "Lain. What do you know of how you feel toward them? You've been too busy thinking of home and praying." He burst out laughing.

"And my prayers have been answered," Lain laughed too. Escalante began to fear trouble ahead; their laughter had been full of tension.

Escalante heard Lain crunching twigs as he strode off into the darkness to his own blankets. Lord help us all, Escalante thought. First their doubts and cowardice, now their lust. Why must there always be some problem of the soul?

Why can't they just ride hard during the day and sleep well at night and enjoy the way to California for its own sake?

Escalante knew why not, though. He himself had wanted women often enough, badly enough, to know why Lain was so bothered. Still, there was a time and place for everything. He prayed there would be no more to Lain's wanting women than just one night's hunger and careless talk of it.

His sleep was troubled; Lain's problem could well become everyone's problem.

Chapter 16

Dominguez woke the next morning with fever flaring in his bones, but he claimed he was not too sick to travel. The Uintah guide, however, had decided in the night that he did not want to go. He too feared the Comanche.

"He can't do this," objected Escalante. "He must be reasoned with, made to see how much our future lies in his hands. Andres, please assist me." Escalante strode over to the guide.

"What do you want me to say?" Cisneros came up to Escalante and Andres at this moment.

"Father, why not speak through this old one here," Cisneros suggested, pointing to the man who had appeared the night before. "His face is kindly. I trust him. Must be something about his age and bearing."

Escalante bit off the end of a cigar and lit it. He found that he agreed with Cisneros. "Andres, tell the old man that unless the Uintah accompanies our party, no letter will be written. Tell him also that if the Sabuagana refuse to assist us or stand in our way in any fashion, then the next Spanish they meet will be soldiers, not priests."

Muniz studied Escalante, rubbing his chin. "You're certain that's what you want me to say, Father?"

Escalante blew out smoke. He liked the idea of applying increasing amounts of pressure. He wished he had done so sooner. "Yes, I said so didn't I? Now tell him!"

"They call this threats and coercion, Father."

"I know, Andres. Just tell him."

"Would God approve?"

"I don't know. You tell him and I'll answer to God."

"The things they say about you are true, Father. You'll do anything to achieve your goals."

"Most anything."

"But suppose—"

"Tell him!"

Muniz shrugged and turned to the Uintah. Escalante's anger was visibly rising and he looked ready to fight. Few of the Sabuagana listened; most just went about their morning business, uninterested in the entire affair. The Indian children passed each other on errands while the women sat cross-legged, preparing the morning meal.

Andres finished his translation. "The Uintah says he must think it over, but I'm sure I've made it clear he has only one option—to be our guide."

"I think he'll come," whispered Escalante as he watched the Uintah conversing with his Indian brothers.

Miera shrugged. "We should only be thankful we're going."

Escalante turned to Dominguez, eyes bright and avid, but the older priest was distressed at what Escalante was doing and looked away. Escalante's eyes slid over Olivares and came to rest finally on Cisneros. Cisneros smiled, a look of approval in his eyes.

Two younger Sabuagana were now arguing heatedly with the Uintah.

"They're upbraiding him," explained Andres, "trying to make him go."

Cisneros walked over to one of the loaded mules, flipped back a pannier and withdrew a fine steel hunting knife. "Why not bribe him with this?"

"Good thinking," Escalante grinned. He took the knife and held it before the Uintah. "Andres, this excellent knife is his if he chooses to lead us. Tell him we go with him or without him. He gains nothing by refusing, but a good knife and perhaps a great adventure to enrich his old age if he agrees."

Lain rode up just as the Uintah accepted the knife in exchange for future services; the Spaniard had been tending the cattle.

For a moment when he spotted the rather hostile Lain, the Indian seemed to regret his decision. Escalante saw it and told Andres Muniz, "He has five minutes to decide. If he isn't ready to go by the time I finish my smoke, we take the knife back and leave without him. Make it clear to him."

Andres spoke at length; the language barrier was disappearing fast.

The man looked from Escalante to Andres and back. His face was a battleground; in the end the knife cut down his fear and he nodded hard.

He turned and entered his own brush hut for a few moments. When he came forth he said a tender good-bye to a greying woman who appeared after him and handed him a red fancy-weave blanket, which he proudly displayed to the other Indians and then flung over his shoulders.

The men were all mounted now and a mule was waiting for the Indian. A little boy had climbed into Dominguez' saddle, but the priest was feeling so sick he hardly noticed. One of the Sabuagana tried to pull the boy back down to the ground, but the child held fast to the saddle. Dominguez reached his hand out to protect the child and in so doing unknowingly took custody of the boy.

Lain tried to yank the boy from the saddle, but with no success. Dominguez finally intervened. "Let him stay for now. He'll change his mind when he gets out of sight of home.''

"Or we can let him off at the lake," Cisneros agreed. "He's probably a Uintah, as his leggings are similar to our guide's. I wonder if it is his child."

The little boy was now speaking to the Sabuagana. They responded sharply, but their scolding had no effect on the child. He repeatedly called to a young woman who sat perched high in a cottonwood.

It was the lovely young girl from the first afternoon, Escalante realized. It seemed that the little boy was her brother. She climbed down from the tree and walked toward Dominguez' horse.

This produced an uproar among the Sabuagana. They had all drawn away from their huts, cooking fires and chores in the grove to watch the departure. They tried to hold the girl away from her brother, but she struggled and made some headway. She was prettier than Escalante remembered her, Moorish almost in her darkness, with features straight and fine. Even in distress a certain girlishness and even shyness stood out. Lain rode forward, blocking her path. "What does she want?"

"I expect she wants this little boy, her brother," Andres drawled.

"Should she have him?" Lain leered at the young body.

"Yes," retorted Cisneros, riding forward.

Several Sabuagana were now arguing with Andres, who spoke in turn to the priests. "She wishes to accompany her brother but these Indians care greatly she does not. It seems she is betrothed to one here, the son of an elder."

"You are sure she chooses to leave?" asked Escalante.

"Very much, it seems," observed Cisneros.

"She can't come." Miera spurred his horse forward. "It's bad enough to think of taking the boy. I say we give them both to the Indians to hold and ride away."

"I say we bring her with us," Lain smirked.

"Not possible," pronounced Escalante. "She at least must be left behind." He moved his horse toward the Sabuagana elders. The animal was growing restive, stepping high, swinging its giant rump. "Give the Indians this." Escalante handed Andres a length of plaited riata from his saddle. "Tell them to tie her. The girl stays behind."

She had reached her brother and was clutching one of his hands, her cheek drawn unconsciously close to the inside of Dominguez' thigh. It was evident she thought the white men would bring her along.

Several Sabuagana approached her with Escalante's leather rope. They slipped it around her head and nearly choked her pulling on it.

Cisneros' heart went out to the girl. As she struggled against the riata, he remembered Lucrecio Muniz with the bear. This one had become an animal too and lost her feminine charm. She clawed, spat and shrieked. Cisneros' sympathies shifted to the Sabuagana. They secured her finally, but when Lain came to take her brother from the saddle, Dominguez shook him off. The child was silent, watching his sister, holding tightly to the saddle.

"He does not really care to leave, the little boy," the old priest insisted. "He will come back on his own. We're wasting time. Let's get going. Ride a little way into the distance. Let him come along. Out of sight of his dear sister, he'll probably get scared. In any event, we're gaining nothing. I myself don't think it would be so terrible if he stayed with us."

Escalante made a few final presents to the elders, thanked them and promised them God would be with them. Cisneros helped Lain gather the cattle, while Miera and Andres took over the pack train. The party made their way out of the cottonwood grove northwest toward the plain, Andres leading the Indian guide's mule and teaching him to ride. The lessons amused Andres. This was the first adult male Indian he'd ever seen who could not ride. With the newness and commotion the Uintah's spirits seemed to lift. Soon he eased his grip on the saddle horn and began to sway instead of jounce.

The terrain became more lush as the plain broke into numerous valleys. Small streams ran through the valleys, which were dotted with marshes. Bright berries glistened on bushes, beaver ponds terraced the gullies. At midday it was obvious the little boy did not wish to return to the Sabuagana.

It was also obvious the party was being followed. From time to time a figure would appear on a distant ridge, but however often Escalante rode back to investigate, he found no one.

At one point, when Escalante wanted to query the guide about this puzzling development, he said to Andres Muniz, "What is this Indian's name? We can't go on calling him 'the Uintah' or 'Hey, you.'"

Andres laughed. "He has a name all right, but I can't pronounce it and neither could anyone else."

"Does it mean something?" Escalante asked.

"Yes. It means Pony with Wind Hooves. Fast Horse, you could say."

Dominguez spoke up. "We must baptize him and give him a Christian name. It would be fitting to begin our conversions with our guide."

"I say call him Silvestre after Father Escalante," Juan de Aguilar called out. He reddened self-consciously as he made the suggestion. "It's good luck to name him after our leader."

The others chimed in with him, so Silvestre it was, by acclamation.

Dominguez made a face. "We'll name the next one after you," Escalante chuckled.

"Over my dead body," Dominguez laughed back. "Every time I'm called for dinner, he'll come and eat it."

As a guide, Silvestre was not too highly skilled. Escalante suspected that sometimes he was as lost as the rest and shamming it. Escalante wasn't too alarmed, though he thought it a pity he was not so good a guide as a rider; the Indian had already graduated to a horse. But even if the Uintah did not know precise routes, Escalante believed he had general knowledge of the country that would prove valuable.

Silvestre made up for uncertainty with amiability. Miera still did not trust him and told Escalante that depending on his guidance might yet prove to be a grave error.

"You suspect he'll stab us in the back?"

"Perhaps. I'm not so certain he's vicious, but I do think that between his fear of moving too far from home and his desire to please us and get more presents, he'll run us around in circles. He says he knows where he's taking us but I don't know if I believe him. You wonder too; I can see it on your face."

"This far from home," Escalante returned, "who among us really does know his way?"

Miera kept silent and rode on.

Lucrecio Muniz took up singing, to everyone's surprise and nearly everyone's regret; he sounded like a French nun with indigestion, Dominguez remarked.

Andres would ride past his brother and slap him on the back of the head, laughing and begging him to stop. Lucrecio would hold his silence until Andres was past and begin again. He was very fond of one particular ditty about a frog that wished to become a star in the heavens but could never hop high enough.

Cisneros was alone in encouraging him. He told Andres to leave Lucrecio alone to caterwaul as he wished; the noise gave him comfort in the wilderness and made him think of his wife less often.

"But he discomfits the livestock as well as the men," Andres complained.

"They enjoy it."

"The men?" Andres hooted.

"No, the cattle."

And it actually appeared they did. They kept quiet and clustered around Lucrecio when he sang.

Simon Lucero had taken to being very rough on the cattle, snapping his shortened whip at them and calling them vile names. Their slowness and dullness seemed to enrage the small person; or possibly it was their size. His whip often snapped backward and whacked his own horse.

Early one afternoon Escalante was amused watching Dominguez' style of riding. The priest seemed to be clowning, leaning low from his saddle as if trying to pluck flowers growing beside the trail. How unlike him, Escalante chuckled.

"Dominguez, that's pretty daring horsemanship for such a stout priest," he called. "Pluck one for me while you're at it."

Suddenly Dominguez lost his grip and toppled from his saddle. His horse jumped and then trotted off. Dominguez bounced on behind, one foot caught in the stirrup. His cassock rolled up like a shade, showing a white rolling gut, a camiso and baggy underdrawers that tied at his knees.

Escalante spurred his own mount and leaned from his saddle to seize the bit of Dominguez' horse. "In God's name," Escalante scolded, "you should know better than to try that. You're not some trick-riding cossack."

Dominguez did not answer. Escalante rolled from his saddle and dropped beside him, praying that his colleague had not cracked his head as fear of disaster gripped him.

As Escalante tugged the stirrup loose, Dominguez waved feebly and croaked, "I'm all right, except that I'm dying."

Dominguez was shivering as if to rattle himself to pieces, yet the day was hot. "You are not dying, Father, but your fever is fulminating again. Why didn't you say something?"

"We don't cover the miles to Monterey by stopping for my fever all the time, Escalante."

"We won't get to Monterey at all if you don't call a halt when you should, Dominguez. If we'd stopped earlier it might have taken only a day for you to recover. Now you're so ill, who knows how long it will be?''

Dominguez smiled.

"Don't smile at me," Escalante snapped. "I am very angry with you. I mean it."

"As well you have a right to be, I suppose."

Escalante stood. He loosed a fierce whistle between his teeth, the call of a wild bird. Those who were riding ahead pivoted in their saddles. Escalante waved them back and shouted, "We're stopping for the day. Someone help me make a shelter for Father Dominguez and his fever."

They camped in a cottonwood grove. Dominguez was very sick by this time. Escalante asked him whether he could stand and support himself by holding onto his saddle. Dominguez tried but fainted, falling on and pinning Simon Lucero.

"Get him off me!"

"Yes, yes, Simon. Don't worry, you'll live," Escalante soothed him. Juan de Aguilar and Lucrecio Muniz lifted Dominguez and Lucero disappeared, shaken and humiliated.

Dominguez began to babble. "Please care for the child. Please keep him with us on our way." His shaky right hand kept tracing a cross as he repeated his words over and over.

The boy sat cross-legged beside Dominguez, as though he knew his safety was in the hands of the plump priest, and watched with great curiosity as the men made camp.

They called him Little Lain, after Joaquin, partly as a joke and partly because they couldn't pronounce his Indian name either; it was even worse than Silvestre's.

Lain was not amused. "Of course you would give him my name. What other is possible? I think I shall fancy him as I would a son, if I had one. And beat him the same way, too." He bared his teeth.

As they were unpacking and settling in, Andres Muniz called to Escalante. "I've found some things you should look at, Father. I haven't shown them to anyone until now, although perhaps I should have.''

"Such mystery," Escalante chuckled. "What have you found?''

Muniz reached into his saddlebags. When Escalante recognized the things he pulled out, he was suddenly troubled—even more than by Dominguez' sudden relapse.

"Matchlock pistols and homemade ammunition, all very old." His eyes flashed. "Just *how* old would you guess, Muniz?'' The Franciscan hefted one. "And for God's sake, where did you find them?''

"In that ruin, back where we found your friend the hermit. They were wrapped securely in a shredded old oilskin. I found these also." He unrolled his bed pack and pulled out three bows, then reached into his saddlebags again and took out several arrows. "They are so old I don't even recognize the fletching patterns. Comanche, perhaps. I really don't know.''

"Can you guess how old they are?''

"I'd say at least a century.''

"Beautifully intact, if they are that old," Escalante sighed. "Perhaps because the air is so dry.''

Andres Muniz rubbed his chin. "Perhaps.''

The others gathered to touch the weapons and wonder aloud about their origin. The firearms were clearly Spanish.

Finally Escalante cut off the speculation. "How did Spanish arms this old get out here? Who could have brought them? If Muniz is correct in his assessment of their age, we may have hit on a real mystery. No Spaniard is supposed to have been here so long ago.''

"Someone may have come out here more recently with them," Miera offered, not in the least fazed by all the excitement.

Muniz shook his head no. "The leather covering them is too old and the dust on them too thick.''

Escalante didn't want to make too much of this, but his

head was reeling. He thanked God that Dominguez was sunk in deep, feverish sleep, for he didn't want to alarm him with this new mystery.

Miera and Andres Muniz showed them to Silvestre and asked whether he knew how they might have come to be in the centuries-old pueblo. Silvestre studied the pieces, holding them close to his face. No. He didn't know how they came to be there. He couldn't even guess.

Stupid Indian, Miera thought, sucking on his pipe. "I recall hearing of several parties from California that got lost and were never heard from again. But I do not know of any particular party. I haven't seen the records." He tapped ash from the pipe. "One bunch was supposed to have been a train of civil servants, minor officials and their wives, posted to Monterey."

"Yes, I recall hearing the same thing. How many years ago would that have been, Miera?" asked Escalante.

"No more than a hundred. But as I say, that's only rumor."

"A lost party of men and women a hundred years ago." Juan de Aguilar's awed voice sounded very young. "My God, think of that."

"I am thinking of it," Simon Lucero announced. His voice cracked as he spoke and the others laughed with loud relief. This new discovery began to seem less mysterious and intimidating.

"Do you recall how many were supposedly lost, Miera?" Escalante asked.

"Fifty or thereabouts, I believe."

"And their baggage was never found?" Escalante touched the old matchlocks. "And no more of these."

"No, Father, I don't think so. As I recall, the story says they vanished, poof, with everything—and not much of practical value at that. Silks, laces and fine leathers are not the ideal clothes for the wilderness in winter."

"If these people really existed at all," Escalante added.

"Please, all of you. No one must mention these old weapons to Father Dominguez, at least not until he's feeling better."

Escalante was silently wondering whether the find was important enough to merit sending a man back to Santa Fe with a report, as Lain surely would wish. The thought died young as Silvestre began shouting unintelligibly and staring at the stand of cottonwoods near the stream.

When Escalante looked to the trees he muttered, "God help us, it's true. Bad luck does come in threes. First Dominguez becomes ill, then the matchlocks, now this."

"Did you say something, Father?" Lucrecio Muniz asked.

"Never mind, Lucrecio. Go and fetch that girl and bring her here."

Standing almost invisible in the shadows of the cottonwoods was the girl they had left tied with a leather riata among the Sabuagana.

Escalante had to admit it; she was truly beautiful. Her dark hair was in wild disarray and her buckskin dress was badly tattered. But those eyes—like round moons—sweet yet alluring. She can't be more than fourteen, Escalante guessed, but oh, Lord, she can still bring us plenty of trouble, trouble of the worst kind. God, give me strength and wisdom.

Even the cool Miera was surprised. "What cunning the she-devil must have, to get out of those leathers and away from the tribe."

"Perhaps they've let her go on purpose now that they know we're too far away to bring her back."

The boy ran to his sister but they did not embrace. The men stood in a row, watching without speaking. One by one they looked to Escalante. "What do we do with her?" Cisneros asked.

"Oh, let her join us, if she must," Escalante roared at no one in particular. "We're not going to lose time bringing willful girls back to their homes. Agreed?" They all nodded, some more enthusiastically than others. "Good. Don't anybody argue with me right now. We have enough trouble dumped on us for one day.''

Cisneros and Lain were the loudest to agree; just what Escalante had been afraid of. He knew the sound of men hungry for a woman. He wouldn't be able to chaperone her, either, if it was as he feared, that she would be as willing as they. She would never be coming, he thought grimly, if he could think of anything short of death to keep her away.

The following morning Escalante made an entry for September 15, 1776:

> We are putting up with much cold and damp, surprising weather for September. However, we are high in the mountains, so perhaps inclemency is to be expected. We are unable to move from this location still, because Father Dominguez remained feverish and fatigued, still suffering the aforementioned illness, upon awakening today. This means we will not be able to take a side trip we had planned to a canyon near the Uncompahgre Plateau, so named because there is said to be ore bulging from the earth there. It seems that many years past a party representing the governor brought back metallic rocks. At the time no one assayed them. One opinion, supported by the accounts of the Indians who inhabit the area, is that the rocks were silver ore. This occasioned the name of the area, Sierra de la Plata.
>
> We covered only a little more than eleven miles before stopping yesterday. This is slow going. I pray for better progress tomorrow and health for Father Francisco Atanasio. Amen.

Escalante took a new sheet and started to write a postscript. ''I am deeply concerned for Don Juan Pedro

Cisneros. . . .'' But he crushed the paper into a ball and bounced it into his fire.

It would be unfair to the man and his wife and family to speculate on paper on sordid suspicion alone. A man shouldn't be maligned for his thoughts. Mendinueta and the bishop in Mexico City hadn't sent him into the wilderness to record gossip. Even if a sin had occurred, they'd have little interest in it.

Nevertheless, Escalante prayed the girl wouldn't bring disaster.

Chapter 17

A turning wind came through the cottonwoods late that night, but only Dominguez, weak and spiritless, was awake to notice. It was a wind that would not return for weeks, the first cold wind of fall. It carried with it a grey feel, as though from a pond icing over in the mountains, turning the leaves a certain way, slightly changing the shape of the trees.

Dominguez lay on his back, barely conscious of the moon and stars. His fever had passed, leaving behind a fusty smell as though a parade of horses and elephants had passed close by him. Discomfort in his stomach and bowels caused him to shift from side to side, but his pain was gone. It was nearly dawn. With a warm mist rising from the ground came the scent of dead fires. Dominguez began to wonder if he had been left behind.

God has punished me for something, he thought, casting his memory through his years in Mexico City and all that had been so placid and orderly in his life. In his delirium he had imagined animals gathering around him, dogs and beavers, even bears. He remembered marveling at how the animals knew he was not going to die. It seemed he had counted them and been amazed at how many there were.

He began thinking of Marquez, the hermit the men had told him about. He had been angry with them for not coming for him immediately when the hermit was found. Trying to imagine what Marquez looked like, he began to think the man was there, watching him from behind a fringe of willows or a cottonwood.

Dominguez rolled over completely to one side and for the first time fell truly asleep. A crane flying over the distant plain under the moon and twinkling stars began to call. Another answered.

It was dawn when he awoke again. Miera was sitting by his side.

"I thought you might be dead." Miera poked at the earth with a stick.

"I am not dead," Dominguez sighed. "Do we leave today? No doubt I could be prepared to travel."

Miera shook his head. "Father, sometimes my spirits waver, I must confess. Escalante would lead us forward to attack hell with a bucket of water. I admire that. But I am getting old, as you are, and have lived a full life, but I wish to see my wife again, not to perish."

"I'm sure we shall not."

"I see now," Miera went on, "that I'm more a colonizer than a trailblazer. I fear this will of Escalante's, Father, for it often seems stronger than his love of God."

"More a colonizer than a trailblazer," Dominguez echoed. "Well said. I sometimes see myself in the same way." Miera shrugged; he had understood that about Dominguez long before.

Dominguez rolled onto his back. "I've had to put my trust in Escalante because without him I couldn't proceed. We have no choice, my friend, except to trust. God is the higher master."

Miera nodded. Breakfast was being prepared and eventually other members of the party came to check on Dominguez.

The Indian girl, who had slept nearby, brought him bitterroot tea and the little boy made him more comfortable with a pillow stitched from bark.

The men spent the day butchering another of the cattle, hanging out strips of meat to dry and salting the rest. The men were covered with blood by the time the task was finished. Flies swarmed and the smell of blood, fat and intestines in the sun was palpable.

Propped on his elbows, Dominguez studied first one man, then another, trying to delineate and understand the apparent tension among them. The men seemed less chatty than they had been. There were fewer jokes and taunts than before.

As he studied them at their butchery and fire-tending, Dominguez came to think Pedro Cisneros had changed more than any of the others. Dominguez had always considered Cisneros a serious man. The others too appeared to have noticed the change in Cisneros, for they kept their distance for the most part, and when they spoke to him at all it was with studied politeness.

Dominguez noticed that the young girl was now clearly a part of the expedition. She must have joined us while I was in my delirium, he figured. He had the distinct feeling that she was involved in the changes he saw in Cisneros and the others.

Escalante was approaching; Dominguez wondered whether he saw things the same way.

Escalante squatted beside Dominguez with a bowl of fresh-made beef broth and offered to spoon it for him. Dominguez snorted and sat up to take the bowl himself. "I see we have a visitor," he remarked.

"More than a visitor; she's one of us."

"I won't ask you to explain why you allow her to stay. I trust you know what you're doing." Making sloppy sounds as he ate, Dominguez went on, "She may be only a child, but there's something about her. She has the charisma of a worldly woman—and these men have been without women for some time now."

Escalante grunted. "I've noticed."

Dominguez sipped more broth. "Will the Sabuagana come for her? Is she going to bring trouble?"

Escalante shook his head. "I doubt that. They've let her go. They probably hope she'll return to them, but she wants to be with her own people. That's one of the reasons I said she could come with us."

"She should be allowed to go back to her own people."

"I suppose we'll have to give her another name too," Escalante mentioned.

"That's how it's done." Dominguez licked his lips as broth beaded on his chin. "That's our rule. What is her old name, anyway?"

"Andres said it means Laughing Bird."

"It's a pity we have to change it."

"Yes," Escalante agreed. "It's really quite nice."

"But it doesn't quite suit her. She's no laughing bird, that one." Dominguez tilted the bowl and drank the last of the broth from it.

"No, not with those knowing eyes."

"Considering your experience with women, no priest should be a better authority on knowing eyes than you, Escalante," Dominguez snickered. His own eyes were bright for the first time in days as he smiled in mischief. "But seriously, Father, does her being here mean trouble for us?"

"Explain what you mean."

"Trouble among our men. Before the fever took me they were an easy-going bunch. When I came out of it they were not. I think this Laughing Bird is the cause."

"I'm not sure, Father. I've wondered myself. I pray she is not. But even if she is the devil, aren't we strong enough to deal with it? If we can't handle a discipline problem and protect a young girl, we shouldn't be priests and we shouldn't be leading this expedition to Monterey. Have more faith, Father.''

"As usual, Father, you are correct."

They rode out the next morning with Dominguez belted into his saddle and proceeded once more onto the plain. Miera rode on one side of Dominguez to provide support in case he fell from his horse. Escalante took a position on the other. The children trailed behind, the boy on a mule and his sister leading it. The rest of the men rode on ahead with the horses and cattle.

At one point Miera said, "I wonder if we'll be safer with these children than we might have been without them."

"Hardly," Escalante snorted.

Dominguez cast him a reproachful glance. "How do you mean, Miera?" he inquired with careful courtesy.

"They were born out here. They know all sorts of things: how to find water, how to pick a path up a mountain, even how to behave as guests of another tribe. Besides, it can't hurt us to be seen traveling with healthy, happy Indian children."

Escalante smiled grudgingly. "Just what I needed, a silver lining. Thanks, Miera."

That afternoon, stopping beside a small dark creek for a meal, Joaquin Lain followed Laughing Bird when she disappeared beyond a nearby ridge looking for firewood. She was bending over a greasewood bush looking at a gopher when he came upon her. She straightened up and she stared at him forthrightly, then looked away. Cisneros, who had followed Lain, stood on the ridge and heard him speak.

"Come to me, little widgeon, my duck of desire. Do not fear me and do not try to run away."

Cisneros' face burned with shame and anger, the words sounded so common and foolish. Lain was humiliating himself and somehow Cisneros seemed to share the breach of manners. Cisneros also realized he wished it had been himself who spoke to her first.

Lain was brushing the flaps of the girl's vest with his fingers. He tugged them open to reveal her breasts. She took a step forward as though welcoming him. Then she put one hand on his arm, punched him hard in the midsection with the other and ran away.

Cisneros took after Lain, who was giving chase. The girl ran like the slim silent shadow of a hawk gliding over the sage. Cisneros and Lain, hampered by age and heavy boots nearly to their knees, made noise and lost ground.

Lain turned when he heard Cisneros coming. Surprised and angry, he threw up his hands to defend himself. Cisneros hit him hard with his open palm and Lain stumbled backward. Laughing Bird had stopped to watch.

"You dog, you thief, you raper of virgins!" Cisneros was gasping hard. Lain tried to hit him but missed and Cisneros slugged him. His chest expanded with anger and he began to shriek still viler epithets at Lain.

"Leave off and let me have her first," babbled Lain. "I've trailed her here; she is mine by effort."

"Is that what you think? That I stop you only because I want her for myself?"

"Everyone else will think so too." Lain smiled with contempt. "After all, isn't it the truth, just a little?"

Cisneros roared, "You swine!" and charged. Lain turned and fell; he drew a small dirk from his belt, dark with the blood of the slain bull. He lunged at Cisneros but missed. He lunged again and fell again. Cisneros drew his own knife as Lain got to his feet. Laughing Bird, who had been giggling softly, stopped.

"My cousin is your wife," growled Lain.

"Yes," Cisneros hissed, forgetting the girl in a sudden coolness, thinking only about his own skill with a knife.

"Imagine her watching this, if you can." Lain taunted as they circled each other.

"You bastard."

"She would choose you, Pedro. Let me have the girl."

"It's true I am married, Lain, but the girl is not yours to have."

Lain was staring at him, rising slowly from his defensive crouch. He raised one eyebrow and the knife dropped to his side. "Married? Yes, you are. And so your sin of lust is greater. Remember this, Pedro, if you take your pleasure of this one."

Cisneros' knees became weak with a different sort of anger, a frustration so great he forgot himself. "Married for what," he shrieked. "I love my wife, but she'd rather have you, cousin. I have always known, though I've said nothing. You've known it, too."

Lain was backing away. He said nothing, but the loss in his eyes had changed to victory. He looked over his shoulder to see Cisneros stabbing his own knife into the dirt.

The Indian girl was standing near Cisneros but staring at Lain. She wasn't so pretty after all, Lain thought. To hell with her. He knew what woman he wanted. And if she wanted him too . . .! He shrugged and returned to camp.

Cisneros and the girl returned minutes later with tinder for the fire. Lain and Andres were eating together and Andres was suppressing a smile. Cisneros stared stonily at Lain but said nothing of what had happened.

Cisneros and Laughing Bird shared a cooking fire with Miera, Dominguez and Escalante. The boy ate with Silvestre. Cisneros had come to understand a few words of Sabuagana. With these and with gestures he tried to communicate with Laughing Bird. He didn't have much to say, however, so for the most part they ate in silence. The girl ate quickly, sometimes pressing mouth and tongue to bowl, but she waited for the others to finish.

"When you were in the seminary," Escalante asked Dominguez, "were you taught in Latin?"

Surprised, Dominguez looked up from his bowl. "No. I was both born and ordained in this hemisphere. I was taught in Spanish."

"Curious."

"Why do you ask?"

"Why do I ask? Because even though I too was taught in Spanish and ordained in Mexico City, I find myself thinking in Latin and dwelling on church music."

Dominguez looked at Miera. "This happens, you know, saying the Mass, reading one's breviary. I too from time to time find intimacy with the tongue." He turned to Escalante. "I suppose I should have realized you were ordained here, but I didn't. You were born in Spain."

"Yes, In Treceño, in Santander. The most beautiful mountains in the world are there."

"But you studied and were ordained in Mexico City—at Convento Grande, of course."

"Of course. But though I was taught in Spanish, there was enormous attention given to Latin while I was there. How they tortured us with irregular verbs and St. Thomas Aquinas in the original. Some of the teachers took pride in being better Latin scholars than they had even in Rome. They passed their torches of scholarship to our hands, whether we wanted them or not."

Dominguez grinned. He remembered what it had been like.

"Do you ever think of Santander and the mountains there?" Cisneros asked. "Do you ever long for home?"

Escalante resumed eating. "No."

Cisneros smiled wryly at Dominguez. Miera, glancing from Escalante to Dominguez, shook his head.

Cisneros could feel Andres and Lain watching him as they lounged by their fire. The hairs on the back of his neck still tingled at the thought of his encounter with Lain. He felt divorced now from his softer self; a new sharpness rose in his soul and marked his face.

Lucrecio came carrying silver cups filled with chocolate. Lucrecio always made the chocolate, at the beginning of the journey with great deliberation and not much skill, but now quite nicely. He brought the cups, all marked with the owners' names, to each man in the party. The Indians watched with great fascination, but when offered sips of the chocolate, immediately spat it out. They preferred their own teas.

Silvestre, squatting on his haunches, cocked his head to give his good eye the best advantage. Andres always mimicked this, sending the men into peals of laughter.

Cisneros allowed the Indian girl to take the dishes from his lap in a way that seemed almost domestic.

He realized the others were laughing at him and flashed them an angry look, then walked over to Andres, who was laughing the loudest. Andres' eyes grew cold, but without menace or aggression, and he immediately stopped laughing.

"I think it best you do not speak or laugh at me," Cisneros warned, his voice trembling.

Andres broke the line of his gaze and spat casually on the ground. "Why not?"

Cisneros said nothing, feeling the fool. Andres kept silent too, but the spirit came back to his eyes, and with it the snickering glint.

"You two shut up! Now!" boomed Escalante, lurching up from his fire, stepping toward Andres and Cisneros, who stared at each other. Cisneros was gently patting his knife in its sheath.

Escalante addressed the entire camp. "We cannot have this dissension." No one appeared to be listening. "Take heed of my words, men. I've never been more serious in my life. It's not easy being out here, so far from civilized life, but you all knew how it would be when you signed up. Please. No one can possibly benefit from such anger and hatred. You must try to be more civil to one another. That is all I have to say—and I hope not to have to say it again."

When the meal was over Lucrecio washed the dishes with sand and rinsed them in the clear dark waters of the creek. Trout wafted through the shallows, rippling like leaves in the current.

"Let's catch some trout for a little variety," Simon Lucero suggested. The party was ready to leave, but Little Lain slid from his mule into the grey of the shallow water and stepped with great delicacy toward the rippling fish. Flies had come out of the trees in the afternoon heat and the horses were stamping and swishing their tails. The dust the cattle raised ahead came billowing back through the grove.

"What is Little Lain doing? Make him get out of the water and on his mule," Escalante demanded.

"He's baptizing fish, Father," said Andres. "Watch and you'll see."

The Indian was standing perfectly still in the heart of the shallows, dipping his hands slowly into the water. The fine muscles of his arm articulated, and with great swiftness a brown flash of trout came flipping out of the water. Lucero jumped off his pony and whacked the fish against a rock. Little Lain produced another and one more after that.

"We are surrounded by magic," Cisneros said. He looked at Lain. "It reminds me of my servant with the bear."

"I suppose he has stroked them into a stupor."

"I suppose."

Something had passed between Cisneros and Lain, a reborn friendliness that greatly surprised them both. Holy Mary, said Lain to himself, he truly believes he doesn't have Estella. That she loves me. He is prepared to surrender.

The fish were soon gutted and split and staked to a board to dry. With the board strapped to Lucero's saddle, the remaining men, Laughing Bird and Little Lain finally moved out of the grove into a country of ridges and sage-covered swales. The party began stringing itself out over miles of terrain, the camp for the evening not too far ahead. A breeze kept the mosquitoes and flies off the horses and the air was fresh and clean. The mood of the party was jovial and soon the men broke into conversation.

Cisneros found himself alone with Laughing Bird. He did not look at her but she delighted him with her presence.

"This makes me happy," he said aloud. "I wish always to be like this, the whole world stretching out before me, and all time. I can choose or not choose. I can pass through life without a care."

The girl edged before him and spoke. He understood almost nothing of what she said but was happy just to look at her, study her face and the wildness of her hair. He cared not to see her expression, really. He wanted only to sense her there. Her eyes were full of light and fancy.

On impulse the pair rode down a small valley that grew wide, then rounded, and finally came to a stop. On one side was a small copse and a tiny spring. Cisneros and the girl stood in the sedge grass staring into the calm water, and then suddenly they faced each other. She seemed quite small to him but she laughed eagerly.

The touch of Laughing Bird's skin was a shock. She smiled encouragement. Stretching on the ground, they gently stroked each other's skin. Desire and wonder at the slimness of her legs moved through Cisneros like a mixing current. She looked him straight in the eyes, smiling with happiness. She parted her lips and kissed him. He tried to dispel his thoughts of Estella and failed. "But what difference does this make? It is not me she wants anyway, but Lain," he muttered.

Laughing Bird looked strangely at Cisneros, trying to understand him. "Do you not want me?" she asked timidly in her language. She took his face in her hands and looked deep into his eyes. Cisneros could no longer resist her. He pushed her gently back down in the grass and took her hungrily.

Chapter 18

Cisneros and Laughing Bird had gotten lost and didn't appear until the next day, when the rest of the party retraced their trail. And now, reunited with the party, Cisneros thought how close they had come to being truly lost and he thanked God.

They had been riding for hours in and out of canyons, Miera following closely behind Silvestre. Miera had been eyeing the canyon walls very carefully for signs of valuable ore when he yelled at Silvestre to stop. He slid off his horse to investigate the strange objects that lay off to the side of their trail. At first he thought they were boulders, great knobs of bleached stone. Then he saw they were striped. He picked one up and banged it against the rock wall. It shattered into hundreds of tiny bits. He realized then what these objects were. Just bones—but incredibly large, too large to be from any animal Miera knew of.

"Father Escalante, come look at this." He ran toward Escalante hauling one of the ancient bones.

"Father," Miera yelled again, but Escalante was on a bluff watching a hawk soar lazily over his head and did not hear. Miera shaded his eyes. Something was *in* the bluff that totally amazed him.

"Jesus, Mary and Joseph." He crossed himself.

All outlined and articulated in the sandstone bluff was the skeleton of some gigantic lizardlike creature. He had never imagined such grotesque ugliness. Stepping backward in surprise, Miera's feet trod on more bones embedded in the ground. The whole earth seemed to heave as though some huge thing beneath him were trying to get up. Miera's hackles rose before he realized it was illusion born of surprise and uneven footing.

"Miera," Escalante finally called down, "what's going on?"

"Come down, Father. Quickly!" Miera looked around, fear engulfing him, and signed the cross again. "There are things here you must see."

Escalante spurred his horse to a gallop to meet up with Miera.

"I have never seen such a thing," Miera kept saying. "Who lived here once, do you suppose?" Escalante shrugged.

"Could the huge animals not live here still?" quavered Miera. Glancing at the skeleton in the bluff, he suddenly lost his nerve. Animals much larger, he imagined, were approaching from over the next hill. This small valley was only a minuscule fold and they would be trampled by a monster too big to notice them. He glanced wild-eyed at Escalante, who did not notice his distress, but spoke blithely.

"Have you ever seen such wonders? These beasts were as large as houses."

"No, I haven't." Miera's voice was getting shrill. "Nor, ever even heard of such things."

"Well, I have—something similar, at any rate. Calm down, Miera, they've been dead for eons. I know that in the coldest northern parts of Siberia they sometimes find tusked beasts in glaciers. They look like elephants, but with hair as

long as a young senorita's and teeth, eyes and flesh—everything
—as it was when they were frozen thousands of years ago.''

"Thousands of years ago? All due courtesy, Father, but
you exaggerate. To remain perfect for thousands of years? As
though never dead?''

"Yes. Something like that." He paused. "It grows colder
there than you have ever known, colder than you can ever
imagine. It continues for years on end. And as you know,
cold preserves.''

Miera wrestled with the notion, conquered it and accepted it. "What do the finders do with these beasts?''

"They eat them.''

Miera sucked air in disblief. "How can meat so old still
be fit to eat?''

"As I said, the cold preserves, and enough cold preserves permanently." He also told Miera about the dinosaurs.
Almost nothing was known of them, he explained, but the little
that was recorded was based on study of such bones as these
very ones before them.

"You believe that these bones may have come from one
of these dinosaurs?''

"It seems the most likely explanation.''

Miera crossed himself and appeared to be on the threshold of tremor. "Is it possible that such beasts still exist in this
region?''

"Anything is possible." Seeing the dread on his face,
the priest added, "But not at all likely. If such creatures still
live, someone surely would have seen them and commented
upon them. So large a creature, even if it wished to, could not
possibly escape notice for long, not even in these spaces.''
He smiled. "No mention of them appears in the folklore of
any natives I know. If there were indeed such marvelous
beasts as dinosaurs still in existence, we would surely have
heard about them. I am willing to swear they no longer
exist.''

"Who back home in Santa Fe will ever believe we found such gigantic bones?"

"They might believe it if you sketch them well and describe them with the intensity you feel for them at this moment."

Miera smiled. Sketch and write. Yes, he was a good artist. They'd believe it, all right. He felt calmer already.

When they overtook the others they found that Juan de Aguilar and Silvestre had ridden ahead and returned with news of Comanche signs on a river bluff about five miles away. Miera immediately suspected Silvestre of conniving with the Comanche at a trap, but he held his tongue.

Cisneros and the Indian girl were obvious; they wore the same rapt look, although handsome Cisneros seemed darker and wilder, while Laughing Bird was paler and somehow more demure.

"No doubt they have hidden themselves in each other." Andres did not quite trouble to speak under his breath.

"He's hidden himself inside of her at least," Aguilar snorted.

"I hope he has the pox, but really I couldn't care." Lain spoke quite mildly.

You're lying, Escalante thought. The hatred leaking from your face tells me you're lying. You care, all right. He had a fearful intuition of trouble.

"Sign of Comanche petrifies me," confessed Dominguez.

"The traces were old," Escalante said. "I've come to know the difference."

"Tracks on a bluff?" asked Andres. "They've been watching us. Tell this one-eyed mutton Silvestre that if he's tricked us he's a dead man."

"Tell him yourself," blared Lain. "Only you can speak the language."

"Wait," Escalante commanded. "I believe Silvestre. Don't get all excited until we know for sure."

They were all gathered on a wide, grassy knoll that divided as it dropped away. Silvestre was standing to one side with Little Lain. Lucrecio Muniz stood near them mending a bridle. Silvestre looked into the distance, restive as a deer.

"The worst thing we can do is nothing. I choose to believe him. If there are Comanche ahead, they can't be far. It'll go better for us if we're moving than if we're caught standing here."

Lain quarreled with this suggestion. Escalante stood before him, staring hard into his eyes, his anger rising. Lain yielded finally. "All right, but I don't like it."

"Do you have a better idea?" Escalante was still testy.

"No, Father."

"Then lead, follow or get out of the way, Lain."

"Give us the guns, Father," Lain demanded. "They don't do us any good against Comanche all wrapped up in skin on a mule's back."

"No. Lord, man, you don't have the intelligence of a cactus. We don't know whether there are Comanche ahead, and if there are we don't know whether they're hostile. We're not a war party or a punitive expedition, remember? If there are Comanche and they see us coming armed, peaceful or not, they're sure to expect an attack."

"By the time we find out whether they're hostile or not, they'll have our scalps," Lain yelled, his face close to Escalante's.

"How many Indian fights have you been in, Lain?" Escalante demanded.

Lain struggled with the answer and finally admitted, "None."

"I've been in about ten and narrowly escaped ten more. I've come to know when they're about to jump and when they're not. There's a certain smell to the air and the country. At this moment I don't smell it. I believe they're there, somewhere ahead, but I don't smell war."

"But simply carrying the rifles doesn't mean we're going to use them."

"The Comanche don't know that."

"Just seeing our guns might make them leave us alone."

"Sight of them for a Comanche is reason enough to attack. They always need more rifles. Trust me, Lain. God knows I don't have the time to argue."

Lain shrugged. "I suppose I must."

The party began to march once more. A new alertness possessed them and they traveled without speaking, scanning the ridge tops and bluffs. They peered at clumps of trees in the distance until their eyes blurred. They saw no Indians, though, no smoke or dust or human trace. Miera rode up beside Escalante.

"I wish we had carts," he said. "We could take those bones with us all the way to California. I know they are lost forever now."

"Perhaps there are others."

Miera turned in his saddle to look back at the lands they were leaving. He wished he had marked the place where those bones lay.

The party reached the banks of a wide, muddy river. Miera calculated their position with his astrolabe. "It's just one more river somewhere between Santa Fe and Monterey. I can determine no name for it on our charts."

"We've named a number of other forgotten places, so we might as well name this one, too." Dominguez went on to propose San Cosme as benefactor, and the River San Cosme it became.

Silvestre came riding in, waving the tack from a Comanche horse. He had found the cold remains of a small fire too. "I don't believe it's a war party," he said. "There were no medicine sacrifices among the ashes of the fire."

Escalante examined the harness and agreed. "I don't believe this is the kind of harness they use on war horses. This leather is heavy, more for a travois."

The river did not appear deep and Escalante and Miera, riding upstream, soon found a ford. The pack train went into the sliding waters first.

Some of the mules began to bray; then one of them hit a deep spot. Cisneros' horse staggered into water over its chest. In alarm, Miera and Escalante started riding along the riverbank. The cattle entered the water next, seeking its coolness, but the current, which was faster than it had seemed, swirled their tails out around them and sucked at their feet and legs. Cisneros turned backward and was shouting at Lucrecio to guard the cattle.

Simon Lucero, perched on his tiny saddle, plunged into the river with a splash. Little Lain and Laughing Bird laughed hysterically. Dominguez came trotting up behind Miera and Escalante. Silvestre the guide had already reached the other side.

"Silvestre, what are you doing?" Dominguez called to him.

Silvestre had waded back into the river and was waving his arms at the pack train.

"Trying to get them to swim," guessed Miera, thinking that perhaps Silvestre had not tricked them after all.

Escalante drove his horse into the river and set out across, cassock swirling out from him like a blanket thrown into the air. He expertly prodded his horse to swim and flattened out in his saddle. Together, horse and man floated into the current, angling straight for the pack train. Cisneros was off his horse now and also swimming. Miera, staring into the hoofprints along the bank, had a sense that the river was rising. Then, peering upstream, he realized he was right. "God save us, this cannot be," he yelled.

"What?" Dominguez called.

"Look, will you? Up there. The river's rising, that's what." He was pointing upriver, where a swell had formed and was rolling down the surface of the river. The hoofprints were filling on the banks and the water seemed suddenly to run faster.

Escalante had nearly reached the lead mule when his own horse went under and began to thrash. Helpless and frightened, the mules, horses and cattle screamed in a frenzy that echoed down the river. A gap appeared in the line of mules and hooves stuck out of the water. The cattle were floating singly and in pairs away from Lain and the others, away from the protecting bank.

"Perhaps I should start across," Dominguez proposed in an unusually calm tone.

"No, Father!" Miera yelled.

"I think I'd much rather take the chance than be left behind."

Little Lain and his sister were floating down the river holding hands. They moved şwiftly in the current but Laughing Bird deftly grabbed hold of a hanging branch. Together they scrambled to the other side. Cisneros had reached water only up to his waist, leading his struggling horse behind him. Andres, however, had vanished. No one saw him enter the water; no one saw him get out. He was just gone.

"Well Miera? I think we better go." Dominguez started to hitch up his cassock.

With one last look at the towering bluffs, Miera entered the water, followed by Dominguez. "I suppose we must."

Miera could feel the water inching up his legs, pouring over the tops of his high leather boots. His horse plunged sideways, regained its feet, slipped again and lost its footing for good. Miera leaped clear and swam hard. He could hear Dominguez splashing behind him but as the cold water entered his ears he lost all thought of the priest. The shock of the ice water infected his mind with panic and despair. Death was breathing on his neck.

"Keep swimming," Miera told his horse as he himself flailed and splashed in the water.

His clothes were unbearably heavy; his boots were pulling him under. He filled with rage as he realized his own boots were drowning him. As his head went under, his hand slipped away from the saddle. But his anger gave him strength and he was determined not to let the swift current take him.

With a fishlike wriggle of his body, he surged forward and grasped the horn of his saddle again. He could taste the water now as though it came through his skin. He kicked powerfully as he swam along with his horse. Finally he made it to the bank and scrambled up, gasping for breath. Cisneros and Escalante pulled his black stallion safely to shore.

At last able to think of his companion, he turned back to the water. Dominguez was unhorsed and flailing.

"Dominguez, Dominguez," Miera puffed, "go this way." He pointed downstream at an angle toward the western shore. "That's how I made it. Paddle hard with your hands; flutter your feet."

There was no answer from Dominguez. He continued to struggle against the current and lose ground. Miera stumbled down the riverbank, followed by Escalante and the others.

"Father Dominguez! Can you hear me?" Escalante shouted. Still no answer.

The river continued to rise. Dominguez could hear the far-away, muffled voice of Escalante as he bobbed up and down in the near-freezing river. He still held onto his horse, but he was losing strength and helpless to respond. Still, an almost peaceful feeling came over him. If this is how I am to die, he thought, it's not so bad. He seemed resigned to death, knowing it was too far to the other side of the river.

But his horse was not so ready to die. He kicked Dominguez hard in the ankle and bucked violently, and with his remaining strength hauled Dominguez toward the still water of the shallows. Then the horse lurched to its feet, water pouring off its saddle and spouting from the stirrups as from open jugs. Dominguez lifted his weakened arms from the water and pitched forward onto the gravel bank. He fell exhausted and did not move.

The men rushed to him. "Is he alive?" Cisneros asked.

"Father, it's Miera. Can you hear me?"

"Are you all right, Dominguez? Speak to us, please!"

Dominguez could hear all of them but didn't choose to respond just yet. He rather liked the attention. He groaned a bit, then managed to roll over on his back. He opened his eyes and looked at the blue sky and the puffy rolling clouds above.

"You're all right, Dominguez. You've made it safely across, but you certainly gave us quite a scare," Escalante rallied him.

"Glad to have you back, Father," Miera beamed. "Thought you were a goner."

Slowly and with stumbling grace Dominguez got to his feet, the weight of his wet robes nearly toppling him again.

"Perhaps you should rest, Father," Cisneros suggested.

"I am just fine. Please, just leave me be," insisted Dominguez.

Recovering from his scare, Miera felt sorry for Dominguez and marveled that he had seemed almost happy in the water.

He took off his boots and emptied them. "I'm afraid to turn around to see how the stock and the pack train have fared." A mule and several cattle had drifted by him as he sat on the bank.

"The hitches were fastened," Cisneros said gloomily. "I fear we have also lost Andres."

Miera covered his face with his hands. "Lord, I hope not."

"As I do as well, I assure you."

From where he stood Miera could see only two mules and three head of cattle. The great alluvial gravel bed was barren as the moon. The tall bluffs cast a shadow and the green of the bushes along the bank was almost black in the dim light.

Escalante reached Miera's side, wringing gushes of water from his robes. He struggled out of them and then used his shift to cover his nakedness. The wet cloth trailed behind him like a thick, unwieldy tail. He squished with every step.

As Miera, Cisneros and Escalante drew closer to the rest of the party, the folds of the riverbank were revealed to be deeper than they had appeared from the other side. There were cattle and mules concealed in them.

"This is not so bad as I feared," Cisneros told Miera. Three mules rose unsteadily at their approach.

Lain, Aguilar, Olivares, Simon Lucero and Lucrecio had built a fire near the bluff and were drying out their clothes and packs. Much that Miera had given up for lost was spread on the ground to dry. The rifles were safe and the gunpowder dry.

They heard rocks clicking together and turned at the noise to see Andres, barely alive. He was soaked, looked as though the wetness had entered his bones. His sly trapper's eyes were nearly popping out of his skull. A miasma of fear of death arose from him.

"I nearly drowned," he puffed, "but I think I'm all right."

"You don't look all right, man," put in Cisneros.

"Good heavens, Andres," Dominguez exclaimed, "you're worse off than I am. Let's go to the fire and warm ourselves."

More wood was gathered and thrown on the fire. Everyone breathed a sigh of relief, including the stock, which huddled together for warmth.

Miera watched as Escalante and Silvestre left to inspect the trail the Comanche had made, hoping to avoid attack.

"We should follow them; they'll be waiting for us," Miera told the others. Dominguez groaned.

"It'll be dark soon. There's no point in leaving now," stated Aguilar.

Dominguez looked up from the fire. "My robes will never be dry and my hat has floated away. I never went anywhere without my trusty hat. And now it's gone," he sighed mournfully, "and my tonsure will get sunburned."

"Perhaps we could make a skirt for you, Father Dominguez," Lain joked, "the way these Indians do for themselves."

"I'm more concerned about my hat." Dominguez took him seriously. "I've worn skirts for most of my life. Didn't anyone see where my hat went?"

Miera put a hand on his shoulder. "You lost your hat four days ago when you were out of your head with fever."

"Oh?" Suddenly it struck the old priest funny, and before he finished laughing they had repacked the mules, gathered the cattle and begun their climb. After several hundred yards of tough uphill going, everyone was sweating and complaining, even Escalante, who surprised everyone. "I hate this. God is spanking us all for something or other."

Aguilar was particularly taken aback. "Father, you hardly ever complain."

"Well, I'm complaining now," Escalante growled.

The climb was even more difficult for the animals. At one point a horse and mule, tethered together, bunched up at one turn in the trail. The horse took offense and bumped the mule, which in turn reared and kicked, opening a deep cut on the horse's flank. The horse screamed and backed, pulling the tether tight. The mule resisted, digging its hooves into the trail. The horse backed off the trail, but the mule held fast to its footing, its legs trembling. The shrieking horse hung on the tether, swaying back and forth over the cliff's edge. Just then, the mule's hooves slid loose and it looked as if they would both go. The tether snapped, though, and the honking mule staggered to safety as the horse plummeted into a gully.

It all happened in seconds. Escalante and the others watched as the horse bounced over and over down the incline, thrashing for a moment when it finally hit bottom, then was still.

Lucrecio immediately scrambled down, even before it had finished its fall. Olivares, silent as he had been for several days, nimbly followed him.

Lucrecio called up to the others, "By some miracle he

isn't dead. His neck is a mess, though. Some of the bones are showing through.''

Without a word to the others, Escalante pulled out his rifle and put a bullet straight through the agonized creature's chest.

"Father," Miera said reproachfully, "you are a priest. I would have put the beast out of its misery. It would be more fitting."

"I am the leader of this expedition, my son. It is fitting that I take such responsibilities. The good God knows it was an act of mercy."

It was still light when they decided to stop and set up camp for the night. It didn't take long, for the men were so exhausted they just opened their bedrolls and went to sleep.

With energy far beyond his strength, Miera stayed up to plot the position of the party with his astrolabe, as he did every few days. He totaled the distance they had come from Santa Fe. "It's more than seven hundred and fifty miles," he announced. He referred to meridians plotted at Monterey and calculated that they had at least a thousand more to go. He didn't mention this to the tired men for fear they'd not want to continue. He himself was so dismayed he found it difficult to sleep. He woke to hear Silvestre calling out to someone far away in the darkness. Beside him, Escalante was awake and listening also.

"Miera?"

"Yes, I'm awake, Escalante."

They listened to Silvestre awhile longer. "We're near the lake," said Escalante. "The Indian told Andres earlier."

"Why is he speaking into the darkness?"

"There are others out there, he thinks."

"Comanche?"

"Uintah. He's telling them something about us, I believe, telling them we come in peace."

Silvestre's voice sounded strange, almost like a white man. Who is this man Silvestre, Miera wondered, drifting off to sleep.

Chapter 19

The party was not as close to the legendary salt lake of the Ute Indians as Silvestre had believed. He had been lost, it turned out. He explained later how different places looked the same to him and how the similarity confused him a great deal. For three days he had worn the red blanket his wife had given him, in preparation to greet his brethren in great style and splendor.

The men of the party were disappointed, but not so deeply as Silvestre was. As he explained, "You are not disappointed because you have not seen this lake country. I have."

Again and again the party crossed Comanche tracks. They found a place where Indians had stretched prone on a bluff, watching their approach from only a hundred yards or so away. Silvestre was again suspected of having led the party into a trap. He was still wearing his blanket, and Miera and Andres concluded it was some sort of signal to the Comanche. They challenged Silvestre, saying he was either treacherous or just plain stupid.

Silvestre replied angrily, "I am neither of those things

you say I am. I am simply lost.'' He had come to understand
Spanish well. He clearly discerned Miera and Andres' attitude
toward him. He took off the blanket sadly and folded it away
as a gesture of honor.

They were in the high country and the nights grew chilly
at times. Yellowing trees announced the arrival of autumn;
the date was September 20, 1776.

They passed through a canyon where mud swallow nests
covered the walls like miniature pueblos. They reminded
Escalante of the buildings of Santa Fe and made him a little
homesick.

They had been climbing constantly higher for days. Miera
calculated that they had come more than nine hundred miles
from Santa Fe. From a range of low mountains they had a
panoramic view extending, it seemed, to the end of the world
in all directions. Then, on a high range, they all became
aware that a dramatic change had come over the land. Something was different, something they could not explain. Until
then, all the streams had flowed eastward. Now they ran to
the west.

"It's as though we've crossed the top of the world,"
marveled young Juan de Aguilar.

"Something like that, but not quite," Escalante said.
"You notice a difference in flow whenever you cross a major
mountain range."

Nonetheless, Escalante's easy explanation could not di-
minish the wonder of the view and the phenomenon of streams
suddenly changing direction.

"Listen, everyone," Miera called out. "We're some-
where in Colorado. This is the backbone of the Americas.
East of it the streams feed the Atlantic, and to the west, the
Pacific. That's all. Now, can we get moving again?"

Everyone agreed they should keep moving. Not only was
it starting to get cold, but according to Miera's calculations
they still had plenty of land yet to cover.

They continued toward another blue mist of mountains far beyond. Large antlered creatures, bigger than elk, began to appear in the forest. Escalante killed one and they ate ravenously of Andres' delicious stew with potatoes, roots and special spices. Then they took a much-needed breather while the rest of the meat dried.

They were traveling twenty-five to thirty miles a day now, even over rough passage. The soil in this region was clay, and when there was rain it turned slippery and was particularly treacherous for the horses with riders.

Silvestre at last was truly familiar with the country. "I feel redeemed," he told Escalante. "I also feel worthy of wearing my red blanket once more."

Escalante felt Silvestre deserved still more for his work, bumbling as it had been at times. He gave the Indian and Little Lain each another yard of woolen goods and some long scarlet ribbons. Silvestre tied the wool about his head, letting the two long ends hang loose down his back. He then strutted before the men and horses, showing off. He was once again a happy man.

Smiling discreetly, Escalante told Dominguez, "I swear, the way that madman is parading about he reminds me of the Mercedarian Fathers, who dress up as ransomed captives on their feast day of Our Lady of Merced. They wear robes and rags such as his."

Dominguez laughed with a rich heartiness that Escalante had never known him to exhibit before. "The outdoor air and lean diet are improving both your disposition and your health."

Dominguez thumped his chest. "And you know, I too believe it is. Except for my fevers, I've never felt better in my life."

Escalante warned the others not to make fun of Silvestre. "His pride and satisfaction are good for other Indians to see. It tells them we're friendly."

On September 23, 1776, Escalante and the others had

their first glimpse of the lake about which they had heard so much from Silvestre.

They clambered up an incline and came out from among pines and cottonwoods onto a broad bench of stone that Dominguez estimated to be as large as the grand plaza in Mexico City. And there in the hazy distance was a sheet of water that stretched for miles over the country in resolute blueness, looking huge even from across the enormous flat valley between themselves and the lake.

Andres Muniz gasped and some of the others crossed themselves. "If it seems so large while we are yet so far away, think how big it really must be. It's an inland sea, is it not, Father Escalante, Father Dominguez?" he asked.

Dominguez nodded; he had never seen or imagined a body of water so big so far inland.

Escalante called out, "The sooner we reach there, the sooner we'll appreciate how large it really is." He set off at a gallop. The others caught his enthusiasm and followed.

Throughout the day as they progressed, puffs of smoke so slight they needed backdrops of trees to be seen rose into the summery air from mountaintops, from ledges and from down in the canyon.

"I presume they announce our arrival," said Escalante.

"Let's hope it's nothing more," Cisneros grumped. The smoke signals made him uneasy; he felt like a man who was being talked about to his face in a foreign language. They had vanished, though, by the surprisingly warm grey day on which the party reached the valley floor.

Foothills mounded away from the mountains, and these they took at their ease. Sage bushes, some quite tall, impeded their progress, but they paid no attention, staring as they were at the valley.

It stretched southward forever, it seemed to Escalante, almost to the sea. Because of the clouds and the greyness the lake haze was nearly all gone. The lake was wide and even longer than wide; the end could barely be seen. They kept dropping lower and lower, Silvestre ahead in his blanket. Even the animals seemed excited.

As they reached the valley floor the sun broke through the grey mat of clouds. In this new light great plumes and planes of smoke seemed to be rising up from the grass. At first Escalante and Dominguez, now at the head of the column, thought it came from village fires, but there was too much of it rising too uniformly from the ground.

"What do you suppose we're seeing?" inquired Dominguez.

"They're burning the fields."

"But why?"

"They fear us, I think. They take us for a war party, perhaps, since we're on horseback. They're burning the pastures to make a barrier and drive us back. In Europe it's known as scorching the earth before your enemies. The Russians are supposedly masters at it."

"I think we surprised them," Miera observed. "There are big gaps between their fires. We can easily get through."

These fires had a great deal to do with the unusual warmth of the day. They came into sight as the party reached the valley floor. Smoke obscured them from above, but at eye level, lines of orange were plain to be seen crisping across the meadows. Mostly, however, the ground was just smoldering as the fires had put themselves out.

Silvestre's sweat ran from under his lank hair. He was signing and shouting in very loud Spanish. Escalante asked him where his tribe was. Nothing could be seen for miles except smoke and desolation. Silvestre, however, simply pointed ahead toward something they could not see. Escalante squinted but only the blue of the lake rose up to dazzle him. Deer ran before the lines of smoke and so did small rodents so numerous they seemed like a breeze moving through the grass.

Escalante, Dominguez and Silvestre passed through great curtains of smoke, the rest of the party strung out behind. The fields burned fiercely about them as they picked their way through the clusters of flame.

The valley was flat and as they drew closer to the lake it appeared to be partly composed of marshland. Ducks, geese and cranes flew up from the tules and willows. Beyond the scorched earth Escalante and Dominguez saw beaver and muskrat wandering over the hills. In the slough of a small river a type of rodent they had never seen before plunged into the water and swam to the opposite bank.

"I don't see the least sign of habitation," said Dominguez.

Escalante turned to Silvestre, who seemed lost in thought. "Where are your people, Silvestre?" The guide just stared straight ahead as if he had not heard.

The few trees in the valley grew in brakes, although several enormous cottonwoods grew singly in the meadows. The rest of the party was just beginning to pass through the veils of smoke. Once more Escalante marveled at the size of this valley; so much smoke had seemed only like haze. He tried to envision the inevitable meeting with the chief of the Uintah, choose the words he would say. God's grandeur and the eerie aptness of an Indian welcome had often moved him in unpredictable ways. Floods of scripture began running through his mind, remembered bits of statecraft.

At such a moment he was certain no man in the entire world could possibly be as happy as he was. He was truly glad he was a priest serving the Lord. After so many years, he could still be greatly moved by the same wonders that had moved him as a youth. God had not seen fit to take from him the one most valuable gift of all—God simply had to be good.

At that moment of revelation, Escalante saw his first buffalo.

"Blessed saints, Dominguez! What is that creature?"

"Look, there are others," Dominguez shouted, sweeping his hand toward the plain.

Silvestre had urged his horse into a trot. The majority of these shaggy beasts were on distant hills, and at first Escalante thought he was pursuing the buffalo. Then he saw campfire smoke in a brake of trees. He had no time to point this out to Dominguez, however, because Silvestre had picked up speed again. Escalante's own horse quickened. They were galloping now, drumming on the earth, bits of sod and small rocks flying out from under their hooves. The campfire smoke in the trees was fast approaching. Escalante turned in his saddle and saw Dominguez laboring along behind him and the pack train still farther back. He nearly lost his seat when his horse took a gully in one stride.

Over the rush of air in his ears Escalante could barely hear a voice. Silvestre was calling out to the Uintah, who now appeared in front of the brake. Escalante and Silvestre were gaining the trees when Escalante realized the Indians were armed. Quivers of arrows showed over their shoulders and they held lances and bows. They wore elaborate clothing and seemed quite different from the Sabuagana. They are white, Escalante thought with alarm, but then realized the white was mud. It had dried on their faces, also streaked with gashes of brown.

Silvestre had already reached his people and nearly fallen off his horse. Their bows were still drawn, their arrows ready. Then they recognized him.

"I don't believe I've ever seen Indians like these," Dominguez panted. He had just caught up.

Silvestre had dismounted and taken off his red blanket. It was being passed around for admiration. He stood in marked contrast to these other men, but as Escalante studied him Silvestre did seem to become more and more part of his tribe. Silvestre loosened his hair, shook it back over his shoulders, and then beckoned to the priests.

"Come, Fathers," he called. "Come greet my people. They await you and apologize for their rudeness with their weapons. They feared we were hostile."

"As we supposed," Escalante nodded.

"I suppose we should go forward," Dominguez spoke

with some trepidation. Escalante was already spurring his horse forward.

The Indians wore buckskin jackets and leggings, and blankets of rabbit fur. Escalante was excited in a way strange to him. Underneath the mud on their faces the Uintah were fair-skinned by comparison to the Pueblo and Hopi Indians. Trappers traded with the Sabuagana, he knew, but to the best of his knowledge no white man had ever visited these Uintah Indians.

"We wish to convert you to the ways of the one true God. We come in peace." Escalante mixed Spanish and the few Ute phrases he knew and embellished his speech with sign language. He saw the faces of the Uintah change from stony to receptive and kind, persuaded by Silvestre's attitude as much as by Escalante. Escalante looked closely at his guide as Silvestre's transformation continued. The man seemed to assume stature and elegance. At home among his people, Escalante realized, leading an expedition and wearing fine clothes, he becomes important—to his people and to himself.

Escalante began speaking again but the Indians cut him off. They wished to take the padres to their village, which could be seen among the thin silvery aspen. The willow huts were many but the village was quite deserted.

Escalante had white glass beads and bits of cloth in the pockets of his robes. He marked the Indians' fascination with the beads. They made noises over them and gathered to peer over each other's shoulders as they held the beads up to the light. They understand the cloth far more easily than they do God, Escalante thought.

"They're humble and receptive, I think," the young Franciscan remarked to Dominguez. "They'll take instruction nicely. I don't sense restiveness, do you? Or any fear of new ideas?" Dominguez shook his head.

Escalante sighed. In a way he now respected the Uintah less than he might have, had they resisted or laughed when he first told them of God. Was it possible that people who accepted His word so easily and quickly really believed it? Or cared?

The Indians followed Escalante as he looked about the village. They were saying things to him, nice things, he believed, which Silvestre was trying to make him understand. He turned and spoke to them of God and His Son, Jesus. When a young woman stepped out of one of the willow huts holding a baby, he spoke of Mary, Mother of God and he explained baptism.

This is the joy of the wilderness, he kept thinking, this simplicity and the finding of what has never been seen before. He could spend his life discovering tribes like these, the divinely appointed arrow of God.

"You are my friends," he told the Indians. "I shall always be yours." As he walked through the village they followed behind. "You are my children," he said, even more moved. "This man"—he took Silvestre by the shoulder—"has led me to you and one of you shall lead me on. God shall have all of what you have. His Name shall be spoken in every grove. This is His, this wilderness. We only pass through, explorer and Indian alike."

Escalante suffered a return of the distaste he had often known at this moment. Why is it, he thought, that although I truly believe in God, I so often feel a little like a liar when I tell them? I think that one should not first introduce God as a trade. My horse is better than your horse; my belief is better than your belief. If I were they, I would never buy a horse, let alone a religion, from me, with my false unction. If nothing else the approach is an insult to my own dignity as well as theirs. There must be a better and more respectful way to approach people you hope to convert, but after ten years I still do not know it. God is love. Therefore it is inevitable that you must hawk him as a love potion. He grinned, enjoying a brief fantasy of himself peddling love potions at a fair.

The Indians seemed quite impressed by Silvestre's high standing, so Escalante elevated him further. He gave him a set of beads. The Indians were smiling as they repeated their greetings, shaking their lances and bows. Then they bowed their heads and beat their breasts, which amazed Escalante. White men used this same gesture, which proved to him once more how God made all men in His image.

They had reached the edge of the grove of trees. A gentle decline stretched away toward the lake of infinite blue. There were white conical hills at the edges, and tiny dots—Indians, perhaps fishing in boats and on the beaches. He looked at the white mud faces of his Indian hosts and remembered their early aggression. It seemed trivial now.

"Do you know how long it has taken me to find you?" Silvestre had taught the Indians to say "Father," and they were murmuring it now.

More Indians were coming across the plain and between the columns of smoke. With eager benevolence, Escalante found he longed to harvest their souls. Still, discord persisted. Was he God's messenger or God's gypsy, as Dominguez and others had indeed termed him? Well, perhaps he was both. If God chose his messengers from the gypsies, so be it.

Chapter 20

Late that afternoon the chiefs of the Uintah, three old men with bits of rabbit fur braided into their hair, told Father Silvestre Velez de Escalante and Father Francisco Atanasio Dominguez that the Uintah wished to live with them and give all of their land to the Spanish. They warned the priests that the Comanche were approaching with blood in their hearts, but together with the Spaniards, the Uintah would go forth and punish them.

"Ah, the Comanche are the devils here. Perhaps this is why they're so eager for the word of God," was Bernardo Miera's cynical response. "They want us to fight their wars for them."

"They're sincere, Miera." Escalante answered curtly; Miera's own doubts too closely matched his own.

"Also, they are defenseless," Miera reminded him. "They're not interested in God, only in our strength."

Escalante told the chiefs other priests would come to take their place and live among them always. For a time the party would remain among the Indians beside the lake, but then they must continue onward.

They were seated in a hollow run formed by buffalo hooves over- the years. A strong breeze was up, blowing thistledown and sedge through the air above their heads. It was still light, but just barely. The hollow held the warmth of the big cook fire. The days were shortening but the valley was much warmer than the mountains. The Spanish were sharing their rations with the Indians, who were curious about the taste. The Indians themselves ate a porridge of seeds, bits of hare, birds and fish. The meats had revolting colors and textures, and Dominguez had to look away when the Indians tore at them with their teeth. The flesh of the fish, however, was a beautiful pearl color. Escalante was amused at Dominguez' discomfort. The younger man had eaten rancid Indian stews before. He took up a piece of meat in his fingers and gulped it down, pretending to enjoy it.

"You're doing that on purpose to make a fat man ill," Dominguez chided. "You can't make me believe you really like it."

Escalante rolled his head and laughed.

The Indian women did not show themselves. They stayed deep in the dim brake, cooking their own meals. They wore buckskin jackets and long grass skirts. They looked almost like Spanish women with mantillas of black hair cascading down. Escalante found himself at the edge of the buffalo hollow looking over the edge. A fire in the wilderness miles beyond the farthest mountains had changed the sunset into a blanket of mauve.

"The wonders of God never cease to astound me," said Miera, who had joined Escalante.

The priest watched Juan de Aguilar leading the horses to a spring in the sagebrush. Behind him the others squatted on their haunches with the Indians at the cook fire.

"Why don't the women come close?" Escalante asked Miera. "Why do they show no interest?" Miera shrugged. Escalante remembered the Sabuagana, the women standing just beyond the fires, their musk in the smoky air. The reticence of the women perplexed him. He had never known the women of any other Indian group to remain like wraiths in the shadows.

He was still filled with the peace he had sensed in the valley of Utah Lake, as they had come to call the big body of water. "These women must be brought to God too," he finally said to Miera. "They mustn't be slighted of their salvation."

Miera shook his head. "I wouldn't like your work at all."

"Why not? You're one who loves work."

"Yours is far too abstract for me, Father, and demanding. Soldiering and painting are easy for me. Peddling an idea is the most difficult labor of all, and it gives you no relief. I've never yet seen a priest who could give himself a rest from working on people's souls."

"Father Escalante." It was Cisneros. "Come quickly. You're needed badly. Father Dominguez is ill once again."

Escalante leaped up from the fire and ran with Cisneros as Miera puffed along behind. They ran past another fire and Escalante was surprised to see Simon Lucero inside a circle of squatting Indians, lecturing them with self-important gestures. Escalante heard "mission to the sea" and "for Spain and God." Even sitting, the Indians were almost as tall as Lucero standing. They clearly did not understand a word he was saying, but it did not seem to matter to either themselves or Lucero.

Dominguez lay on his blankets just beyond the fire. Several explorers and a few Indians clustered about him like angels watching over a Botticelli martyr.

Cisneros explained, "He felt challenged, Father, and had to eat some of that Indian porridge, as you did. It doesn't seem to have agreed with him."

"Dominguez?" Escalante squatted with the others.

"I'll recover," came Dominguez' weary voice.

"I wish your illness could be my own."

"Oh, don't be silly for once, Escalante. That's the sort of thing we priests are always saying to each other. You do not want my illness and I wouldn't wish it on you." He grabbed Escalante's wrist and grinned. "See how rough and common I'm getting out here?"

"Cisneros says you're ill."

"The illness isn't much to worry about, I don't think. Only a sickness of the bowels. You and your iron stomach and Indian stews."

"I suppose I shouldn't have teased you, eating it."

"I don't think I'll need more than a day to recover."

"Of course, just as you only needed a day to recover from your last illness." Escalante pulled Dominguez' nose. "None of your heroics, do you hear? You'll rest for as long as I say you must, whether it's one day or ten. A sick man in the saddle does us no good. In fact, he's a detriment. He doesn't pull his load, and he requires more than his share of help. I've told you all this before."

"I recall that was my speech to you in the hut in Taos two months ago."

"It was," Escalante agreed.

"But you didn't listen to me; not for long, anyway. Why should I listen to you?"

"Because you and I are not the same. You're used to being obedient. I'm not. That's one reason why I'm out here, remember?"

The others turned their heads from Escalante to Dominguez, back and forth, as the two bantered. Miera said, "We could use the time to make some side trips. From the little I've seen of this lake and this valley, a city three times the size of Mexico City could be built here. This valley will be invaluable to the crown. I estimate that lake to be about sixteen miles wide and forty long—enough water to keep a city going forever. I'd like to have more of a look at it."

"I wouldn't dream of depriving you, then, Miera." Dominguez rolled himself in his blankets to sleep.

When Escalante awoke the following morning, the sunshine was intense enough to scald the eyes. Hoarfrost was brilliant on the meadows. The other men were sleeping around him, resembling bodies gathered after a battle. He smelled Uintah cook fires and rolled from his blankets, wanting some of their breakfast.

Soon the other men began to stir under their blankets. Cisneros rose to check on Dominguez. Laughing Bird had gone to bring water from the spring. Escalante could hear Dominguez and Cisneros talking, their voices quite distinct in the early morning air.

Lain swore and Olivares turned in his blankets. A flock of ducks flew overhead. It grew so quiet Escalante could hear the horses cropping grass.

At breakfast it was decided to explore the lake. "I'll need only one or two men," Miera said, "in the event of trouble. I'd like one to be you, Father Escalante."

Escalante looked toward Dominguez and hesitated.

"Oh, go ahead, Father," Joaquin Lain urged him. "I think the word of God can wait for a day. Your wish to go is naked on your face. He'll be well cared for while we're gone."

Escalante did wish to go but was not certain he should. There seemed to be something sarcastic in Lain's voice. But imagined sarcasm was no reason for staying, and in the end Escalante nodded. He would go.

Escalante helped move Dominguez to a place where he could be with the Uintah and instruct them without having to get up and move about too much.

Silvestre, as it turned out, refused to guide them. Having brought them to the lake, he wished only to stay with his people. He told Escalante, "I have carried out my end of our bargain, Father. My days of being your guide are over. I thank you for your gifts and your friendship.''

''As I thank you for your service to us.''

''Then we are no longer obligated to each other.''

Escalante could not argue this, so he sought out the Uintah chiefs and bartered for a new guide. Some cloth hired a rather silent young man for one day only.

Escalante, Miera, Lain and Olivares rode with the guide from the hollow into the warm autumn day. They galloped down to the lake, the horses inspired by the acres of curing grass, the men eager to explore. Escalante was still touched by the beauty of the deep blue lake.

They rode all day, along the shores and through the conical hills of salt and the marshes. Finally they reached the end of the lake, where a large river emptied into a bay. Miera made drawings, took sightings and kept exclaiming at the many species of duck. There were white geese in some of the inlets that Escalante thought looked like swans.

''Where do you think this river leads?'' Olivares wondered aloud.

''Perhaps back to the Gulf of Mexico,'' Miera joked. He designated the river as the Saint Nicolas in his mapping notes.

''Would that it did,'' Lain grumbled. ''I could climb aboard a log and float there.''

The Uintah guide, on foot, had come back to join them and stood looking up at their faces.

''Miera, ask him how far away the other end of the lake is,'' said Escalante.

Miera failed to communicate, so Lain and Escalante took turns trying to make their question understood, but they failed also. With their limited vocabulary, they did manage to learn that the lake at the north end became a river that fed into a huge salt lake. The guide outstretched his arms and leaped from side to side again and again, to express multiples of his arm spans.

''I think he's telling us that the great salt lake is still

many times larger than this one before us," Escalante finally concluded.

The guide also managed to convey to them that it was so salty a man could float in it as a stick floats, with no effort, and that strange animals roamed its shores.

Miera tried to describe for the guide the large bones he had found with Escalante weeks earlier. Were the animals roaming the lake of a size such as that?

The guide did not understand.

"A lake of salt water." Lain shook his head. "Bigger than this one, even. Imagine it."

Escalante did. The idea of a lake so salty it was thick made him think of hell. "We were taught in the seminary that there are landslides of salt in hell to prohibit anything from growing," he remarked.

Lain was intimidated. "Do you believe that, Father?"

Escalante thought for a moment, then chuckled. "Only as a fable, I think, not as a real landscape."

"Even if hell is like that, I'd still like to see this lake of salt."

"So would I," Escalante laughed, "so would I."

They slowly rode back to their camp. There was no moon but passage was easy. The guide trotted along beside their horses. Ducks called high overhead and coyotes loped past them in the darkness.

"It's almost the end of September." Lain shivered against the night chill. "We've been gone two months. I wonder just how far it is to Monterey."

Escalante wondered also. "Perhaps exploration of the salt lake has to wait. We really should be on the trail as soon as Dominguez' condition lets us." He was a little sad; he did want to see the salt lake. As far as he knew no white man before had ever even heard of it.

They reached camp well after dark. The others had held

dinner for them; over it they demanded to hear every detail of what the scouts had seen.

At the end of the evening, when everyone grew drowsy and went to his blankets, Escalante took his writing desk to the fire and lit a cigar. He sighed over it, for it was one of his last dozen. Then he began another journal entry. He noted that the entire Valley of Our Lady of Merced surrounding the fresh-water lake was sheltered, arable, wooded, warm in chilly weather and generally ideal for a mission settlement. He noted too that Utah Lake was watered by four sweet-water rivers flowing down the surrounding sierras.

> Utah Lake, according to reports we receive from the Indians, is joined to the other far larger salt lake by a narrow passage through the mountains, which we have named the White Sierras of the Timpanogos. This other lake reportedly covers many, many square miles, and the water is supposed to be harmful and extremely salty. The Indians maintain that one needs only to wet oneself with the water and immediately itches and burns wherever the water has touched. According to the Indians, there live about the lake some people who would be called spell-casters in our vulgar Spanish idiom. They speak the Comanche dialect, eat only herbs and vegetables and drink only the water from the numerous fresh springs and crystal outlets about the salt lake.
>
> The spell-casters and the Uintah we know are not enemies. However, they maintain neutral distance between each other. Some time ago, a party of them killed one of the Uintah men. . . .

Escalante suddenly stopped writing. He had the feeling that someone had silently come very close and was now watching him. "You scared the hell out of me, Andres,"

Escalante growled. "A man can get killed sneaking up on another like that."

Muniz came from the shadows and hunkered down on his heels before Escalante. "Do you ever get lonely, Father Escalante, and wish you were not a man?"

"What? Not a man? How do you mean, Andres?"

"Do you ever wish you were an animal or a piece of rock or a woman, even?"

Escalante was puzzled and disturbed. "No. Why do you ask?"

"Just curious," Muniz replied, seemingly lighthearted and quite happy. "You always seem so content with yourself. I wondered, are there times you're not? That's all."

"You all right, Andres?"

"Yes, Father. I'm just fine. Good night." And then he was up and gone as quietly as he had come.

Escalante wrote no more beside the fire that night. He smoked his cigar down until it burned his fingers and was too short to hold. Was the man going out of his head? Or was Escalante simply misreading the things he had said?

He was chilly still, and he realized it was no longer the superstitious chill Muniz had engendered. His right side was also hurting—just a little. He prayed his own illness was not recurring. Two sick priests would never do.

Time for bed, he thought. A good night's rest was what he needed. A day like this one will make a man imagine all sorts of things.

Chapter 21

In the days of Dominguez' illness much had been accomplished. The men explored more of the lake and took great pleasure in fishing in the small fresh-water streams surrounding the Uintah territory. They discovered several new species of waterfowl and rodents near the lake and brought back a number to the village for Miera to sketch and describe in his notebook. More presents were given to the Indians in an exchange for language lessons, and of course the word of God was spread.

To conserve the cattle and provide a little variety as well as to amuse the men, Miera and Lucero put together a hunt. It amused them that the Indians should compete for the privilege of guiding the hunting party. They were more than eager to help the explorers, having heard from Silvestre that the Fathers kept the Comanche away.

Dominguez was recuperating fast and the party would leave soon. The priests called for their last gathering with the Indians, explaining that farewells were always said in advance to ease the way for a dawn departure.

Everyone assembled in a buffalo hollow. Even the women came out of hiding for their last chance to hear the word of God.

When all was quiet, the Indians began to recite a prayer Escalante had taught them. The Spanish words, spoken by so many voices, produced a hush among the explorers. Dominguez and Escalante were tremendously pleased with the progress they had made in converting these Indian souls. They never imagined it could be this easy.

And now it was time to select a new guide for the party. Cisneros laid out a blanket and a hunting knife upon the ground. Suddenly the murmuring stopped and stillness dropped into the hollow and nestled there. One of the Indians, a young man with tufts of quail feathers on his rabbit vest, stepped forward from the rest and indicated his desire to be chosen to guide the explorers westward. He took up the blanket and the knife and then looked at Escalante.

"He's the one," Miera announced. "We have a new guide, everyone. He looks perfect."

"What shall we call him?" asked Dominguez.

Escalante remembered Silvestre all at once, his strange upward staring eye. Silvestre remained silent in the crowd.

Andres, by now quite fluent in Uintah, asked the chief what the name of this Indian was. It was unprounceable for Spanish tongues, as were most other Uintah names, so it was decided their new guide would be called Jose Maria.

Escalante remarked to Dominguez, "We've given Christian convert names to everyone but our little seductress."

"Let's leave it at Laughing Bird for now. A Christian name wouldn't seem fitting anyway."

Escalante nodded. "She's a tough one. Her very manner resists conversion."

"And clothing and just about everything else besides," Dominguez laughed.

*   *   *

Some time later it became apparent that Andres Muniz was not among them. No one fretted over his absence at first, but after an hour passed Escalante admitted he was worried. He asked the Uintah to search for him. One of them returned only a few minutes later saying he had not gone far. He was among the Uintah huts, masquerading as an Indian himself, babbling nonstop in Uintah.

A look of pain crossed Lucrecio Muniz' face.

From time to time throughout the day Muniz came back to camp, but he spoke only Spanish to Escalante. His face and gait seemed askew, but in Escalante's view he was still calm as he had been the night before with his baffling questions concerning fantasy and identity.

Escalante reassured Lucrecio. "If he gives us trouble when we leave, we'll simply tie his hands to his saddle horn and take him along whether he likes it or not. I promise you, we won't leave him. I think he'll be all right again once he hears Spanish all the time. We'll undoubtedly see more of this from him as he immerses himself in strange languages. You should be prepared for that."

"I will be." Lucrecio shook his head. "But I find it so difficult to believe. Big brother has always been the strong one." Then he looked intently at Escalante. "If he makes trouble and refuses to come, I'm not certain we should tie him to his saddle."

"Why not?"

"If he's gone out of his mind, it might be better for him, and for us, Father, to leave him here until he's feeling better again. He can catch up to us. Or we can pick him up on the way back. Or I can come back alone and fetch him later, after Monterey."

"You're considering abandoning him, is that what you're saying?"

"I'm considering that a man with demons in his head is no good in the places where we have to go, either to himself or to us. Lord, suppose he goes berserk some night and cuts us all up in our sleep?'' He bit his lip. ''I think if we took a vote, Father, as we did before on Olivares, you would find the others agree with me.''

Escalante said slowly, ''Don't let your jealousy of your brother make you cruel. There are other ways of proving you're as good than deserting him.''

''That's not fair, Father.''

''That's how it seems.''

''Were you not a priest, I think I would ask satisfaction for that insult.'' Lucrecio's face was warped with anger.

''Let's both thank God, then, that I am a priest. It spares us both.''

''You're accusing me of perfidy and betrayal of my own brother.''

''I'm accusing you of nothing. I know you love your brother. I'm simply saying that the rivalry has grown too great. Your wish to surpass Andres is making you willing to leave him behind. You forget that he might be in even greater danger if we leave him here. What makes you think the Uintah are so willing to nurse a discarded white madman? They may just throw him from a cliff if he's too troublesome. Did you think of that? Besides, he needs to be among his own people.''

''I tell you he'll be all right. Once he's rested he'll probably follow us and catch up.''

''So then, why not bring him along and spare him the trouble?''

''Damn you, Father, I'm truly thinking only of what's good for my brother and the expedition.''

Escalante lost his temper. ''Don't you ever curse me again, Muniz, or you've had your last sacrament. I'll excommunicate you. And don't try to tell me how to run this expedition, either. We're not leaving anyone behind unless he's dead. I've brought you all out here, and with God's help

I'm going to get all of you back. And one other thing. Don't even propose a vote or the dice, or I'll break your face." The priest brought himself up short. "There. Now are you happy? You've made me commit the sin of anger. I'll be saying Hail Marys on my poor sore knees for a month for this. Damn me? You mind your tongue and take your orders."

Escalante saw Lucrecio's fist bunch and start for his belt. Escalante caught the fist in his left hand and grabbed Lucrecio's upper arm with his right; he lifted his left knee and pressed it against Lucrecio's elbow. The force snapped Lucrecio's arm out straight and left him a choice: resist and see his arm unhinged at the elbow, or roll in direction of the force. Lucrecio rolled and Escalante boosted him all the way over his knee and slammed him flat on his back. As Lucrecio struggled for air, Escalante turned to the watchers.

"Is there anyone else who wishes to talk to me about leaving Andres behind? No? Good."

Miera was doing his best to bottle his laughter. He had enjoyed the show, and besides, he approved of the exercise in force.

There was movement among the Indian men and women. One of the three old chiefs came forward with a token, a painting of clay and ocher on buckskin. Escalante and Dominguez had asked the Indians to make such a thing, using whatever figures and styles they liked. The Holy Office in Mexico City, they thought, would be charmed.

After the exchange was made with some ceremony, heads were bowed and hands raised into the dying sunlight.

"My God in heaven and all the saints above," exclaimed Escalante, examining the token until it was grabbed from him by one of the others.

"What is this?" asked Dominguez, running up in surprise.

The token showed priests and Indians and even horses,

drawn rudely but with much charm. Above each figure tiny red crosses were inscribed.

"How have they come to do this?" Miera asked in amazement.

"Has the mystery of God's ways shown itself again?" Dominguez wondered.

"Perhaps they understood our preaching better than we feared." Escalante was remembering the crosses on the wall inside the gate at Santa Fe where the wounded soldiers had been dumped as well as the bloody Hopi wars. That was all so far away now, and the Uintah had restored his faith. "Who could have taught them this?" he asked Dominguez quietly.

The older priest shook his head. "It is proof, I think, of the soul's divination."

Escalante was not so convinced of this, but he gave thanks anyway, both priests leading the rest of the Spanish in a prayer. The Indians had begun to depart.

Escalante was depressed. He feared he now knew the answer that Muniz had once refused to give: how and where Indians had learned about God and Jesus.

If Muniz did not know, why his dodging and riddles? And if he had indeed known, why had he refused to tell? Was there something he feared in the question itself?

Escalante was quite certain the Uintah knew the ways of God and Jesus Christ not out of divine intuition but because someone had already been there to tell them. He suffered an emptiness in the gut. It occurred to him that if Muniz knew and did not wish to tell, Escalante might be sorry he had ever asked. But even so, who were these mysterious missionaries?

Later that evening Escalante saw Andres striding into camp carrying a small deer across his shoulders. There was a hole in its chest oozing blood. "Meat for the pot," he announced. He had shot it that afternoon. He told everyone not to take seriously his odd behavior of the day. It had been a game, a diversion to amuse both the Spanish and the Indians.

"Well, he's back," Escalante told Dominguez. "At least one trouble is ending well today."

"I don't understand it. Now he seems to be as normal as you and me."

"Don't believe it for a minute."

"I don't."

Chapter 22

The morning dawned grey. The air was chill with autumn and the long yellow grasses were crackling with frost. Damp smells rose from the dead fires.

Two of the best horses from the remuda were gone and so was Andres Muniz.

Lucrecio's lip curled in scorn when he spoke to Escalante. "So much for your promise to get every one of us through to Monterey, Father. You can't very well take along a man who's no longer here."

"And you think this now makes me seem boastful and foolish."

"A little."

"Well, I do feel somewhat boastful and foolish. And frustrated. Does that please you?"

"A little. My back still hurts and remembers. The ground was hard."

"The fact that your brother is gone and you have no idea what might happen to him doesn't matter."

A look of sadness and pain formed on Lucrecio's face. "Father, of course it's a concern. But your feeling of what's best and mine are different. I still believe that for the greatest good of Andres and this party, it's best we separate. I can't explain why he's suddenly so unbalanced, but he is. That's the truth of it. And in that state, he's of no value to either of . . .'' Lucrecio choked and could not finish.

When he was calmer he continued. ''I ache for him, Father, even though there are times I do want to kill him. But don't worry about him out there alone. No matter how unbalanced he may be, he is a survivor and the wilderness is home to him. He has the same love for it as you do yourself.''

Lucrecio spoke to everyone now. ''My brother is as good at hiding in the wilderness as he is at surviving there. And if he should decide he doesn't want to be found, there's no point in looking.'' Lucrecio clapped a hand on Escalante's shoulder, not hostilely. ''Father, I'll be awhile forgiving your insult and forgetting the easy way you got the best of me. But that's neither here nor there. Getting under way is the important thing. And I say it's best to go without him. If we wait for him we may never get to Monterey at all. He's not coming back this time, not for a long time. The measure of his determination to leave for good is the fact that he took two horses.''

Escalante asked the Uintah men to search for Andres once more, telling them to be gentle with him if they found him. The Uintah seemed to understand. One man took his own head between his hands and shook it from side to side. Silvestre interpreted the gesture. ''He is saying the jug is empty,'' Silvestre explained.

This time the Uintah did not find him. They told Escalante that the trail left by the two horses went southwest as straight as an arrow flies. To catch him, pursuers would need horses at least as fast as Muniz' own.

Lorenzo Olivares and Bernardo Miera, in an odd show of alliance considering their dislike for each other, offered to go after Muniz together. "If anyone can find a man out there, the two of us can;" Olivares remarked.

"The *three* of us can," Escalante grunted, lips tight. "Do you want to make it four, Lucrecio?"

Lucrecio shook his head. "Three of you are enough."

They rode out a few minutes later and easily picked up Muniz' trail; it did indeed take them southwest in an almost straight line. Muniz' dedication to one easy-to-follow direction encouraged Escalante. "Perhaps he isn't trying to hide from us at all."

"Perhaps he knows he doesn't have to try," Olivares called out over the sound of their horses' hooves.

"Eventually he has to rest the horses. That's when we'll catch up."

"Perhaps."

The three rode side by side, first cantering, then walking, holding that pattern to make time and spare their horses. They covered the distance swiftly.

They came finally to a stream so wide and slow it seemed at first that it was a long lake. Trampled mud, fresh horseshoe scars on the stones and the indentations of boots and knees left the message that Muniz had stopped to rest, water the horses and kneel to drink.

No tracks marked the other shore. Muniz had gone into the stream but not out the other side. "I'll ride upstream; you two go down," Escalante ordered. "Fire a pistol if you find where he came out." But he had an empty feeling they would not find the trail again.

An hour later they regrouped at the spot where they had parted. Olivares shrugged.

Escalante stood in his stirrups and squinted against the sun to the southwest. "He knew we were following. He was playing with us. He knew he could lose us exactly when he chose. I'll bet my last cigarro on it."

Miera wiped perspiration from his forehead. "You win."

Olivares added, "As Lucrecio said, Andres is a good mountain man. If he doesn't want us to find him, we won't."

After a while Escalante wheeled his horse back the way they had come. "Lucrecio is right. There's no point in searching further. On to Monterey." Then, knowing no other way to rid himself of his anger and frustration, Escalante yelled at the hills, "Bastard!"

The next day dawned chill and bright and the morning was a polished jewel. There was sadness and concern over the loss of Muniz, but the men were also eager to get moving again. Juan de Aguilar said he personally would be willing to stay one more day in the event that Muniz came back, but Simon Lucero objected. "No. We've waited enough." The others signified agreement. Yes, they had waited enough.

Just before they saddled up, an incident left Escalante once more doubting whether they were indeed the first white men to come so far north.

An old man had been brought down from the mountains, where he lived by himself in a cave. He had seen much and knew the way north better than Jose Maria. He spoke through one of the chiefs, who in turn spoke through Cisneros.

"You shall see much more with me as your guide than you would ever see with him," said the old man, pointing to Jose Maria. "There are men living beyond us who are neither Comanche nor Uintah. They are not Indians at all. They wear blue clothes and speak a language that is not Ute. They worship different gods."

The shriveled old man had hardly any teeth, but his eyes were so bright with the joy of description it was a while before the party noticed he was blind. Even Jose Maria listened in silence to his recital.

"I'm sorry, old man," Escalante replied, "but how can a blind man guide us? Even if we could look after you. If we find these so-called blue-clothed men, we shall be indebted to you for sharing your knowledge with us."

Escalante went to his pack and pulled out a strip of ribbon for the old man. He received the gift with delight and bowed with great dignity to Escalante and the others.

And so it was with great sadness the Uintah Indians watched the party leave, waving stiff-fingered good-byes. They chanted their Spanish prayer as the white men rode into a fresh swallowing mist, grey as the smoke on the day they had ridden into the valley. All thought of sun on the fields and meadows, on the bright blue waters of the lake, was forgotten. The sun would return, but the Indians suspected only the slowly turning wheel of memory would ever bring back the white men.

The rode southwest, men and beasts strung out over a quarter of a mile. The line sometimes bunched up on itself as a caterpillar does. Escalante announced they would forgo the side trip to the vast and legendary salt sea across the Timpanogos Sierras to the north. Winter was leaping on their backs. If they hoped to reach Monterey before snows filled the mountain passes, they could not afford to stop or take side trips. Everyone accepted the decision. The disappearance of Andres Muniz had increased their urgency to be on with their mission.

Jose Maria was a good deal more capable than Silvestre had been. He could follow game trails and he rarely led the party in great wandering circles. He was a shy, upright man, but at times the party missed Silvestre and his one-eyed silliness.

Cisneros no longer rode at the head of the column, but kept to the rear beside Laughing Bird. Lucrecio hardly seemed to notice his brother was no longer among them. The others wondered where he might have gone, sometimes with a pang of regret. Cisneros was good at languages, but Andres had had the gift of tongues as well as good humor and great competence.

Cisneros and Laughing Bird were now speaking Spanish to each other. Escalante noticed this one afternoon and real-

ized Cisneros must have been teaching her. She spoke with
such precision and spacing that Escalante wondered whether
she actually knew what she said. Speaking broken Castilian,
sitting her horse so straight, she seemed almost prim.

"How. far. do you. think. a river. is. from here?"

"Why do you ask?" Cisneros asked.

"Water. I can. smell. I think. one there is. close."

Cisneros nodded. "Probably."

And soon they reached a river, just as Laughing Bird
predicted. Escalante was deeply impressed. What sharp nose
and ears she has, he reflected. He wondered whether the
ability to smell water could be learned.

The sky was dark with the promise of rain, clouds so
dense and purple all other colors became delicate traces.
Ducks flew south down the sky as though pulled by invisible
strings. The party followed the river, entranced by its sounds
and sights. Miera guessed that it eventually fed the Colorado
River. Just before a cold, damp darkness descended, they saw
a grove of cottonwoods and a spring and they camped
for the night.

Cisneros sat at the base of a cottonwood talking to the
Indian girl while they ate supper and watched the last frag-
ment of sunset disappear.

"Where do the clouds come from?" the girl asked. Her
Spanish stumbled. "How . . . how large—Is how say it,
large?—do you wonder they are?"

Cisneros smiled at her, his heart inexplicably sinking.
How pretty she looked, how demure, with the gloom making
her features seem fine. "I feel so bad sometimes about teaching you Spanish."

"Bad," she repeated.

"It's a hurt in the heart," he tried to explain. "Since
I've taught you Spanish, I can now speak to you of love
as I would speak with my wife. It makes the betrayal seem
all the more treacherous. In Spanish, I tell her I love

her. It doesn't seem right that I should be using Spanish to tell you the same thing.''

Laughing Bird did not comprehend. Cisneros sighed, then went on, talking to himself as much as to her. "You make me know my own sins. I see myself in all my weakness and fear but do not seem to care. How do you do this? Is it because you are so strange?''

"Strange?"

"Yes, but familiar too. More familiar than my wife. You have enchanted me, brought out my base feelings. Sometimes I wonder how it is possible to love two women."

The girl grinned and for a moment Cisneros was afraid she had understood what he had said. He looked over his shoulder, then back at her. Her eyes were bright but blank. No, she had understood nothing. She had just tossed Escalante a smile.

"You have made me know the error of my ways and miss them all the same," he went on. "I cannot see any longer what I once was, except in memories of my wife. My sin is enormous, though, and I have taught you Spanish as penance for my delights. Eventually we shall be able to talk with ease, and then I shall be lost."

"Spanish." The girl smiled hugely.

When it was completely dark and the others had drawn their bedding closer to the fires, Cisneros and the girl embraced. However, they did not let their urges go further for the moment but lay placidly in each other's arms.

The girl put her hand on his chest, twined her fingers in his doublet. All thoughts of Estella, Zuni and the wrath of Escalante went away.

A crow lifted from the cottonwood above Cisneros' head and into the night, cawing. All the cottonwood branches were full of crows; the darkness was their blackness. He imagined a very large crow, he and Laughing Bird lost in the feathers of its breast. There were no stars, he noticed. They were all obscured by clouds.

He reached for her, and she slid her hands into his doublet in a manner so proprietary he had to smile. He let his own hand stray over the cool slimness of her thighs. She made a noise, a tiny baby grunt. He felt the small of his back loosen. She slid her legs over his leg and he could feel the delta of her coarse hair. A warmth and a wetness were evident there. She had moved between his legs and begun to ascend his chest, rocking back downward to engulf him. He let his legs go flat and was swallowed up inside her.

She was moving above him, pressing down with rhythm. His throat was parched and his own breathing rustled with the sound of leaves. Leaves did rustle past his ear in a spiritless breeze. The Indian girl was making tiny, childish sighs and grinding against him with a purpose.

Then he rolled on top of her in the blanket. Cool air hit the sweating flesh of his bottom like a gentle slap. Something had stirred him at the deepest root of his heart. He had never felt like this, even with Estella. Their passion erupted all at once and their breathing grew hoarse. All the blackness had lifted away. The crows were gone. There were colors now in the darkness, and a single star.

They lay covering each other with soothing caresses. A few distant coughs sounded from men dozing by the fires. Cisneros panicked. Oh my God, they've heard us and they're laughing. Then he realized this was guilt. Nonsense. They're too far away to hear us anyway.

From far off in the darkness, winding across the land like a thread, came the almost human howl of a coyote.

They camped for the next two nights without water and one of the horses died. Cold night winds now swept through the tawny grasses and the light seemed to have totally changed. One day at dusk, after a brief rainstorm the sun came out and they passed through a change of country. There were some bushes no one had ever seen, with a berry very much like the chokecherry. The sun appeared and brilliantly lit everything.

Escalante had moved away from the column and was holding his face up to the dying light. The horses, brushing through on a trail barely two feet wide, released the pungent odor of chamisos and threw up a tantalizing haze.

Where do these trails lead to, Escalante wondered to himself.

On impulse, with the rest of the party easily within sight, Escalante took one of the trails branching off from the main one and rode down a shadowy draw. He could see from the way these soft hills were formed that a prairie lay off in the distance. He would reach this, he knew, no matter which trail he took, and so he proceeded with very little care. He rode down the draw and under a tree into a thicket of willows. He got excited, thinking water was near, and pressed his horse through the willows, which had already turned gold. He watched for the large antlered moose, which they had often surprised. Escalante had seen one break up the pack train and nearly cripple a horse.

He pushed through the willows into an open space that in spring was probably a pond. Several Indian women with baskets of berries were seated among the grasses.

Escalante's horse shied, tumbling him through the air. He fell heavily on his shoulder but was not hurt, only stunned. Looking up, he saw three Indian women. They had bones in their noses and their hair was plaited with leaves and grass.

"Who are you?" Escalante asked in every language he knew.

They shook their heads as though shaking the sound of his voice away and retreated into the willows. Escalante stumbled to his feet and followed them.

"Come back. I'll not harm you." The willows were snapping at his face. He could hear the women ahead of him as they hurried through the brush. Their voices did not seem unkind.

"Stop. I come in the name of the Lord. Stay still. I come in peace."

The bushes seemed tall and springy in this section of the meadow, and they slapped his face harder than others as he pushed a path among them.

Escalante suddenly wagged his head in exultation and broke out laughing. With the problems of Dominguez' health and Muniz, he had not had a good laugh in days. He realized that he missed mirth when he had none as some men miss their wine.

Escalante rubbed his chin, fancying the women were playing hide-and-seek with him. If they were playing with him, perhaps they would also welcome contact with him. He sensed no hostility or reluctance, only good nature playing itself out in the hiding game.

They clearly were not frightened by his appearance, and this awakened old doubts. Why didn't they find him frightening—unless they had already seen or heard of white men?

But ah, Escalante sighed, of course. Our Uintah hosts would have spread the news of our presence and our coming among all of their neighbors.

All right, Escalante chuckled. A game they want; a game they'll have. He leaped into the air and bumped sandaled heels together, the air billowing beneath his robes and giving him the feeling he was soaring. He felt as good as he had playing games as a child. He was euphoric; the feeling was restorative. "Putting it simply," he cried aloud, "I feel great."

As he had at times before, Escalante believed God was the wilderness and the wilderness was God and he had made a good choice for himself in loving both.

In the spirit of the game with the women, he began thrashing about the weeds, growling and scratching his armpits, jutting out his lower jaw and showing his teeth.

All children love a friendly monster, Escalante thought, and perhaps these women are still children enough to love monsters too.

I'm an ape, he thought. They've never seen an ape. I'm a friendly one, though, and friendliness is what matters here.

Away among some scrub trees Escalante heard giggles. Three figures broke from the greenery and fled, screaming in glee fueled by mock fright. Their wet wash trailed behind them.

"Arrrghnnnngh," Escalante roared and loped after them, lifting his hem to clear his ankles so he could make speed. He shook with laughter as he ran. How like my grandmother I must look, trying to run in a dress, he thought. Another laugh shook him. Grandmother could probably run faster, too. He prayed none of the other men would show up and see him making such a fool of himself.

The three women ran on, looking back, shrieking and bounding like does. Escalante stopped, panting. There was a fourth. Where was she? Escalante dropped into his hunting-ape crouch once more. He leered and lurched. He scratched his armpits. He spun about and rubbed the top of his head as though he were the stupidest ape ever to swing through a tree. He cupped one hand around his chin and the other hand around his elbow. He frowned and growled and mixed in whatever words he felt might be appropriate. "Now where can that woman be? Why won't she come out and let me catch her?"

The woman herself answered. A giggle sounded from beyond a fallen willow with a trunk as big as a sewer main.

"Ah ha," Escalante cried. He hoisted his rough wool skirt one more time and ran toward the willow. He hurdled it; normally it would have been an easy flight for him. This time his hem caught on the point of a broken branch. Like a ball on a short string, Escalante was jerked to a stop in midair. As the cloth parted he plunged down into the shrubbery on the other side of the willow trunk.

The landing was soft. The woman yelled and then gasped as her breath whooshed out beneath his weight.

"Ah ha, I've found you," Escalante shouted. In wriggling about to lift himself from her, Escalante only tangled both of them further in his robes. Somehow her head was caught against his groin inside the loop of his rope belt. When he tried to pull the rope loose, she twisted herself some more and her face pushed against Escalante's feet. She bit a big toe. The two rolled over and over down an incline, grinding the woman's soggy laundry into the soil. When they finally stopped rolling, she was still somehow tangled in his robes and rope belt, and he was captured in muddy tangles of washing. Their faces were only a few inches apart.

Escalante was on top of her, his feet twisted up with hers. Some of her many braids were stretched across her face to form a sort of mustache and beard.

Escalante imagined his breathing had suddenly stopped. She was a beauty, riches enough for any man. He studied her face. The woman seemed to have quit breathing also. She was examining him in turn. His Franciscan skirt was ripped and the shreds were blowing about his waist. Escalante felt scorched where his bare thighs were rubbing hers. The cool of the breeze and the stickiness of their skins, moist with sweat, diverted him.

She smiled then and suddenly bit his nose.

Escalante at first thought it was only more of the play he himself had initiated. Then he realized it was more than that. She made no effort to move his body from her own. Escalante realized there was something powerful about the moment and the meeting, something physical.

He felt the sun warm on his back. Neither of them moved. Whatever happened next was up to him, Escalante realized, child's play or lovemaking. That was the clear message. She parted her lips to show white teeth and pink tongue.

Escalante was startled by her directness, so free of guile. She was not seducing a priest for the sheer mischief of it, nor acting out some fantasy of finding God. She didn't even know what a priest was.

Escalante smiled. She smiled in return, puzzled by his silence and delay. He had to decide. What was he going to do with this ready woman with teeth as white as pearls? Which road would he choose with her? Child's play or love play? Wisdom or foolishness?

He knew he still had one other choice: neither.

He could turn passive and priestly and not even touch the woman. Stillness and passivity were always effective. He had learned it long ago in defending against unwelcome advances.

"Lord," he muttered, "I find priestliness just beyond my reach at this moment." It had been a long time since he had been with a woman. Cisneros' affair had often touched him with the awareness of his own needs.

What might the saints and martyrs have done? Put their hands into a fire, Escalante grinned, that's what they'd have done.

He made his choice then. He responded hotly to the woman's wiggling and wrestling, feeling as though he were suddenly bursting with aggression. She responded with a laugh, wicked and encouraging.

He pulled her to him and enfolded her in the tatters of his robe. He would put his hand into a fire later. At that moment, the woman's skin against his own was heat enough. Escalante chuckled at his joke. The woman laughed too; she caught the mood if not the meaning.

The joking soon ended and Escalante took the young woman into his strong arms. She discarded the little she had on and proceeded to do the same to Escalante. She loosened his robe and let it fall away from his muscular body. She sighed throatily as she fingered his chest. She soon let her tongue do most of the work and Escalante was released into a world of passion he'd not known for years.

He soon rolled onto her and engulfed her mouth with his own. He marveled at her rounded breasts and gently flicked the nipples with his tongue. Soon they were both ready and she parted her legs to meet his hardness. They reached the heights of passion in a powerful explosion and she held onto Escalante as though she feared she would fall off the world if she let go. As the intensity of their union subsided the beautiful young woman hummed sweetly and began rocking her body against his.

Chapter 23

Long after the girl had departed Escalante sat where he was, savoring the afterglow. The other Indian women had come back to peer through the willows at him, but finally they had drifted away and Escalante was left alone. The setting sun was crisping the leaves of the willows in a nearly audible way. He got up to depart only when the head of his horse appeared. His eyes focused and he stared at the horse, which seemed to have come back for him. It was getting late, he realized, but the presence of the horse made him enormously happy. Something in the universe cared for him.

When he swung into his saddle he noticed the stickiness in his groin. He should have been marinating in guilt as Cisneros was, he knew, but he found that he could not flog himself, even for God, with honesty. He banished guilt as an enemy alien.

He laughed again, reveling in the euphoria of insight.

"I'm two Escalantes, by God," he told the horse. "I'm Escalante, lusty and wise in the ways of the world and the minds of men, my own mind in particular. And I am Escalante the devout, every bit as superstitious and childlike and as much in need of a stern God as the very people I come to serve.''

He rode on. ''And my two Escalantes constantly strive for dominance of me.''

And finally, ''I've known both my Escalantes separately for years. Why have I just now met them both together for the first time?'' He laughed once more. ''What a revelation to come from rolling in the grass with an Indian woman.''

He called out to the clouds. ''God, Your Worship, is this Your doing? Is this Your way of teaching me something about myself? Are You telling me I must choose one Escalante or the other?''

The horse moved on, carrying Escalante without guidance, but the priest did not notice. He was still reasoning. ''It's as Dominguez told me in Santa Fe, a long trip in the wilderness is enlightening. I may yet learn which Escalante I am and which one can serve God best.''

It soon grew dark and cold, but the horse had no trouble finding its way. Ambling through the chamisos, the animal sniffed out the rest of the party before Escalante even saw the fire. He heard unfamiliar voices and stopped to listen. He did not recognize the language either. He listened hard for hostile tones; he might better serve everyone by not riding in immediately. If these Indians were indeed hostile, it was best they not know of the enemy in the darkness. After a few moments he concluded that the voices were friendly and spurred the horse forward once more.

Indian men with the same near-Caucasian features as the women of the afternoon were grouped about the fire. They had bone plates in their noses and ears and several carried elaborate nets that appeared to be made of sagebrush.

Escalante dismounted and addressed Dominguez. ''So. Are these perhaps the blue-clothed Indians who aren't Indians at all, according to our guide? Rubbish. They're another of the many kinds we're going to find out here.''

''They do speak something close to Uintah,'' Cisneros

said, "but not the kind we've heard before." He had been speaking with a barrel-chested Indian who appeared to lead the group.

The Indian carried a metal lantern that gave off a gentle light through its design of pierced metal. The pattern startled Escalante, the lines were so typically Spanish. A question of familiar content disturbed him. How do Indians who supposedly have never met Spaniards design Spanish lanterns?

The pitch torches were giving off a wonderful cedar smell and the lantern glowing so civilly reminded Escalante of his mission church in Zuni. Attempting not to be too specific and alarm the men, Escalante mused, "Where do you suppose they found such a lantern?"

"The hermit Marquez had one like it," Cisneros recalled.

"Yes," Lain agreed, "but these aren't white men, although they could fool me in dim light, with their beards and their fair skin."

The Indians told them they were camping nearby. They were a hunting party, far from their home village.

"Strange that these Indians are bearded," Miera said suddenly.

Escalante laughed. "You've just noticed?"

"Of course I have not just noticed. But I've just considered the meaning of the beards. These men might be part Spanish, or at least European. Most Indians don't have beards. And what about their blue clothing?" Miera persisted. "We've not seen any Indians wearing so much blue before, either."

"In any case, they don't seem as friendly as the Uintah and may decide to fight. We must try to bring them the word of God, but be on your guard for the least sign of hostility." Escalante turned to smile at the Indians as he finished speaking.

The young priest did not make an entry in the expedition journal that evening. He sought Dominguez instead. "I have to ask you to hear my confession, Father."

"Escalante, I can see that this is something serious. Don't tell me. It is possible that you could have found temptation even out here?"

"Just come away from the others with me and I'll tell you. I found it, all right."

They stopped beside a stream, the moonlight rippling brightly on the gentle current. Escalante knelt before Dominguez. "Bless me, Father, for I have sinned." He spoke frankly of his afternoon with the Indian woman.

Dominguez heard him, absolved him and levied a penance of five thousand Hail Marys. "And I don't care if it takes you a year to say them. You deserve far more than that. I'm dismayed and angry with you. I'm sure God is too."

"God will forgive me, Dominguez. It's his job."

A few minutes later they were companions once more, their feet swishing in the chill stream water, their sandals forgotten.

Dominguez spoke reflectively. "The more I know you, the more you worry me. When men sin, we're supposed to suffer and repent. You sin and you repent, but you never really suffer."

"If you mean, do I feel guilt, no I don't. I did once though. There was one woman in particular when I was at the Convento Grande in Mexico City."

"Mexico City." Dominguez repeated the name fondly as if speaking of someone he loved.

Escalante put his face into his hands, remembering. "A certain Dona Tranquila. Nothing ever passed between us but pure love. It happened shortly before my final vows. I was seventeen."

"That's when it usually happens to young men: just before final vows. It's an almost predictable hazard of the priesthood."

"She was older, twenty-five. Can you imagine considering a woman of that age older?"

"When you're seventeen, twenty-five is considerably older."

"She broke if off and asked her family to return her to Spain for an extended visit with family in Valladolid. I threatened to leave my order and follow. She clamped her hand across my mouth to prevent me from speaking such nonsense and scolded me:

" 'You're not in love with me as much as you're afraid of commitment to your priesthood. You're only weeks from ordination and you are suddenly filled with fear. You doubt yourself and your calling. Well, don't use me to pry yourself loose from your vows. Have the courage to do so on your own, if that's what you finally decide you must do.'

"Then the last thing she ever said to me was, 'We have never even so much as kissed, you and I, so there's been no carnal sin, only a small one, if loving each other is a sin at all. And the truth is, Silvestre'—she called me that—'you really do not wish to leave the priesthood. You are it and it is you. And we both would indeed be sinning if we took you from it. You'll never forget your Tranquila, but you'll be glad forever that you didn't follow your foolish and uncertain heart for me. You're going to be a fine priest, a different sort, I think, and sometimes unpopular with superiors, for you have proud and headstrong ways and you think for yourself. But you'll be a fine priest one day, possibly even remembered in history, while others more conventional are forgotten.' "

"She was wise beyond twenty-five years, Escalante."

Escalante raised his face from his hands. "I was crushed for months, the unhappiest ordainee with the darkest secret in the history of our order, Dominguez." He looked at the stars. "But do you know what happened? I came to realize Dona Tranquila was entirely correct in all she said, and I thank her to this day."

Dominguez started to speak again, but Escalante waved his hand. "Let me finish. When I finally confessed this love, I was told I should feel an enormous burden of guilt. But I didn't. My conscience had cleared as soon as I decided to stay with the priesthood. And not to bore you with long explanations and rationalizations, I have never felt guilty since, after being with a woman. Repentant, yes, since I believe God would prefer I not do it, but not guilty. I'm a man of physical desires, which I control most of the time. But occasionally I do not. I believe sincerely that God understands my need. In return for this indulgence, I seek to serve in the way I know best, helping others to see the greatness of God in the forces and monuments of nature. Dominguez, once I confess and repent these affairs, there is no remorse. I am free. I don't think God would want penances from us if he did not intend to wipe the slate clean each time we pay them.''

Escalante kicked at the water in the stream. ''And Dominguez, I couldn't go about God's business in the wilderness at all if I spent my days wallowing in my sins. Does that answer your question, why I sin and repent but do not suffer? A priest who is always suffering is useless.''

Neither spoke for a while; then Dominguez sighed. ''Yes, that explains it. But I'm one of the old-fashioned ones, so for me that does not justify it. . . .No, no, don't speak. Now you let me finish as I let you. You confuse your own will with the will of God. And you compound your sins by refusing to ask his forgiveness. Falling in love with a woman is a little thing, Escalante. If one does not act on the love, then I think God can tolerate it, as long as you love Him more. But fornication is something else, a truly grievous mortal sin. Once is supposed to be enough to damn you to hell. And you think you can do it over and over and remain stainless?''

''I don't know.''

''Holy Mother of God,'' Dominguez roared, ''the Inquisition would have a fine time with you.''

When he had quieted, Escalante asked, ''Aren't you ever tempted by anything?''

Dominguez chuckled. "Yes. Lately I think constantly of that sherry we had at dinner that first night in Santa Fe." They laughed. "And that's been about the extent of my sinning throughout my life, Escalante. If I have one sin, it's gluttony. Do you know, I've never been with a woman."

"Perhaps you ought to try it sometime before you die, old-timer," Escalante joked.

"Never mind," Dominguez snorted. "This is no time for humor. Don't even speak of it. You are a vulgar gypsy sometimes."

"But much as you hate to admit it, you like me," Escalante replied.

"Touché, Father, touché," Dominguez chuckled.

The next morning there was frost on the ground that the horses licked and savored, and a wild and sweet pungence in the air from the smoke of the Indian fires. The party prepared to move on. The Indian women were among them now; they had come into the camp during the evening. Several wore muddy garments. They giggled at Escalante, Lain noticed. "What do they find so funny?" he asked.

Escalante choked on his coffee. "Either I'm the handsomest man they've ever seen or they've never seen a man wearing a dress before."

"But only the four with the dirty clothes are making the fuss," Lain pointed out. "Especially the one with the big white teeth."

"I don't understand it either, Lain," Escalante fibbed.

Then awareness dawned on Lain and his mouth formed a silent "O." Escalante's heart sank when he realized that Joaquin Lain understood, but the next moment Lain was smiling and had laid his fingers across his lips.

At the head of the column muster, the Indians were saying good-bye. They told Dominguez they wished to live among the Uintah if that would bring them closer to this God the priests spoke about so much and so lovingly. They would do so even though relations with the Uintah had not always been friendly. The expedition moved out an hour later.

They came to a place where the hills ended and the white land stretched before them. The vastness was intimidating. Shielding his eyes to scan the distance, Miera remarked, "It's almost enough to make one believe the world is really flat after all, as the sailors believed before Columbus. I myself almost fear we'll fall off if we proceed."

The sight of it discouraged Escalante. He leaped down from his mount and touched the tip of his tongue with some of the white earth. He sighed. "Why this, O Lord, why this?" The sand had a terrible brackish taste.

Standing, he told the others, "I've heard of these salt flats, but I never imagined they could be so vast. Bigger than that salt lake we heard of, I'll bet my last cigarro."

"That must be some precious cigarro," Miera joked. "You've wagered it several times now."

"This entire country must have been an ocean once," Escalante reflected. "Otherwise, how could there be so much salt in the earth?" Miera nodded his agreement.

That night, October 2, 1776, Escalante wrote in his journal that he had not the heart to push the men out onto the salt flats so late in the day with so little promise of sweet water anywhere in the land ahead:

> In the late afternoon light we imagined we saw water nearby after all, a lake or a swamp not detected earlier. We hurried to it and found imagination to be a traitor. What we had taken for water was in truth more of the same white terrain, parts of it salt, parts of it saltpeter and parts of it dried alkaline sediment. We moved on farther southwest over more salt flats about twelve miles. We eventually stopped because the horses couldn't go on without water. There was some occasional pasturage for them, but barely enough.

We have given the name Salt Plains to the land
on which we camp. We have picked up some amaz-
ing white sea shells. Do wonders never cease? Shells
clearly of the sea found a thousand miles from the
sea. We can only conclude again that there was
once a body of salt water here. . . .

The ruthlessness of the terrain was complicated by colder
weather. Some nights were bitter. Nonetheless, Escalante
welcomed the cold in a perverse way. "The colder it is, the
less water we'll need," he told Dominguez. "We won't
sweat it away."

That night they broke out the clothing from the winter
packs. And two nights after that, the cold and the short water
rations triggered the violence that had been brewing between
Joaquin Lain and his cousin Juan Pedro Cisneros.

Chapter 24

Cisneros was bringing dinner from the fire to Laughing Bird and Lain kicked out as he passed. Cisneros staggered and fell but somehow managed to roll onto his back without spilling the stew. He sat legs apart holding the bowl like a chalice.

Lain snarled, "Do you ever carry food to your beloved wife, my cousin, as you carry it to the slut?"

"I don't have to," Cisneros spat back. "I have peons such as you to carry it for me."

That was all it took. Lain rolled forward from his seat by the fire and landed atop Cisneros. This time the bowl emptied over both men.

Later no one remembered seeing Lain draw his knife, but it appeared in his hand. He thrust down with both hands. Cisneros shoved a fistful of stew into Lain's eyes and rolled aside; that was defense enough. When Lain's knife touched down, it stabbed only salty earth.

Cisneros wrenched a hatchet from a stump they chopped wood on. Eyes glittering, he very slowly backed off, beckoning Lain to come for him, holding the hatchet ready to open Lain's head if he dared to attack.

The two danced a sort of minuet, actually seeming to bow, teasing each other with kicks and reaching out with their weapons in choppy strokes that cut only air. The other men stood and silently formed a circle as though they welcomed the violence.

Escalante had been tending his horse, which had gotten salt under its saddle and been rubbed raw. When the shouting began he thought he might permit Lain and Cisneros to brawl without interference. Perhaps the fight would bring Cisneros to his senses. But when Escalante saw the knife thrust and the axe raised, he bellowed, "Stop!" He lifted his torn skirts and bounded toward the group.

He reflexively reached into the fire and yanked out a large flaming brand. He leaped between the two fighting men just as Cisneros swung the hatchet at Lain's shoulder. He missed, but Lain was off balance; he fell and supported himself with one hand while slashing with the other.

Cisneros was the first victim, since he held the advantage that had to be defused. Escalante swung the log like some blazing battle mace, hard against Cisneros' leather-vested chest. Cisneros reeled back and dropped the axe so he could brush away the sparks and cinders clinging to his clothing.

Lain saw him defenseless and leaped at him, his arm straight out holding his knife.

Escalante yelled, "No you don't either," and slammed the fiery club across Lain's wrist. The force of the blow broke the brand, Lain's charge and nearly his arm. He fell and rolled forward, dropping his knife in order to nurse his wound and slap at the sparks that had burst from the log and showered on him. He shouted that he had thought Escalante had come to help him punish Cisneros for his sins and crimes.

Straddling both men and feeling silly holding what was left of a burning log, Escalante prayed the rest were not deluded as Lain was about his intent.

"This fight is over," Escalante told them quietly, "and

any man who believes otherwise must account first to me and then to God for his foolishness.''

The others shuffled and Lucrecio Muniz tried to make light of the fight. ''They wouldn't have really hurt each other, Father. We'd have stopped them.''

''Stop talking rot,'' Escalante ordered. ''Now everybody get to sleep. If you behave like little boys you'll be sent to bed like little boys.''

There was hesitation as resentment colored the faces like masks in the glittering firelight. For a moment Escalante feared he might have accomplished not discipline but a mutiny.

It was Simon Lucero who spoke next. ''And any man who doesn't account to Father Escalante and God will have to account to me.'' He swaggered before them and cracked his whip.

Escalante was astonished. He would never have expected such support and good timing from Lucero.

''And I'll stand on a box to do it,'' Lucero added.

There was a moment of dead silence and then everyone was laughing, Lain and Cisneros included, and the tension dissolved. Everything was all right again for a while.

Escalante was not finished, however. He knew there was one more thing to be done to profit from the incidents of the night.

He spun Cisneros about and pushed him off into the darkness, shoving him hard between the shoulders each time Cisneros tried to turn or to ask, ''What is this?''

''What is this? This is something I should have done the day it first became apparent you were going to undo your pants for an adolescent Indian girl,'' Escalante growled between his teeth, ''that's what it is.'' They kicked up ghosts of salty dust as they lurched through the moonlight.

When the firelight was only a flicker far behind them, Escalante spun Cisneros about and hurled him against the trunk of a starved pine. ''This is far enough. What I say here is for your ears only.''

Cisneros smiled bitterly. "Spare me your lecture about Laughing Bird. I think I'd rather discuss her over hatchet and knife with Lain."

"Stop talking like a child." Escalante slapped him twice across the face, forehand, backhand. "And if you ever tell anyone that I have struck you to shut you up, I'll put the Inquisition on you." Escalante spun in a circle and faced him again, hands pressed tightly as if to squeeze out the words.

"Listen carefully, man. I'll say this only once. If you have to sleep with this child, do it. I've decided not to try to stop you and I'll see to it that no one else does. I'll leave it to you to answer to God and your wife, who will certainly hear about it. To keep order on this expedition—"

Cisneros interrupted. "I'll take her and leave the expedition if you just order it."

Escalante backhanded him again. "You will not leave this expedition. Since we lost Andres we need every man. And by God, I think we need her more than you. She has instincts about this wilderness that we'll never understand or develop."

Cisneros nodded, bowed his head and studied his feet.

"So. What I have to say is this. Sleep with her if you must. But take her off somewhere and be discreet about it. This exhibitionism can't continue. I won't have it. You are disturbing the others. They are jealous. There is bound to be trouble. I have heard talk that you're going to share her with them, whether you wish it or not."

"Over my dead body."

"That's what I fear. Lain came close to killing you tonight." He stared into Cisneros' face. "So this is how it will be. If you cause one more incident because you're not man enough to control yourself before the others, she will sleep, ride, eat, do everything from now on within arm's reach of Father Dominguez or me. You won't even get close enough to touch her hand. And if you insist on causing trouble anyway, you'll travel bound and gagged.'' Escalante turned his back and walked back to camp.

In the first bleak light of morning, Escalante learned he had lost one more man during the night.

"It's Jose Maria,'' Miera told Escalante. "He's just vanished. Poof. Like that.''

"He was disturbed to the point of tears over the fight between Lain and Cisneros," Escalante said. "Did you see him constantly crossing himself, even though he doesn't understand the gesture?'' Escalante tightened his lips. "Do you think the fight had anything to do with it? Frightened him off, perhaps, thinking he might be next?''

Miera packed his pipe and shrugged. "It's as good a guess as any. Does it matter why? He's gone and we need him.''

"Is there any point in looking for him, Miera?''

Miera shook his head. "He's like Andres. If he doesn't want you to find him, you won't find him. It's obvious he doesn't want you to. He wouldn't have left us otherwise.''

White chalk cliffs stretched for miles and the grass tasted so salty the horses wouldn't even drop their heads for a sniff. The sky had been striated with dirty clouds for days but it never rained, though it was often dark for a long time.

They checked the stars with Miera's astrolabe whenever the heavens appeared through the cover of clouds.

"I still have no idea where we are,'' Miera confessed to Cisneros and Escalante. They crouched in sleepless misery before the fire, the others all silent in their blankets. "We've kept turning west and then south and west and then south again, but nothing seems to free us from this terrain.''

One morning the clouds cleared enough for the men to see mountains covered with snow in the far distance. Miera didn't like it. "I wonder if that snow is there all year long, or is it fresh?''

"I think you know as well as I do,'' Escalante chided

him. "It's fresh. Winter has already come to those high passes in the sierras. At least we won't be thirsty there."

Nonetheless, the news troubled everyone into a state of quiet depression. Snow in the passes meant the way to Monterey would be much more difficult, if not impossible. They might have to take long routes around the mountains instead.

Their bowels were still tortured by brackish water and the horses were weak. The thought of turning back so clearly demoralized the men that Escalante called an early halt after traveling only twenty-five miles. The combination of physical and mental stress was proving too enervating for them that day.

Escalante once again felt bad himself and his gait was rocky from fatigue. Nevertheless he moved among them, forcing a steady step and easy-going manner, and aided those who suffered most with the salt sickness. There was not much he could do to make them comfortable, but he arranged packs for their beds, straightened their blankets and gave each some of the precious little fresh water left in the skins. Finally Escalante was too feverish himself to do more and he lay down with the others.

Dominguez watched it all from a low hill. Darkness was drawing across the plain like a curtain of dust.

The old priest stayed on the hill a while longer, amazed at his own well-being. Cisneros and the Indian girl had left to scout once more for water. Besides himself, they were the only healthy ones left.

Dominguez got up finally and started down the hill toward the spring. The gloom of darkness was beginning to depress him. He stumbled over something lodged in the earth and fell.

He dug out and examined the object, which was quite large and not easy to uncover. Turning it over and over in his hands, he was amazed to discover it was a Communion chalice. At first he could in no way believe this, but the more he examined it the more he accepted what it was. It was very old and was made of lead. He wondered how it had come to be there and who had brought it, and he recalled Escalante's suspicion that other Spaniards had indeed been there before them. He was convinced no Indian could have ever made such a chalice, not without knowledge of God and Christ, and only white men could have instructed them.

Dominguez said nothing about his find. He wanted to show it to Escalante and discuss its meaning first.

Then Cisneros and the Indian girl came back into the camp. Lain was feeling better and Lucero and Olivares were improving. Cisneros threw down two ancient rusted weapons. It was then that Dominguez called to Escalante and told him to get himself up no matter how woozy he felt. Something important demanded his attention.

Escalante was in fact feeling better. The sleep had helped. He was not convinced the alkali water was the cause of his illness. He had drunk very little of it, only the very minimum to prevent dehydration. He was running an intermittent fever and his lower right side just above his leg pulsated from time to time as it had in July before his seizure in Taos.

"We rode until we could see a change of country," Cisneros was telling the others. "We were too tired to go farther, so we came back. We think there is good water ahead. At least we saw trees."

Escalante wrapped his robes about him against a shivering chill. "What are these weapons you've found?" He was turning one end over end, trying to identify it through the rust.

"Pistols. Matchlocks again, I'd say. Very old. They remind me of that hermit and the weapons we found in his hut."

"How old, would you say?" Escalante spoke reluctantly, almost deciding he did not want to know.

Cisneros shrugged. "Perhaps Miera can tell."

But Miera was baffled too. "God only knows how old or where they came from."

It was then that Dominguez went to his saddlebags and brought back the lead chalice. "Here's something to stand our hair on end."

Escalante crossed himself. The thought that they were not the first nagged once more.

"Why lead?" Cisneros wondered.

"That's what disturbs me most of all, I must confess," Escalante answered. "Deliberate blasphemy, possibly, and the suspicion chills me. Who out here would know enough about God and His son to blaspheme in the first place? A chalice is supposed to be of silver or gold, not of lead."

Everyone discussed the possibilities and probabilities for another hour, with no conclusions that satisfied anyone. The theory of a long-ago, lost and unchronicled party traveling from Mexico to California came up again and again as the most likely answer.

Escalante's fever climbed again and the throb in his side took up its beat. He excused himself and walked unevenly back to his blankets, feeling sleepier than ever he had before. He prayed angrily that he be allowed to be well again. He swore to himself that it was his body and his expedition, and well or not, he was going to take both wherever he chose to take them.

Just as he was about to sleep, Escalante sat up so quickly his blankets flew off. Suddenly he felt wide awake. He called to his colleague, who was settling into his own blankets, "Dominguez, do you hear music? Far away?"

Dominguez cranked himself wearily to one elbow and listened to the night. He made it clear that he was only doing so to humor Escalante. "No, no music. Really, Escalante, how could there be music out here?"

Escalante listened once more. At first he heard only the sounds of night breezes and animals and felt foolish. Then: "There. You have to listen very hard before it fades away, but it's music. Reed instruments and something tinkling, I think."

"It's your fever you're hearing, Escalante," Dominguez insisted.

Escalante was stubborn. "Miera, do you hear anything?"

"It's only the wind through the trees and rocks, Father."

"Miera, get Laughing Bird out of Cisneros' blankets," Escalante commanded, "and bring her here."

"Only to set your mind at rest, Father," Miera grunted. He was back with Laughing Bird in a few seconds. Cisneros followed, nervously demanding to know what Escalante could need of the child in the middle of the night. He was trying to appear confident and in command, but he was obviously fearful that the priests had decided to separate them.

"Stop blathering, Cisneros, and ask her this for me." Escalante pointed out into the darkness. "Ask her, does she hear any but ordinary night sounds out there, far away?"

"Father?" Cisneros was puzzled.

"Just ask her!"

Cisneros translated. When Laughing Bird comprehended what Escalante wanted of her, her face took on the look of someone who has what someone else badly wants. The smugness made her ugly. She knows I need her superior senses, Escalante thought. She will charge dearly for this later, but never mind that for now.

Laughing Bird clapped both hands over her ears to demand silence from the others. She moved away from the group and tilted her head into the saline evening breeze. Her hair lifted and settled like a cape in the drafts. She turned her head one way, then another, as if seeking the direction of a sound. She paused for a long moment, then began moving her head slowly back and forth again.

What a fine show she makes of this, Escalante thought, taking far longer than she must. Never mind that, either. Let her do what she must, only come up with an answer. He wondered whether it had been fever. He now heard only breezes stirring up dust devils from the salty land.

Laughing Bird wheeled and faced the group. She clapped

her hands to her ears once, then made fists, thumbs pointing down toward the earth.

Miera took out his pipe. "Try to sleep off your fever, Father. She hears nothing but the night."

Escalante was catapulted from a dream of a man screaming by the awareness that a man really was screaming, and in great fear.

It was Simon Lucero, bowlegged in his undergarments. Lucero's mouth was an open funnel tilted toward the sky, screaming and screaming.

The others were sitting up and kicking blankets aside, yelling, What? What? Lucrecio Muniz was shaking Lucero, trying to soothe him with rough comfort.

Lorenzo Olivares was the only one organized, pulling his armpit holster into place and checking the priming and loads of his pistols.

It was a dawn of grey light. Escalante needed a moment to focus on things. When he looked beyond the camp, he saw what had frightened Simon Lucero so.

Escalante almost felt like screaming himself. A ring of men leaning on pikes, swords and long muskets circled the camp, a tight ring leaving no way out.

Escalante noticed several things in sharp detail. The weapons they carried seemed very old and cumbersome. They wore random skins and cloths, and capes of woven grass, but their clothing bore a hint of European tailoring of a time gone by.

They started walking then, tightening their circle. They numbered a hundred or more, Escalante estimated, pretty heavy odds against his own nine.

Then a coldness not born of fever shook Escalante. He was not surprised to see the men suddenly there in the pale dawn light. It was as though he had known they were coming for a long time. They were not Indians, but white men.

Chapter 25

Escalante had kicked off his robes during the night to cool his fever. Naked he had slept; naked he arose. The cold wind whipped him and brought on violent quaking. But all in all he was feeling better.

He reached for his clothes. They were in a ball. Wind-blown leaves and alkali dust filled the creases. Then he snorted. There was no time for fine tailoring. He ran wearing nothing but sandals and skin to the long mule packs that held the carbines he had smuggled from Santa Fe against the expressed wishes of the Bishop in Mexico City.

Escalante did not pick at buckles and knots; he had plucked Miera's short cavalry sword from its saddle sheath as he ran and he butchered the fastenings of the packs.

The ring of strange white-skinned men grew tighter. Escalante could make out nostrils and eyeballs. Some had mustaches and spade beards cropped in a clearly Spanish manner. They seemed in no hurry, as though they expected no serious resistance.

Escalante tore open the oiled skins swaddling the carbines and tossed the first to Miera. Olivares, still the unshakable one, was snatching open the packs with the powder and shot.

Escalante shook two rifles in the air. "Come and get them. Form a square. If it comes to shooting, five load while four fire, one on each side of the square."

Escalante pushed a weapon at Lucrecio, but he did not even try to catch it; it hit his chest and fell.

"Lucrecio, for God's sake, don't stand there like a dummy, man. Pick it up and use it."

"Father," Lucrecio babbled, "you're naked."

Escalante picked up the carbine and shoved it at him again; this time Muniz took it. "You've seen naked men before, Lucrecio."

"Never a priest, Father."

"A priest has nothing special to show. Now go." He turned Lucrecio and pushed him at Miera, who slapped powder and shot into his arms.

Olivares was pulling the horses to the square, the tethers of two in one hand, three in the other. The horses went up on hind legs, pawing air, frightened by the shouting and running. They seemed to smell the strange figures of the ring and not to like what they smelled. They communicated their fear by lashing their heads back and forth.

Olivares forced them to form a square of their own. "Get them down," he told the others. "They're our barricades. We'll shoot from behind them."

He yanked down on the bit of a big brown stallion so hard the bit drew blood. Another horse balked, standing despite Olivares' cruelest twisting of the bit. Aguilar brought the animal down by whacking behind the knees with his carbine.

Escalante shouldered the remaining bundle of carbines, took up two other loose ones and ran for the square. He had never been more frightened in his life.

The strange men were now at the perimeter of the camp. Escalante noticed another detail. Many of the tunics were cut broad in the shoulders and bore epaulets in the tradition of Spanish military dress.

"I should be one of the riflemen," Simon Lucero called to Miera. "I'm the only one short enough to stand safely behind a horse. I'll have the steadiest aim."

"By God, you're right, little man. You can shoot, too; I've seen you." Miera handed the first loaded weapon to him. "No one fires until ordered," he called out. "We'll wait till they fire on us."

"What are we going to do, let them sit on our laps before we defend ourselves?" Lucrecio Muniz was feeling tougher.

"That's the idea, son," Miera answered. "The closer they are, the easier they are to hit."

Escalante was grateful for Miera's calm and gave thanks that there was one combat veteran with him. Miera was also an experienced quartermaster. He said, "Here, Father, bare skin is no uniform for fighting."

Escalante had been loading but he looked up. Miera had brought him his robe. As he pulled the garment over his head, Escalante heard Lucrecio demand to know why they weren't firing on the enemy. Miera explained again that they did not know they really were the enemy as yet.

Escalante stood proudly and yelled in Spanish, in Uintah, in Hopi, in English, repeating himself in every language he knew. "Halt. That's as far as you come without identifying yourselves."

They halted; it was eerie to see. One moment they were walking and the next they were not.

Escalante was baffled. "Which one of them signaled? Did anyone hear a command?" No one had.

No matter, Escalante considered, as long as they've halted. He turned about slowly, studying the ring for sign of traps and treachery, but saw none. "All right. Good." Then he shouted, "I want you to know this. We come in peace." Escalante called out "peace" in all his languages again.

"We show arms only because you surprised us and we don't know whether you're friend or enemy." He repeated the word friend, over and over. He tried to determine who were the leaders but could not. No one was distinguished by manner, position in the rank or dress. Escalante paused and continued. "Peace. If you do not fire, we do not fire. If you do, we shall—and our weapons are superb. Peace, I say again. Peace."

"Don't forget, '*in nomine Patris*,' Father." Dominguez whispered.

"In the name of the Father and the Son and the Holy Ghost, amen," Escalante obediently called. "Peace."

Then there was quiet as the two groups faced each other waiting. The dust blew, crossing the circle, making Escalante spit grit from his teeth. His fever was down and he felt strong, a fortunate change when it was needed most.

"They just stand there and look at us. Why don't they say something or do something?" Lucrecio hissed.

"They're being polite," Lucero replied, sighting down his carbine across the horse's ribs, "allowing the guests to have the first word."

"Well, I don't have the patience for it," Lucrecio asserted. "This is driving me crazy. A fight I understand. Waiting I do not."

It was Miera who interrupted. "Wait now," he kept saying. "Wait. I think it's going to work out all right. No firing until I order it. Wait now. Do you understand? Wait." His tone was soothing.

"You're crazy to hold fire," Lucrecio yelled. He squinted down his rifle barrel, sighting on a grass cape.

Miera kicked the barrel. The flintlock mechanism gouged a deep bloody track across Lucrecio's cheek and the bullet wounded a tree.

Escalante looked at Miera. He didn't want to shoot but he shared Lucrecio's jitters.

"They haven't fired on us as yet." Miera still used the

same soothing, low tones. "If killing is what you want, they could have massacred us all in our sleep." He rubbed his chin. "Now, they're tough and they're not to be trifled with, but I'm sure they're not looking for a fight. Remember, it's their territory and we're trespassing."

In the silence there was only the sound of wind and the wheezing of the horses.

"I'm with Lucrecio," Juan de Aguilar whispered. "I don't want to wait and find out." Escalante took Aguilar's rifle barrel in both hands and turned it down. "We'll listen to Miera and take the chance. Keep the weapon ready but don't shoot before the signal." Escalante added quietly, "I'll personally castrate you if you do. Understand?"

Aguilar made a face and nodded.

Miera was rubbing his chin. "Father, which one of that bunch would you say is the leader?"

"I can't tell, Miera. That one there, perhaps. The others seem to stand apart from him, as if they're showing respect."

"I'd say the one off there just a hair to the left of that needle rock. There's something about him. He's older."

"Like you yourself, you mean," Escalante snorted. "Not every old-timer is a leader, Miera."

"You'll both soon find out," Dominguez interrupted. "Look."

One of the strangers was breaking the circle, walking toward them. He slung his musket under his arm as he came, lowering the muzzle and holding it by the barrel.

"He's coming in peace," Miera sighed.

The man was young, about twenty, Escalante estimated. He stood just outside their position. He smiled brightly and held out both hands palms up, signifying peace. He turned slowly about with the eloquent body of a showman. Inspect me. Look me over. I am probably a freak to you, as you are to me, but I enjoy seeing and being seen.

Then he moved closer. He pointed at one of the prone horses and nudged it gently with his toe. The horse raised its head, eyeballs huge; it was still frightened. Olivares pressed it back to the earth.

The man made a sweeping gesture at the men standing silently in the ring. He laughed lightly, then abruptly stopped and smashed a fist into his palm.

The suddenness and intensity of the movement were startling.

"I think he means our horses are a joke as protection and he and his forces could smash us any time they wish," Escalante guessed. "What do you think, Miera?"

"It looks that way."

"I say shoot him, then," Lucrecio blurted. "Let them know it will cost them one man at least, before they even try."

"We're not even sure they want to, as I keep telling you, Lucrecio," Miera explained again. "It's a game. He's trying to scare us. And besides, they probably could run all over us if they decided to. But I still don't think they want to. Not now, at least."

Dominguez crossed himself. Several of the others did the same. Escalante thought, we are all staring at this beautiful young man like a bunch of peasants seeing a prince for the first time. "All right, everyone," he said quietly. "Stop the gawking and stand tall. We'll give him some intimidation in return. And some style. We can put on a show, too. Miera, your carbine. Snap it to me, smartly now. The way you'd do it at parade inspection."

Miera straightened and his arms shot straight out. The carbine flew to Escalante and stung his palms as he caught it.

Escalante pointed at a tree some fifty yards off. He made certain the young man was watching the right one. Then Escalante put the carbine to his shoulder and blew a large bird off a branch without even seeming to take the time to aim. The horses flinched at the blast.

Escalante blew away the powder smoke and chucked the weapon easily back to Miera. Next, smiling as the young man himself was smiling, Escalante pointed to one of the men forming the ring, then another and another and another, and finally swept his arm to include them all and drew his finger across his throat.

The young man's face tightened. It was Escalante's turn to smile, strut and parade. He jumped across the body of a downed horse, held his arms up and turned about before the young man to allow a reciprocal inspection.

The stranger did not appreciate it. He had lost face before his own. Escalante's one gunshot had as effectively killed his image of strength as the bird. Nonetheless he smiled as if Escalante's ploy meant nothing.

Smiling when you don't mean it, Escalante thought, is the essence of diplomacy, here as in Europe.

The rest of the men in the ring showed no response to Escalante's shot, apparently to spare their emissary and themselves humiliation. The young man turned to address them all. He raised his arms to command their attention and stood beautifully straight. His black hair shone in the sun.

When the man spoke, Escalante felt excitement fill him. He had never heard such words. They sounded like Spanish spoken with an Indian dialect.

Questions filled Escalante's head, and many explanations presented themselves. Number one among them was the one that postulated earlier unrecorded visits by Spaniards untold years earlier.

Dominguez and Miera also noticed the bastard child of Indian and Spanish and leaned forward to listen, hoping concentration would reward them with understanding.

Escalante studied the man while he spoke. The build and features were clearly European, not Indian. The skin where it met the clothes was so fair as to be called white, but the face and hands were rather dark. Perhaps he was just bronzed from the sun.

The young man finished speaking and gave a signal, whereupon the rigid disciplined circle became a broken, un-

even line, then dissolved altogether. The men approached
Escalante's group, their weapons inverted as the first young
man's had been. They seemed eager to meet the strangers.

"I think we were both wrong about the leader, Father,"
Miera said. "It's not the old man or the other one. This one
here is their chief, and he so young."

"Keep the weapons ready and the horses in place until
we're certain this is no trap," Escalante answered. "The
Hopi win battles by pretending peace, then knifing you while
your back is turned."

They watched the men walking toward them and silence
once again became the only communication. The groups studied each other, the Spanish gawking like children, the others
maintaining more restraint and coolness, but still aboil with
curiosity.

After minutes of silent study, it seemed as though everyone had something to say. The roar of voices reminded
Escalante of the bullfighting in Mexico City. He decided to
take a chance on peace. His horses were standing unattended.
There were so many of the newcomers surrounding each of
his own party that organized resistance was no longer possible. Defense would be a joke. Escalante slung his rifle muzzle down to indicate that neither would he attack. He looked
to Miera for support. "I think things are all right."

"For now, Father." Miera did not sling his carbine. He
seemed to hold it carelessly but his finger was near the trigger
and the flint was still cocked.

Juan de Aguilar was host to four more. They were
bending over to examine the locks of his weapons and stroking the wood and metal as soldiers of any two armies meeting
in the field have always done, Escalante realized. They were
talking only inches from each other's faces and it was plain
that Aguilar did not understand a word of their Spanish-Indian
sounds, as they did not understand Aguilar.

Escalante did not like the way some looked at the new
saddle carbines. "They want them for their own, all right,"

Escalante remarked to Miera, and decided to put his own at the ready after all. He no longer felt like putting so much trust in peace.

Simon Lucero collected the largest gathering of all. The new men apparently could not believe in a full-grown man only as tall as a child. They looked at him and touched him gently as though he were a breakable toy.

Escalante became aware that Olivares was standing beside him; he too held his carbine ready. The flaps of his two shoulder holsters were tucked back so he could get at the pistols. "You've got something on your mind, Olivares. What is it?"

"Look at their belts, Father. See what's hanging there on some of them."

Escalante felt bitter liquids rise in his throat. The dark patches that had at first seemed to be pouches of some kind were human scalps. One on the leader's belt was tied in a braid fastened by rosary beads.

A bent silver crucifix caught the sun. Just like the one Convento Grande gives all the new priests when they take their final vows, Escalante thought. Now, where on earth. . . ?

Chapter 26

Escalante and the young chief stared at each other. It was as though no one else were there on that useless alkaline earth. The young chief's mouth curled, but not in a smile. There was no affection there, though there was respect. I've beaten you the first time we meet, Escalante thought, and you're not going to let me forget it or rest yourself until you've gotten something back from me. Let me make your way easier.

Escalante smiled and extended both hands to grip his and then bowed. The chief understood and was somewhat mollified. As one leader to another, Escalante had showed respect.

The young priest refused to think about the human scalps, of which the chief wore three. He would worry about them later. And the rosary.

"We can begin our friendship with names." Escalante spoke in Spanish first, then in Uintah and Hopi, knowing full well he would not be understood, but demonstrating that he knew Indian languages and Indian ways. "My name is Father Escalante." He pointed to himself with exaggerated gesture, as a mime might do. "Father Escalante."

The other understood. "Father Escalante."

"You have a good ear," Escalante commented. "Your pronunciation is nearly perfect."

The other responded with a name that sounded so Spanish that Escalante sucked in a breath in astonishment. Colonel of what, he wondered.

"Coronel," the young man repeated. "Coronel." He did not gesture and point to his chest as Escalante had done. He had his dignity to consider, Escalante supposed.

Escalante was aware of an intuitive kind of understanding shared by himself and Coronel. He imagined he knew the man's feelings and wishes to a degree, even without talking or signs. He was convinced Coronel understood him too.

So when Coronel looked at a small rise of ground like a throne by the stream and gestured, Escalante knew exactly what he meant. Coronel wanted to sit and talk with Escalante alone in a meeting of two chiefs. Escalante bowed and the two leaders stepped together over to the knoll.

The rest was not so easy, for even though there was intuition and understanding between them, specific information required struggling with words, hand signs and symbols drawn in dirt with sticks.

Messages were missed and misunderstood. In frustration they often had to wipe the air clean with their hands and the dirt clean with their feet and start over. But each enjoyed the struggle for communication. In Coronel's strange-sounding words Escalante could gradually discern more and more of the shape of his own native tongue. In the end Escalante knew who Coronel and his people were, and the knowledge filled him with wonder.

One of the first things Escalante learned was that Coronel's knowledge of the history of his own people was sketchy and at times fanciful. No one had ever kept records, and oral tradition is naturally altered over the years at the whim of the tellers. This much was clear, however:

Two hundred years before, white men such as Escalante and his eight, in numbers as many as the rocks on the plain, had come through the land searching for the fabled Seven Lost Cities of Gold. They had trusted themselves to the lies of an Indian who persuaded them to appoint him their guide. This party had failed, according to legends, having bogged itself down in wars with the tribes.

"Where did all of this happen?" Escalante asked.

Coronel replied with a sweeping gesture that took in the entire region. "In other words, you don't know precisely where." Escalante knew he would receive no better answer.

Coronel continued. The main party of white men returned south to Mexico under its gallant leader in the bright metal armor. But some of them, with permission of the leader, elected to continue the search for Cibola. They found only great hardship. They suffered through two fierce winters and remained alive only with the help of some Indians who showed them how to find food and build shelter against the worst of the weather.

In the third spring, according to Coronel's legend, the white men in armor decided for reasons now lost to memory to stay forever among the Indians. Coronel suspected their ordeal had bent their minds and made them mad. For whatever reason, they stayed, took Indian brides and melded Indian ways with their own. However, they never lost their pride in being white. They refused to become part of any tribal society, instead forming a clan of their own.

One of their ways was to make war and take what they pleased. It was dangerous behavior from a small, new clan and met with resistance from most of the tribes. The white clan was frequently put to rout and even slaughtered in spite of their firearms.

However, those who survived seemed to be the stronger for the hardship. They would lie low until their numbers were replenished and then go out to plunder again. Legend held that the whites had passed through several such cycles of victory and defeat, decimation and repopulation.

Eventually they became totally nomadic. They shunned

the security of the pueblos for the risky but exhilarating life of raiding. They kept some prisoners as slaves and killed the others.

"And this is what you are today," Escalante commented, his head reeling. Coronel nodded. So was Attila the Hun, Escalante reflected.

Coronel sensed Escalante's disapproval and hastened to explain that they had also kept many of the legendary customs of the ancestor whites such as dancing, politeness and horsemanship. They still preferred the dress of the ancestor whites and still treasured the old weapons, which they had carefully kept clean, oiled and repaired.

They had learned by much trial and error to manufacture the black sand from powder of burnt wood, dried bird dung and a yellow mineral boiling out of hot springs to the west. Ah, thought Escalante, impressed with their ingenuity, the charcoal, saltpeter and sulfur needed to make gunpowder.

However even with the utmost care, the weapons were one by one exploding or wearing out, Coronel sighed. They had far fewer weapons now than he remembered as a boy. He hoped one day to find some way to replace them, he said; his envy of the newer guns was naked again.

Coronel described himself and his clan as rich in ceremony. They celebrated feasting, hunting rituals and fertility rites. "You will see them during your stay with us," Coronel promised.

Coronel's assumption that they were going to stay jarred Escalante. It sounded more like an order than an invitation. He did not like the finality in the voice but he kept his peace on the subject.

Throughout, Escalante had avoided looking at or mentioning the scalp with the rosary and crucifix at Coronel's waist. But finally Escalante saw a place for it in their dialogue. "Do you know the significance of this object?" Escalante fingered the shining icon.

Coronel did in a way. He replied that his people told

legends of a Great Spirit and a Son who had died for all of the men in the entire world. The silver object Escalante took so seriously was, Coronel recalled hearing, the symbol of them. However, Coronel had never seen any manifestation of this Great Spirit or His Son. Further, he knew of no one who ever had, even in their legends. True, he knew these gods had been important to the ancestor whites and that they had believed with their very souls. However, their faith in the religion of the ancestor whites had grown dim over the decades and now even seemed a little silly.

The Great Spirit of the Indians seemed more real. He manifested his presence through harvests and horses, famines and plenty, all things a man could easily see and understand. The Great Spirit's likes, dislikes and wishes for man were clear.

"Have you kept none of the religious practices of the ancestor whites, then?" Escalante was thinking of the lead chalice and the rosary on the scalp at Coronel's waist.

Coronel thought about the question. Yes, some; those that were fun, such as the drinking of fermentations and pretending it was blood. Christianity? What was that?

Escalante, with conversion in mind, cautiously asked whether Coronel would like to hear more about the Christian God of his own forebears and come to know of His love and mercy and the promise of eternal salvation through His Son.

Coronel smiled and shook his head no. There was something so positive and secure in the negative response that Escalante decided not to press it, as he and Dominguez had pressed other Indian groups they had met thus far along the way.

The others have been impressionable and ready, he thought, but Coronel and his group are not. They're sophisticates by comparison, European cynics whose conversion cannot be bought with gifts of cloth and beads and promises of love and salvation.

Escalante wondered aloud, "Over the centuries, have

your people in their wanderings ever preached to other Indians of these things? Have you traded weapons or religious
articles that still might exist today?''

Coronel shrugged. Of course.

Escalante marveled at the ways of God once again.
Coronel's people had actually been pagan missionaries of the
faith, and if Escalante contemplated long enough, he could
believe that God Himself had appointed them.

There was but one area in which Escalante and Coronel
could reach no agreement. ''These scalps.'' Escalante touched
the one bearing the rosary beads. ''Do you take scalps often?''
From time to time, Coronel answered, but only from brave
men. The scalp of a brave man contained much power.

Escalante asked, did Coronel ever wonder if this was a
false belief and a justification for useless viciousness and
bloodletting? Could Coronel not understand that perhaps they
held no mystical power at all?

Coronel studied Escalante's face intently and shrugged
elaborately. He could not even begin to comprehend such an
absurd question.

Escalante inscribed nine crosses in the dirt. Then he de-
stroyed each by digging in his stick. Coronel pondered; then
his mouth split in a smile. He understood.

He shook his head. No, he and his clan were not interested in wiping out Escalante's party. They did not seek a
war.

Coronel and Escalante had built a small vocabulary of
shared gestures and words by this time, and had begun to
understand each other. Coronel managed to convey that he
and his clan could have killed Escalante's group at any time
during the night, and in fact still could if they were willing to
suffer heavy losses to Escalante's fine weapons, simply
because of great superiority in numbers.

Escalante pressed the question. ''That means peace for
now, today. What about peace tomorrow? Will we still be
friends then?''

Coronel shrugged. Who could promise such a thing? But remember, sometimes fighting was the only thing that mattered. That philosophy gave Escalante an unpleasant feeling in the gut.

They were reaching the end of their talk when Escalante asked, "Have you any idea who your ancestor whites were?"

No.

"They were Spanish."

"Spanish," Coronel repeated, forming the sounds exactly as Escalante did.

"Yes, Spanish. As I am. As the rest of my men are. We're all related in a way, even after two hundred years."

Coronel's expression did not change. Escalante realized the man had no notion of what Spanish meant or who the Spanish were. Furthermore, he did not really care.

Escalante was just dropping off that night when he realized he still had no idea where the rosary with its bent crucifix had come from.

Both groups spent the morning at the spot where they had met but settled in separate camps to rest after the excitement of the meeting.

Escalante's group bracketed him at the breakfast fire. While the meat fried and the coffee brewed, they all demanded to hear about the solitary meeting Escalante had had with Coronel.

Escalante told them, "This may be the most astonishing thing you've ever heard." He paused, then began. "They're not the survivors of some party lost long ago on the way from Mexico to California. They're a mix of Spanish and Indian. The white heritage seems to dominate throughout. And they go back further than we have imagined."

He paused again. "To Coronado. Nearly two hundred and fifty years ago."

He was chuckling at the changes bending their faces; he must have looked the same to Coronel.

They were all familiar with the explorations of Francisco Vasquez de Coronado to the areas now called New Mexico, Arizona and California. In 1540 he had set out to find the mythical Seven Lost Cities of Cibola with their streets of gold.

Escalante assumed they knew Coronado had eventually aborted the search. He recounted how some of the party were fired by the lies of a Plains Indian they called the Turk, who told of still another wealthy kingdom he named Quivira. These men elected to continue the search and Coronado approved. They split from the party and tramped off, never to be seen or heard from again. It was assumed they had been butchered by Indians or had perished in the mountains. After a few decades hardly anyone even remembered who they were.

"Well," Escalante concluded, "they didn't find any gold but they didn't perish either. We've just met their children" —he stood and pointed—"and there they are."

Dominguez whispered, "And this accounts for the mysteries of the lead chalice and the Spanish weapons found in places where no Spaniards are supposed to have been as well as the rumors of God that seem always to precede us among the Indians."

"Yes."

"Breeders with Indians and themselves," Miera frowned, "until their souls and even their language were lost. Incest." He shuddered.

"Among other exotic practices, so it would seem," Escalante agreed.

"I cannot express the fear and uncertainty I feel at this moment," Dominguez put in. "Who back home in Santa Fe will believe such a thing?"

"Possibly nobody," Escalante conceded.

"I can think of no better time to lead you all in prayer, for our souls and theirs," Dominguez suggested.

"Ours first, please, Father?" Aguilar piped up.

They formed a circle on their knees. Dominguez told them they had never needed God on their side more than they needed Him at that moment. He adjured them to add their prayers to his and then began, "*Pater noster*. . . ."

After they had prayed, Escalante confirmed Miera's earlier mistrust. "I've asked Coronel for reassurances. All he would say is no war for now. They have no reason to and they don't feel like it."

"But?"

"But he couldn't guarantee beyond the next five minutes. I say this: if he suddenly feels the whim to fight us, he will."

"That's what's wrong with giving young people leadership," Miera snorted. "I get the feeling that fighting isn't a horror to them any more, it's a way of life. He'll fight us even though he doesn't consider us an enemy, for the sport of it, simply because he wants to. For the sport of it. That's the most terrifying enemy of all."

"And because he wants our weapons, Miera. Never forget he needs them. If we're careless he'll try to take them."

"Then why don't we get out of here? And if they try to stop us, shoot our way out?"

"Because these people probably need God's word more than any I've ever met."

Later that afternoon, Coronel assured Escalante that he and his clan would show the Spanish the best way through the mountains to the West before the winter snows built walls across them. But first the explorers would stay with the clan to enjoy its hospitality and share its customs.

Once more Escalante had the feeling Coronel was giving an order, not an invitation. Coronel did not even seem capable of imagining refusal.

Escalante suggested to his group that they all go along without argument. The possibilities for conversion of the clan were too exciting to pass by. Dominguez agreed. His eyes glittered and he bit his lips as if tasting the challenge.

Juan Pedro Cisneros and Lorenzo Olivares objected. "We've got a little experience out here, as you do, Father," Cisneros argued, "and we say we shouldn't put our necks in the noose pursuing lost Christians for their own good. It's not for the good of ours. They're going to turn on us and you know it."

Miera broke in. "I too say we shouldn't go with them. But this isn't the moment to run, not with a hundred of them practically sitting in our laps."

"And now I outvote you all." Escalante's jaw was set. "Whether we have a chance to run or not, we're not leaving until I order it. Forgive my bluntness, Cisneros, Olivares, but our mandate is to convert Indians as well as to find the way to Monterey." He looked toward Coronel's group spread out on a gentle slope. "No one I've met in my life needs God more than they do."

"But does God need them?" Lain snorted. "I'm not even sure they have any souls left."

The subsequent behavior of the clan was so correct it made their fears seem foolish.

There was no hostile word or gesture on the march. The clan's hundred followed at Coronel's young, boisterous pace. Escalante and his group were left to trail along with their pack animals. There was no sense of being required to follow, but still, Escalante felt they were being carefully watched along the way. He was certain some were following unseen, put there by Coronel to block any sudden retreat.

Late in the afternoon they entered a valley between embracing hills. Here the soil was sweeter and the water fresher than what they had just left. In the distance there was another lake, not nearly so large as the lake of the Uintah, but still good-sized. And here, too, was the encampment of the white Indian clan, where the women and children and animals lived while the men went foraging.

Miera was impressed by the organization of the camp and the lean-to hide shelters. "The layout is a good defensive military model. Julius Caesar would have liked it. Strong points for defense, all the supplies gathered safely toward the center, all of the horses grazing where they can be guarded easily and pulled inside in a hurry."

"Don't forget Coronado was a military man," Escalante reminded him. "And Coronel says they've kept all of the best ideas of the ancestor whites."

The clan bore no Indian or Spanish name; it traditionally refused to take one. The early ancestor whites had preferred to call themselves simply the clan, or so legend said. And what had been good for one generation had been good for the next for nearly two hundred and fifty years.

For their own security's sake, Miera chose a campsite separate from the clan's. It was on a rise abutting the valley wall, fairly defensible, with a good field of rifle fire and a rough exit up the steep hills to the outside in case they were boxed in and had to run. Escalante thought the choice was brilliant.

Several days passed as the clan enriched life for Escalante and the others with gifts of fish and fresh meat. They told Lucrecio Muniz and Simon Lucero where to find good grazing for the horses and mules. The clan women came to do the washing.

Escalante noticed the women were as handsome as the men, tall and fine-featured. They had inherited the best looks of both Spanish and Indian bloodlines, with the white predominating.

Joaquin Lain, Lucrecio Muniz and Juan de Aguilar were strongly attracted to the women. It seemed odd to Escalante, but it was Simon Lucero who attracted most of the women.

They were charmed by his size and sought him out to pamper him. It was to Lucero they brought the choicest cuts, for Lucero they scrubbed the clothes the hardest, and to

Lucero—as early as the first night—that they most readily offered their personal favors.

Escalante and Dominguez had free access to the clan village. They went every day to talk of God and Christ and the bliss of Christian salvation. Everyone they talked with listened politely and at length, but no one seemed to comprehend. Dominguez was especially discouraged and angry. "We can talk until we're blue and they encourage us, saying yes, yes, yes, and then in the end they ask, 'Jesus Christ *who?*' Are we stupid or are they?"

Escalante smiled wryly. "Neither. They're just not about to listen to us. They're not such primitives as all of the others have been. You forget. They've got Spanish blood."

Escalante noticed that one particular woman came to him each morning and each night to work and to cook. Her hair was always heavenly scented and her smile suggestive. She often brushed against his robes. She would touch Escalante's silver crucifix as if hoping he would take time to explain its symbolism. At times she caught and held his eyes. The sexual signal was as loud to Escalante as a church bell on a Sunday morning.

So was the possibility of betrayal. A man with a woman in his blankets was an easy capture—or an easy murder by the woman herself.

Escalante went to Coronel. He thanked him for being so generous with his women. He requested, however, that Coronel relieve the women of their work in the Spanish camp. Such pampering was not good for discipline. They would get soft and lazy. Surely Coronel, as a leader of men himself, understood this. No insult or offense to the clan was intended.

Coronel flashed his fine white teeth. Of course he understood. The women never came up the hill to the camp again. Lain, Lucrecio and Aguilar were merely disappointed, but Simon Lucero fell into a fit of depression at the loss. Never had his lust been so satisfied and he feared it never would be again. Escalante never admitted he was responsible.

Juan Pedro Cisneros was openly amused at this development. Once again he was the only one with a woman. Lain snarled, "Don't be a fool, flaunting it." And for once, Cisneros took good advice.

Escalante told Miera he thought the night watch should be tightened up and that every man should sleep with two rifles loaded and ready to cock in addition to his sidearms. Miera applauded the idea.

Twice Coronel took Escalante hunting. He showed Escalante how to steer a horse with his knees across the flats after deer and to know just when and how the deer were going to swerve. The herd would slow down just enough at this moment for a man to drop a riata over a pair of horns and send the owner crashing to the earth. This part of the life in the valley exhilarated Escalante. Coronel was a good companion and Escalante liked him as much as he had ever liked any man. It was too bad he could not trust him.

Several times Escalante asked Coronel to keep his promise and show them the way through the high sierra to the West. On each occasion Coronel smiled and said there was time, plenty of time.

Escalante noticed too that always there seemed to be some of the clan at the mouth of the valley. Perhaps they were only grazing their horses or fishing the brooks that shone there, but Escalante had the feeling they were lookouts, stationed there to detain the Monterey expedition in case it tried to leave before Coronel permitted it. He could not be certain, though. There was no incident to point a finger at.

Escalante chose to accept the risk of attack inherent in staying rather than the risk of trying to leave. Besides, there were souls to harvest.

In balance, Escalante found more to keep him in the valley with the nomad clan than to drive him away.

The problem of breaching the clan's cynicism and putting them on the road to God fascinated him and he wanted to stay until he licked it. He found support in Dominguez, who said he had known from the start that the road to heaven was more important than the road to Monterey.

But finally there occurred an incident that showed Escalante how mistaken he had been.

Chapter 27

Two men ran up the hill to the camp with a summons from Coronel. There was to be a celebration of the full moon that evening. The nine Spanish and their two Sabuagana were to come and share it with the clan. Again it was more command than invitation.

Only three went down the hill that night: Dominguez, Miera and Escalante. Little Lain and Laughing Bird sat in darkness outside the camp. Their rifles rested on logs and aimed at the path from the village. They had the horses with them, saddled and ready to go. The pack mules were loaded and milling in the dark.

This was Escalante's idea. In case the clan planned to use the full-moon celebration as a diversion while they raided the camp and seized the firearms and livestock, Escalante wanted everything out of their reach and ready for flight.

"We'll explain to our hosts that the others are sick with bad-water fever again and that it's past the children's bedtime." He nodded to Olivares and Lucrecio Muniz. "Watch everything with Miera's glass. At the first sign of mischief, you two send Little Lain and Laughing Bird up that hill and over the top with the supply train. You'll come charging into that camp like conquistadores to get us out.''

''I still think we should just ride from this valley as quickly and quietly as we can,'' Miera growled.

''It's you who weren't certain they were enemies, remember? No. No running while it's possible we may convert them. We'll stay a few days longer and ride just a little faster to Monterey later, if we have to.'' He wagged a finger at the clan village. ''If we do have to run, we'll all meet again at the fork of those rivers about ten miles south of where we first met Coronel's people. There's fine cover there, and it's back the way we came. We've been so eager to go on they may never guess we didn't.''

The celebration had already begun. Escalante could hear tinny, reedy music as they approached and he recognized something about it and grabbed Miera's arm. ''There, that's it. That's what I was hearing the night you all said I was delirious, just before the clan surrounded us.''

At the edge of the lake, where wind blew foam onto the beach, men and women danced stiff and aloof on a floor of pine from just-cut trees. Musicians grouped at one end played on lutes, reed flutes and small drums crafted in European patterns but lopsided in shape and producing warped sounds. The steps and dance patterns were very old. They were nothing Dominguez or Miera recognized, and both said they had danced old dances as children.

Groans mixed with the music, but Escalante could not determine the source. He thought it was probably part of the ceremony.

He stopped abruptly, filling with sudden anger. The others drew up beside him and formed a line abreast. Escalante had seen that full-blooded Indians were pressed beneath the planks, howling and sobbing with pain. The priest had not known there were prisoners; he had not seen any. He could only assume they were recent captures, brought in by riders who had arrived that afternoon—perhaps expressly for the ceremony, he grimly reflected. The music continued, the dancers performed their wooden *danse basse et macabre*, and the groans seemed almost palpable.

The dancers could all have been out of some old Spanish court except for their grisly floor and one other thing: they were almost naked. His anger receded and Escalante stood stock still, mesmerized by the madhouse aspect. They wore ruffles of grass like shirts of a style Escalante had seen only in sixteenth-century court paintings.

The women also wore skirts of grass, but their loins were exposed and painted white. The men for the most part wore no nether garments; their genitals too were accentuated by paint. They carried antique matchlock pistols in their sashes; Escalante could not help making the comparison between their firearms and their naked members. He found the thought grotesque as the costume.

The women had draped their heads with rotted mantillas rewoven with their own long hair; their faces too were painted white.

The dancers occasionally grinned and their lined faces looked like skulls as they paced their slow steps. Most of the audience was talking behind fans, some sitting in chairs whose designs were perverted from the European. Some of the dancers waved to a hideous old woman who sat with her legs spread and fanned her naked crotch. Under the dance floor the glittering anguished eyes and the cavernous screaming mouths were truly alone at the party.

Escalante was aware of being shaken by his shoulders; Miera had seized his cowl. Escalante saw the hand coming at his face and took two backhand slaps across the mouth. Miera shrilled with disgust, "There! Is this enough reason to get out of here, Father? Enough?" Escalante shook himself and nodded. He wondered where his mind had gone, watching the dancers. "Forget their souls, Father," Miera raved, "they don't have any."

The dancers continued prancing and dipping by the light of the ancient lanterns. Finally Escalante surrendered to revulsion when he saw the sodomy in the audience. His temples throbbed with his anger.

"Father," Dominguez spluttered, "if this is what they see as the tradition of Spanish court dance, I shudder to think of the Mass they must hold with their lead chalices. Miera's right. I concede. There's more here than nine men and two children can ever do for God. We leave *now*!"

Escalante saw Coronel watching from across the floor, his lips curled back over his brilliant teeth. When he knew Escalante had seen, he began to laugh.

Coronel shoved several of his dancers aside. He knelt and struggled with one of the half-round pine logs. His muscles showed cords under glistening skin and his knees trembled straightening up under the dead weight of the log. He hurled it aside.

Coronel knelt again and reached into the space below the logs. He pulled and more logs rolled. A handful of hair emerged, then a head with growling mouth, the torso, the entire body, crucified upside down on a cross of logs. Coronel wrestled the crucifix erect.

He pulled the hair to turn the head so that Escalante could see the face.

Escalante felt the scream swelling deep inside himself.

"Curse you and all your kind and your immortal souls to hell forever. *Amen*!"

Coronel grinned and shook the head by the hair again. Even though it was upside down and shimmering with lights and shadows, there was no mistaking the agonized, still-living face of Andres Muniz.

Chapter 28

A horse came flying across the dancing platform, its feet neatly tucked up. Two more followed, tethered behind the first. They kicked bark chips loose from the logs and bludgeoned the dancers aside. Some of the lanterns lofted through the air and fell on the leather lean-tos, whose skins turned into fireballs.

Escalante saw Coronel go down under the first horse. Andres Muniz on his cross was lost to Escalante. It seemed he had been thrown against a group of dancers, scything them all to the log floor. Escalante tried desperately to think of a way to rescue him. He just hoped Andres was in good enough shape to sit a horse. They would lose enough time hacking all that rope off him, without having to pack him out of there besides.

Another four saddle horses came charging onto the lake shore from the other side, a man riding low to the lead's neck. Escalante recognized the Cossack style of Olivares. "Climb on! Climb on!" the horseman bawled.

Escalante pushed Dominguez into a saddle; the horse was running before Dominguez fairly had a grip on it.

Escalante threw himself across another saddle on his stomach and flailed away, battering dancers with his fists and the first organized clansmen with his feet. He blessed Lorenzo Olivares and God, who must have told him he was needed at that moment. He saw that Coronel was up again.

Olivares threw a set of reins to Miera. Two of Coronel's dancers tried to wrench the leathers from him, pressing Miera to the animal's side. Using the horse as a support, Miera kneed one of them in the whitened groin—nice obvious target—as the other wrapped himself about Miera's head and shoulders.

Escalante had righted himself in the saddle and a certain ferocity set in. He turned his own mount back to grind to paste Miera's assailants. His robes flapped in the air behind him. He canted up from the saddle, standing straight on one leg in its stirrup. He came on at full gallop and held his arm straight and rammed the swarming Indian's face with his fist. He felt the impact and the snap of the neck deep in his wrist, elbow and shoulder.

The man was lifted off Miera's back, arms everywhere, before he crashed to earth. Escalante boosted Miera into the saddle and then more clansmen were on them both.

Fires raced to engulf still more leather tents, moving faster than Escalante had ever imagined fire could fly. A woman ran from one with an infant, her hair aflame. Sparks from it rode the wind across the dancing platform and ignited the dry grass gowns of the dancers.

Escalante saw that the way out along the lake shore was filled by Coronel's men moving toward him shoulder to shoulder. They held ropes to snare the horse's feet. The horse sensed the danger and did not want to charge them. He reared and wheeled and Escalante felt himself slipping from the saddle.

Miera was also in trouble. He had picked up three more men who held onto his legs. Miera had both his own and Dominguez' reins in one hand and was pushing his fingers into a pair of white-ringed eye sockets.

To Escalante's great relief, Dominguez suddenly came to life. He stood in his stirrups, grabbed the lower jaw of one of Miera's attackers and twisted until the man had to let go or take a dislocated jaw. Miera and Dominguez were moving again. The third man fell from Miera and horseshoes opened his face.

Escalante heard Joaquin Lain and Juan Pedro Cisneros yipping off to his left and then primeval bellowing. A longhorn galloped red-eyed and panicky, running with head low, trying to shake off the man who wiggled on one horn. Blood ran down the man's legs and the horn into the beast's eyes.

Three more bulls followed, pulling down tents with their racks. One of the clansmen pushed his matchlock's muzzle against the side of one and fired. The ancient weapon exploded and killed them both, but before it died the bull arched its back and kicked and left another enemy with one foot twisted backward.

Escalante heard more hooves and hollers. Lucrecio Muniz and Juan de Aguilar were pounding along behind and whacking fiatas against the animals' flanks. "This way, bull, this way!" Aguilar turned them to the dancing platform, where the crowd was thickest. The logs had caught fire and some of the dancers rolled across them like sausages on a grill. A few lucky prisoners managed to crawl out from under the logs.

Escalante had seen stampedes. A rampaging longhorn was a terrible engine of war. They used their horns as pikes, prodding with their lowered heads, kicking or trampling anyone they couldn't gore. To Escalante it was exquisite horror. He ached as a priest for the injured and killed; on the other hand, as a man betrayed, he thought they had it coming. And once they had tasted battle, the bulls, never good-tempered, were full of rage and blood lust.

Escalante choked on smoke and wiped the sting from his eyes. The noise was enough to pain the ears. He followed on the tail of a huge old bull that cut a swath through the clansmen, who trampled each other to get out of his path.

Escalante looked down into the bell of a matchlock blunderbuss and at the face with squinting eyes that seemed to float over the muzzle. He kicked the weapon. The muzzle flash scorched his face, and as he slapped at the pain he almost went out of his saddle again. Ahead he saw Miera rallying the others, circling an arm high above his head, turning his horse in circles so it would be difficult to grab. Escalante galloped to them, elbows out wide. He was spitting soot and the eye on the scorched side of his face was puffing and closing. "We're not leaving Andres behind."

"Andres?" Lucrecio howled.

"Andres."

"Here? Where? Let me get him."

"You and I are going back and take him from them." He turned to the rest. "If everyone goes, we have a fine chance. But whether we all do it or just Lucrecio and I, I promised you I'd never leave anyone behind if I could help it. Anybody else coming?"

He did not wait for an answer. He turned his horse. Lucrecio was there beside him, face alight with battle lust and glee at the news. Escalante heard the others shouting and grouping behind him. He shook his shoulders and settled in his saddle. He knew they would come.

Fires incinerated the shelters. The smoke, as much as it made Escalante want to retch, provided fine cover. Formed into a wedge with Miera at the point, they moved among the fires and back to the dancing area, where Escalante had last seen Andres Muniz with Coronel.

The herd was still doing its terrible work. The clansmen tried to bring the bulls down by throwing fishnets across their horns to tangle and confuse them, but the cattle shredded the nets and mobbed the throwers. Most of Coronel's men were too busy with the stampede to think of the men on horseback.

Miera and Escalante went side by side through the flames flickering up from the log platform. A burning man blindly clutched at the horse's legs and missed. Coronel was still

there, raging at almost the same spot, holding Andres Muniz'
hair in a cruel twist. The wooden cross had fallen with
Andres on top, cruelly lashed to it. It was as if no one had
moved, and Escalante realized how few minutes had passed
since it all began.

Escalante saw a firearm blaze and heard its flat boom.
Olivares' head seemed suddenly to have been pulled backward. He clamped a hand to his forehead and black trickled
shining between the fingers. Miera ran his horse into the
formation. Its hooves chopped at chests and thighs as Miera's
stabbing sword moved in swift figures of eight, down one
side, up, down the other. He hit the man who had shot
Olivares. The man fell, his head cloven.

Olivares was rocking back and forth but staying erect.
"It's all right," he was shouting. "All right." So much
blood, Escalante thought; it does not look all right.

Then men and horses rode into the crowd screaming.
The mounts did terrible damage with their hooves and the
men on their backs fought with grim single-minded purpose.

Olivares' horse stumbled and fell, but Olivares kept his
legs to one side so they would not be trapped under it and was
hanging on. The black streams from his head wound spread
spiderlike on his face.

Olivares rammed one of his pistols under a man's chin.
The face puffed out and split. His horse was barely on its feet
again before Olivares hooked his leg across its back.

Escalante pivoted in his saddle, tight with fear, feeling
sweat soaking his body beneath the heavy woolen garment.
He was looking for Coronel still. He had decided he was
going to drag him away too, if he could find him, along with
Andres, and end his perfidy and betrayal. Coronel was in
sight for a moment, face lined with rage, trying to climb over
his own confused men to get to Andres once more. Then he
was swept back by a movement toward the lake and Escalante
lost him in smoke and shadows.

Miera was hanging down the side of his horse now,

hacking the ropes that bound Andres Muniz to his cross. His sword point cut into Muniz' ankle and red colored the ropes. Miera hesitated for a moment, but Muniz yelled hoarsely, "Never mind that. Cut, man, cut." Miera swung his blade again and bits of rope flew.

Muniz kicked the last ropes free, then kicked his cross too, in reflexive rage. He stood for a moment alone, with no one near him.

"Andres," Escalante bawled. "Come on up." He extended his arm and Andres caught it with both hands. He dug in his heels with both legs slightly bent and used the forward momentum of Escalante's horse to catapult himself over the horse's back, riding Escalante's arm as a pendulum. Eyes full of tears, Escalante saw that Andres had done it very well. Good! He was not hurt.

Escalante felt the man hugging his waist. He yelled to no one in particular, "I've got Andres." He pulled the bridle hard to make the horse wheel, making certain the others had heard him. He saw that Juan de Aguilar's horse also had gone down in the charge. It was up again and facing off with Aguilar dragging behind, holding a stirrup with both hands. He was not struggling to remount, but letting the animal bolt and pull him free.

Miera was calling quietly, "Steady now, steady. . . . Form the wedge again. . . . We're going out the way we came in . . . In tighter there, Lucrecio, that's it. . . . Form the wedge. . . . Move only on command." He kicked an attacker in the head as he circled, primping the formation. Then he yelled, "All right—*now*!"

They moved ahead together. Escalante hurdled a mound of men trying to claw them to earth. He was blinded for a moment by smoke, which also robbed his breath. Then the horse was gaining speed and the air was clear and clean and the noise diminished behind him. No one blocked his way. He was out of the camp.

Escalante looked about. Miera was there, whacking one

last attacker with his sword. Lucrecio Muniz was riding to meet Escalante and shouting, "Big brother, big brother."

Escalante counted. They were all there, coming together. Dominguez, to Escalante's great surprise, was riding with great energy and daring through the moonlight.

Escalante exulted. He was shaking with residual fear, but he felt about as exquisitely excited as he ever had. He recalled hearing of a rare euphoria after combat. We've escaped, Escalante was thinking. Somehow we've really escaped.

Then a horse and rider came out of the darkness ahead. There were flashes of flame from a line of weapons.

Escalante veered his mount to avoid the other and he knew the turn had been too sudden and that he and Muniz were going down. Other horses and men hurled themselves at the group, splitting it. As he landed on his back, rolling to avoid being flattened under the horse, Escalante saw Miera and Dominguez lifting Andres between them and fading into the night. Lucrecio Muniz was using his carbine as a club against two Indians while Andres danced about trying to mount up behind him.

Escalante knew what had happened: Coronel had kept his guard in place at the mouth of the valley after all, and they were riding to assist in the fight at the camp. The two parties had collided in the night.

Chapter 29

Escalante was alone when day came. He was walking his horse toward the confluence of two rivers he had designated as a meeting place in the event the group was split up, as it had indeed been. Olivares had sent Simon Lucero, Little Lain and Laughing Bird there with the pack animals and spare horses when it was decided to attack the clan and liberate Escalante, Miera and Dominguez.

Escalante prayed he would find them all at the rivers. He no longer felt so exultant. In fact, he felt awful. Even with every person and every supply horse salvaged, the expedition would still be in trouble, he reflected. Coronel would almost certainly be coming for them. He wanted the rifles too much. Besides, the Monterey expedition had lost all of its cattle. They would have to live off the land. With winter coming, it would be increasingly difficult to find food. And to top it all off, Escalante was wallowing in guilt and remorse over leaving the Indian captives to their fate. There wasn't a single blessed thing they could have done, as he perfectly well knew, but he felt the burden anyway.

From out of nowhere, a lead ball struck Escalante's

horse, taking away half its head while it drank from a sour stream. It died and fell on Escalante in the water. The priest found he could not raise his head high enough to breathe. Lord, he thought, I do not want to be drowned and pickled in this salt stream under a dead horse. He braced one leg against his saddle and pushed. A brass tack buckle opened his ankle to the bone. A fan of red colored the water. His yell of pain came out as bubbles.

Free, Escalante floated belly down, lifting his head only as much as he had to in order to gulp down some air. He cautiously looked about, barely moving his head, trying to look as dead as his horse.

He heard the splashing of a carefully moving horse. Escalante imagined it lifting its hooves high from the water and easing them back in. Its rider was gentling it with faint whispers. A bend in the stream and the brush growing there separated them.

Escalante looked to the bank of the stream. There was no time to stand and run. Sheltering rocks and trees were yards away. The horse and rider would round the bend before he could hide.

Escalante took another deep breath and lowered his face into the water. He prayed he looked like a corpse. He became aware under water that the rider's horse was not moving. No sound of hoof against rock was magnified by the water. Escalante allowed his head to roll gently to one side. Water would move a dead man's head that way. He squinted, only for a second. Water filmed his eyes, but he could see the rider was alert, studying both man and horse. He was reloading before moving closer. Escalante let his face twist slowly back into the water. He prayed he was not floating into purgatory.

He opened his eyes. The enemy horse's hooves looked like four undulating sticks stirring up clouds of muck and plumes of bubbles. The clansman approached, keeping pace with Escalante's drift. The hooves sounded thunderous in the water.

Escalante prayed the man would not just shoot him in the back for safety's sake. Escalante tried to imagine the man deciding whether it would be a waste of shot.

Pressure built in Escalante's chest. He knew that in a few more seconds he would have to breathe again whether it was convenient or not.

He decided the man was cautious. If nothing else he was going to watch long enough to be quite certain that the man floating in the stream was, indeed, dead.

Escalante's chest ached and he saw square shimmering patterns. He knew there was only one thing left for him to do. He canted his body to one side, obeying the nudge of drift and current. He sculled and shot under the horse between its fore and hind legs and seized the man's left foot in the stirrup. He stood up in the water and pushed the leg straight over the saddle, left hand locking the knee and the right twisting the stirrup loose.

The rider in his leathers and grass cape had been leaning over the right side of his horse. Escalante just continued the motion and shoved him head first into the water.

Taking in great gulps of air, Escalante dived between the horse's legs and came down on top of the rider, whose foot was trapped in the stirrup. The horse leaped. Escalante felt a numbing in the hip and grunted. The beast had kicked him. He put the enemy between himself and it. The man was screaming, trying desperately to shake his foot from the stirrup. The matchlock lay in the water. Escalante's opponent was getting battered as his horse thrashed.

The foot finally jerked away from the stirrup and the man stood, feathers of water forming on his elbows. Escalante plunged toward Coronel, his enemy, through the shallows, fighting to carry the weight the water added to his robes.

Suddenly Escalante was howling in a rage he did not even know he possessed. He lunged. Coronel was reaching back over his left shoulder for a long knife. It was then that Escalante made his move. He hit him, a long arcing punch

that came up from his knees. Escalante hit him again before
he splashed down, and bits of tooth and blood sprayed the air.

Escalante yelled, "I trusted you. And this was where
you were leading us all along. You . . . are . . . the . . .
Antichrist."

He pulled Coronel from the water and pounded his fist
into his face again and again. Coronel tried to stand but
twisted and fell under the barrage. He worked his way to his
knees and there he stayed, leaning into the current. He had
both hands clamped across his face and he began to sway
back and forth and moan. Most of his lower jaw was on one
side of his face. Escalante had broken it at both hinges.

"I trusted you," Escalante repeated, not caring whether
Coronel understood. "You knew all along that you were
going to try to take our guns and our scalps. You were going
to use Muniz to bargain for the weapons and then turn them on
us and dance on our faces and crucify us. When did you take
Muniz? How long did you have him? Since before you met us?
I'll bet you did, you scum. Ah, you make me sick."

He gave Coronel's jaw a good shake and took his horse.
He turned for one last look at his fallen foe and for the first
time clearly saw the crucifix. It looked slightly chewed and
had "Fr. F. G." carved in the soft silver in big letters on the
back. Escalante had seen it many times in past years.

A wild killing rage possessed him. He had never felt like
this. His blood roared and pounded as the fury infected his
body as well as his mind.

He had no weapon. He had to find one! He looked for
something to use to kill Coronel and his eyes fell on the
rosary again. He thought, I can strangle him with that.

Then shock engulfed him. Blasphemy! What he could do
to atone? He could never confess the urge to do murder with a
rosary. And Father Garces' rosary at that.

He sighed. This, his penance, would be hard.

"Coronel. You said none of your people had ever seen

or heard of a manifestation of the Christian God. Well, here is your miracle: I'm not going to kill you.

"But if you don't hand up that scalp and the rosary *right now*, I am going to hit your jaw some more."

Coronel's hands shook with haste to be rid of his prize.

When Escalante rode out of sight, Coronel was kneeling and moaning in the stream. The priest could not resist a parting blow.

"Think of me when you eat!"

Escalante found the others at the fork two days later. He had ridden cautiously, doubling back on his own trail several times and riding stream beds as often as possible, even though they added miles to his route. He did everything the Hopi had ever taught him about dodging trackers.

They were all there, peering at him from behind rifles and logs. They didn't stand to greet him. All were too tired from the riding and fighting. Lucrecio and Andres Muniz sat beside each other drinking coffee.

"So much for your brother's ability to stay out of trouble, Lucrecio," Escalante said. He felt the anger of relief. "I can't think of any way to tell you all that I apologize for my foolishness in remaining among them, hoping to convert them, except to tell you outright. I apologize. There's no point in trying to describe to you how awful I feel about it. I can't even describe it to myself. Miera, you should have shaken me sooner and harder, and I should have listened to you anyway." He could not bear to speak of Garces yet. The governor would be the first to hear.

Dominguez led them in the rosary, the penitential psalms, the litany and orations. As before, they formed a circle, but this time all faced outward. Instead of clasping their hands, they held their saddle carbines. They were are all afraid.

Later, as they described how they had gotten to the meeting place, Escalante learned that Andres Muniz had been a difficult capture after all. He had dodged the clan people for five days after they had first seen him riding alone. They stalked him in relays and Andres had no sleep during the entire time. When they finally boxed him in a ravine, he killed three. They subdued him only by rolling rocks down on his head.

And Dominguez, it turned out, had saved both his own life and Juan de Aguilar's just the day before during a skirmish on the plain with three pursuers. Dominguez explained he had taken up what seemed the only likely weapon for him, namely, the heavy silver altar cross. Using it as a mace, Dominguez had clubbed two attackers unconscious.

"I may have killed two men, but I feel no guilt or contrition," Dominguez concluded. "I didn't even pray for their souls. Why is that?"

Simon Lucero spoke up. "Father, you're not even sure they're really dead. You didn't stay long enough to find out. So give yourself benefit of the doubt for once. In this case I'll bet ten pesetas that God will too."

Escalante bit his tongue.

Cisneros had been the one riding Escalante's horse during the flight. The mount was in good condition, but "What did you do with my saddlebags?" Escalante asked. "I think this is as good a time as any to smoke my last cigarro."

Chapter 30

They turned back in late October. Escalante indicated in the journal that the decision made him want to weep. It was one of the times of black despair in his life. He judged himself a failure, forsaken by God, in whose name he had undertaken the venture. However, the hard evidence piling up daily told him they should give up the dream and go home.

Today was a day of constant suffering. The north wind blew without letting up. It brought the bitterest cold thus far, and even the best of our garments were not proof against it over the long range. They will not be warm enough for us if we are here when deep winter sets in. Considering this and the loss of our remaining food animals, we are simply not equipped to deal with winter in these northern passes. Also, as we speak with the Indians we meet along the way in Utah, we hear no word of Spanish Fathers or Spanish missions in the region.

This tells me that Monterey is still far off. According to our maps and the positions Miera plots with the astrolabe, this is true. We clearly have many hundreds of miles to go to the west before we reach the Pacific.

Snows have already buried the mountains. Every sierra is robed in it. I fear the passes will be closed to us if we attempt the crossing, and we might be forced to winter in the mountains alone and without food or shelter. We are very low on essentials. We would run the risk of dying from hunger, if not cold.

Also, supposing we do reach Monterey by the grace of God, despite the adversities mentioned above, we would not be able to return to Santa Fe before next June, 1777. . . .

This was too long. They had promised the Sabuagana, the Uintah and the Ute to send other priests bringing the love of God to them. Another year or more would be too long to make them wait. They would begin to lose faith.

Miera fulminated and Escalante saw qualities he had not liked when they met some time back. Miera was capable of twisting fact to win his way.

Miera now insisted that no matter what the maps and latitude positions set by his astrolabe indicated, Monterey was far closer than they knew. They could reach it within a week. It would be a crime against church and crown for them to give up when they were so near.

Everyone was shoulder to shoulder about the fire to extract warmth and shelter from each other. They had named the place the Little Valley and River of Saint Joseph. It was in southern Utah. Ice and snow bit their faces. The ground was iron hard. The horses and mules snorted and stamped in the cold, eyes full of dumb discomfort. They stood side by side as though expecting a blizzard.

Miera shook his head. "No, Father Escalante. With luck

at finding food and forage and hides, we can last out the winter in these mountains if we have to.''

"With all due respect, Miera, no,'' Escalante insisted. "Only two days ago you estimated the distance to be many hundreds of miles. Now you tell us it's just around the next tree. Miera, listen. Even turning back, the expedition isn't entirely a failure. The paths we've found and the mistakes we've made will make it easier for those who follow. There's no doubt in my mind that there's a northern passage to Monterey. My maps show it. It's just that we're not going to find it this year.''

Miera would not listen. He began gathering his belongings and saddling his horse. He looked deep into the face of each man in the party. Then finally he looked at the two priests.

"I don't dare to argue, Fathers, with the rightness of your decision. This journey was conceived in the offices of the church, although the state is represented also. You have your duties, but I have mine. This northern route must be secured for deep and complex reasons, as you know. English and Russians, as we speak, are in California to destroy us. Our gains in this new land must be anchored by a line of settlement and trade.''

Miera yanked up on his whip and pulled down the great capped stirrups from the saddle pommel. He turned to face the group once more. "You can say what you wish, decide as you may among yourselves, but I am going on. I'll take only enough for one man from the stores. Any who wish to come with me are welcome. But to repeat what you have said to us many times, Father Escalante, whether anyone comes with me or not, I'm going.''

After a while Lorenzo Olivares and Andres Muniz stood and untied their horses from the remuda.

Lucrecio Muniz turned and stared at the mountains. "If you go this time, big brother, I worry about you no longer. Don't expect me to—''

Andres Muniz interrupted, "This is not craziness as it might have been before, little brother. From the start I believed in this mission. I still do. And I believe we should keep going."

Simon Lucero, after sitting in silence, tugged at Miera's sleeve. "I'd come if you ordered me to, Don Pedro. After all, I am in your employ. But I'd prefer not to."

Miera said warmly, "You've been a fine companion thus far, Simon. I'd go anywhere with you. It's just not destined this time, I guess." Miera seized Lucero's hand. "I'll see you back in Santa Fe soon. You still are in my employ as far as I'm concerned."

Escalante considered beating Miera unconscious and packing him home across his own saddle. Then he realized he had no right to stop him. In turning the expedition back, Escalante had in a way relieved everyone of obligation to stay with it. Each man could now make his own choice. He only wished they would not. He feared for them.

Finally, in the dark of a stormy noon, it was time to go. Miera bid everyone good-bye, no hard feelings, and turned his big horse away. Andres Muniz and Lorenzo Olivares followed. Andres swung in his saddle and looked back at his brother. Lucrecio did not even wave farewell.

Mist closed in about the three. A storm was moving in over the mountains.

Escalante and Dominguez and the others rested themselves for the return journey for several more days. At night they posted watch in case Coronel tracked them. Escalante plotted a straight route back to Santa Fe. Snow fell for a night and a day and the cold was the bitterest they had yet known. Then, at daybreak on the third day, they packed up the sparse remnants of their camp and chased their grazing animals.

Cisneros and Laughing Bird had gone out the afternoon before to scout the way. The party followed their trail south-east. The air grew warmer as they moved down from high altitudes.

They were moving through a picturesque valley with good water in the foothills when Juan de Aguilar, the last in line, spotted two riders behind far in the distance.

"Company coming," he shouted, lifting his carbine from its saddle scabbard.

Escalante stood and shielded his eyes against the sharp sunlight to study the two. The thought that they might be outriders from Coronel sent a jolt through him. After a minute he sat again, saying, "Never mind, Juan. Put up your gun. You wouldn't want to shoot two old friends."

They were waiting, their horses patiently pawing the earth and nuzzling each other, when Miera and Olivares came back.

Miera reined in with a flair, legs straight in his big stirrups. Olivares was behind him. "You made good time. We had to race to catch you," was all Miera said.

Escalante looked at him, waiting. Finally Miera admitted, "I've gotten too old to survive a winter in this desolation. Three days of this cold nearly killed me. I couldn't sleep at night, even with every blanket. And this is only the beginning. I smell the worst winter we've ever had coming up."

Escalante knew there was more to come so he waited.

Miera rubbed his chin. Contrition came hard for him. "Let younger men finish what we've started. You're right about what we've accomplished already, Father. The things I've seen and noted thus far are worth nothing if I go on and get myself killed. The notes and maps won't do anyone any good rotting out there with me. That was the vanity of an old man talking the other day."

"Olivares?" Escalante asked.

"It was a choice of going on with a madman or coming back with Miera." He shrugged.

"Andres isn't coming, then?"

Everyone turned to Miera. "There's no need waiting for

him. He's going on to Monterey alone. He still believes he's immortal out here.'' Miera turned away.

Lucrecio Muniz cried, ''Damn him.'' He spurred his horse and cantered east toward Santa Fe.

''Let's all go home,'' Escalante said and started after him.

Chapter 31

They rode back through the gates of the Santa Fe presidio on January 2, 1777, just one day too late to celebrate the New Year. They were coated with ice and marinated in weariness.

One of Dominguez' own mission priests did not recognize him at first; the explorer had grown a beard, was fifty pounds lighter and was smoking a cigar.

Word of their coming had been brought by outriders from missions they had passed along the way home. There was a ceremony in the governor's mansion. The smell of cedar wood, mountain holly and holiday food filled the room and made the very windows of the place shiny with good cheer.

Servants and men on official business passed by the open door of the reception room with an air of expectation. Everyone wanted to be near these men who had just come back from so important an expedition. Adult voices were as subdued as those of children when they spoke. No one mentioned the fact that they had not reached Monterey.

Later, in a private audience, Escalante and Dominguez presented Governor Pedro Fermin de Mendinueta with the

Uintah deerskin drawing, surreal with pagan and Christian symbols. Mendinueta studied the drawing in detail. He was familiar with Indian artifacts and admired the gift. "Even in dull candlelight it's beautiful," he said. "I sometimes think that we Spaniards are the barbarians. But still, we must teach them to leave out their pagan totems."

He carried the drawing to a table upon which he exhibited his favorite Indian objects. Compared to weapons, clay cookware and leather goods, the drawing seemed almost mystical.

It would go to Bishop Diego Nadie de Escobar in Mexico City later, but for now it was his, and he savored it. Escalante liked the man for his feeling about Indian work.

"Don't feel as though you've failed, even though you didn't reach Monterey," Mendinueta told Escalante and Dominguez. They sipped coffee with the sherry Dominguez had remembered so fondly. "I assure you, neither the civil authorities nor the church officials behind the Monterey adventure feel you've failed, even though the original goal was not met. Perhaps it was too unreasonable. You shouldn't have been sent so late in the year."

Mendinueta polished his temples with his fingertips. "At any rate, no gloom over failure. Celebrate success instead. That's an order. For you did succeed, you know. You've opened up lands none of us knew anything about. The mineral logs and maps Miera drew up are invaluable. You've found treasures out there to keep church and crown in new wealth for centuries. People are coming to realize that gold and silver aren't the only valuable metals. When I think of the copper alone, I marvel. Gold is only for money and jewels. Copper is for building cities."

Mendinueta raised his glass to them. "Fathers, in the name of my government, I salute you. When a northern route to Monterey is eventually found—and mark me, it will be— I have no doubt that it will be built on your passage. And when I think, too, of all the souls you've brought to God, there's only one thing to say. Well done, gentlemen. I can think of no higher tribute."

As they were leaving his office a few minutes later, Mendinueta called quietly to Escalante, "By the way, Father, my cousin sends her regards. I'm pleased to be able to tell her you're fit and well. You do remember my cousin Rosalinda, don't you?"

Escalante remembered. He searched the governor's face for malice. He found only a slight smile on the face of one man telling another there are no hard feelings. Escalante reddened nonetheless.

Back at the reception in the great hall, Escalante found he was growing uncomfortable. By temperament, he did not belong there. He was bored. After a while, he found he was no longer listening to the questions fine ladies and gentlemen asked in politeness about Indians they really held to be savages.

Escalante wished he had some thick maize beer instead of brandy and the sherry Dominguez loved so dearly. He missed his mission in Zuni. He missed his Indians. He missed the feeling he had waking up in the morning and seeing the wilderness stretching out to the end of the world.

How quickly I've forgotten how bad it was out there with Coronel, he thought. I've been back inside a city for only a few hours, and already the old discontent returns to unsettle me.

Escalante knew it was time to leave when he realized he had ignored a question from a lieutenant governor, a fop and a ninny. Escalante made excuses. "I apologize for my rudeness, Your Excellency, but I was thinking of something important."

He fired up a cigar and sought out Miera, who was standing proudly in his trail clothes beside his wife. Escalante liked seeing Miera this way. He liked seeing all his men proud, wearing their rough clothes as laurels.

He turned, looking about the hall, studying each of them for a moment. Miera. Dominguez. Lain. Lucrecio Muniz.

Aguilar. Lucero. Cisneros, miserable with his wife and Laughing Bird in the same room.

"Miera," Escalante grinned as though nothing of special importance was on his mind, "I've been thinking. Do you recall that place where we decided to turn back, where you were so angry at me?"

Miera did.

"Well, I've been remembering things. And do you know, a certain notch in those sierras to the north keeps coming to mind. . . . I wouldn't say for certain I saw what looked like a clear passage there, there was so much snow at the time, but do you know, according to our Indian map, that was just about where a pass should have been. And I would swear that for one moment, when the sun was right. . . . Oh well, it was probably nothing but an aberration anyway. . . ." He let out a laugh full of good health.

Miera's eyes crinkled in pleasure.

"I have the feeling the spring thaw will be early this year, Miera," Escalante went on. "And I've been wondering. . . ."

Dominguez came between them. "Stop wondering. Do you realize we could be there in a month, with good horses and dry terrain." He laughed. "The first of May would be a good time to set out, wouldn't you say?"

Escalante raised his glass. "Father Dominguez."

"Father Escalante," Dominguez replied.

Epilogue

It was a dream, and as is so often the way with dreams, it never came true. The first of May 1777 came and went with no party to the West ever formed. Everyone had other business. Escalante was in Mexico City bringing the expedition journal and the Uintah drawing to Bishop Diego Nadie de Escobar.

It was the same the following year. After that the dream of returning west to open the passage to Monterey remained that, just a dream cherished by eight men who had fulfilled only part of it.

Escalante remained the bridge that linked them. From each he received news from time to time and to each he passed along news.

Juan Pedro Cisneros did not stay long in Zuni. One day in February of 1777 he walked from the office of the mayor, packed a bedroll, food and clothing and rode west without saying good-bye. He knew he was losing his wife and children forever, but he decided it was the price he had to pay for the thing he wanted most. Laughing Bird and Little Lain had left a few days earlier to return to their Sabuagana people; they were homesick. Cisneros followed.

He tracked the boy and girl for a week, and then one day he glimpsed them ahead, specks on horseback moving along a ridge. They had not seen him. There was still time to turn back, but Cisneros shouted to them and took the step he would never be able to retrace. When she turned and saw him, Laughing Bird stopped and waited as though she had expected him to come all along.

Joaquin Lain was appointed mayor of Zuni after Cisneros deserted it. He filled the unexpired term, then stood for election on his own and won.

In time both canon and civil courts declared Juan Pedro Cisneros legally dead and his wife a widow. It was said that this was one of the swiftest declarations of legal death ever in New Spain. It was also said that a certain interest in the proceeding on part of the mayor was helpful in winning it; Joaquin Lain and Dona Estella Cisneros were married a month after.

Lorenzo Olivares did not return to his home in El Paso. He settled in Chihuahua instead, a discouraging distance for his wife's family to travel looking for him. In Chihuahua no one cared that he had once tried to kill his wife. He became a storekeeper, and a good one, it was said. He lived with a woman who bore him many children.

Bernardo Miera became a widower late that winter of 1777. Dona Mercedes suffered a stroke that completely paralyzed her left side. After a period of rapid degeneration she died. Some interpreted the death of Dona Mercedes as a further sign from God that the expedition had been ill-omened and that Miera himself should never have gone.

Rubbish, Miera snorted; nonetheless, by his own admission, "My wife's passing has taken the rawhide out of me." He wrote to Escalante with the news and said he was certain Escalante would understand why he did not quite feel like exploring again that spring.

Instead he turned intensely to his painting. He also began

fleshing out his trip notes and drawing fine maps for the use of future expeditions. These chores filled his days for a good long time.

Simon Lucero resigned from Miera's employ and opened a public house in Santa Fe. A generous low-interest loan from Miera himself provided most of the financing.

Lucero called his place the Iron Dwarf. He prospered, providing memorable meals and clean rooms to travelers on the Santa Fe coach. When asked why he chose to be an innkeeper, Lucero replied that he had long ago accepted the fact that food, and not women, would be his vice. He had decided that the only person he could depend upon to feed him as he would wish was himself, and the Iron Dwarf kept the food handy and good and the money rolling in.

Lucrecio Muniz took Simon Lucero's place in Miera's employ for a while. He eventually joined the Mexican army, became a career soldier and served with distinction in the wars with the Apache and Comanche.

Lucrecio seldom spoke of big brother Andres, but when he did, it was with great sadness.

Juan de Aguilar remained in Santa Fe, working at times as blacksmith or trail boss for pack trains. He left the city in spring of 1778 and nothing definite was heard of him afterward.

His family in Santa Clara always suspected he had ridden east and joined George Washington's Continental Army to fight in the American Revolution, then in its third year. It was the family's belief that he fell during the battle for Charleston in South Carolina.

Father Francisco Atanasio Dominguez was a changed man after the Monterey expedition. He found the hard life he led for five months more to his liking than the cloisters of Mexico City and the conversion of the outlands Indians more his sort of challenge. He withdrew his petition for early retirement, requested and was granted posting to missions on the frontier and spent thirty more years as a missionary. As he told Escalante, the life was "his only hope for keeping the weight off.'' He never did give up the fine sherry he liked so much, however. He said it went well with Escalante's damned cigarros.

He confided in Escalante that his new outspoken intolerance of mismanagement had brought down the wrath of disgruntled brethren he had disciplined on inspection tours of Franciscan missions. Administrative charges had been leveled. Dominguez said there was a possibility that he might never be *persona grata* in Mexico City ever again. And he was not.

As for Father Silvestre Velez de Escalante himself, in April of 1780 he set out for Mexico City for medical treatment. The fevers that had troubled him throughout the expedition and after were more frequent. The pains in his lower right side were of longer duration and increasing ferocity.

At Parral, the mining city in Mexico noted for its clean and healthful air, his right side seemed suddenly to erupt in flames and his fever mounted quickly. He remained in Parral to recuperate and rest, but he never left the city. Instead he died a few days later, only months shy of his thirtieth birthday.

Andres Muniz was the only one ever to reach Monterey. In June of 1779 Escalante received notification from the Franciscan mission there that a certain mangled body had been found rolling in the breakers outside Monterey Bay. Judging by the clothing, it was assumed the deceased was a sailor fallen from one of the ships in the port. The note reported that the man was buried outside the hallowed ground of the cemetery.

No one knew where he was from, who his family was or whether he was Christian. His only identification was a piece of parchment found in a shirt pocket. On it was the name Andres Muniz, followed by eight others including that of Father Escalante. It was evidently a roster of some kind, the note said, perhaps of men with whom he had shared something important.

Seventh Powerful Novel in

THE AMERICAN EXPLORERS
Zebulon Pike

PIONEER DESTINY

by Richard Woodley

It was a trail that led ever westward, into the trackless wasteland of the Louisiana Territory. Zebulon Pike began his journey as a young man, yearning for fame and glory, too idealistic to understand the motives of his superior, General Wilkinson. Not even Clarissa Pike could convince Zebulon to turn down the challenge of a courageous mission. Dangers stalk the trail as Pike discovers a traitor among his ranks . . . a battalion of Spanish sharpshooters . . . and a Mexican general who owes a debt of gratitude to General Wilkinson and a man named Aaron Burr. Only the sensuous Juanita Alvarez can tell him the bitter truth—that he has been betrayed by those he trusted most. . . .